Tightrope

Tightrope

Four Novellas

TATAMKHULU AFRIKA

Mayibuye History and Literature Series No. 72

Published 1996 in southern Africa by Mayibuye Books, University of the Western Cape, Private Bag X17, Bellville 7535, South Africa.

Mayibuye Books is the book publishing division of the Mayibuye Centre at the University of the Western Cape. The Mayibuye Centre is a pioneering project helping to recover areas of South African history that have been neglected in the past. It also provides space for cultural creativity and expression in a way that promotes the process of change and reconstruction in a democratic South Africa. The Mayibuye History and Literature Series is part of this project. The series editors are Barry Feinberg and André Odendaal.

ISBN 1-86808-307-1

PREVIOUSLY PUBLISHED
POETRY:
Nine Lives (Carrefour/Hippogriff 1991)
Dark Rider (Snailpress/Mayibuye Books 1992)
Maqabane (Mayibuye Books 1994)
Flesh and the Flame (Silk Road 1995)
The Lemon Tree (Snailpress 1995)
Turning Points (Mayibuye 1996)
NOVELS:
Broken Earth (Hutchinson 1940)
The Innocents (David Philip 1994)

ACKNOWLEDGEMENT
With financial assistance from the Royal Netherlands Embassy and the Swedish International Development Co-operation Agency (SIDA).

TYPESET BY USER FRIENDLY
PRINTED AND BOUND IN THE REPUBLIC OF SOUTH AFRICA
BY THE RUSTICA PRESS (PTY) LTD, NDABENI, WESTERN CAPE
D5217

The Vortex

For Jo-Anne and Cecilia
who helped tighten the nuts and bolts

Covertly, he watched Sep eat. As he had done for most of his going on for eighteen years. Quite a trick – the sly surveillance of one who otherwise had a power over him more immediate than God's. Flick the eyes up, rake them across the hated face, lower them, still blankly seeing, back to his plate. Cool.

He had never been able to decide which of the face's features he liked least. The cold as an adder's eyes, the fleshy, pore-pocked nose that had once belonged to the alcoholic that had become the teetotal born-again, the as fleshy, spittle-flecked lips that chewed and chewed, flowering out, snailing in again like an anus excreting a turd?

Again he gathered himself for the leap into the face of the man he called 'Dad', but this time she warned – a tiniest clearing of the throat – and he eased. They had never discussed this – had never discussed even the father he had never known – but she was an alert woman behind the submissive façade, and intuition had told her what he was about and the cough had first come as an involuntary effort to protect – and had stayed.

'What are you doing today?' Sep asked, pairing his knife and fork, neatly, on the plate, tone already challenging, eyes looking past him to a point somewhere above his head.

'Nothing,' he mumbled, dropping his fork, hands suddenly twice their size.

'Nothing! Nothing!' Sep mimicked, voice dancing, weaving, ready to jab. 'Nothing is right! *You* are nothing!' Then he smiled, angrily, finding a cleverness on his tongue. 'And nothing *for* nothing. When are you going to get off your behind? Find something to do? Earn your keep?'

'Work is scarce, Sep,' she said, her voice patient with the patience that knows it will be to no effect.

'So is he.' Sep pushed back his chair, grating the legs along the floor, stood up to go. 'Proper endangered species, our boy! Nothing's good enough for his hands.' Carefully he buttoned his jacket, picked up his lunch-box from the stand beside the door. 'But enough is enough. Come the end of the month – no job? – *out!*'

They looked at one another for a long moment after the door had slammed.

'He won't,' she said, leaning over to stack the plates.

'I wish he would,' he muttered, shoving his hands in his pockets, trying for cool. But the eyes stayed child's.

'Don't talk big,' she said. 'Where would you go if he did?'

'I've got friends,' he said, lifting his chin – then stopping short as he wondered if he had said too much.

He had. 'Yes,' she answered, voice unfazed, but face seeming to come at him as the bones set. 'And if they are the kind of friends I think they are, he *will* have you – and don't look to me to stop him then.'

'But what does he expect me to do?' he cried, hearing himself whine, hating himself for it, but it taking him like a bodily urge. Why, he wondered, was he forever so miserably not like Ray? 'He's okay. Been in that railway job his *whole life* – who's gonna get him out of it now? Got so stuck it's like he's in a crash. Gonna need the jaws and a torch! But I'm the new generation white shit. Blacks are numero uno now when it comes to work. Blacks are numero uno, full stop. He knows that, and it's okay by me, though it may not be okay by him. Oh, Ma' – and he jerked his hands free of his pockets and pounded his fists, softly, intensely, on the tablecloth – 'Why did you have to marry such a creep? You could-a had your pick. You still look great – even now. Why *him?*'

He began to think she would never answer him. Straight-backed, stilled as one of the porcelain figurines she so loved and that, in their dozens, strolled, raced, courted, or merely, exquisitely, stood on the heavy ball-and-claw furniture of her generation, she hardly seemed to breathe. Outside a biker kick-started his bike, but she gave no sign that she had heard though the sound erupted around them with the violence of shattering glass, and it was only when a fly circled the plates between her hands that habit spurred her to wave it away.

'I don't love Sep,' she said, not looking at him, hands again quiescent about the plates. 'But I don't hate him either. It's only when there's hate, that being together gets too tough. Your father gave me love.' Fleetingly she glanced at him, turning only her eyes. 'Then I lost it. They say it's better to have loved and lost than never to have loved at all. Well, maybe. Personally, I don't feel like risking it a second time.' Again she waved away the fly. 'I'm comfortable with Sep. He made a mistake once. Showed me too much of himself. Now I know more about him than even his mother did. That should make him hate me, and me him. But it doesn't. It's like I'm his priest or his God. Like some funny kind of a love. After all, how much closer can you get to a person than knowing all there is to know about him or her? How much more of a sharing does one want? How much more of power, if it comes to that?' Now she turned to him, fully, the pale, usually placid face tense, a rare anger in her eyes. 'I'm fed and I have a roof. Sep does not beat me, though we have our rows, and I'm left in peace more than most women are. At my age, that means a lot. Maybe it's enough. So watch it, Johnny. Don't muck up things between me and Sep. I am your mother, but there are things I am not letting go of, even for you.'

Then she rose, gathering up the plates, and he stared at her, shocked, seeing her for the first time, feeling he had been struck. She's *hard*, he thought. I never knew she was this hard!

At the door, she turned and it was as though she had read his mind when she said: 'Don't look at me like that. Nothing's changed. It has always been like this. If you saw me as something other than I am, that's because you are still too young to see straight. Or maybe you just *want* to see me as something I am not.' Carefully, usual calmness regained, she re-balanced the plates in her hands. 'Look, Johnny, as your mother I should not be talking to you like this, but, the way things have been going between you and Sep these past few weeks, it seems there is nothing else to do. So let me tell you – straight – if to be hard when the time comes for that, is to be a survivor, then I'm a survivor. And if living with someone because you need bread and a bed is no better than being a woman of the streets, then I suppose I'm that too. But it's not for you to complain. I'm letting you have your fair share of the bread, if not yet of the bed, and there's no reason why things should change unless, as I said just now, you in some way or another – in *any* way or another –' she paused, lending weight to the words, 'come between me and Sep. By which I am meaning right now – don't antagonise Sep to the point where he turns against me because of you. And remember something else I said just now – Sep *is* hard on you, but he won't all that easily throw you out for a reason I hope you will never have to learn. So stick it out for both our sakes and get words like "creep" out of your mind.'

Again she made to pass through the door. Stood a moment, silent. Then said, almost tiredly, like a mugger's victim surrendering the last coin: 'I am much younger than Sep, you know. As, of course, you *do*

know. I could have had my pick, you said. But what you *don't* know –
and I am telling you now so that you can see how serious is this thing –
is that Sep is far richer than you ever thought and I am the major –
and I mean *very* major – heir to his estate. If I die first – well, it was a
gamble that I lost – but if I outlive him, then there will be *cake* to share
out instead of just bread.'

And with the slight, guileless smile he had always believed to be just
that, she at last went through to the kitchen and he heard the plates
clatter down into the sink.

He had been an unwilling scholar. So pathologically so, that Sep –
ultimately exasperated and more than a little prompted by the equally
obsessive desire to save and hoard money – had at last acceded to his
pleas that he be taken out of school and be allowed to look for work.
But he was bright enough and would probably not have been so
obdurate about schooling had he not harboured the somewhat
childish and braggart belief that earning his own money would deliver
him from being ground between the dual millstones of hegemony and
rejection that was Sep. He had, therefore, fully – even vividly – grasped
all that she had said, and his first reaction had not – as she had
seemed to fear – been estrangement, but rather the reverse: a feeling
that, for the first time, she *was* his mother, and not just the wife of Sep.
This sensation of a new closeness was strengthened and, perversely,
illumined by the knowledge that although there was much of his
mother in him, her steel was not. He was the marshmallow, moody
one – the unknown father perhaps? – and although he hungered for
anchorage as much as she, his was the anchorage of dependency,
while hers was a rooting in her own self, her own independent right to
live.

By calm and silent tooth and claw, if need be.

His second reaction was all hers. Slipping into the rat's nest of a
room that Sep, with typical pomposity, called his 'study', he stared at
the small wall safe to the right of the shelves with their swelling library
of pentecostal books and tracts. The combination lock and solid brass
handle seemed to glimmer, recede, return, in the half-dark, inviting
his waiting hand to touch, to stroke. But he fought back their siren
voices, his habitual, mortal dread of Sep persuading him that
somehow, somewhere, a trap had been laid and his slightest spoor
would become as known to Sep as it would undoubtedly become
known to Sep's God.

'Wow!' he breathed, softly, at last. 'Rich!' and turned and went,
quietly, out of the study, the house, not greeting her, though he heard
the hoover snoring in her and Sep's room.

But all the way through the growing quiet, workday suburb in which they lived, hurrying past the oddly faceless houses with their sad attempts at being other than the same – a gauche architectural cliché, a plaster monstrosity on a patchy lawn – he saw the safe, the shine of the brass, the enticing, secretive combination lock, heard himself saying, again and again, 'Wow! Rich!' pretending – though not realising this – that, for the first time ever, he and Sep were as one.

And when he saw Ray waiting for him at the corner of Main and Fourth, as they had arranged, his heart surged with a fresh excitement and he thought, 'At last it is *me* who has something to tell Ray!' and his shadow grew long.

❋ ❋ ❋

Ray's reception of his news was as disappointing as it was odd. When he spoke, extravagantly, of the by now grown legendary wealth in the safe, Ray's face blanked as though a shutter had been wrenched down over an inner self. And when he enthused about the admirably tough mother he had never known he had, Ray merely looked at him with a skew, wry smile that made him feel like the talking fool that he had hoped he no longer was.

His finding these reactions puzzling was, as he was later to admit to himself, clear proof that, despite his on and off contact with Ray for the past almost two years, the latter was still but the outwardness his eyes saw – the skeleton that he then fleshed out with a Ray that existed solely in his own fanciful and idolising mind.

It was in the second last year of his schooling that he had first become aware of Ray. Then fifteen years old and still three years short of the matric he was never to achieve, he had been adjudged old enough for Sep's stultifying authoritarianism to be somewhat relaxed, and he was told that Sep and his mother would no longer be taking him with them when they attended the Saturday evening shows at the posher of the two local cinemas, but he could now attend the Saturday matinees at the same cinema, provided he was accompanied by boys of his own age of whom Sep approved. Since the boys of whom Sep approved were, inevitably, the boys he disliked most, these matinees had become as much a mortification as a gratification of the spirit, and he had suffered them until desperation sparked in him a rare courage and he had dared one Saturday to attend the matinee alone.

Returning, jellied with dread and frustrated that (as he should have foreseen) any pleasure the film could have afforded him had been aborted by his fear of what was to come, he had found to his disbelieving delight that neither Sep nor his mother questioned him concerning the film or who had accompanied him, and that Sep had, in fact, finally become bored with the surveillance he had himself imposed. His mother had eventually made plain in all ways other than words that she had guessed what was going on, but she never told Sep, and on the odd and rare occasion when Sep (who was basically and arrogantly convinced that no one would disobey him anyway) did still question him about the film or who had gone with him, he would (as later became necessary) quote from a newspaper review of the film, or he would name a boy of (by Sep's standards) excellent family that Sep did not, however, normally contact in the short term.

So disobedience had become practice and it was not long before he paid his first visit to the cinema he had been forbidden to attend. Originally a skating-rink patronised by, mainly, the poorer white Afrikaner youth, it had in later years evolved into the Rinko Theatre – a tawdry 'pleasure palace' that smelt of dust and mice and was patronised (at its matinees, at any rate) by a second generation of the same youth. Invariably the foyer would be plagued by sand and papers that the wind whisked fretfully about, but inside the dim lighting hid the flaking gold-coloured paint and the murals that spoke of an earlier age.

He had loved it. Some common gene in him had responded to its shoddiness, a fierce hunger for escape from the sterile, moralising domination of Sep had feasted on the extravaganza of the murals, and the lingering child in him had revelled in the Western shoot-outs, the macho cowmen who loved their horses more than they did their women, the kung fu knockabouts, and all the other essentially guileless crap that, all too soon, was destined to be seen for what it was.

Ray had been the doorkeep even then, halving his ticket as he went in, handing him his pass-out at interval, but it was months before that which reached, took, returned, meant to him anything more than just a hand. Matinees were never less than full house and, keen as he was never to be late, he had been but one of a jostling, unseeing throng of devotees of a like mind.

But, one day, he *had* come late, hurrying, panting a little, still stressed from a day of bruising encounters with Sep. The foyer had been deserted, save for the 'ticket-girl', ensconced in the no longer so very ivory tower of her kiosk – and Ray, who was chatting her up with the brazenness he was later to know so well. She had been brassy, lard-white, ripe as a fruit, blotchy cheeks showing through even the powder's heavy flouring, dyed carrot-red hair intricately coiffed. Buffing her nails, elaborately indifferent to the ready blandishments, reaching for an ease fragile as an egg's shell, she had, nonetheless, been very much aware of Ray, had valiantly, if uncomfortably, grappled with the new South Africa in which race was no longer the spindle round which history revolved.

He had known at first glance that Ray was not white – so sharp had been the contrast between the girl's almost harlequin pallor and Ray's richly olive skin. But more than that had not registered as he frantically fumbled in his pockets for the ticket money, ears already attuned to the seductive clamour behind the closed auditorium doors. Then Ray, hard beside him at the kiosk, had held out his hand for the ticket, saying, 'Okay, kid, let's tear her right here,' and a lazy resonance in the voice had struck a chord deep inside him, and he had looked up with something close to a start and faced Ray fully for the first time.

And Lucifer, fabled prince of morning, had plummeted from the heavens a second time.

It had been as flame to straw. Could not have been any other way. The steady purposefulness under the calm that was later to draw him closer to his mother, and which so signally he did not himself possess, had immediately been evident also in Ray, but to an enhanced degree. Ray's purposefulness had far outstripped his mother's and became a savageness of cold eyes that did not warm even when the mouth did. His mother, as he had put it to himself in another way (though not in quite those terms), was the patience of the spider that waits, while Ray was the stalking cat's quivering about-to-spring.

There had been a stirring in his genitals as the full power and ruthlessness of Ray's personality struck him, and Ray had sensed this, the black eyes alerting in response and the head, with its close-cropped frizzy hair and ring in the ear, inclining barely perceptibly his way. But, for once, Ray had been wrong. There had been no lust to warrant the sardonic half-smile with its missing front teeth ('the better to suck with,' Ray would many months later mockingly explain), no reason to tilt the doorkeep's fraying cap more jauntily over an eye.

What had passed between them was no more than his acknowledgement of the awesomeness of the other's strength, his shamed admission of his own inadequacy, the involuntary desire from the central powerhouse of his flesh to stretch out a hand that it might savour Ray as it would the hide of some leonine and (to him) immaculate beast. He had, after all, felt the same stirring when playing with the grown-tame alley-cat that he loved and had taken in, but that Sep and his mother loathed and forever drove from the house.

Nevertheless, an obsession had been born and the flesh had not lightly relinquished the territories it regarded as its own. So, during the week following an encounter which (as he soon discovered) was only an event of any significance as far as *he* was concerned, he had lain awake for long hours of the nights, listening to Sep shuffle like a pervasive genie from room to room and wanting, with a soundless crying that increasingly became a lamentation of the flesh as it was of the heart, to escape from a house whose darkness was wholly of the heart, and whose walls held him back from a shape that beckoned and that was neither man's nor woman's, though it bore a face like Ray's. And towards dawn of the Saturday of the show, he had slept and had dreamt that a sea of wolves seethed beneath the window's ledge and soundlessly willed that he be of them, and he was and they had run, as soundlessly, under a round moon and the needlepoints of the stars, and all the wolves' eyes had been the eyes of Ray and their snarls had shown that the front fangs were gone. And when he woke, the bed under him had been wet with his seed and he had been replete – and he had also been afraid.

The dream had not, however, deterred him from what was to become his pursuit of Ray, it being open to him to interpret it any way he wished, and Ray's turning to him a blind face at that day's matinee had only lent a more desperate intensity to his wish to have Ray as his friend. It had, however, required almost every ruse in the book (including the essentially feminine one of dropping something in the hope that Ray would draw his attention to it) before Ray again differentiated him from the rest and, with an amused tolerance, tossed him the occasional 'Hi!' Even this small yielding on the part of Ray had enormously pleased and encouraged him because Ray was at least five years his senior and (as his mirror each morning savagely reminded him) his tending-to-be-chubby face with its spaniel-sad eyes was in spectacularly uncharismatic contrast to Ray's own honed and hungry look.

So, coming out from the show one Saturday – coming out last in the hope that Ray would notice him – it had been almost with disbelief that he had heard Ray ask, "Hey, kid, you want to help me lock up?' Dumbly he had nodded and then walked along beside Ray as he closed and bolted the various shutters and doors, straining with a near-physical painfulness to find something to say, but suddenly and maddeningly without words. Ray, too, had been silent, although (he had sensed) not uncomfortably so, and when the last bolt had been shot home, he had followed Ray's curt jerk of the head into a small storeroom beneath the stage.

Here, at a cracked and stained washbasin with a strident tap, surrounded by a forest of old theatre seats and filmic bric-a-brac, Ray had washed his face and hands and then, with conscious flagrancy, bared himself as he changed his uniform for T-shirt, sneakers and jeans. But his strict upbringing under Sep had not prepared him for such intimacies and, although not unaware of the mechanics of sexuality and as versed as any when it came to the sniggering erotica of the toilets at school, he had embarrassedly looked the other way.

Still buttoning up his fly, Ray had then come to stand squarely in front of him and he had stared at the near-naked woman sprawled across the T-shirt's psychedelic red.

'So,' Ray had asked as though in follow-up of a previously unspoken question and answer between themselves, 'what's it then you want from me, kid?'

'Nothing,' he had mumbled, not looking up, more than ever flounderingly reaching out for words he could not find.

'Nothing? Jeez! Casing me so hard for *nothing*? What would'n you do for *something*? Come *on* – I'm norra poes, you know. What's the deal?'

Then he had known he *must* answer. 'I just like you,' he had at last got out, still not looking up. 'I thought we could be friends. I don't have any friends.'

Again he had heard the whine in his voice. Hated himself for it. Hated the imbecilic sound of his words in even his own ears. 'How must they not sound to Ray?' he had agonised. But Ray had grown strangely still, legs splayed, fingers still twirling the top button of his fly.

'Old man's a shit, huh?'

The guess had been so right, he had stiffened, startled, and Ray had smiled. But a little grimly. As though at a tale too many times heard.

'Okay, let's go,' he had said, and they had locked the storeroom, and eased through the concertina-iron of the great gates closing off the foyer, and locked these too. Then they had walked all down Main and turned right into Fourth, and followed Fourth until its smarter houses deteriorated into ever shabbier semis, and the skins of its people had darkened, chameleon-style, and they and that which clothed them had become indistinguishable from the surrounding penury and decay.

Eventually, end of the street in sight, chemical ochre-and-yellow of the usually invisible mine-dump towering over the squat roofs, Ray had stopped, pointed at a two-storey, featureless block of flats whose seemingly doorless entrance gave onto a booming dark, and said, 'I kip here,' and left him, not once looking round.

Standing alone on the cracked and weedy pavement fronting the flats, papers and other offal restlessly about his feet, he had not felt offended that Ray should have left him so summarily, had begrudged him even the customary courtesy of 'Ciao!' On the contrary, he had felt that, by taking him down Fourth, Ray had made a statement of some kind, had permitted him to come closer than he had, at that stage, dared to hope. But the flesh, too, not missing a trick, had swiftly moved another step in its subverting of his adolescent idealisms, reminding him that although he had looked away from Ray's nakedness, he had been vividly, even wistfully, aware of it and had not subsequently easily forgotten the fingers twirling the button on the fly.

Wisely or fortuitously, he had been correct in his assessment of Ray's intent. The latter had, indeed, opened to him in a meaningful if still incomprehensible way, and although their contacts had still been confined to the Saturday shows, it had no longer been necessary for him to trap Ray into acknowledging that he was there. In fact, Ray had even begun to listen (or pretend to listen? – he was never quite sure which) to the increasingly easier flow of his chatter during the intervals, and the locking-up after the show had become a small ritual in which he actually did the work while Ray shed his uniform in the storeroom and then shared a cigarette with him before going home.

Ray had not, however, again invited him to accompany him down Fourth to the flats, and when he one day suggested that he would like to, Ray had said, 'Nah, it's not your scene,' and when he rather sullenly asked what did Ray know about what was or was not 'his scene', the latter had turned on him with a hard impatience he had not before shown. 'Look, Johnny,' he had said, 'maybe you got more schooling than me, but I'm thinking you know fuckall about a lotta things I know like you know your hand. I got a woman down there and I'm thinking a woman is one of the things you know fuckall about. And even if you did – she's not your kind of woman – at least not yet. Or maybe never for all I know. Look, kid' – and his tone had grown even harsher, crueller – 'I'm neverminding leading you, as the preacher says, to hell if that is what you want. But you are still a baby, kid. And soft like a baby. How can you know where you want to go? And besides – it's not only the woman – it's – it's other things as well' – and he had paused, relenting a little – 'So cool it. If talking to me at the shows does something for you, makes your old man taste a little less like shit in your mouth – then *okay*. But don't want more from me, kid. I'm not a very giving guy.'

Then, the gates to the foyer locked, Ray had turned to go, pinching out the butt of their cigarette, flipping it away with forefinger and thumb. But *he* had not turned in the opposite direction up Main, and Ray, sensing this, had paused, asking, peremptorily, a little surprised, 'Okay?'

'No,' he had said, his voice breaking a little like the boy's it still was – like the boy's he so much wanted it no longer to be. 'I want to be where you are, Ray. Hell is hell. What makes you think you can lead me to a worse hell than living under a shit like Sep?'

Ray had stared at him, almost with shock. Then, 'Weird!' he had muttered – and again – 'Weird!' and had left him cursing himself for having said too much.

But he had not said too much. At the next matinee, Ray had spoken to him with less of condescension and more of warmth, and on his returning from the 'Gents' at interval, Ray had nudged him, lightly but familiarly, in the crotch, whispering, 'Close up there, kid,' and he had looked down, reddening and grinning like a loon when he saw that he had forgotten to zip up his fly. Back in the seat in the auditorium, he had found flesh sitting next to him, also grinning, but not like a loon, as it reminded him that this was the first time that Ray had ever touched him, and why, it had asked, was the physicality of that touch still lingering when it was the spiritual bonding that had been sought? He had not been able to answer that, had, in fact, hardly been able to hear the voice – feeling, as he did, both exhilarated and unsettled by a dark singing of the blood.

On the Saturday after that, locking up after the show, Ray had said, 'Let's go down Fourth,' and though his heart had leapt at this fresh evidence of acceptance, he had pretended to no emotion as Ray had pretended to none, and had similarly held his tongue when Ray confided in him that though a doorkeep's job paid shit, he stuck it out because the theatre was one of the places where he made the contacts that brought him the *real* bread. Here, though, an involuntary puckering of the brows had given him away, and Ray had broken stride as he loosed his short bark of a laugh and said, 'Yo, kid, where you been all your life?' Then added, 'How must I make out with a larnie like you?'

It had been a measure of the increasing understanding between them that he should not have been angered by the harsh thrust of those words – had sensed, rather, an affection in them of an inarticulate kind – and he had waited for Ray to say something more, but the latter had stayed silent as they turned into the forbidding maw of the flats and climbed the echoing litter-strewn steps to the second floor with its doors on either side of a long corridor that had stretched from a present dimness into a near-night. The smell of masala and onions had clung to the walls, had, indeed, seemed to permeate them like some exotic mortar for the bricks, and that, and an underlying stench of urine and sweat, had emphasised the widening gap between the ambience he was so impulsively abandoning and the world of Ray that the gloomy corridor, and the doors like the doors of cells, had suddenly encapsulated in the most uncompromising and disheartening way. But he had fought back that queasiness as they passed between the doors, trying not to hear (or, at least, not to be too receptive to) the tumult of basic domesticity (or as primitive revelry) that those doors restrained – and, above all, trying not to betray by the least outward sign that he was fighting to hold onto a dream as he would have fought to hold onto his life.

So they had come to the door of Ray's own two-roomed flat and Ray had turned the knob onto a barrenness of uncarpeted floor, a paucity of trashy furnishings that he had found impossible to associate with the flamboyant personality of the man he sought to know. What, he had wondered, *did* he actually know of Ray? Were there any who were still linked to him by blood, or did he swan it alone in this incongruous backwater of despair? What did he do with all the money that the 'contacts' he had spoken of allegedly so lavishly bestowed? What *were* these contacts and what did they pay Ray *for*? How *real*, in fact, was this man his loneliness pursued like some hungry stray?

There had been no answers, only a further unfurling of reality as Ray had crossed to the still closed bedroom door and, without knocking, had flung it open to reveal the one ornate object that the apartment held – a bed of bemusing opulence and, rising from it, a woman whose unsubtle scent had suddenly and cloyingly overlaid the same onion-and-masala smell that he had noted in the corridor and that seemed to have been apportioned to all the flats. Slowly she had come forward, barbie-doll-blue eyes drowsy under the heavy lids, extraordinarily pretty face marred by a too richly rouged, sullen mouth, surprisingly undyed ash-blonde hair in as oddly uncaring disarray.

She had also been fat. Unedifyingly, almost disablingly, fat – the entire skeleton, with all its articulated artistry, submerged in the undulating blubber of the buttocks, belly and breasts.

'I go for the kilos,' Ray had later confessed. 'Easy and soft. Like the roll round the wors,' and had laughed, making it clear that the woman would be but one of the many who had shared the bed.

'This is my friend Johnny. Greet him nice,' Ray had then ordered, and she had come close to him, eyes slitted, mouth in storm, and he had seen that there were fine wrinkles round her neck and that the blue, cold eyes were also old. Then she had leaned forward and pecked him on the cheek and the not too clean silk gown had momentarily gapped onto a grossness of naked lard from which his every sensibility had shrunk, and a sourness under the scent had trumpeted of genitalia as unwashed as the gown.

'I said greet him nice,' Ray had repeated, not raising his voice, but an inflection in it as deadly as the cocking of a gun.

Her eyes had widened then and she had brought her mouth to his, thrusting her tongue against the innocence of his teeth, backing off, a fine sweat suddenly on lip and brow.

'Better,' Ray had approved and, as she passed him, he had palmed the flopping buttocks with a violence that savoured more of assault than caress.

'Her name's Dolly,' he had added, as though she was incapable of speaking for herself – as though she was a pet dog or cat.

Suddenly pity for Dolly had moved in him. Suddenly that pity, that softness that essentially was him, had been pitted against the dark pitilessness of Ray, and he had turned away his head to hide the conflict of which the other was still unaware, but would be so quick to detect from even one rash glance of the eye. For a moment what was and what was to be had balanced on a knife edge of conscience that could have swung him either way – had seemed weighted to take him from Ray – but then his eyes had met those of Dolly who, unasked, was setting out a half-full bottle of very fine brandy and three china cups of varying design. She has been covertly studying him and, trapped by the unexpected swing of his head, was still staring at him with such a consuming and incomprehensible hatred that it had struck him with almost the force of a physical blow. Shocked, he had looked down, the ashes of his pity for her, the ashes also of what he had once been.

Then Ray had swept aside the brandy and cups, commanding, 'Nah! Make tea!' and she had brewed and served them tea, and they had sat drinking it – so unlikely a trio – he, Ray and the girl – indulging Ray's sudden and cruel as it was endearing whim to play the master in his own home, to emphasise that it *was* a home, and not just a whorehouse or shebeen. And to show off with pride (and the concomitant sense of his own inferiority) his white, domesticated slave.

The following Wednesday had been Ray's day off, and the first of many such days that he was to spend with him. There had been no *asking* him on the part of Ray: merely a matter-of-fact instruction to meet him at the corner of Fourth and Main at such and such a time. Ray's peremptory takeover of him, far from upsetting him, had been the gratification of his deepest need, and he had been unable to recall any earlier day in his life that had afforded him so unalloyed a pleasure, or such a sense of fulfilment in and acceptance by a being other than himself. Paradoxically, through enslavement he had been freed.

That is until, day drawing to its close, he had found (as was so often to be the case in his dealings with Ray) that there was a sting in the tail.

They had taken an early bus to centre town, he bunking school (that being a common practice with him by then). Had played the video games, played pool. Lunched, royally, on junk food, jostling the new South Africa's polychrome crowds. Sat a second time through a kung fu flick in one of the last remaining sleazy cafe bios with its shadows and shapes, snoring tramps, smooching, down-at-heel boys and girls, perverts and pimps. ('Gotta see the ending,' Ray had said, 'never got to see the fucking ending, watching door at the Rink'.) He had thought it would be a yawn sitting through the show again, but Ray had enjoyed it so much, it was like it was the first time for him too. Indeed, Ray had not at all seemed like his twenty or so years that day. More like his own age, but sassier. Whistling up a black girl with her painted-white lips and a white girl with lips black as the black. It had been cool, and it had not been cheap. But Ray had paid for them both. Every time. 'I got the moola,' he had said, 'and moola's for getting what you want.' Again a query had surfaced in him about the origins of Ray's bucks. But, quick as a fish, it had fled, not spoiling his day.

With the sun lowering, and beginning to think about Sep and getting home, Ray had jerked his head and they had gone into a downtown coffee bar: cramped, hot, black bar stool sticky under the arse, black espresso's bitter mud in the mouth, languid men with womanly hips pressing close. Ray had grown very silent then, face older, harder, than twice his years, eyes vigilant as a hawk's.

At last a man had come to them: middle-aged, big-bellied, soft and white, eyes running like hares under their lids. Slick as an oil despite his bulk, he had drawn Ray aside, whispered, glancing over at him, whispering again, but Ray had shaken his head, expostulated, hands voluble as any words, turned to go. But the other had restrained him, nodding, tip of the tongue flicking out to moisten the full lips, and Ray had come to him, pressing a note into his palm, whispering, 'Bus fare. Ciao, kid.' And had left.

Back home, he had lain until deep into the night, watching Ray and the fat man crossing the street, driving off in a car that had seemed to him as long and black and silent as a hearse, Ray not once looking back. At times he had wept – boy again – the carapace he had filched from Ray ripped, bloodily, off.

He would not, he had decided, see Ray again.

But that Saturday, as though his feet had taken him there with a volition all their own, he had found himself back at the Rink, and Ray, uncharacteristically, had come to him first, punching his arm, ignoring his averted head, urging something into his hand. Looking down, he had seen two R50 notes.

'What's this?' he had whispered, voice hoarse, head at last reluctantly turning to Ray. 'I don't want anything of yours.'

'Look, Johnny,' and Ray had gripped his shoulder so hard that he had winced, 'cut the shit. I know you are mad at me, but business is business, kid. The big gut in the coffee bar is the one with the dollars. But you don't get him easy. He likes them young. Like you. He wanted you, kid. But I said, no, you are my old lady's by her second man – *white* man, see? – and you are not in the trade and I don't *want* you in the trade. But he can have me instead. And when he saw that's the way it's gotta be, and him with the hots by then, he said, okay. And that's your share. Strictly halfies, kid. Because you were the bait. Enjoy.'

For long moments, he had stared at the notes in his hand. Stared at them as though they had a venomous life of their own, shaken, no longer so much by grief, as by something that had felt suspiciously like jealousy and most definitely had been rage.

'He could have given you nothing, you know,' flesh had hissed, dancing like a small tokolosh at his side. 'And, besides, who needs who?'

Crumpled and soiled, smelling faintly of Ray's too sweet aftershave, the notes had nestled, waiting, in his palm.

'You really want to give him up?' flesh had goaded him again. 'Give back the notes then!'

But his hand had slowly closed over them and Ray, back tearing tickets at the door, had hugely winked, eyes amused – and black as holes.

❋ ❋ ❋

As the end of the month and Sep's threatened eviction of him drew near, he became fearful and prone to increasing bouts of moodiness and despair. Where would he go? Constantly the question beat its small drum of menace in his mind and, in his dreams, Sep's face, inflamed with rage and contorting like an image in a flawed glass, would pursue him with a voiceless and implacable intent. His mother gave no sign that she was aware of his distress, though he made no effort to hide it from her, hoping she would again – and even more forcefully than before – reassure him that Sep would, after all, not make good his threat. Conversely, though his whole life was now centred on him, he did not confide his inner turmoil to Ray, not wanting to betray his true and shaming capacity for terror to a man who, apparently, did not know what that word meant.

And yet – though so convinced that the worst possible scenario was upon him, and sickened as he was by the very thought that that scenario might also entail his being separated from Ray – he made no real effort to find work, save for an occasional lacklustre standing in a job queue, or answering some interviewer's questions with a signal lack of interest in the work he ostensibly sought. This was partly due to the fact that he did not really believe that he *would* find work, but mostly it was because he was increasingly becoming involved in and enchanted by Ray's devil-may-care and hedonistic lifestyle and could no longer conceive of himself being straightjacketed in the kind of eight-to-five respectable occupation Sep would insist he choose.

He was now able to spend much more time with Ray than when he had first got to know him. At nearly eighteen and, thus, now more man than boy, it had become plain even to Sep that still to compel him to go to matinees with little kids, was not only laughable and cruel, but would reflect badly on Sep's public (and carefully cultivated) image of the indulgent and loving stepfather who had the welfare of his charge at heart. So, also mindful of the fact that crime had radically increased since the first all-race elections, Sep had (in his own best interests, rather than magnanimously) given him permission to attend one evening show a week, provided it was not the Saturday evening's, when he would be expected to keep an eye on the house while Sep and his mother took in their own regular weekly flick. He had promptly chosen Ray's day off of Wednesday so that he could spend not only the day with him, but also the evening up to the time of coming out of a show it had never been his intention to attend. An added bonus, however small, was the ticket-money given him by Sep which he then pocketed or, with a savage satisfaction, spent as much on Ray as on himself.

Sometimes, in a nightclub or coffee bar, someone (nearly always a man, one or twice a woman), whom Ray had already contacted at the Rink, would approach Ray and, as on the very first occasion, he would be left sitting alone. Quite often also it was someone unbeknown to Ray (always a man, middle-aged, or even hoarily beyond) who would approach *him*, and Ray would glance at him, inquiringly, though fully expecting him to (as always) shake his head, when Ray would say, 'Nah, he's mine,' and (the 'half-brother' story having proved too difficult to sustain) then grip his knee with a possessiveness designed to show in what way he was his. Then, if the client chose Ray instead, Ray would again leave him alone, provided (as Ray always said) 'the guy looked like bucks and was not a Rocky Horror show,' and the next Wednesday (and again as at the very beginning) Ray would hand him his 'cut', which, however, was no longer 'halfies', but twenty five percent, since, as Ray had almost apologetically explained, 'I gotta woman to look after, kid. Also rent and stuff. So I reckon it's only fair you're one in four. Okay?'

'Of course, it's okay,' he thought, but still he felt like a pimp, and there was a duality to his taking the money that tore him even further apart. On the one hand was the natural hunger for pleasure and trendy gear of the youth whom Sep starved of all 'extras' save the price of a cinema ticket once a week, and, on the other hand, was the reluctance to deny himself a *sharing* with Ray that substituted, however inadequately, for the sexual communion Ray so freely lavished on others and that, each time he was left alone in club or bar, wracked him with a jealousy and hurt he could not help, yet sensed was as committed and damning as would have been any intimacies of their flesh.

Then there was his fear of Ray contracting Aids. On the face of it, this was a more selfless anxiety than the others, but, in reality, it was not, since Aids, apart from accidents or murder, was the one of the dark Angels of death most likely to prematurely rob him of Ray. Although, by virtue of his upbringing, still a virgin (and his perception of Ray's promiscuousness thus still too academic to arouse in him a sufficient condemnation of it, or to wake in him a fuller appreciation of how much of a pimp *he*, in *his* turn, had become), he was well aware that his fears for Ray were far from groundless, but when he, embarrassedly, but spurred on by his anxiety, had asked Ray if he used condoms during intercourse, Ray had scoffed, 'Nah! naked snake, kid! That's the way they feel it and that's the way they want it!' Then, more banteringly than cruelly, he had added, 'Look, kid, I dunno what you do when we split. But I'm thinking that's still one dead snake there' – and he had touched him, teasingly but not ungently, in the groin – 'But that's your scene, and though I don't get it, it's okay by me. Kind of cute – for a change.'

The last Wednesday of the month turned out to be also the day before the scheduled confrontation with Sep and his dread at the imminence of the event could no longer be contained. Increasingly it showed in the wild swings of his moods, the unnatural brightness of his eyes, the slight yet perceptible trembling of his hands. No less predatorily aware than usual, but as averse to involvement in another's woes as he was secretive about his own affairs, Ray had at first pretended to a deaf ear and as blind an eye. But then a particularly dysfunctional laugh provoked him beyond endurance and he blurted out: 'You on drugs, kid?' Startled, not so much by the question as by the accompanying almost wolfish grin, he violently shook his head, but Ray, now acutely aroused, needled him until, at last, broken down and voice broken as his will, he told it as it was, ending with the inevitable 'Where must I go?'

For a fraught moment, head lowered, Ray's long, not overly clean fingernail scratched at the plastic top of the table in the supermarket cafeteria where they had bought burgers and milk. Then he let out an explosive breath.

'Look, kid,' he said, still not looking up, 'I'm not thinking you're fingering me for a kip. Or maybe you are, but don't know. But know or don't know, you got me in a dwaal. Do I say "fuck you, what are you to me?" or do I say "Come, kid, doss down between me and my whore?" Now I can't say "fuck you", just like that. Because why? Because – have I gotta say it? – you kind of like a kid brother to me now. But if I give you dak, what do I do with you? What do you do with me? Look, kid,' he said again, but looking up now, his eyes blackly opaque, 'it's not the woman that's the problem. You stuck it out even with the fat one, and I'm thinking she *was* kinda gross, and now you and Fiona get on pretty good. Though don't let it get *too* good!' – and he grinned in a wry, untimely aside – 'But, otherwise, you only been to the shack when it's quiet. Other times, nights mostly, it gets pretty rough. Like I'm rough. I sell the vino, kid, and the *real* stuff. And' – he paused, fractionally, alert – 'I sell drugs. And when an ou in the flats gotta kêt he wants to fuck, but his wife must not know, and Fiona and I are going out, I rent him the bed. That kinda thing, kid. How you gonna live with that?'

But the question had been overshadowed by the bed. 'And you still sleep in it?' he exclaimed, more shaken by this than by any of the other excesses he had learnt, if not to approve, then, at least, to endure.

Instantly, Ray was venomously, lethally enraged. 'Where do you fucking well expect me to sleep?' he snarled. 'On the fucking floor?' – and he thrust up, slamming back the chair – 'Don't come preaching to me, you little poes! Or you can fucking well fuck off!'

Hurting, but still leashed, he followed Ray into the street, walking a pace behind him till he slowed down, allowing him to catch up. But the day was spoilt and they parted later with a polite sullenness and a residual misery on his part that further eroded his capacity to deal with the crisis now only hours away.

So it was that after a bleakly sleepless night, he found himself at the breakfast table with his mother and Sep. Disorientated, weariness surging like a surf in his ears, he stuffed porridge, eggs, sausage, even toast, into his mouth, wrestled their tasteless awkwardness down his throat. He must not, he thought, by the slightest waywardness of behaviour, draw attention to himself, lend Sep an early opportunity to burst into the explosive assault he had surely, with meticulous sadism, preplanned.

His every sense, not to speak of his years of experience of the man, warned him not to look at Sep, to keep his head down, since to lock eyes with him was tantamount to engaging those of a truculent hound. But he could not resist flicking increasingly frequent, subliminal glances across the table's suddenly shrunken width, terrified as a man stalked by an unseen assassin that the awaited wrath would come upon him unawares. But the usual portents – the heightened flush, red and shining like an unripe boil, the savage as a trap's clamping down of his teeth as he chewed, the bloated as a bladder sullenness of the jowls – were oddly, unsettlingly, not there.

Spearing his egg with the fork in his right hand, holding up the morning's paper with his left as he bent to read the front page news, Sep had never seemed so calm, so uncharacteristically at peace with the world. Had he forgotten that this was the end of the month? Or was this a new and subtle strategy aimed at enhancing the shock, the horror, of the sudden turnaround? Morbidly his mind convinced him that the latter was, indeed, the case and a fresh access of dread set his hands and thighs trembling, and he had to clench his buttocks to curb the fart he could feel ballooning through him as the undigested food in his gut rebelled.

But it was then that his mother, for the first time that morning, raised her head and looked at him, eyes clear and serene, telling him she knew of his torment and passionlessly despised him for the magnitude of his fear. 'Bitch!' he whispered to himself with a bitterness that wept like a death of love, and, suddenly, he was no longer afraid. Suddenly he saw himself as his mother saw him – as, indeed, he was – a snivelling not-yet-quite-man, cowering on the slime-bottom of the pit of his shame – and, shocked that the thought should have come to him so late, he wondered what Ray would think of him could he see him now. Shaking, no longer with fear, but with rage at his debasement of his spirit as of his flesh, he rose, not delicately softly as was his wont, but with a scraping of the chair's legs that brought Sep's head round, and went to his room, shutting the door.

There, still armoured in his new defiance, he unlocked his wardrobe and changed into what he termed his 'street gear': the flashy clothing so beloved also of Ray which he had bought with the money Ray had passed on to him from time to time. Never before had he dared wear this clothing at home, always taking selected items in a plastic bag into a public toilet, or, more rarely, down to Ray's flat, and changing there. Now he stood: a Ray-clone – save for the pale skin, the strangely drained blue of the eyes, the straight, fair hair he was forced to cut short when, so desperately, he wished it to be long with, maybe, a ponytail and a little ribbon woven into its strands. He had chosen this most violent T-shirt and tightest jeans, and he noted with satisfaction that his mirror showed his nipples thrusting against the thin, clinging fabric of the shirt, and his genitals so emphasised that they might as well have been left bared – and, in a final challenging gesture, he clipped a small, gold ring into the barely noticeable hole Ray had pierced in the lobe of his left ear.

As suddenly as it had been born, his courage ebbed, draining out of him with an almost audible suck. The house was deathly quiet and he knew with a sick, benumbing certainty that, dressed as he was, he would never be able to walk through his door into the ambuscade of menace beyond. Hurriedly, he made to again undress, but, as if on cue, Sep's heavy tread began to move towards his room and he froze, back to the mirror, as Sep slammed open the door and strode, toweringly, in.

Senseless with a terror he would not have thought it possible for his heart to survive, he stood, rooted, wondering, frenziedly, if (for the first time in their lives) Sep would not merely berate him, but fell him with his fist – or perhaps flay him to a pulp with the solid-brass buckle of the belt he always (and somewhat incongruously) wore. But, hardly less of a shock, Sep stopped short of him, stood, frozen, face turned greyly ashen as an unwashed sheet, incredulous, unblinking gaze ranging over the gear, centring at last on the voluptuousness of the crotch, not moving on. For a moment wrenched out of time, the tableau held, then Sep swept his tongue over his lips and, wordlessly, wheeled and was gone.

Seconds later, the front door banged, and he went out, to find his mother still sitting at the breakfast table, staring at nothing at all. But she turned to him when she heard him come in, and something deep-down moved in her eyes when she saw the gear which he, in his distraction, had forgotten he still wore. 'Yes,' she said, and there was an inflection in the single word that acknowledged an answer to a question, and she briefly, unamusedly, smiled.

'Why did Sep not row me?' he asked, his voice high as a girl's with puzzlement and strain.

'He saw a ghost,' she said and swatted at the ubiquitous fly. Then, when she saw he would not let her be: 'You. He saw you. In those clothes. They reminded him of someone else he once knew.'

Still he would not let her go. 'Who?'

'His lover. I found them in bed together. My bed. He was a rent boy. I never saw him again, but I owe him a lot. He gave me the hold over Sep I'd always wanted and still have.'

He stared at her, stunned as much by her calm as by what she had said. 'But what has this got to do with me? Why must he hate *me* the way he does?'

'It's not like that,' she said, almost pityingly. 'It's more than that. He hates you because he cannot hate you *enough.* You're nearly Colin's age now and, through you, Colin is getting back into his mind and into my bed. On the one hand, he wants you here, wants you for himself – don't go out with this boy or that boy, be home by this time or that time, though you are now more man than boy – and on the other hand, he wants you out of here because his lust is too strong for even his God, and he's still got sense enough to know that if he gives in, that's the end of all he's built up here and, again, I'm the one that wins.' She paused. 'I never meant to speak to you in this way of these things, but' – she looked him up and down – 'I see you have found out all about them for yourself.'

'Up you!' he said, white, as Sep had been, with spite, and cruelly liked the slight faltering of her calm. Then he left the house, still in his gear, but when he came back for lunch, she set a place for him in the kitchen, saying, 'I've asked Sep to give you another month to find work and he has agreed, provided that, if you don't, I'll disown you as my son. In the meantime, you must eat here and keep out of Sep's way.' Then, seeing his shock, she went on, 'It's as I told you before, Johnny. For my sake as well as yours, nothing must come between Sep and me.'

Then, deliberately, she left him alone and he, dully, and with as dull and weak a rage, toyed with his food ('Like a servant,' he thought. 'Or a rent boy!') and wondered if there was any real difference between him and Sep when it came to being bound.

What his mother had expected to achieve by this cumbersome and improbable arrangement never became clear. Had she really so little understood his psychic impasse as to imagine that such a draconian measure would goad him into a more avid search for a job, which would enable her and Sep to be rid of him with none of the adverse publicity that Sep, as a high-up in his Church, could so ill afford? Or had she known that there was no point to it, but did, after all, cherish him sufficiently to want to delay the parting under the cruellest possible scenario that otherwise must be chosen as the lesser of the two evils she and Sep faced? Or had she simply decided to exact revenge for his saying 'Up you!' and, thus, enticed him into an extra and (except from her point of view) unnecessary month of minor hell?

For hell it, indeed, proved to be. And it would have been ludicrous but for the deadly serious issues underlying it all. Carefully as some nocturnal beast, he would plot his way in and out of the house, gauge when it was safe for him to go to the toilet, open his bedroom door, sneak into the kitchen for the meals his mother hurriedly placed before him, then left him painfully to consume, his only knife, fork, spoon, sounding on plate and cup with a loudness that both alienated and appalled. 'Tell them to get fucked!' said Ray, when he confided all this to him, but the question of where he was to go had never been resolved and (from his side, at any rate) was apt to be a sensitive subject since the day he and Ray had quarrelled in town. And so, he counted his cash, and hoarded it, and stuck each day out in the hope of a deliverance he inwardly did not really believe would ever come.

Nonetheless, it was like a slash across the face when, on the evening of the last day of 'grace', he slipped into his room after a visit down Fourth and found all his clothes had been packed into two suitcases standing, ready to be taken up, beside the bed, and, pinned to the duvet, an envelope with his name written on it in his mother's hand. Hastily, he ripped it open, finding in it ten R50 notes and a message on a jagged piece of unruled paper that read: 'I know you think I have no heart. But I have enough not to want to see you leave. So I'll be until late with Sep's mother who is not well. The suitcases and the cash are the best I can do for you. For now. Take care.'

Slowly he pocketed the letter. Then the notes. Sat down on the bed. So she did care for him, after all. His eyes blurred with tears and he lowered his face into his hands and wept with a desolateness that was no longer a boy's. Then, exhausted, clinging still to the carcass of the known, seeing the once coveted freedom for the chill and lowering alienness it, in fact, was, he leant back across the bed, meaning to rest but a while, close his eyes. But the house was without sound: only the great pendulum-clock in the dining room ticking in sync with his heart and the wind screeching a branch of the peach tree across the glass of the window beside his head. He slept.

. When he again opened his eyes, Sep was standing over him, perfectly still, eerily ludicrous in long johns and vest, grey-socked-feet unshod, hair abandonly left wild. 'Jesus Christ!' he thought, mind in flight. 'He's been here all the time!' Then he saw that Sep was not as still as it had seemed. Was, in fact, very slightly swaying – metronomic-ally, not of his own will as a leaf in wind. 'He's drunk!' his mind again, incredulously, exclaimed. 'Back on the bottle after all these years!' and he stared up at Sep like a bird woken too late to the falling upon it of the hawk.

And yet, save for the eyes – bloodshot and fixed as some grisly doll's – the Sep he had loathed was seemingly sunken without trace. 'You are not wearing your pretty clothes,' Sep mumbled, eyes still distantly not seeing him from their other world, drunken tongue the worse for his having taken out his teeth, left them in the glass beside his bed. 'Don't you want to please me any more with your pretty clothes?'

His flesh crawled. Not so much at the whine in the voice, as at the repetition of the word 'pretty' with its connotations of girlishness and liaisons of a stranger kind, and he cautiously tried to raise his body from its exposed sprawl across the bed. But Sep, with a suddenness shocking as a corpse come to life, pushed him back: then crashed down beside him with a violence that suggested his legs had given way.

'You have been cruel, Colin' – and again he recoiled at the archness in the other's tone, felt a fresh horror as he realised that Sep did not even know who he was, was seeing in him the boy-lover of whom his mother had told. 'Why have you stayed away so long? You know she does not give me what I want. Must have. Only you can.' Then, conspiratorially, 'She's not here now. So relax, boy, relax,' and he realised, though with utter disbelief, that what he was feeling was Sep's hands fondling his thighs, and what he was seeing was Sep's erection, tractioning up behind the long john's tight, confining sheath, and he tried to wrestle the hands away, but Sep only chuckled, whispering, 'Still shy, Colin? I thought I had cured you of that!' Then, with a strength he had never before thought the other possessed, Sep was rolling him over, dragging down his tracksuit pants, hooking his fingers in the back of his scants, and he was yelling, as though he would spew out his gut, 'Get your hands off me, you fucking old pig!'

At once Sep released him and he whipped round, astonished at so easy an escape, realising, then, that his voice, and the violence of it, had triggered Sep back to reality, to the now. It had also – to his hardly lesser dismay – triggered Sep back to the inextricably entwined love-hate relationship with himself – and to the doomed, pathetic outreach for the redemption of the Church. Appalled, he watched Sep suck back into the known, detested 'Dad', guessed too late what was to come, too late tried to flee, found Sep screamingly straddling him, hands round his throat, tightening, tightening, as though he would squeeze the sense from his own intractable flesh.

'Whore!' Sep roared like the Wrath of the God he sought, spittle and liquor-fumes flailing from his mouth, 'Satan-seed sent to rob me of my Jesus's love!' and he thought, searingly, dementedly – Ray, his mother, but mostly Ray, flickering in and out of his consciousness like a traffic light – is this to be all there is?

Then she said, 'Sep,' quietly, from the door, and Sep, like a switched-off toy, instantly slumped, rose from him, erection still rigidly unappeased, hunched down on the floor, face in his hands, howled – like a dog, a lost soul, the first, damned man.

And he, cawing for breath, throat raped, also scrabbled off the bed, stood, heedless of the tracksuit pants and scants about his knees.

Swiftly she came to him, pale, composed, only her voice betraying urgency as she said, 'Go now! Quick!' and he tidied himself and, a suitcase in either hand, went out, as one banished, into the street.

As he walked, blindly, still not knowing where he was going or what to do, concentrating only on distancing himself from the house, a thin, black adder of a thought slid through the chaos of his mind. How had her entrance been so neatly timed? Had she ever been away? Had she, far from showing him an unexpected warmth of love, used him as bait in a trap set to bind Sep to her afresh after the past traumatic weeks of strain? Had she, in fact, baited that trap at the *beginning* of those weeks, hoping that his continued and (for Sep) grown intolerable presence in the house, would drive the latter back to the bottle, to the committing of some desperate, compromising deed? Tiredly, he pushed the thought away, thinking 'what did it matter now, anyway?'

Then he was going down Main, passing the Rink, hardly knowing where he was, suitcases dragging at his arms. The show was long since out, but a cigarette's lit tip was glowing, redly, in front of the foyer-gates, and Ray was separating himself from the shadows, taking a suitcase from him, walking at his side.

'About time!' he said. 'Can't fucking well wait here all night!'

*** *** ***

Although Sep had not penetrated his flesh, he had trespassed beyond the flesh and left there his hoofprint and dung. In consequence of this, he hated and recoiled from the thought of Sep more virulently than ever before, and for the first few days after accepting the refuge of Ray's roof and, thus, ceasing to be a mere spectator of the latter's world, he was unable to reveal to Ray all that had taken place on that fateful last evening in what, he knew with all his tissue and every sense, could never be a home to him again. Ray, true to form, never questioned him, and when he eventually, seeking to draw the pus from the wound, of his own accord spoke of that night's events and how he felt, Ray listened almost grudgingly, then, when he was finished, looked at him from a shadow in the corner of the room and said, eyes empty with an emptiness that spoke of a passion beyond the tongue, 'Ja, welcome to hell.'

Which remark he did not explain.

The unburdening, however, proved to be of little help. Was that what Ray had meant by his reference to a 'hell'? Certainly, a torment was to be found in any deeper analysis of how he felt, and he tried not to indulge in this, but there was much of the masochist in him and he probed, as a tongue would a rotten tooth, the ultimate bedrock of his being where still he cried out in loathing at Sep's touch, yet atavistically exulted, was fulfilled, that another's flesh should have sought his flesh and branded him with an evidence that, in his aloneness, he was yet not alone. As contradictory was a heightened sensitivity – uneasiness almost – when it came to another's touch, coupled with an ever easier tolerance of the Bohemianism – and often petty and not so petty criminality and thuggery – that life at the flats demanded he endure. It was almost as though, after his experience with Sep, all else was déjà vu.

Living, so to speak, backstage of Ray's life, all the nuts and bolts mercilessly exposed, it was inevitable that he should start to revise his previous assessments of Ray's role in his world, and, indeed, of the nature of Ray himself. As regards the first, it soon became apparent that Ray was not at all the major player he had seemed. Nor was he as affluent as he had made out. His dealings in drugs and booze were relatively minor, while his occasional services as pimp were more in the nature of favours to friends than aimed at any real monetary gain. The primary source of his income remained the sale of himself, a dealing which he once – spurred by one of the random impulses to which he was so prone – tried to justify by asserting that 'he was the rider, not the horse'.

His freer access to Ray's nature – not a 'true' access since Ray was far too secretive for that – yielded surprises as gratifying as, one in particular, distressing. He had always been prepared to discover, and, in his infatuation, even accept, that Ray abused the drugs he stocked as much as those to whom they were sold. But this, most pleasingly, was not so. In fact, and in a truly radical departure from the norm, he did not even, except for the occasional 'trek', smoke the almost ritual dagga-zoll of – as his mother and Sep would have said – 'his class'. As sparing was his use of alcohol – his other and parallel 'stock in trade' – but he *was* a chain smoker of cigarettes and tried, through rigorous exercise, to annul its effects on the rather fine physique that he knew but too well was not only his main commodity, but his weapon and shield in a marketplace of the flesh that was as bereft of mercy as it was void of love.

Far less edifying was his treatment of the succession of women he, with such an odd persistency, installed as mistresses of his body, as they were mistresses of the pathetic make-believe he called his 'home'. He had been shocked at the time by his treatment of Dolly, but it had not been such as to prepare him for the regular, physical assaults upon Fiona, whom he liked and who liked him. After one of these assaults – which were all the more terrifying because of Ray's complete silence throughout – he asked Fiona why she put up with it. A (for a change) trim, small brunette with matching eyes that should have smiled, except that one was swollen shut, and a mouth that tried, though still crusted with blood, she had shrugged, said, 'What else must I do? There's no going back, come this far. At least, he lets me drink all I want, and it's better than going back to the coast and walking the docks. They beat you up anyway, Johnny, wherever you go!'

On the balance of it, his revised image of Ray should have led to the slackening, even severing, of the bond. But the pull of Ray's personality was too strong and his spiritual as well as material need of him the more profound now that he no longer had a home of his own. Stubbornly, he reminded himself of the better moments with Ray, particularly recalling how Ray had helped him carry his suitcases down Fourth, had spread a mattress and duvet for him on the living-cum-dining room floor, brought him a slug of brandy to still his still trembling hands, grimly, yet comfortingly, said, 'Cool it, kid. There's a lot worse shit in the world.'

And, ironically enough, it seemed that Ray's very weaknesses, now revealed, not only served to maintain the bond, but to heighten it: Ray's relative lack of affluence suggesting a correspondingly greater generosity, his human frailties – reaching out to, entwining with, his own inadequacies – weaving between them a relationship that was more complex, as it was more mature.

And in that lurked a dire peril. Bound now in frailty as well as affection to Ray – and, in addition, no longer a transient, in that he had later used up the money he had brought with him to purchase his own mattress, bedding and bed (and even a small cupboard for storing his personal possessions and clothes), he increasingly became more participant in, as well as dependent on, Ray's all too questionable affairs. So, Ray, busied with other matters and an addict at the door, would ever more frequently toss him the keys to the drugs and shout, 'Hey, kid, help the ou there!' and he would accept the oddly so often soiled and crumpled notes from a tremulous hand, quickly averting his face that he might not see beyond the hand. But the exhausted eyes, the surfacing-beneath-the-skin horror of the skull, would engulf him in a dream, and he would wake, sweating, staring at the blank wall of his own life, listening to the sad night's cessation of sadder sound.

At one stage, thinking to distance himself from Ray's dealings without distancing himself from Ray as his friend, he found (ironically enough) the job of whatever sort that his previous inability to find had led to his banishment by Sep. As a packer of supermarket shelves, his wages were minimal and his tasks befitting more a machine than a brain, and he quickly (albeit guiltily) capitulated when Ray, patently self-seeking and with his usual extravagance, began to berate 'fortune' for saddling him with such a moegoe of a friend, asking what *sort* of a friend was it anyway that would put his – Ray's – interests last when it was these interests that had fed him and put a roof over his head when he was in need?

He was not so besotted that he could not recognise this as crude manipulation, but his morality and will had been eroded by the contentment he had found with Ray, the blissful sense of exchange of a stark servitude for a domination less unwelcome and clear. So he went back to dispensing booze and drugs, even arranging of the odd rental of the bed, while Ray hovered like a ravening dragonfly at the door of the Rink, culling the crowds for a likely lay, often again using him as bait for the teenager-avid straight as well as gay.

Any doubts he might have had about continuing his association with Ray were dispelled when, one morning, walking up Main, he and Ray met his mother, she heading for the Pick 'n Pay further down. Never before had she seemed so bland, so lacking in witchery and deceit, her pallor merely that of a skin starved of sun, her hair old-fashioned in a greying bun. Clutching the old tweed carryall with the wooden clasps that always accompanied her on her trips to town, she very slightly faltered when she looked up to find them upon her, but showing this only through a tightening of the hands, a deadening of the face that intensified rather than violated its habitual calm.

Stopping, all three, Ray close to his side, he and his mother circled each other like cautious hounds. Then she smiled with an easy naturalness that he knew (and she knew) he could not match, and held up her cheek for him to kiss. But he refused, feeling the suitcases back in his hands, relishing the fury that flared in her eyes, watching it as quickly die.

'This is Ray Willies,' he said. Then, tauntingly: 'My best friend. I'm staying with him now,' and Ray held out his hand, but she left it stretched, levelling the score.

'Nice to meet you, Mr Willies,' she said, emphasising the 'Mr', tongue toying with his name. 'I do hope you are giving Johnny *all* he needs.' And left, smile a cold glitter of disdain.

Ray stared after her. 'Bitch!' he muttered, both bewildered and annoyed. 'Who the fuck was that?'

'My mother,' he said through gritted teeth, lengthening his stride, and, for once, Ray was silent in the face of a rawness he understood, that matched his own.

His mother's unwitting buttressing of his relationship with Ray could not have been better timed, because, on the night of the second day after the encounter in town, there began a period of the most bitter testing yet of his loyalty to Ray. It was on that night that Ray quarrelled with Fiona for the last time – a quarrel marked by a nightlong altercation of increasing bitterness that culminated in a single, sickening blow of a fist on flesh and an eerie, almost animal wail. Erupting from their room with a ferocity and suddenness that stopped his breath, Ray then stormed from the flat, leaving the door shuddering in its frame.

By morning, Ray had not yet returned and Fiona came out of their room, lugging a large, scuffed suitcase that clearly held all she possessed, and leaned over him to see if he was awake.

'I am leaving, Johnny,' she said, one side of her face wrenched out of shape, 'and I won't be back. It's the end of the line for me here.'

'But where will you go?' he asked, coming close to hating Ray, his pity and concern for her so real that she broke as before one of Ray's blows, and, covering her face, rocking on her heels, wept with the abandon of a child. Gently, with a matureness beyond his training or his years, he drew her to him, stroked her back, smelling her womanness, discovering her bones, till at last she stopped and drew away from him, wiping her eyes. 'Thanks,' she said, not saying more than that, but taking his hand. 'I'm leaving town, going back to the docks, Johnny. That's a long move from here. So you won't be seeing me again. But I have a friend down there and she'll let me share her room.' She paused, tried to smile. 'Maybe this time I'll get me a *steady* Taiwanese who'll give me enough to tide me over between trips. Who knows?' Then she looked at him, deeply, steadily. 'You love him, don't you?' and when his eyes narrowed and he tried to take away his hand, she added, hurriedly, 'No, I don't mean like that. I don't think you are like that. I mean just *love*, Johnny. You understand?'

Slowly, warily, he nodded, and then she leant to him with a great urgency and said, 'Don't, Johnny! There's nothing there. Or, if there is, it will do you no good,' and she leant over further and kissed him, saying 'Ciao!' and was gone.

For a long time he lay there, watching the sun widen over the dingy walls, deeply stirred – and deeply perturbed by her final words – but at last dismissing these, reassuring himself that although Ray could be inexcusably cruel to others, he had never been that to him, so there *must* be 'something there' and it was not for him to turn against Ray for no reason other than the outpourings, however understandable, of a cast-out and tormented girl.

Midmorning, Ray returned, not greeting him, the smell of liquor pungently on his breath, mouth morose. But he was not drunk and, seeking to still any lingering doubts by hearing Ray's side of the case, he called upon all his courage and, blunt because of his inborn fear of any more powerful than himself, burst out, 'Fiona's gone. Why did you treat her so bad?'

Instantly Ray rounded on him, teeth bared. 'Bad?' he raged. 'Wharra you know about bad? All the time you been with me – you had no woman. I'm thinking again you *never* had no woman. Spit only in your hand. Mr Good can't put it where it wants! So don't talk to me about women or what's bad till you got the snot off your nose. Shoved that meat between your legs where it belongs!' And he strode into his room, slamming the door, the springs singing under him as he flung himself down on the bed.

But in him, too, there was a sullenness and Ray had forgotten that. Deeply hurt, rage and shame blinding him to the consequences of what he did, he got up and began to pack his suitcases, going – where? And he was nearly finished when Ray opened his door again and stood looking at him, eyes still bloodshot, but no longer crazed.

'Wharra you doing?' he asked, his voice hoarse and slurred.

'Leaving,' he said, snapping shut a suitcase's catch, not glancing up.

'Ah! come on, Johnny, don't act like you was a little girl. Can't you take a little rough talk?' and Ray came forward from the door as if to curb him, and he thought, incredulously, did he hear Ray *whine*?

'No,' he said, trying for curt, but already wavering as he snapped shut another catch. 'I am like Fiona. Nobody talks to me like you did.'

'*All right,* then,' and this time he was sure there was, at least, a pleading in Ray's voice, 'I'm sorry,' and then, when still he did not look up, 'Come *on*, kid. Wharra you want? I must go down on my knees to you like a dog?'

The thought of Ray doing that was so incongruous that he found himself fighting off a laugh and reason, returning, said, 'Go for the gap,' and he got up and faced Ray and said, instinctively knowing he had the ace, 'Okay, but I still want to know why you treated Fiona so bad.'

There was a long silence, in which Ray took his prized personal bottle of brandy from the cupboard and poured them each a solid dop. Holding his up to the light, pushing the other across, he, at last, heavily, almost bewilderedly, said, 'You know, Johnny, I'm fucked if I know how to answer that. Let's just say it got so I could feel the bones in her and they hurt. Okay?'

And he tilted his glass and they drank a toast – although neither knew to quite *what* – and, that same night, fat Dolly was back in Ray's bed.

'Jesus! you also sleeping here now?' she said by way of greeting as she carried in her things. 'We going to take it by turns?'

Again, the prospect of such an arrangement was so ludicrous that he wanted to laugh, and, indeed, did – and she looked at him, surprised, and suddenly grinned, and the sulky doll's face was transformed.

It was a good start and it got better, ripening into something like friendship towards the end – for end, inevitably, there was. Often, when Ray was not there, he would sit on the bed in which she seemed to spend most of her time, and they would talk, finding that there was surprisingly much for them to talk about. He told her about his mother and Sep, and she nodded – understanding that – and she told him about her father: a farmer who, out of his bed, was a dour diaken of the Kerk, but, between the sheets, was a satyr incarnate who bred ten children from his fat, complaisant wife ('fat was all I got from her,' she wryly said) and then possessed them as if they were kin to the calves he bred from his as fecund Friesland cows. But he had not stopped there: 'Ma was not enough for him. He still had to have it off with the widow in town. Share her with I dunno how many other holy spooks.'

Equally boldly, she told him of her flight from home, her slow, certain descent into the twilight world of the whore, her experiences in the fabled sisterhood of the streets that turned out to be as capable of treachery, selfishness and deceit as any of the other communities of the human beast. But neither of them spoke of Ray, or their relationship with him, until she one day turned to him and bluntly asked why *he* did not.

'What must I say?' was his (to even his own ears) oddly uncomfortable response. 'He's my friend. He's been good to me. I like him a lot. That's it.'

'Get off!' she mocked. 'That's not it. There's more. Much more. Like he's not just a friend. He's mafia, too, and you don't talk about mafia. Even behind its back. And you don't just *like* him. You've kind of got the hots for him' – and, as he stiffened and rose to go – 'Okay! Okay! Wait for it! I don't mean the hots that gets you into bed with a woman. Or a man. I mean the hots that wants something to burn, and sometimes it thinks bed is the way, and then it thinks, no, that's not what I want. I don't just want your cock. You up me, back or front. I want what's other side of that. *All* of it, till you are me and I am you and neither of us is alone anymore.'

Shaken by her sudden eloquence, the passion that lifted her to a propping on one elbow in the bed, he stared at her as though he was seeing her for the first time.

'Don't look at me like that!' she hissed, transcendently enraged. 'Did you think I've got no fucking brain? That I'm just a fat slob for your Ray to piss in when he wants? And let me tell you' – and the moon-face that jutted to him was momentarily keener than it was round – 'I see your friend with no more shutters on my eyes than he puts the rubbers on his cock. And he's no big deal, pal. He's just a small-time, bluffing-himself rent boy and crook, and the only person *he's* got the hots for is Ray Willies, full stop.'

Panting slightly, she leaned back, replete: but the extravagance of her emotion and words had angered him, left him less convinced than had Fiona of the validity of her attack on Ray.

'Okay, then,' he said, and his voice was chill, telling her that she had overplayed her hand, 'if that's the way you feel. But why, if you've got so little going for Ray, have you come back?'

She sighed, fat whore again, swirling, snagged, in an eddy without end. 'He asked me to,' she said. 'And he's got a better roof than most. And he's a better lay than most. That is, when he's not shoving it into too many other holes. And' – she paused, surprised, as though she had come upon a thing mislaid in a dark room – 'because, though I have no love for him – hate him most of the time – I'm also sorry for him.'

'Sorry for him?' he echoed, surprised as she.

'Yes, sorry for him. Something went wrong there. At the start. Like it did for me. And nothing will make it right anymore. So we're one and the same. Whores,' and her bulk heaved without mirth and she turned her face to the wall and slept.

Chastened, perhaps, by his near-break with him over the departure of Fiona, Ray abstained from any blatant maltreatment of Dolly for more months than he had dared hope. But, eventually, the familiar nightly outbursts of wrangling and assault resumed and Dolly began to show both the physical and spiritual marks of these, and, though still cordial, to react to his efforts to normalise life for her with something of the unresponsive skittishness of a too often beaten beast.

So, it was with a measure of surprise that, on the afternoon before the morning of the end, sitting, as usual, on the edge of the baroque bed, he found Dolly to be less distracted than for some weeks, and he wondered if matters between her and Ray were on the mend. But it was a vagary similar to Ray's that had seized her, and he was startled when she suddenly rolled over onto her side to face him and, with an intentness and gravity that precluded his taking offence, asked, 'Johnny, you been with a woman yet?' The blush that he so hated and that always overtook him at the most inopportune times, answered for him and she said, 'Ja, virgins I smell.' Then, 'But you're no chicken anymore. How old are you, kid?'

'Nineteen,' he mumbled, looking down at his hands, nails scratching at the duvet.

'Nineteen!' she exclaimed, blue, babyish eyes round. 'And no woman yet? Jesus! You're for the zoo!'

'I told you what it was like at home,' he snapped, now, indeed, offended – and annoyed.

At once she was contrite. 'Ja – sure – I shouldn't have said that. It was gross.'

Silence encircled them, anchored them as in ice. He was conscious that she was studying him, but refused to look up. The cheap, made-in-China clock on the table beside the bed, ticked with a shrill whingeing of its ageing parts. A child wailed, somewhere in the flats: a car rattled past in the rutted street. Then she moved, gently, sibilantly, compelling his glance, and he recoiled when he saw that she had drawn wide her robe and, as on the very first day they had met, was exposing to him the huge nakedness of her flesh.

'Want it?' she asked, her eyes oddly shy, though her voice was light. 'For free. A gift from a whore.'

His first thought was to refuse, angrily berate her for forgetting that she was Ray's girl and he Ray's friend, and her offering herself to him in this way not to be excused. But a second thought edged out the first, slyly as a creature of the dusk. 'Here,' it said, 'is a woman who will help you into her, be patient with your ignorance and awkwardness, remove from you the stigma of the virginity you have borne too long, that is making you so much less of a man than Ray, is losing you the full measure of the respect from him that otherwise would have been yours.'

Tentatively, he surveyed the hanging breasts, the elephantine thighs, the belly's sobbing mound, the fabled tuft of pubic hair that must bring him relief, release, but that, dwarfed as it was by the massiveness surrounding it, seemed no more than an anatomical joke, an extraneousness devoid of all mystery and grace.

Swiftly, a shudder ran through him, though he clenched his body like a fist to cover it, and his genitals stayed comatose as meat.

'Don't you want it?' she asked, and now there was a faint plaintiveness in the voice that hurt.

Desolately, conscious of the continuing stubborn inertness of his loins, he wondered how Ray, with his honed, proud physique, could ever have achieved arousal on this spread, amorphous freak. And even as he so wondered, picturing Ray straddling her, covering her, melding his rhythm with the rhythm of her sad, responding flab, he achieved his own arousal, suddenly and independently of his wanting or will, so that he felt as one possessed by a psyche not his own. Instinctively, his hand went out and stroked her belly, breasts and thighs, and the alien in him groaned with a lust that was as alien as that from which it sprang, and he snatched back his hand, understanding, sickeningly almost too late, that what he had sought was not her skin as *her* skin, but as the skin on which had lain – in an intimacy he had never shared – the skin of him to whom she belonged.

'Gangbang!' whispered a dark blood. 'Is that what you want? A baying under the moon?'

Gently, he leant over and drew the robe about her again.

'No,' he said, in answer to her gathering frown. 'Sometimes it thinks bed is the way, and then it thinks, no, that's not what it wants.'

'You for the nuthouse, not the zoo!' she mocked. 'Look at you. Hard on to last all day and you throw it away.' But her eyes understood.

Desire, though, did not. Uncaged, it was not lightly again driven back and his rather smug feeling of noble restraint, of having played the mature man, all too soon gave way to the morose and adolescent

35

guilt of the masturbator that his mother and Sep had so relentlessly implanted in him from the first days of his becoming aware of what he was. Leaning his back against the tiny bathroom's door to keep it closed – its lock long broken and never replaced – he released himself into one of the condoms he kept in the cupboard beside his bed, savage with self-disgust, as resentful of his sperm as of his blood. Then, hearing Dolly's approaching steps, he hastily threw the condom into the plastic rubbish pail behind the door and left the house, walking determinedly nowhere, wading through the litter of the mean streets as though he waded through the litter of his life. 'What,' he suddenly, treacherously, asked of himself, 'am I *doing* here? Drugs, booze, flesh. Is there nothing *else?*' But then he remembered Sep's fingers hooked in the back of his scants and that night he was back, fretfully listening to the last of Dolly's and Ray's interminable fights.

It seemed set to rage all night, Dolly's shrill yapping like a Pekinese weaving through Ray's harsh, demanding yell. 'Always the same fucking thing!' he fumed, covering his ears with his hands, save that this time – as though the two protagonists had themselves grown weary of their routine – there were no blows. And, once, he thought he heard Dolly scream out his name, but this he dismissed as imagination and, at last, exhausted, fell asleep despite the row.

When he again woke, the sun was already high and the flat so silent that he at first thought he was alone. But then he saw Ray with his back to him, brewing coffee, and the bedroom's door gaped onto an emptiness so vividly sensed that it was almost seen.

He stirred and Ray turned to him, his eyes blank as shades. 'Coffee,' he said, his tone remote and cold, and sat down, taking up his mug with both hands. And he rose and dressed, conscious of Ray's watching his every move: his drawing on of his T-shirt, buttoning up of his fly, groping under the bed for his shoes. 'Christ!' he thought, 'last night must have been some ball!'

Then he went and sat down at the table, facing Ray. But Ray did not slide his coffee across to him as he normally would have done. Kept it on his side – and somehow he knew this was not the time to reach, to fetch. This was Sep, second time around.

'Your girlfriend's gone,' Ray at last said, no change in the shuttered eyes. 'Said to tell you "Ciao!" Said to tell you "thanks for a great fuck." Better even than mine. Said to give you this,' and he reached to the shelf behind him and, with forefinger and thumb, mock-delicately dropped on the table between them, the still glutinous condom he had so hurriedly flung into the litter pail.

'Christ! O Christ!' he silently groaned. 'Betrayed! By her! By my own hand! Why am I always so ready to run like a hare? Why did I not flush the fucking thing down the bowl?'

And then he wondered what he should now do. Tell Ray the truth? Betray her as she had betrayed him? Rob her of her small victory over Ray? Somehow, deep down, he knew he could not do this, that he still liked her, whatever her true feelings towards him had been, that Ray deserved the blow she had so clearly dealt his arrogance and pride. And, deeper down even than that, at the very core of his own small ruthlessness (and not so insignificant a conceit), he knew that he would not tell Ray the truth simply because he *liked the lie,* luxuriated in the macho image that Dolly had, unwittingly (or had it been – *could* it have been – wittingly?), created for him in Ray's eyes.

Ray, sensing the turmoil that had seized him, for once got it wrong. Grin as wide as a shark's under the dead eyes, he suddenly extended his hand, saying 'Shake, kid!' and he, wonderingly, took it. 'At last you're right in there with me, kid. "Better than me!" she said,' and the wink, the coyness, were grotesque, 'and I don't have to hang my head for shame for you no more. But,' and his voice took on a warning, though still brotherly, note, 'next time *tell* me what you gonna do, kid, and it's all yours, and no bad smell either side. Or,' the warning grown clearer, aimed, 'better still, fetch your own meat from now. Okay?'

Then he leant back and said, 'Get your coffee, kid,' and this time he reached for his mug, but Ray grabbed it first and, with the same wide grin and unseeing eyes, flung its still scalding contents full into his face. Howling with pain, hands clapped to his eyes, he staggered from his chair, overturning it, and Ray, flinging aside the table, sending everything on it crashing to the floor, was on him, wrenching away his hands, punching him, once, twice, and again, pulping his lips, smashing his nose, further blinding the already blinded eyes.

He did not know it when he hit the floor, lay there for a time forever gone, Ray's boots taking over from the fists, crashing into face, ribs, knees.

It was nearing noon when he began to claw his way back to consciousness of light and sound. His ears sang as though he had been flung into an aviary of birds and psychedelic strobes flashed on and off behind his still closed lids. Then his eyes opened and he saw the flaking ceiling, the shards (some crackling under him as he moved) of the shattered plates and cups, the kettle, lying on its side, a piss of its water snaked across the floor, and, immediately above the still dishevelled bed, the gaudy girlie-almanac that promised improbable delights to a flesh geared now only to pain.

His face stiff under its mask of drying blood, his right eye swollen shut, his ribs so painful he could only breathe in short pants, he tried to crawl across the room to his bed, but the room spun as though his movements had nudged a trigger of some kind, and a china splinter gashed his palm, setting him bleeding afresh, and he, forgetting, cried out, 'Ray!' Then he remembered and a desolateness more terrible than the pain overcame him and he blanked out a second time.

But the coma was lighter now and when Ray crashed open the door, he was almost instantly aroused. The wildly staring eyes and weaving stance of the figure the door framed, seemed to presage a further assault and he shielded his face with his arms and cried out again, but now in a pleading that shamed, but could not be restrained. Then he realised Ray was drunk, was gripping the door's frame for support, was weeping with a soundless abandon that, like the drunkenness, he had never witnessed before, and he uncrossed his arms and stared in disbelief at a man he no longer knew.

Then Ray was kneeling beside him, cupping his face in his palms, saying nothing, save for the silent eloquence of his tears, the as silent scream of his eyes. What does he want of me, he thought, whimpering with pain as Ray desperately patted his cheeks, rolled his head from side to side. Does he think I am dead, wants me to speak, tell him I'm okay? But why should he care? Why should I care? And, for the first time, bitterness rasped through him the thin wire of its iron.

As though sensing this, Ray suddenly lowered his head, sound at last draining out of him in a long groan, and kissed him on the lips, his own slippery with mucus and tears, his breath benumbing with the liquor's stench. The kiss was full and male, spoke only of contrition and grief, and now he, too, groaned, but from the pain of the pressure on his smashed mouth, and when Ray again drew away from him, he saw that the latter's lips were now also reddened with a fresh blood taken from him, and it was as though there had been a bonding as ancient as time.

Then spurred, perhaps, by the groan, reassured that there was still something, feared lost, to be retrieved, Ray wrestled him to the bed, often stumbling, legs splayed, haste hissing through his teeth, and he thought, 'Christ! leave me alone!' as the pain from his ribs clamped round him and his breath shrilled. And yet, through it all, he did not really want to be left alone, was agonisedly content that Ray's hands should unwittingly so maul him, so clumsily swab the blood from his face till the water in the bowl he had placed on the cupboard beside the bed, was as red as the blood. Should, even more searingly, strip him bare to reveal the full damage wrought by the boots, a disabling of ribs and knees that far outweighed the more visible, superficially more shocking, kicked-skew one side of his face. Was this, he wondered, as Ray wrapped him in the thick duvet from his own bed and pressed two Panados into his mouth, the same man that had leapt on him like an animal only a few hours before, and, if so, when would the beast again break loose to rend his spirit even more brutally than it had his flesh?

But he need not have feared. For some reason he was never to fully discern, nor understand, and Ray would be unwilling (or unable) to wholly disclose, the latter had veered from a going to a certain there, to a going to a somewhere that shifted with the unpredictability of a mirage. But this no Paulian revelation, splendour of light on a lonely road, as he was at once to find. Finished with him, Ray went into the bedroom, came back with an unopened bottle of what looked like gin, put this on the table he had summarily righted in the otherwise still chaotic room, sat down. Uncapping the bottle and unsteadily retrieving one of the still whole mugs from the floor, he filled the mug with what, by its cloyingly sweetish smell, proved to be aniseed liqueur, and gulped it down. Shaking his head, shuddering through his entire length like a water-soaked dog, he stared at the wall with glazing eyes, then, more slowly but steadily, continued drinking, mechanically siphoning the remainder of the bottle into his already insensate flesh, striving for the total oblivion that he at last achieved when his head flopped forward onto the table and he slept with a roaring breath that precluded dream. 'Or did it?' he wondered, watching him with the pity and horror of one witnessing a severing of veins.

When he again woke, it had grown dark. But he could still see Ray's body slumped across the table and he called to him. But the fallen silent form did not stir, and that and, above all, the cessation of the tortured breath – was there *no* breath? – filled him with intolerable misgiving and he made to rise and go to Ray, but his battered body rebelled and he fell back, nearly senseless with renewed pain. The effect of the Panados had, in fact, worn off, and he lay there, his concern for Ray ingloriously ceding ground to the mounting agony of his own flesh and bone. Then he remembered that Ray had left the packet of Panados within his reach, and he fumbled for it with his still uninjured left hand and managed to extract and swallow two more of the pills after spilling several on the floor.

A brightness woke him and he opened his eyes and it was day, and Ray was sitting down beside him on the bed, looking, astoundingly, very much the man he had always been, placing his hand behind his head, raising it, holding the mug of coffee to his lips, saying, 'Drink,' saying it again with almost his old impatience when he tried to take the mug and help himself.

Ray had, of course, been right. It was to be another week before he could help himself, and, in that time, Ray fed him, doctored him, helped him defecate and urinate (even buying, or borrowing – he never found out which – a hospital bedpan for the first few most difficult days), and, on the morning after the assault, wash-wiped his bruised and, in parts, bloodied body with a wet cloth, swabbing even his genitals with nothing of the ribaldry that this normally would have provoked. Uncharacteristically unsmiling, though not hostilely so, saying only what had to be said, Ray made it very plain that his was an act of penitence, a proffering by the body of an apology for which all the tongue's articulateness would not suffice.

For that week also, Ray stayed in the flat when not on duty at the Rink, but he did leave it in the night of his day-off, when he thought, with no small a grief, 'Ja, here we go again!' but Ray returned within the hour, bringing back a box of painkillers other than the Panados which he had gone down to buy at the chem. 'Better than the 'Nados,' he said, and left the box beside the bed. During the day, from early till it was time for the Rink – and particularly on the Saturday when his 'regulars' had pay to spend – he sold his drugs and a little booze, and explained that his tjommie was 'sick' and there would be no trade in the afternoons for a while. In the lonely way of the predator, Ray had customers or victims, but no friends (and no 'family' who ever called, or of whom he spoke), so they were left pretty much to themselves and learning to be comfortable with that, and even on the few occasions when the almost redundantly silent telephone did ring, Ray simply said, 'No deal,' in a tone that meant that that, indeed, was what it was. The fact that no woman had been recruited to take Dolly's place did not at first puzzle him because Ray was clearly in no fit state to cope with any further emotional strain, and, on a more self-serving level, it would have been embarrassing for him to be found nursing a flatmate whom his own hands (and boots) had reduced to so pitiable a state. But, by the end of the week, able to again hobble about and the 'highs' of penitence and pardon (though, possibly, not yet of guilt) on the ebb, he diffidently asked who would be 'next', but Ray, again with an almost welcome something of his old harshness, said 'Nah! Fuck 'em!' and he knew he should leave it at that.

His had been a good question, though, and one that still warranted a reply, because, shortly after, Ray back from the evening show at the Rink and both of them already in bed and the lights switched off, Ray suddenly again switched on his light and called, a high note, almost of fear, in his voice, 'Kid, come sleep by me!'

Startled, recalling that he had heard that same note of strain in

Ray's voice shortly before their sleeping for the past few nights, he recoiled at the thought of so sustained and intimate a proximity to one who, he knew, slept 'in the raw' and who, after (for him) so long an abstaining from women, or (darkly the thought crept in) men, might unleash upon him a clone of the crazed Sep who still clawed him in the unexpectedness of dream. 'But he was drunk,' said reason, 'and Ray was only drunk this one time because of what he did to you,' and, 'Did he not touch you like your own hand when he washed you and helped you with your piss and shit, and not once was he Sep, only Ray?' and he knew reason was right, but still he hesitated, for the first time relating Ray's long sexual history with others to his own unsavoured self.

'Kid?' called Ray again.

'No,' he said at last. 'I'm okay here. No fuss.'

Then he heard Ray rising from the bed, padding across the floor, and looked up to see him standing, naked as expected, in the door.

'I'm not asking it for you, kid. I'm asking it for me.'

'But why?' he stalled. 'Why do you want me to sleep with you?'

'Because I don't like sleeping alone. I get dreams. That's why.'

'Then get yourself another woman,' he said, sullenly, and turned his face to the wall.

'Hey! you think I'm gonna rape you, or something?' Ray shouted, voice rising as much in shock as rage. 'I could-a done that a long time ago, if I wanted to. Like I smacked you around the other day!'

But he did not turn back from the wall and the silence lengthened and deepened between them till he could hear the faulty shower dripping a heavy-as-blood water onto the bathroom floor.

'Okay,' said Ray, and he had never before known him to speak in so quiet a tone. 'If that's the way you feel,' and the bare feet padded back across the floor and the door closed.

'If that's the way I feel,' he repeated to himself. 'How *do* I feel?' and even as he asked himself that, he rose and went to Ray and slid into the bed next to him, and Ray said, 'Thanks, kid,' and slept, instantly as a child.

In the morning, he tensed for an otherness between him and Ray: a shyness, an awkwardness, a sense, perhaps, of an impermissibility clandestinely indulged. But Ray was, if anything, easier with him than before and he felt himself respond, and when they, that Wednesday, spent Ray's day-off together, the first since his injuries had confined them to the flat, there were no assignations, no abandonments of him in a lonely stand or bar, and he knew for certain that, like a pack ice breaking up, a pattern that had been fixed was in flux and the ground was flowing beneath them like water and wind.

Later that night, lying beside Ray, sharing with him a last cigarette, as they had done in the seemingly now so distant days of the locking-up at the Rink, he felt that flood sweeping him closer to Ray than he had ever been, felt himself warm in blood and bone, felt his loins swell, and clamped down, crying 'No!'

But Ray, as though sensing how he felt, dragged hard on the cigarette, firing its tip, then passed it to him and, hands locked behind his head, burst out, 'Meat! That's all we are, kid. Just meat. No Big Daddy in the sky. No afters with wings, and stuff. Just a hole in the ground. Gotta have the hole, kid. Cause why? Cause we stink. That's why. But why's it gotta *be* this way?' – and he swung his head, urgently, from side to side – 'All this time, I been fucking meat, and fucking it cruel, because I'm sticking my meat in *more* meat, and I don't *want* it that way. And all this time, I been beating my women, and beating them bad, because *they're* meat and I'm wanting what they don't have. Even my old man was meat, kid. You know that?' – and he turned his face and stared at him, amazed as he expected him to be amazed – 'Ja, he would come from my old lady – and *she* was meat! – breeding more meat all the time! – breeding me – and he would stick his meat up my meat, and me only six, kid – only *six!* And you thought your Sep was the big time? That's why I said nothing much when you told me what he tried. The first time I thought he's gonna be loving me, but he give it me *hard*. Think, kid, he growed me from his seed, then he comes and puts his seed in his seed. Like he's fucking himself. You know wharramean? For years and years he done that till I growed big enough to tell him to go fuck his hand. Now he's dead and she's dead and I never been to put flowers on their holes. Reckon flowers would'n. grow on *his* hole, anyway! And the rest?' – he chopped with his hand – 'I don't wanna know. They leave me alone, I leave them alone. It's better so, though sometimes I wish – I wish –'

'What?' he asked when he realised the sentence would not end.

'Oh, I dunno. Forget it. Wishes don't get you anyplace.'

'And me?' he asked, edging warily onto perilous ground. 'Am I also meat?'

Ray stayed silent for so long a time that he thought he had fallen asleep and he glanced quickly at him as he leaned over to stub out the cigarette. But his eyes were wide open, the whites gleaming wetly in the dark.

'You hear me?' he asked.

'Ja, I heard you. But I'm thinking, must I lie to you or tell you the truth?'

'Try the truth,' he said, his voice more tense than he liked.

'Okay. I'm thinking I was going to anyway. Look, Johnny' – and he stared at him with a grave seriousness that added to his years – 'Love is a big word for a man to say to another man. Maybe too big a word for me to get onto my tongue. And who says I believe in it, anyway? Maybe it's just the hots dressed up to kill. And I mean *"kill"*. But from the start you hooked me, kid. From that day when you said you wanted nothing from me. Wanted just to be my friend. Nobody never said that to me before. Then, the other day when I nearly killed you because of a fat whore saying you was better than me in bed, I turned around. Knew if you *was* meat, you was the first meat I did'n want to throw away when I had my fill. Okay?' – he paused, wrestling, he sensed, with something heavier and darker than he had yet said – 'Now, kid, I'm gonna tell you straight that there's been times when I thought what it would be like to lay with a meat I liked. With *you*. And' – noting his start, his quick drawing away – 'before you get all fired up – thinking Daddy Sep rides again and I been waiting for you all the time in this fancy bed – what about you, kid? What about that hard you got between your legs right now? You think I did'n know? I don't have to feel you, kid. I hear it in your voice, me being no larnie in this trade. But, again, before you wet your scants, hear me, I'm not gonna touch you though I'm thinking if I asked you to let me have you now, you would'n say "No" straight off. I'm not gonna touch you, kid, because' – and he sighed with the effort to get it all out – 'you come so close to me now, I'm not, like my old man, gonna fuck my own meat.'

Then, almost soothingly, he added, 'But don't feel bad, kid. Meat's a mad dog. Leave it loose and it hots for anything, nevermind the shape or stink. And when it's dik, it throws away what's left, and I don't wanna be what's left. Nor you.'

In the clap of the silence that followed, he tried to speak, to say, 'thanks', 'I love you', any sad, damned thing, but his tongue lay slack and nerveless as his loins, and, eventually, it was Ray that, on the brink of sleep, went on, 'I dunno how short's our road, kid, nor where we going, but I'm wishing now I could earn our bread some other way. Drugs, booze, whores – meat! But what the fuck else *can* I do? I'm wore out and growed the way I am. Maybe I *should* wear the rubbers, though. I never *killed* nobody yet. Why now?'

Suddenly, a terrible prescience struck him, and he found his tongue and asked, with a harshness that rang like anger, but was the beginning of the keening that, inwardly, he had so long feared would come, 'But why should the road be short and not long? What are you trying to say?' and, as from some other world, he heard Ray, lifelessly trying for lightness, reply, 'Ja – well – you might as well know it now, kid. I have got it. Top of the class! The Big A.'

* * *

The next morning, trying for discreet, he studied Ray as once he had studied Sep. How slyly, he thought, blood chilled, heart seized, had this thing, whose very name tolled a bell of death, wrought the change that he only now saw, that, through a process of gradual montage, had already become a clear stripping of the flesh from the bone, a hastening of the retreat of the eyes into the skull. How long, in terror and alone, had Ray known he housed this devil's seed, burst now into virulent life, that was to consume him with a mounting rage? Ray never said and he, as uncertain of his own reactions as he was of Ray's, quailing at the prospect of compounding the horror and heartbreak he already felt by attaining a more vivid appreciation of Ray's state, turned inwardly away, yet remained bound as one fleeing in a dream. By nature as reticent as he was inarticulate when it came to the profundities of the heart and mind, Ray, unquestioned, made little effort to enlighten him of his own accord, assuming a hollow flippancy when the subject did, inadvertently, arise. This reserve, with the perversity of all mystery, only served to highlight this matter the more and the ensuing duality of attraction and repulsion stretched him thin as a scream.

There was an occasion, though, near the start of what was to be a long and climactic year, when Ray, unasked, said something as revelationary as it appalled. 'Hey, kid!' he shouted, grinning with the old ferocity that culled him from a softer breed, squinting at him over the breakfast table's sparse litter of unmatched cutlery and plates. 'I'm thinking my old man shafted me worse than I thought. You know I never had no kids, though you never asked. Never had them though it was naked snake all the way. So I'm thinking now my old man, when he was up me, made me woman inside. Like my balls was eggs – you know wharramean? And now I got his devil-baby fucking around in my gut. This devil-baby they's calling the Big A!' and he laughed with a harsh explosiveness that was more hysteria than mirth, and he felt, probably wrongly, probably himself no longer quite sane, that Ray had *set out* to shock him, to rub his nose, like a puppy's, in the shit, saying, 'See, *that's* shit. You don't know it yet. *I* know!'

Ray was certainly still very capable of being cruel, did not go with any theatrical nobility or stoicism through his life's littered wasteland to the even bleaker wasteland at its end. This commonplaceness – this *commonness* – was disappointing to his more romantically inclined concept of how high drama should be, but, as before, it was the bond of shared *frailty* that held, that served to remind him that, basically, this was still the same Ray that he had learnt to love despite all his faults, and not some castrated angel as incapable of excretion as it was devoid of blood.

Even so, witnessing Ray's decline was not a pretty thing. Pathetically, he at first strove to retain his physique – his pride in it – by stepping up his already strenuous exercise routine, but instead, inexorably, he was compelled to relinquish exercise after exercise as thinness became the gauntness of one starved of life and he was reduced to a hanging of the hands between the knees and a muttered, 'Don't feel so good today. Maybe the 'flu.' But it was never the 'flu: more an increasingly virulent and recurrent pneumonic clogging of the lungs, the strangulation of asthma, and, most degradingly of all, a diarrhoea that narrowed his world to the ring of the toilet bowl and drained him still further of the sass that, by turns endearingly or repugnantly, had powered the mercurial waywardness of his will. Perhaps the most benumbing phenomenon for them both, however, was when Ray first lifted his head from the pillows of a morning and the loose hairs on the latter chillingly told of his going bald, and, shortly after, there was the day when, in a trick of light, he saw an insidious greying of Ray's hair, and he got up, carefully, as though holding in a disembowelled gut, and walked down Fourth to a small, ruined shed atop the dump, and wept there with all of the silent abandon of Ray when the latter had held his shattered face between his palms.

When the exercises stopped, Ray, as though tacitly conceding that the body, that had so long sustained him with its power and allure, had now betrayed him, set about its destruction – and his consciousness of its destruction – with the same systematic, though now negative, ruthlessness that had marked the thrust and iron of the days of high noon. Now so wasted that the marketplaces of the flesh at once knew what was wrong and, thus, cast him off like one of the used 'rubbers' that he had, indeed, begun to use, and, in any case, grown too weak and passionless to satisfy a clientele that demanded more than its pound of flesh, Ray began to sequester himself in the flat, to brood, to swing from a manic hilarity to a schizophrenic melancholia – and to enhance these states by the abuse (as he had once so feared he might have to overlook in Ray) of the very drugs he sold. The stench of the 'pipe' and the accompanying booze festered in the flat, as it festered in so many of the other flats in the block, and he thought (startlingly as his mother and Sep would have done), 'Shit. Now we're shit. No place left to go to. Not even down!'

But there was. Ray still had his job at the Rink. Had to lose it. Which, eventually, he did. Sacked. Sent picking his way carefully back down Fourth, thin legs high-stepping it like a mantis's on the prowl, once straight back hunched over like a beggar asking alms, like an old man – or an old whore – like the meat he had once talked about that knew no sex or shape – lurching back, then, into the flat – reaching for the mandrax, the dagga, making him a 'pipe'.

Now there was only the money from the booze and drugs to pay the flat's rent, to buy the barest necessities of food and clothes, to pay Ray's spiralling doctors' bills, and, increasingly, this money was not enough, and he (this time meeting no opposition from Ray) again tried to find a job, but the policy of preferment of blacks over whites when it came to work was now more established and stringent than before, and his hands stayed idle as the skeletal, doomed hands of the man to whom his heart still clove.

Why did it still so cleave? Was it because he relished the reversal of roles, savoured the fact that it was now Ray who leaned on him, rather than the other way about? But that, he thought, would not be a cleaving of the heart in the sense of the heart's traditionally connoting tenderness and love. Did he just stay on because there was nowhere else to go? But this also did not ring true because, in all fairness to himself, he could not find, in any realm of his being, the stony mercilessness and opportunism that this would entail. No, he decided – and was rather too smugly exalted for his own good by this – he could not *but* love the man who, when he one night suggested he take up a stand on the 'beat', said, 'Ja, you do that, kid, and when you come back you'll find me gone, and when I say "gone", I mean *gone*'; or the man who said, 'Fiona's back in town. Asked about you. Knows about me and cried a bit. Go see her sometimes, when there's the big itch,' adding, with a brief flash of a wry smile that tore his heart apart: 'You're better'n me, you know'; or the man who, sometimes, at night, in a stupor of sleep in the bed he still shared only with him, would clasp him in a sexless, beseeching embrace of a child fleeing the dark – or the old fleeing the cold.

He did, indeed, visit Fiona, finding her much thinner than before, thinking, 'Christ! not her too!' She caught, understood, the look, laughed with a desperate gaiety, said, 'No, not yet. And trying to keep it that way.'

'Why you back?' he asked, extending her his hand, but she stretching up, kissing his cheek.

'No steady Taiwanese, Johnny. Just the same old one-, maybe two-, three-night stands. And the trade's all teeth. Shark eat shark and kinky sex getting kinkier and more than I can take. But it's good to see you again, Johnny. Like old times.' Then: 'This social or business? Ray said it might be business. Off and on.'

'Social,' he said. 'And to stay that way. For now.'

'You still the monk, Johnny?' and he looked uncomfortable, and she knew, but did not deride, though asking all the same: 'You must be going on twenty now.'

'Am twenty,' he said. Then, urgently, willing her to understand: 'Look, Fiona, my time will come, but it's not yet, and don't ask me when. But ask me *why* and I'll say: "You seen Ray and you cried."' But she looked blank, and he went on: 'Ja, you seen Ray and you cried. But *why* did you cry?'

'Well,' she hesitated, groping for his sense, for her words, 'death's no mean deal. It's the one you still respect when you spit on the rest, and when I saw Ray and how he had changed, I *had* to cry. For *me,* as much as for him.'

'You still think there's nothing there? Like you said when you went away?'

'Well *death* is there, and so little of the Ray I knew, that perhaps there *is* still nothing there, but a better kind of nothing, if you know what I mean.'

'Yes, I know what you mean,' and he looked at her with a sombreness that stilled, 'and now *you* must understand that you saw him – only once?' – he looked at her, inquiring, and she nodded her head – 'and you cried, but I *live* with him, eat with him, sleep with him, and he like a corpse by me in the bed, and *I* am crying *all the time.* You gonna like me less or more, if I come from a burying that's been a year now, and maybe will be a year again, and I say, "Fiona, I got the hots, help me forget there's death, there's a friend, cover for me while I let death have him to himself for a time that will be for me a nothing, but will be for him a hell?"'

'Probably neither way,' she said, considering, grave. 'But I do understand.'

'Okay then.' He paused, took her by the shoulders, possessed her with touch and eyes. 'Look, things with me and Ray are *bad.* No moola for medicines, rent, the works. Ray's *finished,* Fiona. So now it's *me's* gotta do something – for *him,* more'n for me. *What,* I don't know right now. Jobs are out. It seems the rough way's the only way. So, if something goes wrong for me and Ray's left on his own – promise me – though you don't *have* to – what do you owe me and Ray, anyway? –

you won't let Ray die alone.'

'I promise,' she whispered, not pausing at all, pressing herself to him, 'though it's you I owe, not Ray.'

A few days later, he knew – or thought he knew – what he must do: a two-phase operation of, first, abasement, then assertion, before which even now he quailed, but for which still he steeled himself in the desperate hope that the steel would hold. And, that night, watching Ray blearily surface from the latest surreality of the 'pipe', he said, 'I have a plan.'

Immediately, as though responding to a voice beneath the voice, Ray reared up straight, glared at him with an awareness, a perceptiveness, beyond vision and tongue. 'No!' he said, hoarsely, startlingly. 'No! I did'n like it then, and I don't like it now. I did'n like it then, cause it was not my scene, but I thought about it all the same, cause that's the devil in a man. But there's snags in it, Johnny – a *moer* of them that's gonna get you in the trong quicker than you shit. Like how you gonna open it without showing your hand? Like how you gonna show your hand without skepping blood with it that's bad, Johnny, real *bad*? And I don't like it now, cause it's still not my scene. Nor yours, Johnny. *Nor yours!* And what's more – the vibes are wrong. Wrong, Johnny, *wrong!* You thought I did'n hear you when you bring me this thing, first time? I heard you all right and I hear you now. Leave it, Johnny. Leave it. *Please!*' and now there was a naked pleading in the voice that snatched his breath, and he wavered on a knife edge of irresolution keen as pain.

But then he looked about him again with clear eyes, seeing the squalor and disintegration of the flat, of themselves, of, particularly, Ray, the ravaged body that cried out for the medication they could no longer afford, the bleak shell the spirit had fled that it might die in decency, and he rallied his resolve and said, curtly, discouraging the argument that he knew would betray that resolve, 'There is no other way,' and, that night, Ray again clung to him with the frantic tenacity of one who held to a last of life.

She was waiting for him when he rang the bell. Rang it, he thought, as one who had never before been there, slept there for the most of his life. He had phoned her to ask if he might see her, and she had said, expressionlessly, 'If you must.' She led him into the sitting room, the great clock in the dining room, deeper in, chuckling and wheezing like a senility of time, and they sat down on two of the straight-backed, primly uncompromising chairs, and faced each other as though for a confrontation across the central table's shining glass and Art Deco vase.

'Well,' she said, her eyes meeting his with their usual infuriating calm, but there was a fretfulness to her toying with the plain gold wedding ring 'Why,' he wondered, 'did it never show any signs of wear?' – and there was a distractedness about her as though she listened to a parallel conversation in another room. 'What is it you want to see me about?'

'I need help,' he said, pride rebelling at the old whine back in his voice.

'By which you mean money,' and the sneer was clearly there, though the pale fall of the face did not stir. 'And who really needs this money? You or that friend of yours? Billy something-or-other, was it not? Or has he ditched you for someone else by now?' ('Ah!' he thought, ignoring the final slur, 'she can't remember his name,' and exulted at a small hurdle overcome.)

'No, we're still together,' he said, striving to keep his voice free of the rancour that her attitude and, indeed, the entirety of the old, loathed ambience was beginning to arouse. 'And – yes – we do both need the money. Any money. Even if it's only enough to pay the rent. He's dying of Aids, you know.' ('Forgive me, Ray!' he inwardly cried, but reaching for a pity somewhere behind the façade, recalling she had always been a social worker of sorts. Amongst whites, at any rate.)

'Good riddance,' she said, with no more passion than if she had said, 'Close the door,' and the words hovered in the room like a winged pestilence that nothing would again sweep away, and she, noting the sick disbelief the words had evoked, was at last driven to defend. 'Well, what else do you expect me to say? I am not – and you should know that – as anti-colour as Sep, but I do believe in each to its own, and it's not us whites who are responsible for a thing like Aids.'

'So you are not going to help us,' he stated, more than asked, his voice thick with disgust and the stirrings of a hatred he had never quite felt for her before.

'Look, Johnny, let's not waste time on this. Sep could be back any moment and I don't want him to find me talking to you. Yes' – as he looked up, puzzled and disturbed, knowing it was not yet three in the afternoon – 'Sep does not work anymore. Sacked. And just about sacked by the Church as well. Just sits in his study most of the time. Drinking, hardly talking to me. But' – quick and proud, not wanting from him the pity that he had tried to arouse in her – 'we're not any worse off than before. Sep didn't need the job anyway. Especially after his mother died last year and left everything to him. But he was chief clerk at the office and liked the power it gave him over the others there.'

'So now you gonna tell me the moola's all in the bank for the interest and you can't, like in the old days, go and grab you a handful from the safe there,' and he jerked his head in the direction of the study, sneering with a cunning provocativeness he had never guessed he possessed, 'and pass some on to me who's supposed to be your goddam son?'

Her eyes flashed, then chilled. 'Don't talk to me like that. I'm still your *white* mother, though the country's black and you with a skolly's tongue. And understand, once and for all, I can open that safe right now and, because of Sep's being the way he is, and sometimes not even able to sign a cheque right, take out *more* than before, but I am not going to do that and you will not get a cent from me, now, or at any other time from now.' Then, more softly, bitterly: 'Yes, you are my son – I cannot escape that – but a son I disown, do not want to see again. And it's not only now that I'm disowning you. I've disowned you since the day I met you with that skolly stud and saw how you looked at him and knew what was going on. God help you – and me – but I wouldn't be surprised to hear you've also got Aids, and sitting there, dirtying my chair!'

Quivering with rage, he rose, slamming his fist down on the table's glass, overturning the vase, hearing it shatter into irredeemable shards. 'You filthy bloody whore!' he breathed, and exulted as her face exploded with shock. Then, turning at the door: 'And give my love to Sep. Tell him I hope you'll soon have him dead, so that you can get that piece of paper that's waiting for you in the safe, and he can get a little peace at last!'

'Get out!' she shrieked. 'Get out!' But he took a last, long look at her, savouring the creature now wholly torn from the camouflage of its imperturbability and grace.

When he returned to the flat, carrying the bread he had ostensibly gone to buy, he sensed Ray's studying him: sensed also that Ray knew something had been tried and had failed, and that he would be trying again in some other way. After Ray's first perceptiveness and his refusing to be swayed by it, he had not again discussed the matter with him, but lying, that night, going over the details of the next step in his mind, he knew beyond denial, that Ray lay equally wakefully beside him, was enormously yearning against the opaque shield of his skull.

It was more than a week, though, before he felt sufficiently prepared with regard to operational details, if not with regard to the pounding of his heart, to be able to make the first irreversible move. In that week, he had, perforce, to abandon his last pathetic attempts to conceal from Ray what he was about, it being necessary to absent himself from the flat for sometimes as long as half the night in order to check his plans against the practicalities on the ground. For hours, he would mount a patient (and sometimes not so patient) watch over his old home, identifying what were the constants in the activities there and which the variables that could trap and fell.

It was in that week, also, that Ray suddenly and determinedly abstained from booze and the pipe, thus inflicting upon himself a torment of the spirit and flesh that it was almost unbearable to behold, and the flat became something of the nature of a grotesque Gethsemane in which the unlikely figure of Ray played Christ abasing himself in anticipation of the supreme abasement and abandonment of the splaying upon the Cross. Watching this harrowing extravagance of supplication and grief, he came the nearest yet to aborting his plans, but on the last afternoon before his setting out, Ray, rising after a long grappling on the toilet with his diarrhoea, blacked out and fell, crashing headfirst into the shower tap and gashing open his brow. Tremulous with pity, he carried him to the bed, washed the thin, spent blood from the wound, felt a longing reach, lamenting, back to the first, far days when Ray had challenged him in the little storeroom at the Rink, twirling the top button of his fly, demanding with all of the now fled arrogance and conceit, 'So, what's it, then, you want from me, kid?'

'Not this!' he thought. 'Oh Christ, not this!' and he drew the duvet over Ray who was now struggling to again open, to focus, his eyes, and, with a resurgence of resolve that, he swore through gritted teeth, must not be allowed to again abate, he took from his cupboard a short, dagger-type knife that Ray had given him for his protection when they still walked the perilous fringe, and strapped it to his right shin, midway between ankle and knee. Then he stuffed a heavy sweater and a pair of woollen gloves into a plastic bag, and, taking this up, stood at the foot of their bed, and said, striving to be casual, to be what he had always been and would never be again, 'Ciao – see you later Ray.' But Ray, now again fully conscious, said quietly, flatly, 'Goodbye, kid,' and the two words struck him in the back like two blades as he went out through the door and closed it behind him a final time.

It was dusk when he crept through the hole in the fence at the back of the house and the blossoms of the oleander thicket, on the edge of which he hid himself, drugged the air with their poisonous, almond scent. The image of Ray, drained and bleeding on the bed, stayed with him, steeling him, as the dusk turned to full dark, and another hour passed, and the study window, facing him, and no more than ten paces off, lit with the suddenness of a shout, and he knew supper was over and Sep had fled the table – and probably his no more than picked-over food – for the forgetfulness only the liquor cabinet could still yield.

But he was careful. Waited another half-hour to make sure that Sep had settled down and was not indulging a whim that would see the window darken again. But the light glowed steadily, beckoning 'Come!' and at last he rose from his squatting and pulled on the sweater to both guard against the increasing chill and free his hands, over which he then drew the gloves that would give his touch the anonymity that it craved.

Halfway to the window, there was a rustling behind him, and he whirled, his calm shattered, his breath unsettlingly in his throat, his hand reaching for the knife below his knee. But it was only a cat, streaking off through the long grass – 'alkies don't tend gardens', he irrelevantly, a little crazily, thought – and he relaxed, though perturbed now by a question to which he found no reply: Why had he so instinctively, *lethally*, reached for the knife when he had merely brought it to, at worst, coerce, to, more mundanely, cut the cable of the single telephone which he knew the study held, and whose silencing would give him more time to get away, to stash the money with Fiona before the police, alerted by his mother or Sep, could be upon him and render null and void the sole objective of his mission – which was to help *Ray*, not in any way advantage himself. Or could it be that this almost blatant purity of motive was, in fact, a fraud, that he was, indeed, doing this as much for himself as for Ray, wanted the money as a means to the preservation of his friendship with Ray, and not solely for the alleviation of the latter's misery and pain?

But, here, he was on firm ground. 'Come *on!*' he exhorted himself. 'Can't I also sometimes be not *just* gross? Is the deal not I get the stuff to Fiona for her to look after Ray, then I disappear, maybe taking a *little* of the moola for the road, and never see Ray again, so there's no spoor for them to go from me to him?' Reassured, the justification that he needed as much as he needed courage – that was, indeed, the source of the little courage he could find – back with him, he moved swiftly on to the window, peered over the sill.

Sep was sitting in the swivel chair behind the desk, but had swung it round so that it was facing him, and he ducked down again, panicking afresh, ready to run, mind shrieking, 'Oh Christ! He's seen me. He's gonna shout!' But there was no sound from the room: no whingeing of the swinging chair, scraping of its legs on the floor, turmoil of voices, steps, slamming of doors – only a night bird calling, softly, in the oleander leaves – crooning 'There, there!' to his frightened child.

Even so, he took no risks. Stole around to the other window of the corner-room, again, inch by agonising inch, raising his eyes above the sill. Now Sep's face was in profile to his, the head rigid and hewn as a stair's newel post, and he backed off a few paces till the dark covered him but he could still see into the room, and flicked a small pebble against the panes. Still Sep did not move, was as one dead – or asleep. 'Ja!' he thought, exultantly, 'he's asleep!' and began to raise the old-fashioned sash with a gradualness and stealth that exhausted his reserves of courage as much as it taxed his straining arms.

At last, the sash was fully up, and he climbed over the sill, mantis-leg after mantis-leg, and tiptoed across the room, coming right up alongside the motionless Sep, reaching for his knife, taking up the slack of the telephone line, severing it with a sharp snicker of the blade, thinking, 'Wake up now, if you want!' But Sep did not stir even when he circled the chair and came to stand in front of him, knife held in what he hoped was a sufficiently threatening pose, and he saw that Sep was not asleep, but in a coma, the eyes glassy and void as the windows' panes, right hand still clamped – 'Like a wrench', he thought – round a nearly emptied bottle of Old Buck gin.

Then the realisation of what this meant to his plans, took him up, smashed him down. 'But he must open the safe!' he inwardly yelled, sick with frustration and dismay, and he took Sep by the shoulders, casting aside all caution, shaking him till his head rolled and bobbed, shouting 'Up! Up!' But the head steadied back into its upright, rigid glare as he let it be, and, for the first time, as though defiantly consolidating his state, Sep very slightly began to snore. 'Fuck! Oh *fuck!*' he whispered, burying his face in his hands.

'What are you doing here?' she asked, composedly as though she was asking if he was well, and he looked up to find her standing in the door, only a small pulse in the throat betraying a raging within.

Her calm – his hatred of it – steadied him, though she had hoped, aimed, for the reverse, and, with something of surprise, he recognised a vanity in her born of power, the conceit of the snake's terrorising a bird.

'Come for my share!' he laughed, struggling to hold the hysteria from his voice, but she heard it, moved swiftly to a pace from him, held out her hand. 'Give me that knife,' she said, as tonelessly as before, 'and get out of here before I have the police take you away.'

'The line's cut, whore,' and he showed her the severed telephone line. 'Now open the safe, so's I can have my share.'

'I said give me that knife,' and she edged a little closer, using her eyes. 'Knives are meant for men, not pimps like you.'

Almost elatedly, he felt the last of her hold over him snap under the impact of her words, and he was upon her with the force and ferocity of an unleashed hound, hand, unthinkingly, atavistically, holding the knife to her throat. 'And I said open the safe, whore! *Now!* Or I'm gonna give you this blade!'

Nakedly, steadily, as the blade, all pretence fled, she stared at him, assessing him, knowing him, unafraid. 'You wouldn't dare!' she breathed. 'You? *You* use that knife on *me?* Where would you get the guts from, you fool?' and she laughed in his face, and the laugh was as a gob spat by a commoner tongue. Slowly, savouring, he pressed down on the blade, and it clove the skin, sank a fraction beyond, and a blood began to trickle, thinly, down her neck, pool in the hollow below.

Now she knew she did *not* know him anymore, that the knife was slicing through her throat as her taunts had already sliced through that which had bound them as mother and son. Her body began to shake with an automatic, animal terror, to reek with the sourness of it, and her eyes widened as though to engulf a sky, but the proud tongue would not confess to what the flesh felt, would not plead, merely flatly said, 'I'll open the safe.'

So he released her and she opened the safe, carefully concealing the combination from his eyes, booming the heavy door back against the wall, passing him a canvas bag that rustled reassuringly in his hand, taking out also a large brown envelope which, he supposed, contained the will, holding this to her breasts as though she suckled a child. Carefully he put the knife down on the desk, its blade glistening with her blood, turned to the light to check the contents of the bag, feeling his heart lift at the sight of the tight wad of high-denomination notes that it contained.

Then she was coming at him, knife, snatched from the desk, lunging for his back, startling him in time for him to deflect it to a grazing of his arm, to wrestle it from her as she fought to hold on, panting, opened mouth soundlessly screaming, and yet the whole of her, as at their meeting the week before, oddly attuned to somewhere else: a listening, an expectancy, to her as though she strained towards some wholly other imminence that just might not be in time. Deprived of the knife, bringing him to the floor, he on top of her, she struggled her hand between his thighs, seized his testicles, grinding them together with a viciousness that made him scream, and triggered in her a satisfied baring of her gums. Convulsed with pain, shocked beyond sense that she, his mother, should be brutalising his testicles like any vengeful whore, he plunged the knife between her breasts, again and again, her legs jerking up, enclasping him as in an act of love, till at last she lay still, a froth of blood on her lips, her lungs roaring out a last of air.

He rose into a silence that cried for sound, that was her death's, and he was no longer sane. Hobbling, holding himself, her hand still clamped to his crotch – acknowledging, at the end, its maleness, yielding to it its due respect? – he took up the bag of notes, stood, swaying, looking down at the still insensate Sep, bloodied knife in his hand. Should he kill him, too? What the hell! Already matricide – so – in for a penny, in for a pound? Scrub out *both* witnesses, be freed of the necessity to flee, be freed to go back to Ray, be with him till he died? He bayed, crazily, sobbing at the end, covering his shaking mouth with a hand.

Again he looked at Sep, noting for the first time how he, too, had changed. So very much like Ray had changed: the same shrivelling of the flesh from the bones, pathetic baring of the child that, at the end, was as in the womb, the same incontinences (a stain, he now saw, had flowered in Sep's groin), spittle, mucus, tears. He had never loved this man, but could he still hate what was left of him, this unravelling hulk that was something other than Sep in the shape of Sep? Could he, for whatever reason but that of mercy perhaps, kill what, save for defecation and breath, was already dead?

And yet, with no witnesses left, so much would be solved, he and Ray be spared so much of the trauma and pain that Ray, in particular, might not be able to withstand. Groaning, hand heavy with the knife, he stared at the eyes that unseeingly stared back at him, began, with the force of revelation, to understand that there *were* no more witnesses – that Sep had not *seen*.

But what about the stolen money, the opened safe? Were these not witnesses of a kind, pointers shaping a trail? But he was thinking clearly again, remembering her saying, 'Sep could sometimes not even sign a cheque,' so was it likely that he still knew what was in the safe, and, if did, would he not (knowing her) think it was *she* who had taken the money and been robbed by an intruder where she lay? Quickly, he sheathed his knife, not wiping it, picked up the will where she had dropped it when she attacked him, returned it to the safe, swung shut the thunderous, small door, twiddled the dials.

Halfway to the window, he stopped as though called. 'Christ!' he thought, 'is she still alive?' and he whirled around, heart hammering, feeling his neck hairs rise. But she lay, not moving, where she had died, and he loosed a long breath, turning again to go, but then he saw it was Sep that moved, fiddling with his fly, whimpering like a distressed child. 'He wants to pee,' he thought and, in an access of pity, he turned back, helped the quivering fingers with the buttons, scooped out the genitals and directed the urine's flow into the metal waste container he dragged from under the desk with the other hand. Finished, Sep nibbled his lips, but did not open his now closed eyes, and he stared a moment at the huddle of the genitals in his palm before putting them back and rebuttoning the fly, thinking, 'Is that all? This wrinkling shrunkenness? This cold, small flop like a dead frog? This castrated terror of a dead time?' and put another slug of gin next to Sep's groping hand, saying, not unkindly, 'Drink up, bra. Time to go.'

Outside, notes stashed in the plastic bag he had retrieved from under the oleander stand, the bag swinging from his hand, he felt his spirits rouse despite the numbing horror in the room he was leaving and, yet, would never leave, though he walked the whole of time. 'I am coming, Ray! Hang in there!' his heart sang, reaching out over the grown silent town, the frozen ocean of its roofs, finding mean, beloved Fourth, hurrying down it with the hurrying wind, bounding up the littered steps to the corridor to their door, reaching out …

But they were waiting for him at the gate, idling squad car pulsing like a hornet's sting, just arrived. She had set off the remote-controlled alarm when first he shouted at Sep, and he, not knowing it had been installed after he had left to stay with Ray, had missed out the one factor, the one variable, that trapped and felled.

✳ ✳ ✳

Inevitably, the trial was short, the little black pro deo counsel an uninterested pawn, the sentencing relentlessly swift. 'Little use me pleading innocent,' he thought. 'Money on me, her blood on the knife.' Bail was granted, but set so high that it was of little use, 'and, in any case,' he decided, 'better to cut off now,' though he was to have second thoughts about that, to feel the first touch of a fuller terror to come, when he, so hairless, so very white, intercepted the glances that slid over him in the bath-house or exercise-yard. He was aware as any of what went on in the deeper fastnesses of jails, but it was an academic awareness and its slow sharpening into actuality wrought in him an increasing sombreness of the spirit, and he would wake at night, the cell dark, and glance apprehensively about him at the sleeping forms to see if none crept upon him with a feline stealth. But, as an awaiting-trial prisoner, rather than a convicted felon, he had still not quite crossed the line into the anarchy of a place that was more crowded under the new black government than under the apartheid regime, the previously oppressed but still indigent people exploding now into criminal violence as they sought to seize the material benefits which political victory could not as yet bestow.

Fiona attended most of the hearings, but he was never given a chance to speak to her and, after a brief wave of the hand, she would relapse into the faceless staring of a world from which he already felt irreversibly removed. But the final delinking only really came – chiming in his mind with an almost audible sound of a shattering chain – when the judge, eyeing him with neither pity nor spite across the abyss of the courtroom floor, pronounced him felon for twenty years for (his voice tolling like a bell) 'a most brutal murder – a matricide of singular viciousness for, it seems, no reason other than monetary gain.'

That night, criminal, he crossed the line and, when the lights switched off, they came for him, not singly, but as the grey wolves in the dream of long ago, bearing him to the floor. At the first thrust, he screamed, piercingly, desolately, as a beast entrapped, but then was silent till they were done with him and the cell-boss said, 'Leave it now. Now it's mine.'

* * *

But his master had not been unkind: had treated him as he said he had always treated the wife who had written him from Soweto that she could no longer wait, had found herself another man.

So, when Fiona's message that Ray was dead was smuggled through to him where he sat, sunning in the exercise-yard, it was not unexpected that his master should yell, 'Ithini cwaka! Shut up you fucking shits! Can't you see the wyfie's crying for her other man?'

And they heard, sat in silence, watching, almost in awe, as he keened in the bright sun.

The Treadmill

Again for Jo-Anne and Cecilia
who wanted a sequel.

He fumbled the long, wrought-iron key with its numbered tag into the lock of the door, turned it, went in, humping his bag. After the cell, the room seemed almost extravagantly too large for a single soul and even the busily floral wallpaper, crowding in from every side, did not reduce the room to its actual, very modest size.

Wearily he eased the bag from his shoulders, placed it in a corner of the room, sat down on the bed, palming his eyes. It had been a long day's journey by bus and train back to this point in time, this place where so much had begun, and, after the prison bunks, the thin mattress on the three-quarter iron bed yielded to him with an unaccustomed lushness and he was tempted to lie back on it and sleep a while.

But he knew that sleep would not come – that this room was no haven, no eye of the storm – that the storm was *in him* and that he bore it *with him*, much as he had the bag into which he had crammed the last, few material possessions he could call his own and that 'they' had handed back to him when he had left the jail.

Slowly he got up again – slowly as men who have grown old before their time – toed the fraying carpet beside the bed with incredulous feet – stroked the soiled, peeling wallpaper, the rickety washstand, the wardrobe's doors of packing-case wood, with incredulous hands – tentatively sat down on the straight-backed tokenism of the chair. 'Free,' he thought. 'Free,' but it was only a thought, careful and speculative, joyless as a statistic, bled of meaning as a mantra or a rote.

Going to the window, he parted the curtains, releasing the dust clinging to them, feeling it settle, stingingly, in his nose. One pane was missing and had been replaced by a board and he stared through the remaining three at the tangle of steel rails that surged past immediately below his window and converged on the station platform several hundred metres further on. His room was on the second floor at the rear of the hotel and, even as he stood there, a suburban metro thundered past, shaking the ground and suctioning further papers into the already thickly clogged wire mesh of the security fence separating the hotel from the rails. Within minutes, a second and a third metro barrelled past, bound for the city centre, threatening to bring down the uneasy walls, and he now saw that there was a neon sign at the back of the hotel as well as at the front and it was right alongside his window and poised to flood his room with a maximum of unwanted light. 'Christ!' he thought, reminded of the perpetual light of the jail. 'Home from home,' but there was no mirth in his mind and his heart stayed dead as the still unlit sign.

The aspect of the low-rise suburb onto which the window gave, seemed frighteningly unchanged – frighteningly because that suggested that he had, indeed, come back into a warp in time and that even the dead were risen from their graves. As if on cue, the already low sun, red and unsteady as a balloon floated on a wind, glinted off the chrome of a passing car and his eyes followed it down Main, singling out familiar landmarks, checking only, his heart suddenly hammering, at the intersection with Fourth – sleazy, litter-ridden Fourth that would lead him to where he had greeted Ray Willies for the last time.

Ray. The name tolled in his mind like a bell – tolled as it had so many times before during the prison years – but now there was an urgency, an immediacy, to it that would not be denied and he wrenched his eyes away and stared, almost wildly, out over the streets to the mine-dump that dominated the town. Fallow and yellowed as from a rust, desolately alienated from all save itself, the dump had never been so huge, so sepulchral, as it was now, seeming to rush upon him through the last of the light, reminding him that it was in its shadow that he had gone to mourn when he had first heard that Ray had Aids. Quickly he jerked the curtains closed, almost tearing the tired fabric in his haste, and returned to the bed, where he sat down, face in hands, listening to the metros pass and the roistering in the bar, immediately below his room, swell into the crescendo of the evening's trade.

But it was mainly to the voices within himself that he listened – his mother's, sibilant and fierce, Sep's drunken slur, Fiona's laughing through her pain – and Ray's – always again Ray's – lazy and unflappable – ultimately unhinged – and it was only after the sun had gone down and the sign beside the window had switched on and its expected technicolour light was rapping through the room, that he again became fully conscious of outward sight and sound and lowered his hands from his face and asked of himself, 'Where to now?'

A gust of laughter from the bar, sudden and unrestrained as a rise of birds, seemed to be an answer of a kind and he went out, locking the door, and urinated in the 'Gents', but surreptitiously, as though he had no right to be there. But no one else came in and for a long moment he stared at his image in the mirror over the washbasins, noting how the boyish face that Ray had known had lengthened into almost saturnine and wondering if he should retain the prison crop of his naturally long, fair hair, or let it grow and so betray that the fairness was fast fading into an unseasonal grey. The always melancholy blue eyes were now an even whiter blue, astonishingly akin to the pallid skin, and the melancholy held in the incipient sullenness of one who had been dominated for too long – by rules, warders, bars, walls – and by Jason, the cell-boss, who had claimed him as his personal possession and held onto him with all the bitter jealousy of the deprived. Not, he thought, that Jason had been all that unkind. Only during intercourse, insatiable and impetuous, had he sometimes manhandled him with a brutality that he had later come to understand for what it was and that, therefore, in the end, had scarred his flesh rather than his pride. Almost hungrily, his mind began to reach out to the mellower aspects of his relationship with Jason, but then he thought he heard a step in the corridor and hastily splashed water on his face and dried it on a tissue from a cubicle since there were no towels on the seemingly seldom used rails.

He had been right about the footsteps, but they passed on down the corridor and a door slammed somewhere as he came out and felt his way down the ill-lit, precipitous stairs to the reception area that, when he had booked in that afternoon, had been quiet and deserted save for an off-white youth behind a desk hardly bigger than a booth. All feral teeth and darting glances and hands, the youth had watched him from behind a bowl of dusty artificial flowers as he entered his personal details in the guest book and he had thought, 'Gay,' as he felt the other's speculative eyes prowling over him like flies. He had given a wildly fictitious upcountry address as his place of residence, thinking (with a cynicism that Ray would have appreciated but not have recognised in him) that 'Diepwater Prison' would not go down well in even a place as run-down and unsavoury as this so clearly was. Then he had signed in the allotted column and looked up to catch the youth's eyes with their pants down and, with a perverseness born of weariness and something like despair, said, 'No,' but the youth had pretended not to understand, leaving it to the banging down of the key to answer for him, and he had gone up to his room with a little lift of satisfaction that he had been at a loss to precisely explain.

Now saccharine or savage rock pop was being piped into the area and the growing-tatty, zebra-striped lounge suite and unmatched occasional chairs were mainly occupied by women of different ages but the same faces who surveyed him in much the same way the youth had done, then looked away with the sure instinct of the predator evaluating its prey. The youth was gone and his place taken by a blacker-than-any-black South Indian who bared a gold tooth as he snarled a cigar from one corner of his fleshy mouth to the other and snapped, 'You checked in?'

'Boss man,' he thought and nodded, but the Indian continued to look him up and down, clearly thrown by the fifteen-year-back cut of the shirt and pants he had last worn when he had entered jail and been issued with the regulation prison gear in exchange. Ethnically and sartorially 'with it' to the last stitch, the Indian made him feel like a leftover from a past age being assessed through the bars of its cage, and he breathed a silent 'Fuck you' and strove to not let his annoyance show.

'You "Jackson"?' asked the Indian, stabbing at the still opened hotel register with an immaculately manicured nail.

Again he nodded, meaning to leave it at that, but the pent-up resentment broke free with a volition of its own and he felt his head indicating the surrounding women and heard his voice saying, 'Or did you think I was a client of one of your "girls"?'

Immediately, and dangerously, the other's eyes narrowed and he realised he could not have let slip a more damaging remark because the Indian, in his turn, was now betraying that it was not his booking-in that was of concern to him, but the possibility that he was an undercover agent of some sort who had come to case what was obviously a brothel before it was a hotel.

'Not that it matters to me one way or the other,' he hastily added, but the Indian remained unappeased, thinking, no doubt, that a spy could book in as routinely as anybody else, and, fearing eviction, he buckled all the way and said, 'I was also in the trade once. Maybe could teach the kids here a thing or two,' and he sensed Jason pause in whatever he was doing then, and Ray stared at him with his dead eyes, and he stood, appalled by the opportunism and cravenness of his words. 'Christ! O Christ!' his heart mourned. 'Is this all I am now? Spook with a name? Rent boy's cock for a tongue? It buggering into every stinking hole?'

He felt himself reel, eddy in midstream: no known to cling to, no hand reaching for his own. But the Indian instantly relaxed, smiled, again lifting a lip from the gold tooth, shrugging his shoulders with the inborn exuberance of his blood. 'Well, then you know how it is,' he said. 'Have a good stay,' and rose and went to greet a furtive, well-dressed white who had just come in, parking the long gleam of his car further up the street, and the eyes of all the assembled women followed him like puppets' on a common string as the Indian ushered him into the tiny office behind the desk and discreetly closed the door.

Craving now a drink, capable of getting drunk if he let himself go, he went on into the bar, claimed a suddenly vacated bar stool and straddled it, feeling his buttocks slip over the greasy plastic of the seat. As packed with smoke and sound as it was with flesh, the place seethed with the multi-ethnic mix to which he had grown accustomed during the long years in jail and, for a moment, he felt the twinge of nostalgia of a demon cast out from the hell that had, of necessity, become its home. Women's rights, though, still trailed a dullard last, only a few whores being groped by one-night stands – or one-fuck-stands – if he knew the score – and the ratio of two to one of black barmen to whites and in-betweens was not good enough but better than he had hoped, and his spirits lifted a little – but, again, not enough.

'Sir?' the quiet voice said and he looked round to find one of the black barmen standing before him, eyes cast down, watching a hand push a swab, grey as a disease, through the slopped brandy and beer, name tag, pinned, skew, to his T-shirt, proclaiming him to be 'James'. His hands were beautiful, his face as unsettlingly so – classically sculpted, almost Nilotic nose and lips, dense, oiled helmet of his hair, setting him apart in the true Africa to which only he belonged.

'Brandy. Neat,' he said, wondering at the catch in his voice, handing over his room key.

Carefully, face still composed, the other wrote the key number, charge and date on a small fragment of a cigarette pack, pushed it across for his signature, threw it in a rear compartment of the till and handed back the key. Only then did he look up and he felt an uncontrollable tremor run through him when he saw that the left eye was blued by a cataract and blind. The other sensed his shock and laughed, a gentle, non-combative sound, not averting the eye, and said, 'Don't worry. They all feel like that the first time.' Then, still chuckling, 'Let me serve you often enough and you won't know the left one from the right.'

Served, he realised that he had not stated what brand of brandy he wanted and was, at first, piqued that he should not have been asked, but then he remembered the very low charge that had been entered on the chit and how his failure to respond to this had signified either that he was happy with it, or was a lout who deserved to be served with nothing better than what was undoubtedly, and affectionately, termed the 'house piss'. He smiled then – a wry but first genuine smile that whole first day of being a 'free man' – and decided that he would not, after all, get drunk, not only because of what the nameless concoction – tearing now through him like a rogue coal – could do to his gut, but because Ray (except towards the end) had drunk very sparingly for a man of his 'profession' and 'class', and Jason (who had always been able to pressure the warders into smuggling in liquor for them in exchange for his control of the gangs) had likewise but very rarely gone beyond his self-imposed restraints and – sensing perhaps with a rare insight his own psychic imbalances – had threatened to donner him to within an inch of his life if he found him 'drinking like a tsotsi', instead of with the decorum befitting him as 'his wife'. 'Jason,' he reflected, 'Jason,' the brandy mellowing him, 'fifteen years and what do I know of you?' and he saw James watching him and held up his glass for a refill.

'That one's on me,' said a voice immediately to the left of him and he turned. He was a very small man, but wiry and honed, black, curling hair covering ash-white arms to even the backs of the hands, curiously depthless eyes studying him with the fixity of the drunk or the mad. Warily he noted the black slacks, white shirt, shaven bald as an egg white skull, the betraying puckers in the neck's skin. 'All black or white,' he thought, 'and no chicken anymore. Weird.'

'Why?' he asked as James set down his glass, watching him with alert, amused eyes. 'You don't know me.'

'Of course I know you. All lonely men are the same. And, besides,' and the lips smiled, though the eyes did not, 'I saw from your key tag that you are only two doors up from me and surely one should welcome a new member of our little family of the damned?'

'I'm only passing through,' he lied, hating the sullenness in his voice that made him sound defensive and unsure. Wondering, also, why – instinctively – it was there.

The other laughed, a dry, unfunny bark. 'People who are passing through don't come to a dump like this. Unless they are on the run. Are *you*?'

'Why should I answer that?' he countered, now abrasively opposed. 'I thought you said you knew me. So, go on, *know* me!'

'Okay! Okay! So I don't *really* know you. All I was saying is that a lonely man knows another lonely man when he sees him and as soon as you came through that door tonight, I knew you were a lonely man.

66

And *searching*. Right?'

'Maybe. But who says we are searching for the same thing?'

'Of course we are.' And now the other's knee lightly but deliberately brushed his. 'Again,' he thought, and he was back on the streets, in the bars, acting as a bait for Ray the rent boy.

'What makes you so sure?' he asked, pushing it, pushing aside the leaves to see the face that would hide.

'Look. We are what we are. Each time we move, enter a room as you did the bar tonight, or leave it, in some small way, without our knowing it, without meaning to, we show to others of our kind what we are, what has been done to us or what we have done to others, what, always, we are searching for.' Now he was pressing his knee, hard, against his, wetting his lips with a quick flip of the tongue, straining the expressionless eyes to show what they could not hold. 'Come *on*. I *know* I am not wrong about you. I can *smell* you, man. Smell you like I smell a woman when she's full – *full!*'

That last word, so laden, so nakedly what he did not want to hear, aroused in him more of horror than rage, but it seemed to be only the latter that powered him as he pushed the knee away, said in the flat, tight voice of one driven beyond reason or recall, 'Get the fuck out of here before I donner you dead!'

For a moment the other stared at him in pitying disbelief. Then he got up, slowly, almost tiredly, said, 'Okay. Enjoy your drink,' and went out.

James laughed and he looked up, startled, having forgotten that the other was still there. 'You waiting to be paid?'

'No. I already booked it on his card.'

'Well, book it off again. I want fuckall from him.'

'Can't *do* that. He'll be checking to see if it's there because he'll be *wanting* it to be there so's to get back at you, and he'll be knowing you'll be trying to get if off again so's to get back at *him*. And then *I* take the rap for falsifying his card.'

'Well, drink the fucking stuff yourself then,' and he pushed the glass across and made to go.

Again the other laughed. 'You whiteys faze me. You don't mind a big shit on your hands like apartheid, but go all holy moses when it come to a drink from a poor little homo who's an institution around here and tries the same stunt on *every* new one. So drink up, man, and buy that other drink *you* were going to pay for and forget about old Henry Martins. He won't be worrying you again. Not unless you want him to.'

How quickly, he thought, 'sir' had become 'man'. Was this a

downgrading to be resented or a first yielding to him of a world in which he no longer belonged?

'No,' he said. 'A black man taught me about drinking and he said never to drink when I feel the way I'm feeling now.' The other stared at him, blue eye glaring, seeing nothing, seeing all. 'Yes,' he went on, 'A black man. Maybe I suffered under apartheid as much as you did. Maybe, in ways you wouldn't want to hear about, I suffered a fucking sight more. Maybe I got a black man inside me wanting out. Maybe your tongue's a blind man's, bra James, and the time has come for you to check it out.'

A customer shouted, aggrieved, but the other continued to stare at him, black face composed but aware. Then he turned the glass around and said, 'My name is James Mjozi. I was going to throw this away because you didn't give it to me like a bra. You gave it to me because it was a trash you didn't want for yourself and that's a white man's move. Now you got me thinking two ways.' He paused, eyed the glass, then, suddenly, unsmilingly, downed the drink at a single gulp and turned away to serve.

Tired but no longer so dispirited, he felt his way up the stairs, the reception area below him now darkened and deserted save for a single light over the reception desk and as lone a woman's face that floated like a ghost's in the further gloom. Had he made a friend, he wondered, and, if so, how should he feel about it? Did he really *want* any friends? More specifically, did he want any *male* friends? Had he not had enough of males, of Jason, for the past fifteen years – and would have been twenty if the prisons had not been bursting at the seams and they had decided to let him off the last five? Did not further destruction rather than deliverance, a final confirmation of what he had become, Jason had made him be, lie that way? It was as Henry Martins had said: he was lonely and searching, but searching for the known and the lost, not the alien and alive. He had come back to this town not so much because it was the place of his birth and his whole life before they sent him to jail, but because he was like the soul that, too suddenly and brutally summoned, forever returns to the place and time of its summoning, forever frenziedly tries to complete the deed its grown powerless hands had planned. 'I know all that,' he thought, 'and I know it's sick. But that's the way it is. Has to be,' and he came off the stairs into the corridor and heard the step behind him and, startled, turned.

It was the woman. She had followed him up the stairs and now stood a pace from him, tall, bony body angled forward, hand primping her unsubtly dyed hair, desperate, almost mannish features trying to mellow into a travesty of a smile. 'At least ten years older than me,' he thought, 'and no ways it won't show.'

'You looking for me?' she asked, smile fixedly in place as a wound.

'No,' he said, his voice not unkind as he remembered Fiona and Dolly who had been two of Ray's women in the days before the 'Big A' left him only his bones and his balls.

'You not Louie?' she persisted, her eyes searching and shrewd.

'No,' he said, 'I'm Johnny Jackson and I'm booked into No. 8.'

She slumped. 'Bastard phoned for an appointment with me an hour back. Can't trust nobody these days.' Then, again alert, 'I can see you been around. You want to take his place?'

For a moment, he stood, irresolute, overtaken by events in which he had had no hand. Was this the moment he had been waiting for, the opportunity that might never come again and that must be seized with a last, despairing clench of his suspect loins? But, even as his tongue stirred to say 'Yes,' he panicked, persuaded himself that he was still not ready, that it was all too rushed, that he had no condoms, that she probably (as Ray had always put it) didn't mind if it was 'naked snake' and did he want to go the same way as Ray? And no, he angrily rejected the thought, it was not *he* that might be 'unclean' because, although Jason had never used condoms (Jason and condoms? Christ!), he had been oddly faithful to him and it was now all of fifteen years and still no sign.

'Thanks,' he said, carefully choosing his words, his tone, 'but I just got in and sleep is what I want right now. You don't mind?'

She looked at him, intrigued. 'Mind?' she echoed. 'Me? You *are* a funny one. Don't look like a gent but sure act like one. Like it's you that doesn't mind I am what I am.'

'Could be,' he said and she came forward and took his hand. 'Don't laugh,' she said, and now the smile held warmth, 'but my names are grosser 'n yours. Sharon Berry. For *real*! And I got to drag that around with me for the rest of my life! Ja. Sharon Berry and I'm in No. 10 and anytime I'm free and you want, knock and I won't charge you too high. Okay?'

'Okay,' he said and went into his room and locked the door.

Switching on the light, stopping the rampaging neon in its tracks, he crossed to the window, parted the curtains, stared out at the thin moon hanging low over the dump. The town was still alive with cars, people, walking, talking, last of the metros hammering past, but the dump was a shining, silent world of its own. Corrupted, yet now curiously incorruptible, it was beautiful as a landscape in a dream, as childhood's innocence regained. But he would never be a child again and had grown too brutally wise to bluff himself that he had run away from the offer in the corridor for any reason other than fear of his own, personal high noon.

At odds with himself, plagued by a mounting guilt, he closed the curtains, went to check if the envelope was still in his pack. It was and he made sure that he had, indeed, locked the door and then hung the small towel from the washstand over the keyhole before he opened the envelope and emptied the bank notes it contained onto the bed. They were mainly R50 notes and he counted them twice and arrived at the same tally both times. Then he pushed his hand into the envelope and once again, and with a last of hope, searched for the personal message from Fiona that so achingly was not there. Had 'they', he wondered, somehow managed to extract and destroy it, or had she, prompted by a reason he hoped soon to find out, decided it best to write no more than the instruction on the envelope, which read: 'To be held in trust by the Chief Warder, Diepwater Prison, and handed to Prisoner No. 21176, Johnny Jackson, on the day of his discharge from jail.'

Just over eleven and a half thousand rand still there, he thought, as he put the notes back in the envelope and hid them at the bottom of the pack, which meant, with the almost five hundred rand he had already spent on the journey from Diepwater by bus and train, that she had saved up something like twelve thousand rand to shield him from destitution on his release. 'Jee-suss!' he whispered. 'How many times did she let them fuck her to be able to give me that?' and suddenly his eyes were awash with tears and a harsh, dry sob rasped up out of him like a dying man's, and he wished with an intolerable impatience for morning because she was of his age and maybe still here and, if not, then somewhere where he would *find* and *follow* her – *must* find and follow her because she was his last living link with Ray and all that had been.

Drained, he emptied the old-fashioned enamel jug into the matching, chipped basin on the washstand, and splashed the water onto his face and over his head and the back of his neck and dried himself with the towel he had hung over the keyhole as a shield. Then, it being midsummer and the sweat tackily on his skin, he stripped and lay down on his back on the bed, the rough blanket bristly as an animal's pelt under his buttocks and spine. There was a Bible on the little stand beside the bed and he leaned over and picked it up, thinking, almost surprisedly, that prison had not been *all* bad because, as a boy, he had been a lazy scholar, leaving school before matriculating and reading very little beyond what the curriculum laid down, but, in prison, tedium had driven him to read anything he could find on the sparsely stocked library shelves, and he had often even read aloud to Jason who, though barely literate, had an extraordinarily (and tragically) alert mind.

The Bible, though, had never interested him and he had not been of those who had 'found God' in jail, but now, the many-paged, nearly thick as a brick little book oddly heavy in his hand, he remembered that Sep, his mother's hated second husband who had become a holyroller after a life of abandon that included alcoholism and sodomy, had always said you must open the Bible where (as he had put it) 'your hand tells you' and the first verse you then read would be 'a message from God'. Idly, he tried it and it did not quite work out because the first verse he saw meant nothing to him (unless, of course, God was 'speaking to him' in a code), but the second verse read: 'But I know thy abode, and thy going out, and thy coming in, and thy rage against me,' and this *did* seem to make sense, to address him directly as a voice calling his name across a silenced room.

Despite his disbelief, his certainty that the bedrock of his cynicism was not shifting and *would* not shift, a tremor ran through him and he was suddenly, blazingly, aware of his body's sprawling nakedness on the bed: its hairlessness and whiteness that had so attracted Jason, that Jason had so loved to have under his hands and loins, that yet had remained elements of his own maleness – his body's pitiful denial of what had been done to it in the sating of a need that, in the end, had grown into that which neither of them had been prepared to admit or name. As so many times before, he gathered up the flat, unfeminine breasts, fingered the barren pustules that were their nipples, planed with his palms down the smooth, taut muscles of his gut, handled the genitals that, for all their aggressiveness and adequacy, had never seeded another, whether woman or man. Slowly they began to respond, the penis lengthening as he fondled it, but he took his hand away, reflecting with a bleak humourlessness that he had never found any need to masturbate while with Jason and he was deviate enough without so soon submitting to the most mindless and benumbing non-act of them all.

The metros were no longer passing and a cooler, late night wind began to edge through a chink in the window and under the thinly rattling door, and he switched off the light and the harlequin-neon instantly exploded back into the room. Drawing only the top blanket over him, he placed his hands behind his head and stared up at the ceiling as he and Ray so often had done, talking until late into the night, sharing a final cigarette. The memory brought the loneliness and pain that it always did, but tonight there was a distracting other memory as the rough blanket closed around his nakedness and he sought in it the demanding, but also shielding, massiveness of the Jason that was no longer there.

He had had no option but to submit to Jason, to remain supine as a boy in the hands of some terrible child, because Jason's power over his section of the cells was more absolute than any warder's and disablement, and even death, was meted out to the rebellious with the inevitability, almost, of an act of God. His submission to Jason had ranged from the initial inward scream through sodden dullness to the ultimate acceptance that sex with Jason was an inescapable way of life from which the animal body often derived an animal content and only the mind stayed ashamed. Jason it was who had insisted that, in the summer months, they sleep stripped as he was now because the contesting white against black skins held in a sensual incitement of their own, and that, like the fellatio that had at first so nauseated him, became merely another element in a routine that earned him Jason's protection against the watchfully rapacious lesser members of the gang. In the end, he had even learned what parts of Jason's body to touch or hold in order to tune the latter's libido to highest pitch, and the momentary control which this afforded him over the monolithic creature that he otherwise could not deflect or persuade, had been a source of satisfaction and a means of retribution that had preserved his pride from total ruin. He had, he bitterly thought, become a very adept whore indeed.

But that was Then, and Then – as Jason had so suddenly and startlingly last night proclaimed – was a dead jackal that must not be allowed to prowl again. Heaving in alongside him as he lay in his prison bunk for the last time, Jason had gripped his thigh and he had automatically reached out into the other's warm, capacious groin and commenced the foreplay that he thought was expected of him, but Jason had pushed his hand away and said, his voice measured and strange, 'No, not tonight. Not ever again. Tomorrow you are gone and I will be here many more years. So it is best that we break off *now*. Break free. You of me and I of you. I have used you and perhaps you hate me for that. But I don't think so because you are not a fool and must know how it would have been for you if you had been the woman for *all* of the men. Yes, I have used you, white man. As a woman have you been used. But you are not a woman. You take my seed and shit it out again. You can grow me no child out of my seed. That is because you are still a man. Remember that. *You are still a man.* What we have been doing here is wrong. But, with no women, what else must one do if one is not to go mad? Now you must go from here and say it is finished. It is done. There was no Jason. Jason was only in my mind. Like the things that come to a man in his dreams. That way, the tree will grow straight again.'

'And your heart?' he had asked, daring what he had never dared before. 'Has your heart felt nothing for me? Is it only what is between your legs that has spoken in all these years?'

For a long moment the other had been silent: then he had said, something of the old growl back in his voice, 'You speak perhaps of this thing they call "love"? I have been here too long. I do not know this "love". But I will remember you for a while, will not sleep with anybody else for a while. That is all I can say,' and he had turned his back to him then and, after a time, slept, and, when they came to fetch him, had sat staring stubbornly down at the great pads of his feet until they were about to leave, when he had spoken of the jackal and how it must not be allowed to prowl again.

'Not so easy, Jason,' he thought, staring up at the ceiling as it palpitated in the sign's frantic strobe, feeling still, where Jason had always lain, an emptiness and aloneness whose magnitude immeasurably outstripped a mere day's journeying from Diepwater Prison.

'Perhaps,' his mind ran on, sleep at last closing in, 'I'll believe it's all as easy as Jason said if the jackal stays dead in my dreams.'

Towards dawn, the sign switched off, only silence about in streets and rails, he awoke and thought that he had not dreamt. But the taste of Jason was full and mustard in his mouth and his thighs were glutinous with unwanted sperm.

He wept then – despairingly – as in a sordid Gethsemane of his own – and only rose to shower in the still deserted toilet when the rails beneath his window shook with the day's first wheels.

* * *

Passing through the reception area on his way to the street, he heard the chink of plates from behind a door under the stairs and the conventional aroma of frying sausage and eggs leavened the less prepossessing stench of cigarette ash and booze. His stomach grumbled and spittle was suddenly lively on his tongue, but he did not break stride, partly because he was eager to keep his appointment with his past and, mostly, because he was shy. The previous night's foray into the bar had not seemed so daunting because the place had been crammed with the getting drunk or the angling for a fuck and he had been but another face in a melee that had more to do with desperation than joy. Exposing himself for breakfast, however, would be the equivalent of the proverbial new gun hitting town, and he quailed at the thought of a gaggle of Henry Martins battening on his alienness as they sought relief from the intolerable tedium of their new day. Outwardly freed, he was now the prisoner of his inner self, walking the streets in the nakedness of his knowing what he had been and, indeed, still was, furtive as a felon in a darkened lane.

Shorn of the frail transfiguration of the evening lights, the 'lounge' was both a desert and a ruin and yesterday's youth stood in the middle of it, yawning and scratching under his arms and pretending not to see him pass. But he felt the eyes boring into him as he went through the door and onto the steps leading down to the street, and he yearned to whirl round and angrily question them, but retained sense enough to know that that would betray what the other sought. *What* did the other seek? *'Stop* this!' he raged, and forced himself to walk on, to pretend, after the manner of the youth, that he bore no Jason with him, did not, with his every move, flaunt the latter's presence like a flasher his fly.

At the bottom of the steps, a beggar, matted, black locks quivering like a spider grappling a prey, was rooting in a rubbish bin, pausing only long enough to eye him and bend back in again, summarily, and with an awesome intuitiveness, dismissing him as a wretch hardly less wretched than himself. Now, however, he rebelled and, tapping the other on a shoulder, pressed a coin into his hand, but this bought him no more than a mumbled acknowledgement of a kindness between kin, not the exuberant thanksgiving reserved for the well-heeled.

Smarting, he walked on down Main, struggling with the concept of the present returning to the past – or was it the other way around? – dreading at every step that he would be recognised and shunned, only slowly becoming assured that he knew no one and no one knew him, that he was neither phantom nor flesh, merely a shape amongst many shapes that, usually, encapsulated a man. Slowly, he likewise became aware that the landmarks he thought he had recognised from the hotel window the previous afternoon were not nearly so familiar from close-up, most of them having been refurbished, or changed as regards ownership or trade, or substantially rebuilt within the confines of their original shells. A few had even been replaced by medium- or high-rise other structures that were, challengingly and in their totality, unknown to him, and he quickened his step with a sense of mounting foreboding that stressed him almost as much as did his prison-strictured lungs.

All too soon it was upon him – his rendezvous – not with time but grief. Crossing the front of a furniture shop whose name he remembered but whose new opulence he did not, he knew the great iron gates of the old Rinko Theatre should be next – the gaudy, bawdy, beloved 'Rink' where, as a boy, he had first met Ray and which had been the ambience and anchor for so much of a friendship that had infused them both with a life whose name had been love, but that then had borne a last and fatal flower of murder and disease.

But there was nothing there. Already he was past the shop and there was nothing there. Only a further barren acre of brilliant glass and, behind the glass, row upon row of as brilliant, prohibitively expensive cars that, each time their wheels turned, rode roughshod over the Rink's mangled remains. 'Christ!' he thought. 'It's gone! It's fucking well *gone!*' and the voice in his head was shrill with incredulousness and rage, and then with pain, and he stood and keened behind the blank mask of his face till his very immobility drew to him the eyes that he fled and he moved, unseeingly, on down Main and turned right into Fourth, feeling its pavements coming to life under his heels and time opening before him like a cleaving of the mind.

But, again, there was to be the void, the sullen fleeing from his heart and hands. The small, neat houses, sprinklers twinkling on midget lawns, no longer deteriorated into the hovels he had known, the street's tarmac remained impeccable to its end, the once cracked and weed-grown paving matched the street's immaculateness and sturdy saplings, fussily buttressed against wind and storm, cast the fine lace of their shadows over him as he headed for the flat he had once shared with Ray, heart powering him as though it was the first time. Then the flat roof of the two-storey block was etched against the dump, clear and sweet as a cut in stone, and his heart exulted and he whispered, 'It is still there! At least *that* is still there!'

But it was and it was not. Coming closer, he saw that a heavy glass door threw back the sun from the once doorless entrance and the open space before the block, that had once been a catchment for litter and the excreta of both humans and dogs, now held a smear of green grass with the mandatory sprinkler and borders of cannas in full bloom. At once again estranged, knowing with a sick certainty that he courted only pain, he nonetheless, like an injured beast tearing at its own wounds, went in and up the solid new stairs, subliminally listening for, demanding, even a single echo of the old stair's noisiness, but it was only silence that delivered him, like a shade, to the second floor.

Ray's floor. The old flat. Turn left into the second last door from the end of the long, dark corridor into time. But it was not like that anymore. Would never be again. Now light streamed in through a glass panel in the roof, a picture window in the terminal wall – bright linoleum covered the new, silent-as-the-stairs, pine floors – air freshener, lavender-scented floor wax, prevailed over his memories of onion, masala, urine, sweat – left him standing, desolate and unfulfilled, outside the flat whose number on the door's polished panels was the only link left with a past it no longer held. 'Ray!' he whispered. 'Ray! Where are you? Are you anywhere at all?'

As if in answer, a woman opened the door of the flat, came out, brand name shopping-bag in her hand. 'You looking for somebody?' she asked, her voice as distant from him as her eyes, gold wedding ring gleaming as she tidied a strayed wisp of her hair.

'Yes,' he said, suddenly eager to talk, to share. 'His name was Ray. Ray Willies. He and I leased this flat a long time ago.'

But she wanted no truck with him, drew further away, locking the door. 'Well, he's certainly not here now,' she said, mouth pursed, tight, like a drawstring pouch, sharp, tending-towards-hard features coming at him, bleakly as a blade.

His temper flared then, the long strain taking its toll. 'Hardly likely to *be*,' he snapped. 'He died when you were still a snot at school.'

Her mouth gapped to say something in return, but then she saw his eyes – the animal within – and whirled and strode off down the corridor, heels clicking on the linoleum, back straight – and scared – as though she sensed a reaching of his hand.

'Fucking bitch!' he breathed, expelling some of his pent-up animus, knowing he was being unfair, that she was as much a prisoner of the treadmill as he, not caring at all, though, that she was and that he knew. Then he followed her down the corridor, not once looking back, impenitently content as he saw her quicken her pace, going on, then, down Fourth to where it ended in the ring road skirting the dump.

At the juncture of the two roads, on the right-hand side of Fourth, was a cluster of cottages that once had housed the mine labourers tending the dump, but that had then fallen into disuse – not to say a considerable disrepair – as the dump had extended ever further southwards from town, ingesting all before it with the barely perceptible but certain ooze of its slimes. After his experience with the Rink, he had seriously feared that they, too, would long since have been cast down and, at the sight of them still standing – apparently so very much the same, deathlessly decadent as the twilight characters to whom the mine had subsequently rented them out at a nominal fee –

he paused a moment, overcome with emotion, clutching to him this first real shard of what once had been. 'Christ!' he thought, 'can it, *can* it be that she is still here?' and the renewal of hope after a morning of such misgiving, aroused in him so intense an excitement, so fierce a longing to touch, to seize, to *hold*, that he broke free and found himself almost running towards the cottage where he had last spoken with Fiona, where she had promised to not let Ray die alone.

Standing on the worn, only step, striving to slow his breath, calm his hands, he knocked, too loudly, on the frail, long last painted door, sensed heads turning to him from other doors and steps, heard a kiewiet keening, high up over the dump, as the silence, suddenly all about him, dragged, achingly, on. Desperately, driven by the watching, avid eyes, he knocked again, rattling the door in its frame, feeling his pulse quicken as the curtain in the window beside the door very slightly twitched and a shadow passed behind the dusty panes. Then steps were shuffling closer – 'Why shuffling?' he wondered. 'Is the person – is Fiona – sick? Has she so aged?' – and waited, tensed and troubled, as the door opened and a woman stood there, feet thrust into hugely fluffy slippers, eyes blinking owlishly at the alien day.

'Yes?' she asked, her voice hoarse with booze and bed, one hand instinctively seeking to tame the orange violence of her hair. But he did not answer, stood staring at her with a numb disappointment that she could not understand – and, indeed, misunderstood. 'Jesus, mister,' she whined, drawing the soiled kimono more tightly round her sagging flesh, beginning-to-pucker lips tremulous with petulance and the need for sleep, 'now's not the time. I also got to kip, you know!'

'Sorry,' he said at last, 'but I didn't come for that.'

'You a cop?' she shot back, at once awake, gauging him with her eyes.

'No,' he said, tiredly, 'I'm not a cop. Just came to ask if Fiona Helmsley still lives here.'

'Fiona Helmsley? What do you want with Fiona Helmsley?'

'So you know her!' he exulted, then reined in his gladness, fearful that his need would arouse the desperate predator in her and there would come a devils' haggling over souls. But, even so, he could not quite keep the pleading from his voice as he urged, 'Tell me. *Is* she still here?'

'I asked *you* a question,' she reminded him, her eyes steadily on his.

'Okay! Okay! I want to thank her for a favour she's done me. That's all. No big deal.'

'And I'm thinking it's a *very* big deal,' she countered, her voice

77

knowing and grave. 'You shaking like you are, out there. Tell me, mister. When did you last see Fiona?'

'Fifteen years back,' he said. 'Why?' and the ground gave under him as he sensed, too late, that he had played a wrong card.

'Figures,' she said. Then, 'You on the run?'

'For Chrissakes, no!' he almost shouted, the question ramming into him with a force so nearly physical that he stepped back off the step and stared at her with the haggardness of the fugitive she had supposed. 'Does she know me?' he wondered, and his tongue took over and, with an inevitability beyond his power to control, repeated, 'Do you know me?'

'Maybe. Maybe not. I know so many men.' Then, almost inconsequentially, 'No, Fiona does not stay here anymore.'

'Where then?' he asked and came forward, waiting, but she stayed silent, looking at him with speculative eyes.

'All right!' he exploded. 'So you want something before you talk. Here!' and he fumbled in his pockets, but she held up her hand with a regality that could not be denied. 'Over my dead body,' she said. 'And hers.'

For a moment he stared at her, not comprehending, then his face cried out loud as his tongue rebelled, and she nodded and said, 'Yes. She's dead. Three years now. Buried in the cemetery other side of town. Wait,' and she went inside and came back with a ragged scrap of cigarette pack ('Like my bar chit,' he crazily thought) and handed it to him. 'The number of her grave,' she said and turned to leave.

'What did she die of?' he asked, his voice dull as a wood.

'Guess,' she said, and he nodded and hardly heard her calling after him, her voice gentle as Fiona's would have been, 'Don't take it so hard, mister. We all got to go.'

He knew the cemetery well, it being situated only a few blocks away from the house in the petit bourgeois section of town in which he had been born, and he went straight there from the cottages and found the grave with comparative ease. Grimly he surveyed the body-length mound of eroding soil, the cracked china vase that now held only sand and an ant that frantically struggled to be freed, the small, lozenge-shaped granite headstone that bore only her names, 'Fiona Sherlee Helmsley,' and the dates of her birth and death. 'Shit!' he thought. 'What a way to go,' and promised himself – and her- and *her*? – that, if ever he had the bucks to spare, he would build her a *proper* grave with angels and stuff that would do her proud. But, for now, he could only hate what he saw – hate it that there was no shade-tree to shield her from the blazing sun, no classy marble slab to keep off the rain – and, hunkering down beside the mound, touching its warm gravel as though it was her still warm flesh, he tried to thank her, to find for her the tears he had found the night before, but nothing came and at last he rose and went away, Ray crying to him from his own still undiscovered grave. But, he thought, with Fiona gone and, with her, all else gone, what hope was there now of the healing, of the *resurrection*, that would come through his knowing of that other grave?

A distant clock showed nearly noon, which meant that a day and a night had passed since the Overland bus had stopped at the roadside takeaway somewhere between the two skies and he had been able to buy and bolt down a hamburger-with-chips and a warm-as-a-piss Coke in a can. But although his legs were beginning to flail under him and his feet were coming down flat and hard on paving and tar, his mind was too stressed to acknowledge the body's need, and, on an impulse – 'What the fuck, why not?' – he turned into his old home street and came to stand before a gate he did not know but whose number assured him this *was* it – the house where he had been raised and where the final irredeemable drama had played itself out and his life had unravelled at the seams.

Gone were the pokey sash windows with their frustrating weights, the corrugated iron roof that had begun to leak, the knee-high, untended grass, the tangled oleander stand that had been the haunt of cats, had hidden him on that last, intolerable night. Now a thatch capped the house, impeccable and sleek as a lacquered hair, a generous glass glittered in modern steel frames, a tamed garden satisfied the eye, chilled the heart of the still not quite dead child.

'You got a light?' The voice was so unexpected, so close, that his heart missed a beat and his head jerked round with the guiltiness of an intruder trapped where he should not be. Barely a pace from him, half concealed by the leaves of a hibiscus bush that he could not recall any more than he could the rest of the garden that had so lushly sprung from the buried flesh of a spent time, a crinkled-as-a-paper little man was grinning at him, earth-stains on the knees of his dungarees, a hose, dribbling water, hanging from one brown-as-a-tobacco, grubby-nailed hand.

'Don't smoke,' he mumbled, turning to go, but the little man came forward, leaned on the gate, grinning his wide, yellow-toothed grin, as eager for contact as the dog, suddenly beside him, clearly was not. A high-legged, vaguely wolfish beast, it stood quietly enough, but the neck, hackles rising, was slung forward and low in the odd posture of the predator ready to spring, and a lip lifted in an almost human sneer, baring a fang, and the eyes watched with an antagonism ancient as a baying under the moon. But then the other said something to it, softly, and it at once lay down, muzzle on its paws, dog again, and he remembered how Sep, and even his mother, had hated cats and dogs, and how Sep, in particular, had been born with a wound where love should have been, finding passion only for the shadowy youth, Colin, with whom he had shared his mother's bed till she had trapped them in it and Sep had been delivered into her own largely loveless hands.

'Ja, more don't than do these days,' said the little man and for a moment he didn't know what the other was talking about, having been away such a long way, having had to refocus on the moment and the man with something of the laboured slowness of the witless or the very old.

'Why,' he thought, 'don't I just walk away from this guy? There's nothing in him for me.' But then he thought again and asked, 'You working here long?'

The other laughed. 'Long enough.' Then, a smallest, unexpected edge to his voice: 'Why you so interested in this house? You don't look like a buyer, though you never can tell. But if you are: no ways is it for sale.'

'Lots of shit under that smile,' he thought and anger stirred. 'Wouldn't want the fucking place for free. But, if you must know, I'm back in town after a long time and walking around and I see this place has changed so much, it's only the number on the gate that's still the same.'

'Ja,' and now the edge was gone, 'I didn't like it the way it was.'

It hit him then and he laughed aloud, a genuinely vicious amusement in the laugh. 'Christ!' he thought. 'How Sep and the old lady would have hated this! A Coloured in their little white palace of shit!' and he thought he heard Ray – angry, brown Ray – laugh with him from whatever dark place where he mouldered alone.

Inevitably, the other misunderstood the laugh. 'Ja. I know. You thought I was the "boy". Don't blame you, the way I look. And I signed up the dog because I thought you were a skelm figuring a way to break in. He's a good dog, this. Better than a gun, though he's just a stray I found and raised,' and he bent down and patted the outstretched head, and the hound stirred its tail and loved him with its eyes. 'But tell me: why do you hate the place the way you do?'

Carefully he skirted that. 'Let's just say it's got bad vibes, no matter how much you dolled it up.'

It was jackpot. A key in a lock of time. 'Sure. It was a sad, sad thing that happened here. She dying the way she did, he in the old age home, up there near the park. Going on for eighty now, they say, and crazy as a coot. But the bad name brought the price down and down till I said to my wife, "Who cares about a bad name?" and she said, "Go for it," and I put down my money and grabbed the place with both hands. Say, mister, you all right?'

'No, fine,' he said, 'just fine. Nice knowing you,' and he raised his hand and hurried round the corner and took a deep breath, and let it out again and shook and shook with something that felt like horror but, intricately and incomprehensibly, was a lot else besides. 'Sep *alive?*' he breathed, devastated by an irony too grotesque, too terrifying, to sustain. 'Where do I go from here?' But even as he asked himself that, he felt himself turn, knew his steps were taking him up towards the park, to the one loathsome link with his past that should not have been, that lured him now as a violent blood draws the morbid to its fringe.

Not in the park itself, but set, well back, amongst other as monumental trees, the Home's mock-marble steps, glittering expanses of glass alternating with walls white as hail, spoke to him of wealth, of the wealthy, of Sep. 'Old bastard,' he thought. 'Still got it all salted away. Living on the interest like a king,' and, at once, without penitence, without shame, he remembered the night of his arrest when he had, for the time it had taken him to cross to the gate, held the thick wads of some of Sep's wealth in his hands and, in his turn, became the prey.

'I have come to see Septimus Donovan,' he said, his voice echoless and shrill in the oriental lushness of the foyer, the glacial air-conditioned air.

The receptionist looked him up and down, face adrift in the sargassum explosion of her hair, make-up immaculate as a chrome fitting on a car. 'You a relative?' she asked, not caring that her doubtfulness showed.

'Could be,' he said, but she frowned, sensing insolence in the ambivalence and tone of the two words.

'That is no answer, sir,' she snapped, emphasising the 'sir', 'and I certainly don't remember seeing you here before.'

'Hardly likely,' he snapped back, patience worn thin as a foil, 'seeing I've been gone fifteen years!'

'Look, sir,' and now the 'sir' had a gentler fall, 'be reasonable. Mr Donovan is a very old and very sick man and the doctor has ordered that no one, save relatives and *very* special friends, be allowed to visit him.'

'And how many of these relatives and "*very* special friends" come to visit him anymore? Two? One? None? Come on, miss, answer me!' But

81

she stayed silent, looking down at her hands, only they showing the discomfort which the layered mask of the face could not betray.

'So it's none. But I have come a day's journey to here and it's been fifteen years. And now you want me to go out from here and *phone* Sep to tell him you won't let me in? Won't let him have his first visitor in Christ knows how long?'

'No need to be blasphemous, sir,' she rebuked, scrambling for the moral high ground. Then, more than a little triumphantly, 'And, anyway, he won't be *able* to answer the phone. That is what you don't understand.'

'Listen,' he broke in and something in his voice silenced her, 'all I want to know from you is – do I or don't I get to see Septimus Donovan?'

Mask at last cracked into a rictus of distaste, she tried, then, to stare him down, but he had passed beyond theatricals and, at last, she reached over and pinged the bell on her desk and a very black woman in a very white uniform entered the foyer from a side door and crossed to them, feet whispering over the carpet's extravagant pile.

'You rang?'

'Yes. This is a visitor for Mr Donovan.' Then, turning to him, 'Nurse Ngamlana is Mr Donovan's personal nurse. She'll take you to him. Good day.'

'Jesus!' he thought, following the comfortable buttocks into a lift, following them out again into a third floor corridor that glowed with the luminousness of dreams and smelled of nothing save the sanitised air. 'A *black* nurse for Sep?' and wondered if there was, after all, a hell and Sep's was this sumptuous, air-conditioned jail where the hands of the hated race ministered to even his most intimate and animal needs? But then they were standing before a door whose bland, impersonal lettering proclaimed it to be Sep's and the almost atavistic dread he had always felt for the man beyond its panels, was chillingly back in his flesh and he thrust his hands into his pockets as he felt their old trembling take hold.

'Please,' said the nurse, placing her hand on the knob of the door, but not turning it, 'don't stay too long because,' and he saw now that her face was motherly and deeply kind, that she *cared*, 'this is a man that should die, but he does not know how. If you know him, you must know that he was an alcoholic and that we cured him of that. But our help came too late. We killed the devil in him, but the devil had already had its fill of his body and his mind. Now, each month, his lawyer pays the Home its fees and we wash him and feed him and wait for him to die. More than that we cannot do. So you might wish that you had stayed away as all the others do these days, particularly when he gets difficult, which he often does, when you must press the push button on the other side of this door and I will come. Press it also when you leave, so that I can check on him and lock the door.'

Then she turned the knob and went in, and he followed her and she said, very loudly, 'Here is an old friend to visit you, Mr Donovan,' and went out again and closed the door.

It was an extraordinarily spacious and airy room, bathroom and toilet en suite, carpet as lush as those in the corridor and foyer, bed regal as the baroque oddity in which Ray had serviced his women in the days before the 'Big A' had levelled him to the likeness – and worse – of the liquor-raddled Sep he had so long ago known and now would know again. But, although furnished and appointed to cosset to the utmost whoever was confined to it, the room was still a cell, a lonely place whose desolateness was accentuated by the ceaseless, subliminal murmur of the air-conditioning, the TV screen that flickered, soundlessly and unheeded, on a cupboard beside the bed.

Sep, only his ironically babyish shock of white hair flaring up over the high back of the armchair in which he sat and that faced a picture window that was also a wall, gave no sign that he had heard the nurse or was aware of anybody else still being in the room. Hesitantly, telling himself he was a grown man now, *knowing* he was, but the child in him still very much alive, he rounded the chair, seeming to plunge into the dispiriting endlessness of roofs and grasslands beyond the glass, stood, appalled, staring down at the relic, the myth, the years had spared. This, Sep? He had been in jail when Ray died, had never been able, never wanted to picture him as he had been then, but now he knew and he cowered before the relentlessness of time.

Then the huddle of bones in the chair stirred and he saw that the other's eyes had opened and were fixed on his with the fathomless uninterest of the dead. 'Hello, Dad,' he said, the childish acknowledgement of parental power slipping from him with a volition of its own, but the eyes closed again and he drew up a ball-and-claw bankie with a padded seat and sat down on it, forcing himself to meet the challenge of disintegration that was Sep.

How, he wondered, could he ever have feared this alien thing whose very name sat so uneasily on his tongue, that, in its oddness, had broken free of *any* name? Could he not, even then, have foreseen this terminal shape that lurked under every skin – even under his own skin – that now possessed no awareness other than the absoluteness of its submission to its own decay? Would he also someday come to this: thighs thin as his shins, skeletal hands dangling from a chair's arms, limp flippers of his feet splayed and stalled as a cast-up sea beast's, translucent shell of his flesh barely holding in the long, faltering mileages of his sinews and veins?

Suddenly his own flesh crawled, was aware, and he looked up to find that Sep's eyes had again opened, were looking at him, but now no longer blind. Tongue tasted, struggled, found a voice, said, no louder than a stirring in leaves, 'It has been a long time.'

'Yes,' he said, and tried to smile. 'A very long time.'

'Why did you not come before?'

Taken aback, he groped for words. 'I couldn't come. I've been away. You know where.'

'No, I don't' – was there a ghost of petulance in that? – 'You *could* have come. There has been nothing to stop you for – for- longer than I can remember anymore.'

'Christ,' he thought, 'is this for *real?*' and sat, wondering what he should do next: jog the other's memory or go along with the fantasies of a mind already fled beyond recall? 'How's ma?' he asked, leaning forward, waiting, with something of the tension of the cruel child that would not die, for the fish to run with the line.

'Ma? Why do you call her that? She was nobody's "ma". Nobody's wife. You *know* that, boy. Where *have* you been all this time?'

Exhausted by the unaccustomed effort, the pale stirring of an old rage, the other sagged back into himself, closed his eyes, and he thought, 'Shit!' but then the eyes were there again, glinting with a shard of spitefulness in the deep caverns of the skull, and Sep was saying as though there had been no pause, 'She's dead, boy. Dead. Long time back. Can't remember when anymore. Nor how. Don't *want* to remember anymore because there's a blood there like my brain's bleeding and I dream when I go scratching around in her grave.' Then he began to shake with such a violence that it startled him and he half rose to ring for the nurse, but, as quickly as it had started, the shaking stopped and he realised that Sep had been laughing, had been convulsed with an obscene hilarity that left him breathless and very faintly, inappropriately, flushed. 'Yes,' he panted, 'dead, boy, dead! She thought I'd go first. Then she'd be the head bitch of all the bitches in town. But I beat her, boy. Beat her at the end!' and his eyes closed and he at once lightly slept.

'Old bastard,' he thought, but not bitterly so. 'Done what I couldn't do. Changed his past so's we've got nothing to share and so what the fuck am I *doing* here?' But he sat on anyway, watching Sep sleep, listening to him nibble and suck at his lips 'like he was a kid sucking a jube,' listening to the silence beyond that small sound as it marooned them in the iron of its ice, yet left them more desperately disparate than even at the beginning they had been.

At last, intolerably constrained, wanting now only out, he rose as though he fought back ceiling and walls, began to move, softly, towards the door. But Sep was at once awake, peering at him with bemused and querulous eyes, and, determined to break off from the nothingness that yet so subtly clung, he took Sep's chill, dry hand in his – 'Why only now?' he wondered. 'Why not also when I came in?' – and said, a devious cheerfulness in his voice, 'I must go now. They said I must not stay too long.'

'You lie,' said Sep with the sudden, flat harshness of fifteen years before. 'You are like all the others. Can't wait to get away from me. Can't wait to see me die.'

Startled by such a turnabout, a perceptiveness that was as unsettling as a rising of the dead, he protested, strove to free his hand, said he would come again, winced inwardly at the monstrousness of his lie.

'Kiss me,' said Sep, his voice strengthening, surfacing from its whisper into a clear sound. 'Kiss me! We are not strangers. Only strangers shake hands.'

Hesitantly he leaned closer, placed his lips on the other's cheek, made to straighten up again, but Sep's arms circled his neck, held him back with the frenzied strength of the dying or the crazed, and Sep's mouth was pressed to his, nuzzling it like a beast on heat, and he realised with a shocked and utter disbelief that the other was trying to engage his tongue as Jason had so often demanded of him in jail. Firmly, he kept his lips closed, gritted his teeth, but now Sep was whimpering with such a wordless and desperate need, that, in an access of a pity he had not known he still possessed, he opened his mouth and locked his tongue with Sep's, and wrestled it till distaste overcame him and he wrenched himself loose and made for the door.

'Come back, Colin, come back! Please! I need you, boy! Don't let me die alone!' Sep's anguished cry, shrilling and strained as a dumb man goaded into speech by an intolerable pain, whirled him round. Colin? The shadowy boy-lover of whom his mother had told? The indestructible succubus who had assumed his shape in Sep's tortured mind those many years ago – had done it again now?

Horror seized him then, and a sick rage, and he turned back to the door and rang the bell. Then went out, closing the door. But still Sep's cries seemed to follow him, careening off every immaculate wall, wailing, before him and behind him, like a ravening bird.

Outside, he breathed in, craving the clean air, the cauterising sun. But Sep's tongue, full and fleshy as a penis rooted in the boniness of

85

the skull, still clogged his mouth, his throat, inseminated him with its sourness and his shame.

❋ ❋ ❋

Back at the hotel, he went at once to his room, only peripherally aware that the Indian was nodding to him from behind the reception desk, that a black woman was nudging a broom around between the chairs. From a small window at the head of the stairs, a by now mid-afternoon ray of sun shafted down through the stalled dust of the air, illumining the motes till it seemed to him he was journeying up a mythical path to the – what? – negation? – affirmation? – salvation? – that he had that morning sought and not found – would perhaps, his heart warned, ultimately find only in his own self?

But he was in no mood to hear and, again locking the door behind him, looked around his room and found it quite surprisingly tidied and cleaned. Then he sat down on the bed – always back to the fucking *bed*, he thought, bitterly as one betrayed, and it not so much a vehicle for his rest as for his ongoing apprehension and guilt – and took the envelope of notes from where he had hidden it under his shirt and looked at it, knowing it now for what it was – the means of his survival – in the short term, at any rate – or the cause of his battering and even death if he were to continue carrying it wherever he went. But what else could he do? To leave it, however desperately concealed, in a room as bare as this, in an establishment as accomplished in petty thievery as this undoubtedly was, would be tantamount to handing it to the morning's tramp at the trash bin, and, dismayed that what had seemed so slight a matter should suddenly loom so large, he stuffed the envelope back under his shirt and went down to the 'Gents' to urinate and wash.

Going, coming, he passed no one, and no one passed him, and he slunk back to his room like the last survivor of a holocaust who hears the dead still breathing behind their ravaged doors, and, back on his bed, thought, 'Where to now? Where the *fuck* to now?' Should he go, should he stay? 'Go,' he thought. 'There's nothing for me here. No ending of an old road from which I can go on like there's been nothing between. No skin I left behind that I can get back in. Be the me I was when it was Fiona and Ray – when I loved a man enough to do what I did for him, but could have loved the woman too – and the snake between my legs was not just for pissing through.'

'Yes,' he decided then, 'I must go. Go while there's still money enough in my hand to go. Maybe I should never have come. Only ghosts here, dragging me down,' and he thought of Sep's arms around his neck, his tongue furiously seeking his own, and shuddered, violently as one who dies, and rose to take up his pack and leave.

There was a knock on the door – a soft and questioning tap of the knuckles of one who was not sure – and he froze, immobile as a startled buck before it flees, hoping the unknown summoner would move on, leave him alone. But again the knock sounded, louder now, and he came forward, a little irritably, a little fearfully – with the inborn fearfulness of the prison years – and cracked open the door. It was Henry Martins, seeming even smaller than he had the night before, eyes wide, and questioning as his knock, lips sucked in with the intensity of the impetus to speak.

'Yes?' he snapped, not bothering to hide the hostility he still felt.

'Can I speak to you?'

Martins' voice was soft and shook a little and he realised that the other was afraid, and pity stirred in him as it had earlier on at the climax of his meeting with Sep and he upbraided himself, thinking, 'Sucker! Will I never learn?' But his tone stayed uncompromising and flat as he said, 'Can't see what there's to say. But go on. If you must.'

'Thanks. I just came to say,' and Martins swallowed, pride big as a boulder in his throat, 'that I am sorry about last night. I can still tell my legs what to do when I have had enough. But not my tongue. It gets away from me every time.'

'Like that other meat between your legs,' he mocked, the gratuitous brutality of what he had said shocking even him, and he thought, too late, 'Christ, my tongue's no different from his,' then added, 'But it's been a long day and I want out and I didn't ask him to come fartarsing around me,' and knew that for what it was and wrestled with his deepening shame.

The other looked at him as though he had heard nothing untoward, even, disconcertingly, smiled. 'I'm thinking you'd like to say "sorry" for that, but, of course, you won't. Some can, some can't. So I'm not letting it spoil my day and you needn't let it spoil yours. Unless you *want*. Okay?'

Watching the little man walk off, spring back in his step as though he had offloaded a weight at his door, he felt something – not shame but something more subtle and covert – move in him, compellingly possess him, and was startled by the urgency in his voice as he shouted 'Wait!' Obediently, Martins turned and came back, and stood before him and said 'Yes?' and he knew, as certainly as though the other had spoken, that Martins was aware as he of the irony in the repetition of that single, questioning word.

'But why,' he asked, '*why* did you come to apologise about last night? You were so certain then that you were right about me. Have you now changed your mind?'

Again the other smiled, but now it was a grimace that mocked himself, a little bitter and a little wry. 'Last night was last night and what I believe or don't believe about you has got nothing to do with now. Now is me saying I just don't like pain, whether the pain is in me or in somebody else, and if I have caused the pain in somebody else, then I don't sleep nights till I have crawled like a dog to put it right. Look, Jackson – or may I call you "Johnny" without you climbing the walls? – I don't know how you feel about these things, but there is sadness and there is love, and the sadness is wide as the night and love is little and scarce as the glow-worms we used to hold in our hands when we were kids and wonder why they didn't burn. I do know, though, how you feel about *me*, so – while we are on the subject and whether you believe me or not – let me tell you that I, too – like any other living thing – need love and sometimes offer its other shape – call it "lust" if you want – in bars and other joints when I'm all shickered up and the need in me is dark and wide as the sadness I have just been talking about.'

'So all right then,' he cut in, 'that's the way you say you are and that's the way it is for *you* and I don't want to know. But,' and again he was startled by the urgency in his voice, 'you still haven't answered me about *me*. How do you see me *now*?'

'What does it matter how I see you now? Or how I saw you last night? You are you and only you know what you are. So why don't you ask the only question that counts of the only person that counts? Ask *yourself*: "What am I now?" The mind might try to lie, to con its way out, but the you that is where you-don't-know-where-it-is will tell you the truth. That is if you listen hard enough and *want* to know the truth. Do you really want to know it that bad?'

'Maybe,' he said, 'maybe not.' Then, explosively, 'Look, I've had a long day and I'm not in the mood for all this shit. I ask you a simple question and you come at me like my mind you say will try to con its way out of the truth. You've said you are sorry and I'm saying now that that's okay by me. So let's leave it at that and cut the fancy crap. Better still – cut *clean* because I'm leaving again and, even if I wasn't, there's nothing in you for me. There's some that come together and some that don't. We don't.'

'You eaten yet?'

Disconcerted by the total irrelevancy of the question, he searched the other's face for some sign of a wrong intent, but there was nothing: only a rather sombre concern. 'You not listening?' he asked, surprise negating the sharpness his tone might otherwise have held.

'I'm listening all right. Heard every word. But I would still like to know if you have eaten yet.'

'What makes you think I haven't and, even if I haven't, what's it got to do with you?'

'Well, you haven't been down for supper, breakfast or lunch – for which I don't blame you, the food here being the slop that it is. But it's costing you money and if you had bucks enough to throw away, you wouldn't be staying in a dump like this. Apart from that, you *look* like somebody who hasn't eaten for longer than is good. Eyes way back in your head and cheeks caved in like you're an old lag on the run.'

Instantly his eyes flickered and the gang's tattoo on his left shoulder – two snakes intertwined – 'like Jason and me,' he had always desolately thought – seemed to burn itself afresh into his flesh. As instantly the other checked, with every sense aware that a nerve had been touched, and the floor shivered under him for a space between two breaths as he and Henry Martins stared at each other like two figures in a stalled reel. Then the inborn wiliness of the prison time was back with him and he rushed Martins head-on, blustering his way through, 'No need to call me a criminal,' he snarled, 'because I booked in with only a back pack for my stuff.' Then, remembering what he had observed since leaving jail, 'Lots of good citizens got back packs these days.'

'Okay! Okay! I didn't mean it that way. Didn't even know you *had* a back pack, to tell you the truth. Why so touchy about the least little thing?'

'I told you,' he muttered, the card still good in his hand. 'I've had a long day,' but, under the surliness, as long a breath went out from him as he saw that the other had swallowed the spiel.

'I know and that's why I'm asking if you have eaten even though, as you say, it is no business of mine. Which *I* am not saying because – as *I* told *you* – I don't like pain in myself or others and – though you treat me like the shit I am and I should be clobbering you if I were any other kind of man – or any kind of man at all – you are one of the worst cases of a plain suffering fool that I have seen since I don't know when, and I'm trying to tell you that going hungry doesn't help any and if you were rather to get yourself a good, slap-up meal, maybe you'll see differently whatever it is you are seeing now and let that back pack lie till you've thought it all through.'

'Can I go now?' he asked, elaborately polite, buffooning his way out of a situation over which, somehow, he had lost control.

'Yes. But still you haven't answered me. I was right about you not eating, wasn't I?'

'Yes!' he almost shouted. 'Yes! Yes! I haven't eaten and I'm hungry as all hell and I'm going out of my mind. Now – if you are happy – will you for Chrissakes leave me alone?' and he went in and slammed the door and listened to Martins' soft steps ghosting down the corridor to his own room. 'Jesus!' he whispered, flopping on his back onto the bed. 'Is he for *real?*' but the he that, as Martins had said, was where he did not know where it was, whispered back, 'Who *is* it that is for real? Are you?' and again, 'Why are you so distressed? What is it that you are turning from, will not face?' He could not – *would* not? – answer that, knowing that Martins had gone down the corridor to his room, yet had not moved a step from where he had stood, was still peering up at him, engaging him with a deeply troubling inquisitiveness and concern. Why, he wondered, had he not rid himself of the man as immediately as he would have swotted a bothersome fly, had, instead, stood listening to him with a covert avidity that, in itself, had encouraged the other to go on. And on and *on*, he thought, like a tumour establishing its territory in him, widening it, and he not knowing yet whether it was malignant or benign. Again he wished to take up his pack and go down to reception and book out, buy a ticket for the first place whose name he liked, jump off the deep end, but now the black laxness that had always overwhelmed him after Jason came, was inexplicably, benumbingly, back in him, and he let his mind stream and dwindle on the flow of that apathy till it flickered out and he slept and woke again to a renewed tapping on his door.

'Who now?' he wondered, stumbling, sleepily, to the door, standing, abashed, not understanding why his annoyance should be tinged with something oddly like relief, when he saw that it was again Martins, this time with two plates in his hands, the one upended over the other as a cover and, on it, a green paper serviette that dared him to laugh at it and be damned. 'Fucking thing is *him*,' he thought. 'Kind of proud. Kind of sad,' but, aloud, he said, 'Jesus, Martins, what is it with you now?'

'Just brought you something to eat,' and the curiously hairy hands were thrusting the plates at him, and he was taking them and lifting the top one and finding, under it, three fried eggs in an almost whole circle of fried wors, and a scattering of chips, expertly browned. Instantly his tongue salivated and his belly, savouring the smell of the food like the beast that it was, lunged out, but his mind held back, warning, 'This is a communion one step lesser than the flesh. Don't!' and he opened his mouth to speak, reject, and willed his hands to give back the food, but his hands rebelled, and his heart, taking over, came out of his mouth with a sound like a sob and he turned his back to Martins, horrified and ashamed.

For a moment, there was a silence so intense that he could hear someone turning off a tap in the distant 'Gents' and he swung, as on a gibbet, between desire and conceit and the moment became an hour in his own private hell. Then Martins was saying, matter-of-factly and flatly, carefully skirting the least hint of awareness of anything untoward, 'I'll leave you to eat. I also like eating alone when I can.' Then, 'Bring back the plates if you want and I'll make us some coffee in my room. Otherwise, I'll pick them up later on. Enjoy.'

When the other's door had closed, he closed his own and stood staring down at the food in his hands. 'Fifteen years,' he thought, 'of serving someone else. Waiting on Jason, hand and foot, cock in my arse. Fifteen years of being neither woman nor man. Now this – *this!*' and his eyes blurred and he sat down on the bed, plate on his knees, and took up the plastic fork he found under the serviette – 'thinks of every bloody thing!' – and began to eat with a ravenousness that shocked, as did the tears he could no longer stem.

Finished, he wiped his mouth, fingers, blew his nose, threw the soiled serviette into the trash tin under the washstand, considered whether to return the plates himself or let Martins come for them as he had said he otherwise would. 'Don't,' his mind again cautioned him. 'Don't go to his room. It's a ploy. You know what he is. A plate of food doesn't *change* what he is. Don't be a fool. Let him fetch his own bloody plates, then take your kit and get the hell out of here.'

Carefully he considered that, harnessing intuition to reason, trying to see Martins as naked and stripped down as he could not see even his own self, at last simply gathering up the plates, furtively washing them in the 'Gents' – 'Serving Jason again?' he cynically thought – saying to his mind, 'Go fuck your hand.'

'You shouldn't have,' said Martins, taking the wet plates, betraying no obvious pleasure that he had come. 'Sit down.'

At first glance, the room did not seem all that different from his. There was a carpet underfoot that testified to Martins' long tenancy, but it had seen better days and the standard hotel furniture was too confrontational to be significantly offset or obscured. The curtains in the window were clearly not the hotel's, but although original and colourful, they were almost austere compared to the frilly and frivolous confections he had half expected to find. The most striking addition to the basic pattern of the room was a curtained alcove that housed a rough-and-ready kitchenette complete with midget sink whose waste pipe led nowhere but into a large wooden bucket that surely would have to be emptied somewhere from time to time. 'Probably into the john,' he thought, and remembered that James Mjozi had said that Martins was an 'institution' in a refuge for a mainly rootless 'trade' and, thus, could undoubtedly do pretty well as he pleased.

The exotica that he had always associated with the largely gay world in which Ray had so recklessly harvested rands and, at the last, death, only began to surface when he looked around for a place to sit and Martins indicated one of two black and orange pouffes that served as chairs. Seated, he looked up and faced a framed photograph of a breathtakingly muscular male nude, posture nonchalantly full-frontal, one hand cupping, proffering, genitals as animal and sullen as a stud bull's.

'The photo worries you?' asked Martins and turned its face to the wall.

On an impulse, he rose and turned it back again. 'I have seen more than that – in the flesh – though it's not my scene,' and for the first time the other seemed not so certain of himself, of his control. 'Interesting,' he said but did not pressure the subject further and went into the alcove and there was a rattle of cups and a kettle sang.

'How do you want your coffee?'

'Black. Strong. Three sugars.' Then: 'Who took it?'

'What? The photo? I did. Used to be a professional once. Held exhibitions – here – overseas – could charge just about what I liked. Then I saw darkness the way others see the Light and landed up here, too young for a pension, too old to want to start again and earning just enough interest on what I had saved to keep the Indian happy and pretty up the room. Been in it ten years now. What do you think of it – the photo I mean?'

'Cool but shit, if you get what I mean. Did the guy pump iron?'

'He did. Why do you ask?'

'Had a friend. Born here. Like me, though I've been gone a long time. He used to pump iron. Had a shape something like this ou's and also was not shy about standing around with everything hanging out. But strictly "don't touch". Between him and me, anyway. And his face had a guy living in it. Hate him or love him, but he was there. This one's a doll. Like it's only the body you see.'

'You're right. Except that he was no doll. He was a lout who did you over with bovver boots if you didn't watch out. I didn't watch out.'

'Then why do you still hang his photo on the wall?'

For a moment the busyness in the alcove stilled. 'I could lie to you about that, but I won't. Although *why* I won't, I'm not all that sure. It's because I like what he's holding in his hand.' Then he came out with the coffee and they sat drinking it and he felt Martins watching him with careful eyes.

'You're quiet. Have I shocked you? Should I rather have lied?'

'Look, Martins, I said it before and I say it again: this is not my scene, but I shock about as easy as a dead man.'

The other nodded. 'I like that. Fits you. *Is* you. Maybe that's why I didn't lie.' Then, 'This friend of yours. Where is he now?'

'Dead.' The word dropped between them like a stone. 'Aids.'

'And you loved him.' It was a statement, not a question, and the sound of Martins putting down his cup was gentle as a bell, lightly swung, swiftly held.

'Ja, but not that freak's kind of love,' and his chin thrust at the stud on the wall. 'Which is not to say it never got rough. He was not a good man – whatever that means – and he could be cruel. Cruel as the streets are when the lights go out and it's every jock for himself. The streets were all he knew, anyway – them and the dives and the coffee bars, and the celluloid shit of the old cinema I looked for today and it wasn't there anymore. Once he donnered me up till I thought I was never going to come right again, but he cried about that, Martins, and he gave me *respect*, which I had never had before and have never had afterwards, and which means more to me than love, Martins – or maybe it *is* love, for all I know – and he was *loyal* and shamed me into being the same, and me just a lazy, snivelling snot of a kid who learned how to grow up under a guy who never really grew up himself. Weird.'

'So now you've come back looking for a dead man?'

'Well, you could say it like that, I suppose. But it's not quite the way it is. Fifteen years is a long time, Martins – but it had to be for reasons I don't want to talk about right now – and I was not sentimental sucker enough to think there would be much left of the old trails. But I did expect more than the fuckall that I found and that got me picking up my pack and heading for the door, and I should still be thinking that way and maybe I am, only now there's a kind of laziness in me, sitting here, talking, drinking coffee, almost like I still got roots in this arsehole of a town.'

'But what about your friend's grave? Surely that brought you close to him again?'

'Don't know where it is. Don't know who to *ask* where it is. Ray was a loner, Martins. Cut off by his own blood. In the end, I was the closest thing to kin he had. Worse: I ask around *too much,* and worms will be coming out of a can bigger than the grave I am looking for, and those sleeping dogs will be up and running through this town like you never heard in the ten years you been in this room. Maybe – if I stay – *if* I stay' – he paused, eyes alert and disturbed – 'But tell me, Martins, what am I doing – sitting here, talking to you like this?'

'You don't *have* to. Stop if you want. If you think you still *can.*'

A metro bustled past, couplings clashed in the nearby shunting yards, the silence hummed between them like the just vacated rails. 'Is true,' he said at last. 'It's like I'm halfway having the shits with my tongue. What the hell, look, don't think I'm going funny in my mind, but I was going to say, if I stay, maybe I could make my own private grave for Ray. You see, way out there on the dump was an old shed for the workers and their tools that nobody used anymore and, when Ray was dying, I would sometimes go and sit in there and think about him and I was never closer to him than then. So maybe, even if that old shack's long gone, I could still sometimes go to where it was and sit there and, when I suddenly look up, Ray will be walking towards me over all that red and yellow shit like he used to come walking to me over my mind. Sounds crazy, I know, but it could sort of tie things up for a man and, anyway, these little kid's things only sound crazy when we grow up because it's the *kid's* things that are real, only we can't *see* like a kid anymore.'

'You want more coffee?'

He shook his head. 'So you think I'm crazy,' he said, his tone flat and hurt.

'Of course I do. And it's a crazy I should be laughing at, but I'm not,' and Martins took up the cups and went into the alcove to wash them, tying a flowered apron around his waist. 'And don't get any ideas about the apron. This is my only decent pair of slacks,' and he was coming back, slippered feet padding over the floor like an amiable house cat, the apron still around his waist.

'When did you last shave?' he asked, reaching out an exploratory hand, the movement as casual as it was deft.

The sudden intimacy shocked him and his first thought was to strike out at the hand, but then he saw the other's eyes and there was nothing there save a professional appraisal of the state of a chin.

'Haven't bought a razor yet,' he muttered and realised, too late, that that was a slip – that Martins knew it was a slip – was asking himself, 'What sort of a traveller is this, what is he travelling *from*, that he must buy a razor when he hits a town?'

But the question remained unasked and he thought, 'This guy I can trust,' and he listened with no sense of the bizarre as Martins loosed his chin and said, 'Look, it's too late to buy a razor now and, you looking the way you do, the Indian and that little rat in reception are going to get other ideas and whisper between themselves' – was that, he wondered, a nod at the things which he had left unsaid? – 'But I'll give you a shave, if you want. Could lend you the razor for you to do it yourself, but it's a cutthroat and I am betting you've never handled one in your life. My old man was a barber who taught me to use it when I first had the hairs, then how to use it on his customer-friends in the shop, always hoping I would take over from him when I grew up. But I grew up into something else – into the first shape of what you see now – so I wasn't with him when he died. You want?'

'Okay,' he said, and Martins knotted a towel round his neck and drew his head back into the lean knot of his belly, and he only slightly flinched when the glittering blade first descended and began to sweep the stubble from his chin, cleanly and sweetly as a scythe, and Martins hissing through his teeth and neither of them saying a word. Staring up into the other's face, finding it inward and set as a stone, wholly delivered into hands that moved at the behest of an alien mind, he thought, 'Am I, indeed, mad?' but then also thought, 'Waited on now. Hand and foot. Waited on as once I waited on *him*. Is this how Jason felt all those years?' and the thought was balm to his battered pride and, fleetingly, he felt whole again, and male.

Then Martins was patting the soap from his face with a warm, wet cloth and whipping the towel from off his neck and saying, 'There!' and later they clinked two fine glasses of a less fine wine, and it was only when he closed Martins' door behind him and a bevy of women, passing him in the corridor, looked at him and laughed, that he remembered that Martins was still Martins and that could not be changed.

So, that laughter of the women, thin and spiteful as a roof-iron in the wind, stayed with him after he reached his room, muted the unexpected pleasure that the visit to Martins had lent. Was this, he worried, not again the conspiracy of – what? – 'destiny'? – the timeworn icons of 'darkness' and 'light' – that in the pre-jail years had nudged, *sucked,* him into a momentum of circumstance he could not control? Was this town, after all, his own private Gehenna to which he should never have returned, which he should now with all alacrity flee? Picking up his pack, he swung it, rested it, swung it again, remembered then the pathos of the proffered plate, the kindliness of coffee and wine, the strangely innocent ritual of the shave, and, setting the pack finally down, lay back on the bed and woke into twilight and a trafficking of steps and voices past his door.

'Supper,' he guessed, and was hungry again, and, driven by that as well as by the vague feeling that he must not let Martins down, he decided to claim his place in the dining room for the first time and went to the 'Gents' and urinated and washed his face and hands. Halfway down the stairs, however, he paused, confronted by a minor yet acute crisis that came at him like a blade. Surely Martins would expect him to share his table with him, would greet him with an intimacy that would turn heads and focus eyes. Was he prepared for such a public association with Martins, for the sexual innuendoes to which that could give rise? Remembering the laughter of the women as he had left Martins' room, he knew that the answer was 'No' and almost turned back until common sense admonished him that that was no solution, that he could not forever debar himself from the food, however execrable, for which he had paid. 'Bluff my way in,' he thought. 'Pretend I can't see him because I don't know which way in a strange place.' But he need not have feared. Martins, who was already seated, did not invite him over to his table, merely nodded, went on eating as though the afternoon had never been. 'Cool,' he thought. 'He understands,' but that very understanding aroused in him a deep discomfort, an awareness of himself which did not flatter but against which he was powerless to contend.

Back in his room, he drew the curtains wide, but did not switch on the light, and, taking the chair over to the window, sat and stared out over the town. The pale sliver of the moon was edging down towards the dump and he wondered if the old shed of which he had spoken to Martins was still out there in the wastes, the wind shrilling through its stone sides and iron roof and the door flapping open and shut like an old man's garrulous tongue. The roof and door were probably long gone by now, but the walls could conceivably still be there, unless the contours of the dump itself had changed and fresh settlings of slimes had buried them as finally as had time. Should he really check if anything was still there? *Would* that bring him the fulfilment he had fantasised to Martins that it might, or would it but provoke in him more meaningless pain? The sign's neon jostled, gibbered, round him like a ghostly host – blackness and light – blackness and dream? – blackness and *myth*? – 'Two poles,' he thought, 'and me between, generating what?' – and at last he put on his ancient sweater against the suddenly chillier night air and took a long walk through the streets, only to find it was *he* that then was the ghost, passing, unseen, unheard, through the alien throngs, and, on arriving back at the hotel, he went into the bar, looking for Martins – *anyone* – to whom he could talk and who would affirm that they shared a common flesh and form.

'Bra Johnny,' said James Mjozi, scrubbing the counter between them with a mechanical hand. 'I was wondering if you were still here. Was meaning to check the register later to see if you had booked out.'

'You would have?' he asked, surprised but not displeased. 'But why? You only met me last night.'

Mjozi shook his head. 'I say it again: you whiteys are weird. You believe in what you call "love at first sight", but friendship at first sight is an animal from another star. My people are not like that. They make friends too easily and forgive too easily, which is why we're in the shit all the time. And – yes – I only know you from last night, but I like what I see. You have a good shape and a man's tongue – not like the rest of the dronkies and moffies around here – and one morning – if you stay and if you like – I'll wake you and you must come jogging with me. Two's better than one on the long road.'

'Well,' he said, deliberately skirting the offer of friendship, disconcerted by it, still instinctively embarrassed and repelled by the other's blemished eye, 'I haven't done much jogging, except for – ,' and nearly said, 'except for around the prison yard,' then finished, lamely – 'a k or two now and again.'

'Not to worry. We'll take it slow till the old heels begin to hum. The main thing is the sharing. Seeing things – saying, "Hey, look there!"'

'You talk smart,' he said, awkwardly, wondering how he could get his back off the wall. 'Better 'n me. You a high school boy?'

'Uh-huh. Even higher, bra. Nearly did something right at university once, then the old snake that's got no eyes like it's got no sense, found itself a hole and there's a wife and two kids back home. So the boy with the fancy tongue and big dreams, but a bigger cock, is the two years over thirty cunt – sort of like the two-in-one I'm not, if you know what I mean! – you see standing here now, dishing out the shit to homos and whores. You come for some?'

'No,' he said, 'I'm looking for Henry Martins,' and an instinct subtler than sense warned him that he had said the wrong thing.

At once the other's brows arched. 'Henry Martins? Hey, don't come making trouble here, bra! Forget about what happened last night. I told you: he won't worry you again.'

'No,' he demurred, floundering deeper in, 'I don't want to fight him. I want to stand him a drink.'

Mjozi's face set into a harsh, accusing mask. 'But I thought you were finished with the little creep?'

'I was' – why, he wondered, was the other's reaction so *sharp?* – 'but he came to me this afternoon and apologised and I thought it's only right I showed there's no hard feelings anymore.' Instinctively, he said nothing of the visit to Martins' room, the coffee, wine, shave, the preliminary proffering of food. 'Why?' asked his self beyond the self. 'Why?' and he knew that a shamed citing of his reaction to the women's laughter in the corridor was, here, not sufficient, that there was a motivation beyond that that he but marginally sensed, could not even begin to encapsulate in thought or word.

Mjozi breathed out, but there was, again puzzlingly, something like relief in the breath. 'Listen, Johnny,' and his tone was patient and again a friend's, 'another thing I like about you – and that you made plain as a riot last night – is that you hate gays as much as me, though I daren't show it, being behind the bar, so I'm surprised, bra, that I've got to warn you that you don't stand shits like Martins drinks. That that's like feeding steaks to a wolf with your bare hands.'

But now the extravagant imagery, the almost fanaticism of the tone, repelled him as did Mjozi's eye, and he said, more curtly than he had intended, 'Look, Mjozi, Martins came to me like a gentleman – like *I* was a gentleman – and said he was sorry, and we talked, and now I understand him and he understands me. I *like* being treated like a gentleman, Mjozi, not having been treated like one for the last fifteen of my thirty-five years – so, if you don't mind, I'll be talking to, even drinking with Martins for as long as I fucking well please. Okay?' – 'At last an honourable man,' said the self beyond the self. 'But who are you defending? – Martins? – You?' – and he fled before the turbulent darkness of his mind.

Again the other's face set, but now it was only a face, a tension of skin, bounded by ears, hairline, chin. 'Okay. If that's the way you feel. But surely you'd like to know,' and now there was the tiniest trace of malice in the tone, 'that you'll not be finding Martins here tonight. He left just before you came. With a man. A different man to the one he had the night before. They'll be in his room right now. Ciao, bra,' and, surprisingly, he reached out and gave him the double handshake of more violent times before turning away.

At the top of the stairs, he paused, stared at Henry Martins' shut, silent door. 'Jason,' he thought, and a shudder ran through him like a wind before a storm. 'Only two doors down.' And, that night, it was not only Jason that troubled him in his sleep, but also Henry Martins, coming, stumbling, on his feet of clay, and James Mjozi with his shattered eye.

***

The rapping on the door woke him when night was still greyly in the room. 'Martins,' he at once thought. 'For Chrissake, has the guy got no idea of time?' Then, 'Or is this when he kicks out his boyfriends and goes looking for suckers like me to hold his hand?' The thought was so waspish and perverse that he recoiled from it in shame, but there was also an element of envy, jealousy even, in it that troubled him the most, and he felt the urge to leave, to flee, again welling up in him like a reaching out for spaciousness and light. 'Stay quiet,' he decided, 'and he'll go away,' but the rapping intensified and, at last, it was James's Mjozi that shouted, 'Hey, bra Johnny! You dead?'

'Hold it, I'm coming,' he shouted back, vaguely wondering why he should find Mjozi less irritating than Martins, sensing that, here, he was making a choice of a sort. Hindered by the early morning tumescence to which he was prone, he struggled into scants, vest, pants, shuffled into old sneakers, flung open the door.

'For you,' said James Mjozi, handing him a brightly flowered pair of running shorts. 'Thought you probably didn't have any of your own.'

For a moment he stared at the other, bewildered and barely out of sleep. Then he remembered and his gut flipped. 'Shit! Were you *serious* last night?'

'Of course I was serious. Come, bra. The vest's okay and the feet will have to do, but you got to swop into the shorts or I'll be ashamed to have you running alongside.'

'You don't have to have me anywhere at all. I told you last night this is not my scene. So why don't you just jog back down the stairs and leave me to finish what's left of my kip?'

'You mean that?' Now the other's voice was very quiet, almost sad, and that quietness and sadness cut into him with the sharpness of a guilt that it was nonsensical to feel, yet nonetheless was felt. 'Look,' said the self beyond the self, 'if you are going to stay here – and you *are* going to stay here – you know that – you knew it when Martins shaved you in his room – you knew it when Mjozi said you had a good shape and a man's tongue – you knew it again this morning when you longed to be gone, but with the longing of one who knows he is *not* going to be gone, and got his scants all in a knot because Martins has a man in his room when, otherwise, you wouldn't have given two fucks *what* he had in his room – so, *since* you are going to stay, you need friends or, at least, those who can let you feel you have roots, can make others feel you have roots in a place the Big Wheel has brought you back to a second time. Face it, friend! You are tired now and sick with a sickness that is of the heart and no ways are you going to make it alone,' and, aloud, he said, '*All right* then. Come inside,' and Mjozi

99

came in and sat on the bed and grinned when he turned his back to him while changing into the shorts, and he felt good about that because it showed, he thought, that he understood about the early morning thing and was grinning at him as a man to a man. But it also struck him as almost stiflingly odd that, so soon after returning to the ambience of his youth, he should once again, as had been the way of that youth, be shy of betraying his tumescence to others, when, in prison, there had been such a crude flaunting of erections with the subsequent juvenile ribaldry or more desperate demonstrations of lust. How quickly, he thought, did the past reclaim, imprison him, closing about him its dead hand, its sackcloth of ashes and dust.

Now, the long pants shed, Mjozi had a clearer view of his feet and yelled, 'Hey, bra, where'd you get those soles? Haven't seen sneakers like that since I was at school!' and for a moment all that moved was stilled and he thought, 'Shit! I *must* get new gear today,' and turned to the other as though he hadn't heard and said, 'Come on then, let's go before I change my mind,' and they went down the stairs and into the silent street, Mjozi in front and whistling with a joyousness that lightened his own step and turned his face to the new day.

As they ran, feet slapping the pavements, steps and voices echoing back from the buildings' sides, he was reminded of the prison's exercise yard, but the thought did not distress him, sparked, rather, a small wistfulness that he knew was not warranted but could not wholly deny. Still largely unshared, the early morning stillness was as a water in a dry place and he avidly savoured it, remembering how he had cowered like a bird stricken by a sudden wind as he had emerged from Diepwater into the horrendous cacophony of the world beyond. Mjozi, with his fluid, effortless stride, almost mesmerically chivvied him on and he began to enjoy the running, even to abandon himself to it, the only discordant note being that he sensed that Mjozi was holding himself in in order to help him keep pace, and he was astonished to find himself vowing that he would do this again and try to outstrip the other as his stamina improved. Only towards the end, the east reddening like a pustule about to erupt and the hotel distantly in sight, did Mjozi abandon him, relentlessly lengthening his stride, skimming the earth with the lightness of bone of a bird, leaving him, floundering and ragged of breath, irrecoverably behind.

But, even then, Mjozi's old delicacy of feeling prevailed. Waiting for him on the hotel steps, now almost as wet with sweat as he, but deepened breath still far from spent, he draped his arm about his shoulders, the tough stubble under his arms harshly against his skin, and smiled and asked, 'Again?' and he nodded, but, to himself, shouted, '*Yes!*' not merely because of the physical pleasure the running had afforded him, but because, once again, Mjozi had treated him as a fellow *male*, nudging him as they passed the still infrequent women, commenting on their attributes, greeting them, freely and jocularly, as the new society allowed but all too frequently failed to condone.

Parting, they showered, he in the still largely comatose hotel, Mjozi in the staff quarters in an adjoining wing, and, later, coming down to breakfast, his appetite honed and his lips pursed just short of the whistle of wellbeing to which Mjozi had so freely given vent, he felt extravagant enough to greet even the youth in reception, who dutifully nodded, then turned to him the truer countenance of his spine. 'Fuck him,' he thought, but there was no real malevolence in the thought, and he went on into the dining room to find only Martins was still there and was looking up at him with his eyes set deep and lines of tiredness about his mouth.

'Whore!' The word flared in his brain with the explosive suddenness of a ruptured vein and he recoiled from its loathsomeness as instantly and instinctively as though his own will had played no part in it, but the lesion stayed, and the shame, and a slyness in him that would not be silenced pointed a finger and a woman, passing through reception, laughed on a high, hard note that dismayed.

Then Martins smiled at him with the tentative intimacy of the new friend, but, though aware as he still was of his own wrongness, his own life's ambivalent history, he was also still feeling Mjozi's arm about his shoulders, was again sharing with him the masculinity he had for so long lost, and he found it physically and psychologically impossible to return the smile: could only nod, as had the youth in reception, and move on to his table, where he sat, eyes fixed on what he ate, uncomfortably conscious of Martins' unspoken bewilderment and hurt. Finishing first, the latter stood up, hesitated, the hesitancy drawing the air about them into a knot of questioning that demanded that it be resolved, but still he did not look up, and, at last, he heard Martins' slippered feet moving towards the door, and that soft, almost sensual padding provoked in him an echo of the forbidden word, and he fought it back and miserably chewed his way through the hotel's spectacularly unpalatable food.

But the buoyancy of spirit engendered by that morning's jogging and Mjozi's companionship was not to be that easily subdued and, coming out of the dining room back into reception, he found the Indian gesticulating at the youth, cigar's smoke puffing up as from the stack of a yesteryear's labouring train, and he went over to him and said, 'I'm staying for a while. Will give you a month's notice each time.

But bed-and-breakfast only from now on.'

As on the first night, the Indian assessed him with doubting eyes. 'You can pay in advance? In *cash?*' He nodded and went upstairs and, in the privacy of his room, took out the money and came down again and slapped the notes into the Indian's hand. 'Good,' and the hand closed over the notes with the deftness of a gambler palming his cards and he felt the eyes of both Indian and youth following him as he went back to his room, the one's interested and alert, the other's sullenly inaccessible as stones.

When the bar opened, he checked to see if Mjozi was on duty, and he was, and he told him of the arrangement he had made with the Indian and Mjozi grinned with an honest pleasure and said, 'Got me a proper jogging partner at last. Okay?' and he said, 'Okay,' and, to himself, 'Not yet Ray, but as close as I can get to it right now,' and went out and to town, taking his identity documents and the envelope of cash with him and a spring to his step that had not been there for fifteen years.

In town, he scouted for the most advantageous supermarket sale he could find and went in and bought two sets of shirts and pants that could double as formal or casual, a pair of presentable but not too expensive shoes with socks to match, a sports jacket, two pairs of jogger shorts, a spare vest and scants, soap, handkerchiefs, shaving gear, and – at a separate outlet – a new battery for his digital watch that had blanked out twelve years before. Lastly, he sought out a pharmacy, where he purchased a packet of condoms, thus subtly committing himself to an objective that was still more subconsciously than rationally defined.

Even at the rock bottom prices of the 'everything must go' sale, he found he had spent a considerable sum, and he took most of what was left and opened a cheque account at the first bank that came to mind, which, as habit would have it, was the one where Sep had always banked and where a strongbox had held the jewellery his mother had hardly ever worn. Who, he wondered, had inherited *that*? Certainly not him, but what a windfall it would have been in *these* desperate days! – and he was still fantasising about it, when the fear overcame him that the name 'Jackson' would ring bells as though a fire had broken out in the vaults and the tellers, security guards, maybe even the manager himself, would be slanting their eyes at him and whispering behind their scandalised hands. But no brow raised at the revelation of his name and, along with the relief, a perverse sadness – a hint of horror, even – stirred in him at this so relentless an expunging of what he had been, and he stared at the woman who was opening his account as would, presumably, a ghost and, in the manner of the child that had never quite died, he willed her to look up and *see* the blood with which, so obscenely, he was fouled. And she did look up, but the chiselled enamel of her face did not flinch because *that* 'he' was no longer there, was entangled in the flotsam of a past – a *moment* of that past – in which, alone, it raged and ceaselessly destroyed.

Then, the new cheque book in his pocket the symbol, however transient, of a dignity and status he had never before enjoyed, he bought a hamburger and milk at a takeaway and went back to his room, where he stashed his purchases and calculated how to supplement the hotel breakfasts as cheaply as possible from the last undeposited rands. Maybe a month, he reckoned, and he would have to start drawing money out of the bank again for rent and food, and not even six months and there would be nothing left to draw, and, with the fatalism that was one of the more benign fruits of prison life, he faced up to the fact that the next challenge – matter of life and death, to be precise – was to find a job – *any* job – *soon*.

'But meantime,' he thought, almost jocularly, 'why worry myself thin? If there's work, I work. If not – well – I won't be the first without work. There's millions more and *they* live. Somehow,' and he lay back on the bed, hands behind his head, and said, aloud, watching a fly circle the unlit globe, 'Fifteen years in, bra, and not a day to yourself. So, for Chrissakes, have a couple now and be damned,' and then he remembered Fiona without whom he would have had nothing at all, and his heart went out to her like it was a prayer in all but name.

When he woke, it was late afternoon and he went down to the 'Gents' for a crap and wash, then exchanged his old gear for new pants, shirt and shoes, and looked in the mirror and liked what he saw. Then he put Mjozi's jogging shorts in one of the supermarket's plastic bags and took them with him into the bar, and Mjozi looked up, inquiringly, then recognised him and, hugely grinning, yelled, 'Hey! look at the amadude! Sharp, bra, sharp!' and he mumbled, gruffly, 'Shut up, you tit!' but he was chuffed and it showed.

'Here's the shorts you lent me,' and he held out the plastic bag. 'Thanks.'

'You not jogging anymore?' Mjozi's voice was undisguisedly grieved.

'Of course I am. But I bought my own shorts today. Two pairs.'

'Great, but you got it all wrong about *these* shorts. I didn't lend them to you. I *gave* them to you. A *gift* from me to you.'

'But why? You hardly know me yet. You don't give things to guys you hardly know.'

'Look, Johnny,' and now the other's voice was patience wearing thin, 'you asked me that before and the answer's still the same. I *told* you, with me there's such a thing as friendship at first sight. I either like a guy or I *don't* like a guy. I don't have to go through his pockets and shake him out of his pants to make up my mind. It was that way with you. So I wanted to give you something to prove my friendship and I gave you my shorts.'

'But why your *shorts*? Isn't that a way-out crazy thing to give?'

'No. Psychology teaches you – remember I did go to university once? – that when guys bond, they share something that used to be private, that, for each, was *his*. Like food, a drink, a cigarette. Sometimes even a woman if they're weirdos about sex. But – seeing you were going to jog – I decided to give you my old shorts. Why, you ask? Because they – like all pants – hold the *most* private things a man's got. Work it out for yourself.'

Which he did – that night in bed – coming to the conclusion that the shorts – which he had at first considered giving away as being too kinky for his taste – were, in fact, touchingly akin to the now emptied envelope from Fiona, which he had also almost thrown away, then decided to leave at the bottom of his pack as a last, material link with a dead woman and a shared, dead time. Sleep should have come easily after that, but the huntsman of his heart went further, finding again in the shattered-eyed Mjozi something of the shape of a Ray, wondering with a mounting excitement if, impossibly, the wheel had turned full circle and he was again to savour the sensual innocence of a friendship that had thrust with such unexpectedness and potency from the dunghills of degradation and despair.

In the weeks following, there was evidence that this might well be so, Mjozi visiting him ever more frequently when he was off duty, and he as frequently visiting Mjozi in the staff quarters, where the latter had a room of his own which, although as sparsely furnished as the rest of the hotel's rooms, was kept almost obsessively clean and had posters on every wall of black soccer stars, black boxers, some known to him, some not, and unbelievably beautiful black women who, mostly nude, invited to copulation with a pout of the mouth or a more obvious wantonness of buttocks and thighs. 'Martins in reverse,' he thought and was, then, subliminally unsure whether his feeling less uncomfortable in such an ambience than in Martins' room with its nude male was an affirmation of his masculinity or the other way around?

There was also a TV set of some opulence which belonged to Mjozi and, on it, a slightly out-of-focus photo of a (for a change) fully clothed woman with a plain but very likeable face and, on her either

side, an awesomely lugubrious child. When Mjozi told him it was his
'wife and kids', he indicated the savagely dissimilar other women on
the walls and asked, 'And these?' and Mjozi laughed and said, 'I know
what you're thinking but, actually, I am quite faithful. I love my wife –
love my children like I love myself – and although there *are* a couple of
babes around that I use when I feel I must put it in again or take it in
my hand, I try not to do it too often because I'm wanting my own
woman even when I'm done.'

'And your wife? What if she feels she must have a man?'

Mjozi stared at him, genuinely perplexed. 'But women are not like
that, man! They don't want it the way we do. My wife wouldn't give it
to any other guy. Not if I stayed away for *years*. Thought you knew
more about women than *that*, my bra!'

Quickly he stepped back from the suddenly widening gulf. 'Okay,
wash that out. But, talking about me, why are you so wanting *me* as
your friend when I'm white and there's only blacks on your walls?'

The other was silent for so long that he thought he was not going to
reply, that he had affronted him in some way that was the deadlier for
its not being understood, but, at last, very slowly and surprisedly as
though something that had been hidden was now gradually being
revealed, Mjozi said, 'Man, some question you're asking me there. Is
true – call me black racist if you want – but I *don't* like whites – so why
am I liking *you*? Tell me,' and he leaned forward, taut as a bow, 'you
been around a lot with blacks? I mean deep down? And for so long so
that the blacks sort of breathed their blackness into you and now,
when I smell your breath, it is only my own blackness that I smell?'

Shaken by the accuracy of the other's homing in, he was at first at a
loss what to say, conscious only that he was being rushed into an
extremity, an accounting, for which he was not at all prepared. 'Could
be,' he heard himself eventually say, his tone more sombre than he
had intended, his face swinging aside.

But Mjozi did not question him further. Just grunted, 'So.' Then,
sham-punching him on the arm: 'About you now – anytime you got to
put it in and there's no place to go, tell me and I'll fix you some clean
black tail. Okay?'

He nodded, but did not take him up on that, being still the
fledgling, huddled, measuring the sky, and it was the jogging together
that remained the main facilitation for a friendship that yielded him
much needed solace as he increasingly desperately searched for work,
but a friendship, also, of which, with the inborn scepticism of the
prisoner, he was not as yet entirely assured.

Jobs had been scarce even at the time of his leaving school and he had vivid memories of miserable standings in queues and gruelling interviews that led to nothing but a phone that never rang. But if then had been bad, now was unimaginably worse as millions more of the majority race gained access to the labour markets and the policy of preferential employment of blacks was applied with an increasing stringency to a society that resolutely refused to level out, and despair was starting to bed him at nightfall and to greyly rise with him in the mornings, when, almost a month from his first booking in at the hotel, he saw an advertisement in the 'classified smalls' that read: 'Wanted – security guard to work shifts in politically conservative establishment. Only experienced white males need apply.' Not being 'experienced', he dispiritedly slid mind and eye on down the page, but then the survivor in him, back to the wall, urged, 'Think again. Sure, no experience, but no black competition either. Go for it, man!' and the next morning, the sun barely risen, he was up and hastening down Main to the 'establishment', which turned out to be a small, privately owned supermarket with an encouraging absence of blacks around. There was also a fifty-applicant queue of men of varying ferocity of physique and he thought, 'Shit! what the fuck am I *doing* here?' but he stuck it out and, hours later, stared across a paper-cluttered desk at a woman of about his age who stared back at him from a housewifely face and, surprisingly in English, asked, 'Name?'

Carefully she questioned him and he as carefully lied, realising early on that she was not only probing his capabilities as a security guard, but also the social and ideological background from which he hailed. No, he did not have any testimonials from previous employers because, for the past fifteen years, he had been self-employed. Farming other side the Soutpansberg ('can't get further away from here than that,' he thought), and she nodded then, remarking that he, thus, probably knew all about guns? 'Absolutely,' he enthusiastically affirmed, thinking, '*will* fucking well know by the time I'm finished practising with them on the sly,' but she added that it was not all that important anyway because they only issued the night shift guard with a hand gun and even *she* had one of those at home.

So why was he looking for work now? 'Went bankrupt,' he said. 'The country's in such a mess all round that I couldn't hold on anymore. Had to sell to pay my debts and just enough left over then to get me down to here.'

Was he married? 'Wife divorced me,' he said and was more than a little appalled by the effective flatness of his tone. 'Can't blame her. The years of sukkel,' and again he was shaken by the innate cunning that had prompted him to slip in that particular word, 'wore her right down. Made her old before her time.'

'Sad,' she said and sounded as though she meant it. 'Should we take you, the starting wage is eighteen hundred rand. Would you be satisfied with that?' Not aware yet of the new, high levels of salaries in the country, he could barely restrain himself from shouting, *'Yes!'* and, in the end, his cunning not deserting him, he merely nodded and she leaned forward and asked him what he immediately sensed was *the* question of the interview: 'How do you feel about blacks?'

For what seemed a damning eternity, he considered that. How had those preceding him in the queue answered her? Had they deemed it expedient to speak of 'kaffirs', to angle for the job with the bait of gratuitous abuse? Was he prepared to do that, to betray one of the last, vestigial moralities he still upheld? Betray also the Rays and Mjozis – yes, even the Jasons – of his world? Behind the woman's head was a striking painting of a church, its slender spires seeming to drift in a luminous air. Was she a religious woman? If so, did she, despite the severity of her Calvinist creed, espouse her Christ's legend of love? 'They rule us today,' he heard himself say. 'What can we do? It is God's will.'

'But I'm not even sure I *believe* in a God!' he thought and sat as one who had blasphemed, but she looked at him, very steadily, then nodded and said, 'Leave your telephone number and we'll phone you if you get the job,' and he gave her the number of the hotel, but without hope, thinking, 'The same old run-around. The same old phone that never rings,' and went back to his room and did not try for any other job that day.

In the morning, when Mjozi woke him for the jogging, he was still disconsolate and Mjozi, sensing this, trimmed his usual chatter to the occasional, overly jaunty aside. He tried to respond but his heart was not in it and, towards the end, they were running in an almost complete and increasingly oppressive silence and Mjozi was beginning to glance at him with something approaching alarm. 'I done something wrong?' he asked when they were at last back at the hotel after a run that had never before seemed so long.

'No,' he said, feeling inadequate and ashamed, 'it's just me that's down. This looking for a graft where there's zilch is getting me by the balls.'

'Shit! don't panic so, bra,' and Mjozi, relieved, ran a hand along his arm in the curiously affectionate manner of his kind. Then, unknowingly echoing what he had earlier said to himself: 'There's millions more out there and *they* get by. Even though there's no Mjozi who, if the bad gets to be the worst, will share with you whatever he has to share. So come now and shower by *me*. Don't know why I never thought of you doing that before.'

Uncertainly he followed him, wondering if the Indian – or the rest of the staff, for that matter – would approve. 'Surely,' he reasoned, 'even in a dosshouse like this there must be a rule against guests and staff using each other's showers and johns,' but the lonely – the *frightened* – man's longing to be close to another living being proved too strong and he and Mjozi stripped and went, together, into the still deserted two-shower cubicle and he saw a naked Mjozi for the first time. 'Ray!' he instantly thought. 'Except for the bum eye and the kinky hairs under the arms and in the groin – a black Ray,' and he accepted the sliver of soap that Mjozi proffered him and turned away, fearing that the other would notice – and misinterpret – the emotion that had seized him with the violence and incontinence of a lamentation or a rage. But the image of that nakedness stayed with him – the masculine nipples' insolent thrust, the penis and testicles that unashamedly hung and swung, the lissome aggressiveness of the buttocks and thighs, the belly's flat-as-a-hand – and his heart wept over what had been lost and rejoiced at what it hoped had been regained.

'Hey, how about doing my back for me, bra?' he heard Mjozi say, and he turned and soaped the glistening black muscle of the other's back and reined in the faint tumescence that the handling of beauty or lovableness had always so disconcertingly aroused. 'Now you,' said Mjozi, and again he turned and Mjozi's palms were moving over his skin, but strangely languorously so, and Mjozi's genitals were nudging him with a soft insidiousness as the shorter arms reached up to soap his neck, and horror came over him with the suddenness of vertigo or a flood and he knew it was no Ray that stood behind him, that was about to straddle him, pinion him with the fifteen-year-long shaft of his lust, but Jason, and he tensed to whirl about, to yell, but then the soaping ceased and Mjozi said, soberly, wonderingly, 'What do you know! First time I ever soaped a white man's back!' and laughed and slapped him, hard, and, when he did turn around, he saw that the other was no more aroused than a child playing games.

Trust rooted in him then and he slapped Mjozi back, as hard, his habitual solemnity shattering into an awkward grin, and Mjozi stared at him, a little startled and enormously pleased.

On his way back to his room, the reception youth beckoned him over and handed him the usual scrap of a cigarette pack. 'Said to phone that number,' he muttered and charged the call out to him at three times the normal rate when he asked, heart hammering, if he could use the phone right there. He recognised her voice immediately and said, yes, he could report for day shift the next morning and thank you very much and, still unrepentently manipulative, God bless you, then put the phone down and held out his hand to the bewildered clerk – who instinctively took it – and howled, 'Put her there, pal! I got me a graft again!' Beside himself with relief and joy, he almost ran back to the staff quarters and into Mjozi's room, where he as profoundly astonished the still in the buff Mjozi by clasping the latter to him in an abandonedly unmanly hug, and babbled on till, in the end, he had to turn away to hide the fact that he was weeping like the little kid he had been before it all began. Mjozi touched him, lightly, on the shoulder, then broke out a bottle of high-class booze – 'Compliments of the Indian,' he said and winked – and they drank a toast – one dop only because they were serious joggers and men of substance with jobs to do, and, later in the morning, Henry Martins knocked on his door and said he had heard about it from the youth and here was his hand too.

Guilt gnawed at him then, flawing his day, because he had become increasingly more distant towards Martins as his friendship with Mjozi ripened and, as he took the proffered hand, he felt that his thanks were too effusive and that his guilt showed. Martins seemed not to notice, however, and suggested that they have a drink together to celebrate, but he said, no, he had already done that with somebody else, and only later wondered – not without a measure of unease – why he had been reluctant to identify Mjozi as the 'somebody else'. Nonetheless, feeling expansive as well as ashamed, he suggested that they *could* celebrate by having coffee in the other's room, and Martins readily agreed and he found himself again staring at the male nude and listening to Martins remember that he liked his coffee strong with three sugars and no milk.

Their conversation was trivial and a little stilted as though they had never before sat together in that particular room, Martins only once mildly probing when he remarked that he was rarely to be seen these days. He described then his desperate search for work and explained that he had elected to have only breakfasts at the hotel because it was cheaper for him that way, and Martins nodded and said, Yes, he could understand that and it was a wise move. From his side, he at one stage happened to mention Mjozi in relation to himself, but Martins merely looked at him as though he had never heard the name till now and he thought, 'Uh-huh,' and sidestepped a shit he sensed was lying somewhere close.

Talk dribbled into silence soon after the second cup of coffee that he had felt duty-bound to accept and he stood up to go, and it was then that Martins startled him by saying, straightforwardly and without anger, 'I don't mind most of the things people think or have to say about me, but I do object to it when they take me for a fool. So,' and he smiled to bleed some of the sting out of the words, 'let me tell you that I know exactly why you began to treat me like shit the very morning after we had got on just fine in this same room. Your being here again now is good and I am glad of it, but it doesn't mean that you've changed when it comes to what you were thinking about me back there. Look, Johnny,' and he seemed to stand a little taller, his voice both persuasive and proud, 'you are what you are and I am what I am, and I never said I was anything else but what I am. You might have decided that what I am is more than you can keep down, but if you don't know that there are worse crimes against humanity than who sleeps with who, then that is your problem, not mine.' He paused then, waiting, but there was only a laughter of women passing his door, and he shrugged and held out his hand, 'Well, anyway, best of luck with the job and don't shoot yourself in the foot with the new gun. In fact,' and his tone was no longer bantering but allusive and grave, 'take care not to shoot yourself in the foot in *any* kind of a way because it might just be that I'm the only one around then and you wouldn't like that at all.'

That remark deeply unsettled him – although he was not at all sure why – was, indeed, at a loss as to what it *meant* – and it resurfaced the following morning when he reported for work and they issued him with his uniform and the friendly night shift guard, whom he relieved and to whom he confessed the truth, quickly showed him how to work the gun he was about to hand back in, and, on his own first night shift, gun at last in his fist, he pointed it at either foot in turn and said, 'bang! bang!' as though jesting with a ghost, exorcising it with a disbelief that, somehow, never quite rang true.

Sharon Berry was also among those who congratulated him on that heady day when he got the job, coming to him with her slightly ungainly stride, extending to him a generous whore's hand, and even the Indian almost smiled as he presented him with a cigar which he later passed on to the incredulous beggar at the bins. Only the youth at reception maintained – indeed, intensified – his sullen hostility towards him, and at last he asked Mjozi, 'What *is* it with that guy? Is it just his way, or is there something there I don't know about?'

'Both,' said Mjozi, and laughed, but it was not his usual happy shout: more a harsh, faintly threatening gravel in the throat. 'It is both his way and something you don't know about, and what you don't know about is that he's got the hots for me but I'm not interested, and now that he sees us buddying off together, he thinks I'm having it off with *you* and he's madder'n any woman that's lost her man.'

'*Jesus!*' he hissed and surged to his feet, incoherent with rage, but the other held him back, laughing more in the known way, hand soothingly on his arm: 'Hey, that was a *private* talk I gave you there. So cool it, bra, or you'll be making waves for me more than you do for you. It's the same with that Martins spook, man. The scene's lousy with these guys and you just got to live with it or find some place else to stay.'

Later, he thought – and wondered if he would have spoken out if he had thought like that at the time: 'But Mjozi's wrong there. Henry is *not* the same as the reception shit,' and was faced anew with the moral crisis of whether he should continue with his now again regular contacts with Martins – contacts which he did not talk about when he was with Mjozi, as he did not talk about his friendship with Mjozi when he was with Martins – 'Like a whore with two clients at the same time,' he thought and hated himself that a comparison which was so at variance with the new, macho image he was building should so readily have slipped into his mind – or whether he should let the contacts taper off until he was again estranged from a man he was beginning to like and respect, albeit against his will.

In the end, panicked by the sudden and belated realisation that continued visits to Martins' room could only confirm the reception youth's suspicions that he was the kind of kinky profligate most likely to be having a relationship with Mjozi, he opted for the latter course, pleading the rigours of shift work at the store as the reason for his holding himself aloof. He was not happy with what he was doing, but he genuinely could not think of anything *else* to do and tried to temper the injustice of his withdrawal by greeting Martins with added enthusiasm on the rare occasions when they still met in the hotel dining room, and Martins would respond, then, with a smile that could not be faulted and yet was aware in a manner disturbingly beyond his ability to define.

He now regularly showered with Mjozi after jogging, only once meeting up with another member of the staff: Ephraim Shabalala, who, as cook, had to get up even earlier than any joggers and was usually already in the kitchen by the time they arrived back at the hotel. A huge, uncommunicative black man who reminded him disconcertingly of Jason, he lumbered out of the shower cubicle and watched them undress, eyes still puffy with sleep and mouth slack and morose, then suddenly reached out and fingered the tattoo on his shoulder, exclaiming under his breath and looking sharply at Mjozi who, however, had his back to them, dropping his shorts. Nothing further happened, then, Shabalala walking out without a backward glance, but he was alarmed by the other's obvious recognition of either the significance of the tattoo or the tattoo itself, and, convincing himself that Shabalala would not remain silent about what he had seen, he waited in suspense for the questioning by Mjozi that he was as sure would come.

But the days passed and Mjozi said nothing and relations between them were equally reassuringly the same, and he was beginning to unwind, breathing out an inwardness as long as had been the days, when Mjozi, in his turn, suddenly touched the tattoo while they were showering and said, 'Shabalala says you're in a gang.'

His mind stopped short and he stood, as still, under the shower until, at last, he heard himself ask, 'What else did he say?'

'Nothing. Just you're in a gang. Want to talk to me about it?'

'No,' he said, and his voice was harsh, forbidding further querying, and he waited for Mjozi to express annoyance or hurt, but the other merely shrugged and went on showering, hissing between his teeth.

Later, however, while they were drying themselves off, he *did*, a little plaintively, remark, 'You know, you never tell me *anything* about yourself. Not even the *littlest* things. Like about a wife and kids, or whether you're just a lone guy and why. I'm not one for walking where no one wants, but when are you going to open up a bit, bra? Aren't we supposed to be friends?

'Of course we are,' he said, his wanting to speak, a stone in his throat, 'but – *O shit!*' – and he turned violently aside – 'there's so *much*. You got to give me time.'

'Sure. Gangsters got a lot on their minds,' and he turned quickly back at that to see if the other had said it sneeringly, but there was nothing there save something like awe and he thought, hardly crediting it: 'Jesus! it's like there's lights in his eyes!' and his heart swelled as he understood that, for the first time in his whole life, someone was looking up to *him,* was clothing *him* in a swagger of maleness, of machismo even, that sat upon him as incongruously and as shamelessly as a cloak upon a clown.

So – or so it seemed to him – another strand among the many strands of his supine and ravished ego as a man greened with a new life and stirred between the twin polarities that were Martins and Mjozi – Martins who symbolised the neutered uselessness from which he fled, and Mjozi who personified, as had Ray, the fecund masculinity towards which he reached with a wholeness of the heart as of the flesh. But there was more to it than that – there was a reaching *beyond* that to a feminineness that must be breached and roused – if ever he was to be wholly a man again. He had no illusions about that. Hitchhiking a man for the morning runs, rubbing skins in a shower till the other's maleness came off on his hands – all this meant nothing till, as he deliberately cruelly put it to himself, it was only the man Jackson that was *being* hitchhiked into some woman's bed and the emasculated flail between his legs was doing the simple job of *fucking* for which, primarily, it had been devised.

Was he now ready for this? He remembered the admiration he had seen – or *imagined* he had seen? – in the eyes of Mjozi and an overwhelming assent surged up in him and did not wholly again ebb even though timidity, returning, whispered of caution and compromise and frantically burrowed in the foundations of his new-found confidence when it feared that, for once, it was not going to have its way. He did, however, settle for a 'practice run' – a bomber's reconnaissance of the target, so to speak – and a remaining satirical self laughed outright at such an outlandish thing. But he bludgeoned on, waiting for when he would be on late afternoon shift and the mornings his – each morning reaffirming his commitment to a rite of passage for a retarded youth, observing her comings and goings so as to know when she was most likely to be in and free and he could knock on her door. Did then, at last, knock on her door and Sharon Berry opened it and stared at him, sharply, as though prepared to be annoyed, but then smiled and said, 'Hi! come on in.'

She had clearly been asleep, in her clothes, on the bed – a generous expanse of second-hand kitsch, its twee coverlet not yet folded back.

'I must look a fright,' she said, patting at her hair. Too many times dyed, it had the vivid lifelessness of a doll's, was starting now from her scalp with the urgency of one mourning or in shock. 'Just flopped down like I was dead. You come for a fuck?'

The crudity reminded him of Dolly, the fattest and most raucous of Ray's many women, and he winced as much now as he had then. 'Why,' he wondered, 'does it always sound worse coming from a woman than from a man? Aren't they saying we're all the same?'

He shook his head. 'No. I haven't come for that.'

'You sure? I said you could. Was beginning to think you never would.'

'Yes, I'm sure. Was passing your door and thought I hadn't seen you around since the day I got the job. Wondered if you were okay.' Again he winced, but this time at his duplicity – the lies that surely must be sounding as hollow in her ears as in his.

But he was wrong. 'Why, *that's* nice! Don't get many *social* calls these days. Sit down and I'll make you some coffee. Could do with some myself. How do you like yours?' and he told her, half in Martins' room, half in hers, looking for the ubiquitous curtained alcove with kettle, finding it in the corner opposite the bed.

Finding much else besides. And all of it sad: scarred, unstable chairs, cowering beneath cushions that were meant to be seductive and feminine, but, like the coverlet on the bed, were merely trash, the loneliness of linoleum that was wearing thin and from which the design of flowers and singing birds was bleeding, unstoppably, away, the tiny chest of drawers beside the bed whose littleness mocked the littleness of the private she it held and, on it, an as tiny TV set whose monochrome screen flickered with soundless images of idiot laughter or despair. And, above the bed, the final freak: a framed print of a white man in a white gown, golden locks curling into his neck, a mammoth heart, dripping blood, blazing from his breast, and, under it all, the caption: 'Jesus Saves!'

'Didn't do much for me,' she said, carrying in the coffee and seeing him studying the print, her tone neither bitter nor sweet. 'But then maybe He knows something I don't,' and somehow the capital 'H' was still in the 'He' and he would not have been surprised if she had said she went to church and paid her dues more scrupulously than her saintlier kin.

What *were* they to talk about, if it came to that? The ongoing price of a fuck, old age homes for whores who managed to last out that long? This was not one of Ray's lays whom he had got to know well enough, with whom he had shared the days' routines. This was the ultimate alien and panic stirred in him as he realised that, apart from the sexual urge – or was it, for her, but the sexual *act*? – they had nothing in common, shared no interest upon which to peg more than a random word.

But she was unfazed, probed, chattily, into the petty details of his personal life. How was it with the job? What were the bosses like? *Church* people? Hey, watch out: they could be the worst! And his room? What did he pay the Indian for his room? Why so *much*? Well, why didn't he give up the breakfasts as well then? She, she said, didn't eat at the hotel at all. He explained, then, that he needed a hot meal after the jogging and the takeaways were too far, and she said, yes, she had seen him with that Mjozi from the bar. 'Nice guy,' she approved. 'Always greets me like I'm not a whore,' and went on to say that she only paid a nominal rent for her room, but the Indian took twenty-five percent of her earnings on top of that, which, now that she thought of it, could, in the end, come to as much as *he* paid for his room. But couldn't she hold something back, he asked, and she said she supposed she could, but she was too scared. Where would she go if he ever found out and took away her roof, which was not much of a roof, she knew, but even a flophouse like this was better than nothing at all. And, besides, the Indian made his *real* money from the percentages from the 'girls' and if the percentage from *her* dropped too low, he would only make up for it by raising the rental of her room. Or kick her out. One of the two.

And so, breathlessly, on and on, but always a probing that had to do with his life *here* and *now*, never with his life past. Was this, he wondered, her seeing him as one with the nameless, faceless denizens of the fringe to which she – and, for that matter, even the Indian – belonged? Mostly, though, he listened with only half his mind, distracted by the instinctive rather than intentional flaunting of herself, the short, tight skirt that rucked up over her knees, bared generous expanses of her thighs as she crossed her legs, swung, then, one unstockinged foot with a metronomic insistence that he watch, be *aware*. Sometimes, as she leant forward to make a point, the skimpy blouse would gape and the full, matronly breasts would swell up out of it until it seemed only the nipples still precariously hindered them from breaking free, and, as her voice droned on and successive cups of coffee compounded the wellbeing in his limbs, he slowly was subsumed by her, his flesh against her flesh, his hands moving over her with the harshness of shower water and the softness of soap, and, deep within him, in the black and tideless ocean where volition seethed undriven by any thought, an as black and shining fish rose, stealthily, to the surface, broke from it, and the eye on the side that it turned to him, glared with a sightless light. And he watched it and it watched him, and it sported, but soundlessly, flinging up a spectral foam, and submerged, and clove back up and kept on coming, winglessly winging through an endlessly inner air, and he realised with the shock of a blind man fingering an alienness in a familiar room, that a sly and heavy sullenness was dragging at his loins.

'Christ!' he thought, dismayed. 'Not now! I'm not ready for it *now*!' and he strove to turn the tumescence round, but desire, at the apex now of its ascent, laughed and sleeked him with a playful knowingness and his penis slotted to its fullest length and strained in silent outcry that it should still be so curbed. Caught up in the conflict between his mind and flesh, he did not at once realise that the grown subliminal drone of Sharon Berry's voice had stilled, that the insistent, swinging foot had also stilled, that she was looking to him to answer a question that, clearly, he had not heard.

'I asked if you got a hard on,' she repeated, leaning forward, eyes shrewd and amused.

He started, hating himself that he did. 'No,' he muttered, but his hand instinctively moved to cover his groin.

'Come *on*,' she persisted, 'let me look,' and he tried to fend her off, but she pushed his hand aside. 'Hey!' and now her voice was curt, 'this is not *anybody's* room. This is Sharon Berry's room and she's a whore,' then she slid open the zip of his jeans, observing, again almost chattily, 'Should wear buttons. It's more sexy when I undo them. One by one,' and she reached in and grasped him and said, 'Thought so. You sitting there like there was shit on the chair! You got a condom? I don't allow it without a rubber. Rather die of hunger than the Big A.'

He shook his head. 'I didn't come for this. It's like I said: I just came to see if you were still okay.' Then, reaching for a firmness within himself: 'I'll get a condom from my room,' and he rose, awkwardly, hand in his pocket holding the erection down.

'Not to worry. I got some old condoms here,' and she rummaged in a drawer of the little chest beside the bed. 'Can't have you walking down the corridor with that thing. You'll have the girls running for their lives!' and she chuckled with a bleak humourlessness that was jarringly at odds with his own mood. 'Here let me do it for you. Like with the buttons, it's more sexy that way,' and she leant down and expertly rolled it on and he clenched in a paroxysm of pleasure that was as animal as it was pure: 'Hey!' she laughed, but not ungently so, 'don't shoot now, or you'll have nothing left for me!' Then she laid back on the bed and drew up her skirt, and eased off the incongruously black-lace panties and said, 'Come to mama now,' and it stared up at him like a wound.

Gingerly he straddled her, noting with a somewhat condescending surprise that her thighs, although no longer young and firm, were not the switch-off he had feared, and sought, then, entry, nudging and fumbling till she seized him and guided him in, remarking, with a puzzlement that compounded his shame, that he didn't look it but certainly behaved like it was the first time, and had he not had it off since who knows when? Desperately he nodded and she grunted as he suddenly thrust deep, then dog-jerked on, driven by an exultation that she sensed but could not comprehend, and she warned, 'Hey, easy there, stud. Once it's out, it's out and there's no getting it back. Go slow – slow. Pump a little and rest, pump a little and rest, and don't think of anything when you rest. Just hold in and hold on. That way I won't be robbing you when you pay. Christ! when *did* you last put it in?' Dimly he heard her and, breath roaring, strove, but, at the end, though he sensed it was still too soon, he no longer cared and exploded in her with a shout as much of triumph as of release, then laid his face to hers and wept with the joyous abandon, not of a child, but of a man.

Gradually he slackened, began to withdraw, but she suddenly seized him, drew him smotheringly close, locked her heels behind his back, screamed out obscenities that sounded strangely and profoundly not that, and her body, that till then had merely moved under him in a mechanical routine, ululated with the wildness and ferocity of the dying or the mad.

'What is it?' he hissed, the taste of her in his mouth, his penis, now flaccid and fleeing, struggling to escape her suctioning warmth, his mother, fleetingly but shockingly, again enclasping him as on that last, terrible night.

'What is it?' she mimicked, laugh incredulous and crazed, but body stilling, letting him go. 'Don't you *know?* You crying on me like no man ever did before, is what it is. I was having a high, man. After so long a time I was beginning to think maybe I'm not a woman anymore.' Then she, too, wept.

Sombrely, he looked down at her: the already plain face now unsightly from her weeping, the framing, too auburn turmoil of her hair. What did *he* feel, he asked of himself, edging towards honesty as though it was pain? Compassion? A measure, yes: he was, after all, not a stone: but the swagger of his maleness, at last expressed, bestrode compassion with a cynicism that would not be denied. Love? Shit, no: not even the *liking* was there that could grow into a passion as grandiose as love: and with that admission, the thought that she had been to him more symbol than woman, a doll for the venting of his sperm, he attained to the grace of a shame that momentarily sobered and did not absolve.

Inevitably, it was the triumphalism of the predator that wholly reasserted itself, and, as though sensing this, wishing to subvert it, she said, 'I don't get it. One minute I'm feeling you're as old in the trade as me, the next I'm thinking you've never been with a woman before. *Have* you been with a woman before?'

Brought up short, conscious he was suddenly on hazardous ground, he swung his feet to the floor, playing for time. Then, carefully, letting his annoyance show, 'Am I asking you how many men you have been with before?'

She sighed, tipped a cigarette from the pack beside the bed, lit it, watched the smoke, spiral, fade. 'Okay, I asked for that and – if it makes you feel any better to know – it hurts. But you're still the first stud I have met who's fazed when a woman gets to the top of the hill. Or,' and a small spite sharpened her tone, 'have you never got one that far till now?'

Ignoring her, he busied himself with the condom, then sat with it in his hand, appalled. 'What's wrong?' she asked, his stillness a tangible, third presence in the room.

'It's burst,' he said, his voice distant and strange. 'The condom. It's burst.'

She drew in her breath, sharply – as sharply snapped, 'Shit! You would go at it like you had a train to catch!'

Suddenly the air was ugly with the age-old juggling of blame. 'Don't you give me that!' he hit back. 'It was you who gave me an old condom. Probably should have been in the bin by now. And, anyway, what about you at the end? Flopping around worse than a fish with a hook in your you-know-where!' Why, he peripherally wondered, had he shied away from the precise word? Was this the beginning of a respect for her as the bearer of his seed?

In the ensuing silence, a passing metro's thunder clove the room in two. Then she blew her nose, messily, and wiped her eyes, mascara staining the tissue like black blood from a wound. 'Forget it,' she said, but her voice was sullen and he knew that there was no reason left for him to stay. 'I'm clean and you,' and again there was a spite in her, 'most likely the same. And if there's going to be little footsteps later on – and I say *if* because it's a *big* if at my age – I'll know who's the gentleman I'll be hoping will be gentleman *enough* to want to pay. Otherwise, it's to the quack to put out the light before it gets too bright because a girl can't trade with a kid in her belly and my ma, who's looking after my only one from my steady that died, hasn't spoken to me for a zillion years.'

Awkwardly, he zipped up his pants with one hand and stood, holding the ruptured condom in the other, and she stubbed out her cigarette and again rummaged in the chest and passed him a small plastic bag. 'Here, put that thing in this and flush it down the john. Or throw it in the street if you want. God knows there are enough lying around there as it is.'

But still he stood, trying to frame the last, degrading question, and she looked at him, knowing well what it was that his tongue was struggling so to say. 'Make it a hundred bucks. And if you haven't got it on you, push it through my door later on because I still got to catch up on my sleep. The nights are long.' Then, almost wistfully: 'I'd like to give it to you for free after what you gave me there,' and she indicated the bed, 'but a girl's got to live.'

Now genuinely moved, he leant to kiss her, but she pushed him away, the sullenness back in her, and a metro warned, perilously rounding the bends.

*** * ***

In the months following his successful coitus with Sharon Berry, he rode the crest of a wave that, as in some surfer's paradise, seemed unable to find any shore to shatter it, yet bore, *within itself,* the elements of its inevitable demise: loss of energy, the almost imperceptible but certain flattening back into the desolate sameness of the sea. How long, he was later to think, had been the ascent to the peak, how momentary the balancing there, swift the return to the immobility of past experience – of birth and blood and time.

The trouble – and he knew it – was that he was not, essentially, a sensual or animal man. If only, he thought, he could have *loved* Sharon Berry: there could have been a tenderness to what he had done to her. The following morning, he had bought her a bunch of flowers in an attempt to experience some measure of *post*-coital passion, but there had been nothing – only a sense of guilt at her glowing over the flowers, a turning away from instead of towards her, a feeling of finality rather than of continuance into something still to be.

The climax to which she had brought him – and to which he had brought her – had been too memorable, however, to be simply swept away into the trash bin of time, and, in a desperate attempt to resuscitate it, he had perpetuated the peculiarly male indecency of recounting to Mjozi the coital mechanics – as opposed to the emotions – of what should have been given the sanctity it had earned. This sharing with Mjozi had so incited him that the black sinuousness of desire had again stirred in the quiet recesses of his flesh and mind and he had found himself consummatingly back on Sharon Berry, but this time there had been no orgasm on her part and no weeping on the part of either of them, and the fee had doubled to a more professional two hundred rand. 'Getting too expensive for me now, anyway,' he had thought, feeling more than ever nothing save the aftermath of sated lust as he made to kiss a cheek that was already turning aside.

Also, he did not tell Mjozi of this second visit to Berry, partly because it had proved to be so much less significant than he had hoped, and partly because, although he had laughed it off at the time, Mjozi had seemed more than a little put out by his telling of the first, saying, 'Sharon's all right – for a whore – but I told you to come to me if you wanted tail. What did you have to pay?' and, on hearing, Mjozi

119

had given one of his piercing whistles and burst out, almost angrily, 'You're my friend, but I should let you go on paying prices like that. Jesus! even when it comes to whoring, there are black prices and white prices. When are we ever going to come right?'

So it was that Mjozi, without his even asking him, began to knock on his door on the nights of his rare days off, saying, 'Got us something by me,' and he would go down to find a girl for each of them and a spare mattress readied for him on the floor. At first – though careful that this not be seen – he had been reluctant to play along, fearing a revival of the animalism of the cells – fearing, perhaps most of all, that his new-found masculinity would wilt when faced with so public a display. But it proved to be more of a frolicking with lusty undertones as Mjozi kept up what amounted to a running commentary, shouting, 'How you doing over there, bra?' ebony-black buttocks rubbering up and down, and, deep within him, his own desire, leaping, twisting, blackly gleaming, turning to him its single, burning eye. Again, there was no emotional involvement with whatever woman lay beneath him – in fact, he could hardly remember what these women looked like after they had gone – and if there *was* any growing closer to another, it was to Mjozi and sometimes his image in the mirror would look back at him and ask, 'And who are you now?' and he would shout, 'Fuck off! You have had me long enough. Leave me alone!'

That the opening to each other of an intimacy second only to death, was working both ways, became evident when Mjozi, in the late afternoon of a day that happened to be the day off of them both, came to him, bringing wine, and sprawled on one end of his bed as he moved aside his legs, and, after idle drinking and as idle talk, looked at him very straightly and said, 'White man, I have come as close to you as any man dare and I still know sweet fuck about who or what you are. So how about letting Mjozi into some of your life, my bra? Or have I got to cut my wrists before you trust me with the *big* stuff, and not just the peanuts like cunt and booze?'

'Could be,' he said and thought, 'Uh-huh, which way now?'

'Hey! come off it, man! What's that supposed to mean? I hate it when you talk blind shit that way!'

'It had to come,' his mind ran on, darting this side, that, like a thief in a dead end. 'We have gone too far for me to stay the blank I am now,' and, quite suddenly, he thought, 'Why not? Is there anybody I trust *more* these days?' and, as precipitately, *wanted* to talk about it to Mjozi, to unburden himself of it, to share as much of it as he could in the manner, as Mjozi had put it, of the cunt and the booze. 'Well, what do you want to know?' he asked at last, dangling a hook, fishing for an opening through which to ease himself in.

'Since I don't know *anything* about you, how must I know what I want to know? Just start talking, bra, the way your heart says and as far as your heart wants you to go.'

'The way my heart says and as far as it wants me to go,' he repeated after him. 'But you might not like what you hear. You might like it so little that you will have your boot up my arse before I'm through.'

'Try me,' said Mjozi and wriggled down deeper into the bed and studied the wine in his glass with his good eye.

'Yes,' he thought, 'it might as well be now,' and said, aloud, 'I'll tell it straight – no frills – like there was this kid – me – just out of school, born in this same town. And he had a mother, and a stepfather whose name was Sep and who had been an alky and who mama caught in her bed with another kid called Colin when she got back home too soon. But then Sep found Jesus and left the booze and the kid and went up just this side the angels in the Church, and, being the good Christian father he now was, he treated this kid that was not his – me – worse than dog shit because Jesus wouldn't have liked me the way I was. But the true thing was that I reminded him of Colin and was getting under his skin and playing games with his balls, and it all hung out when the bottle got to him again and he tried to rape me, thinking I was Colin and he pissed out of his mind with the booze. So then I got kicked out of the house for him trying to fuck me, instead of the other way around.'

'Proper whitey move,' said Mjozi, blowing bubbles into his wine.

'Anyway, before you ask why mammy didn't stop me being put out into the street, let me explain that mammy wanted me out there as much as Sep, he having the bucks and old and she wanting for him to die so's she could grab what he left behind, and here's me – *her* son and not his – making waves and maybe giving him ideas about changing his will or even booting her out like he did me. What mammy didn't reckon on, though – she giving me the moola to get me out of town – was that I *didn't* get out of town. My friend, Ray Willies, who was full grown then and worked at the old Rinko Theatre which I see is now long gone, took me into his flat down in Fourth near the dump and let me stay there for free.'

'Hey!' said Mjozi, sitting up straight, draining his glass. 'Not many amaguys would do that today. Sounds like my kind of man.'

'No, he was *not* your kind of man,' and his voice was harsh and hurt, the telling after all this time getting to him more than he had planned. 'He was *better* than you because he was *worse* than you. By which I mean that he not only worked at the flicks: he was also a rent boy and a pimp who would hire out his own bed for whoring in, and he smokkeled in booze and drugs and beat the shit out of the women he slept with, and he once even beat me till I thought I would be crippled for life, then cried over me till he had nursed me back onto my feet. He was a kid who had never been a kid – his father fucking his arse when he was only six – and he grew straight up into being older than I ever hope to be. But he was a kiff friend to me, Mjozi – as close to me, as you just now said, as any man can dare to come – and so he was better than you because, out of his *nothing*, this little coloured shit, as my mother always used to say he was, could give me what neither she nor Sep had ever had it *in* them to give.'

'You were lovers?' asked Mjozi, and the seeing eye was sombre and afraid.

'If you mean what I know you mean, the answer is No, he would've beaten me to a pulp if I had tried. Always said I was like his own flesh to him and he didn't fuck his own flesh.' Then, a little tauntingly: 'Story getting too hot for you now, Mjozi? You want to hear more?'

'You wouldn't want me to *not* want to hear more, would you?' and now it was Mjozi who was harsh. 'Look, I'm not saying I'm this superstud with the golden balls you're so keeping on about, but I'm not stupid either, Jackson, and you know as well as I do that you've got to get this thing out of your system now like you got to get pus out of a boil. So,' bitterly, 'unload it all. Second-rate Mjozi's all ears.'

When, he wondered, had Mjozi last called him 'Jackson'? – and that, and Mjozi's acid reference to himself as 'second-rate', brought him to the sobering realisation that he had gone too far – that his too passionate profession of his feelings for a man that, to Mjozi, was merely a *dead* man – and now also a 'competitor' in a 'threesome' with him – had sounded more sloppy than earnest – had, worse still, given an offence that it might not be possible to again undo. Panicked, beset by the sensation that everything was unravelling beyond his control, that he was sacrificing the living for the dead, he considered cutting it then and there, letting the rest of the story hang, but then thought again: 'Christ, no! there's no brakes left to this thing. What *I* want, or don't want, doesn't count anymore. Leaving Mjozi guessing – making up his own endings – could be worse than playing open cards.'

But his voice stayed sullen with old emotion too vividly again aroused and he still tried to sidestep the climactic issues of Jason and his mother by switching from the then to the now. 'It's been fifteen years since I was last here. Christ alone knows what I expected to find. A ghost? A vibe? As I said, even the old Rink's gone and the dagga and druggie block where Ray used to rent is now so prettied up that they could just as well have chucked that down too. Mammy's dead. Ray's dead. Aids. Couldn't have ended any other way. Fiona Helmsley, who was one of Ray's women that he beat the shit out of but who became my friend and who, because I asked her, was with Ray when he died and I couldn't be there? Well, I found her grave. Some people put their dogs in better holes and Ray's grave I'll never find because only Fiona could have told me where. Daddy Sep's still around. Up there in the home. Sits up, opens his eyes, clacks his jaw, but he's just a doll. Dead as the other three. Still has this crazy fix that I'm Colin the lover-boy. Tried to put his tongue in me like I'm a seventeen-year-old when I left him climbing the walls. Christ! what a jol!'

'Sho!' said Mjozi, refilling his glass, settling back into the bed, and he let out a breath, thinking: 'He's easier now. Am I off the hook?' But it was not to be, Mjozi unerringly homing in with a question he had not expected, that, he realised too late, he had trapped himself into by again saying too much. 'But how come you were not with this Ray when he died if you were such good friends?' The dismissiveness of the 'this' was not lost on him and a sharp, defensive anger stirred deep down at this continuing denigration of Ray, and quickened into spite as he watched Mjozi comfortably tonguing up his booze, and he stressed thin as a wire and Ray somewhere out there where only the worms still knew. 'Stop this!' cried another, saner self from a distant place. 'This is your *friend* sitting here. Listening. Trying to understand. Not an enemy in some deadly war of stealth!' but wine and past time were drawing their red caul over his sense and Ray, risen, was hugely present in the room, reducing Mjozi to a puddle of shadow at the foot of the bed.

'I was not there,' he heard himself say, 'because I was not in town at the time. I was in jail.'

'In *jail*?' and he felt the bed shake as Mjozi jerked upright and stared at him over the rim of his glass, and he thought, 'Steady, softboy. I'm only *starting* to give it to you.'

'Yes. In jail. That's what the tattoo on my shoulder's all about. Mark of Diepwater Prison's worst ever gang. Shabalala probably knows that. Is probably an ex-con himself. But there are some things ex-cons don't speak about for the rest of their lives.'

'For how long were you in?'

'For the whole of the fifteen years I've been away from this town.'

'Jesus!' and Mjozi breathed the name with the reverence that was its due. '*Fifteen years*? What did you *do* to go in for so long? Were you a political?'

'No.' For a moment he wavered and the voice, far back, warned, 'Don't!' but Ray, crowding in close, whispered: 'Go *on*. *Tell* him. You did it for me. Are you ashamed?' and he said, 'I murdered my mother.'

Mjozi's glass canted and wine spilt onto his hand, but he did not notice it and silence was an entity of its own in the diminishing room.

'I had no job and Ray was dying. Got so I had to help him in the toilet most of the time. So there was no money for the rent, let alone the medication that would let Ray go out like a human being instead of like a dog a car's gone over on the tar. I went to mammy for help, but she laughed me out of the house and herself out of my heart. So then, one night, I break into Sep's study where there's a safe with enough moola to keep Ray and me alive for a while, but mammy finds me there, which is fine because Sep's like a dead man in his chair after the booze and can't open the safe for me like I had planned, but now mammy can and does because I frighten her with the knife I had brought to frighten Sep and cut the telephone cord, and she hands me the bucks and hates me with her eyes because she loves the money more. Then she sees the knife I have put down, me not thinking she would do what she does, and, when I look again, she's coming at me with the knife, not knowing me anymore, but I get the knife back from her and we go down onto the floor, she wrapping her legs round me like we are having it off, and I cut her with the blade till she's a nothing that I have never known and me thinking how she's always telling me I'm no man. Mammy wins, though, because she's set off an alarm I didn't know about and the cops are waiting for me at the gate and me with the knife and the bucks dragging me down.' Then he looked at Mjozi, but not seeing him – seeing only a facelessness beyond. 'So I killed my mother and I don't care. Do you hear? I don't care,' but Mjozi said nothing, his eyes rigid in his head, the still tilted glass unheeded in his hand, and he suddenly yelled, Mjozi again vividly there: 'I said I don't care. *Don't care!* Do you understand?'

'No,' said Mjozi, and his voice trembled with the intensity of his distaste. 'I hear but I don't understand. My people don't kill their mothers. This is a white man's thing I am hearing from you – you whom I thought was more black than white,' and he sat up and set his glass down on the floor.

'Don't give me that blacks are better than whites spiel,' he scoffed and Ray nodded for him to go on. 'Hear the rest. So they give me twenty years. (In the end let me off five because the joint's too full.) And chuck me, straight off, in amongst the blacks because there's no apartheid anymore and we're all the same. So what happens? The first night I'm gangbanged so's I don't sit down for a week, then the cell-boss takes me for himself and –' he stopped, suddenly wanting out, wanting to reel back in all that he had so far said, the final hurdle looming impossibly high, but what was, and would not be denied, took him over it with a keening sound that was his and, for the first time, he looked at Mjozi as one who stretches out a hand, '– and,' he went on, his voice toneless and estranged, 'for fifteen years I was Jason Radebe of Soweto's wife,' and turned, then, his head aside and stared at the wall, and did not have to turn it back again to know that the deepening silence meant that Mjozi and Ray had left the room and he was alone.

Later, he sat up, drank the wine Mjozi had left in his glass, drained his own still not empty glass, found more wine in a bottle beside the bed and drank that too. Then, brain dead, he fumbled his way through the shambles of the afternoon. Had he lost Mjozi as a friend? If so, he knew again – as it had once been with Ray – the meaning of loss: the crying of the frightened child loosed, momentarily, into the sun, wrenched back into the darkened room – knew then also the meaning of fear: the beating of the thicket about the prey, the nakedness, the fleeing of that nakedness out into the muzzles of the guns. Would Mjozi, revolted and angered, talk? Flood the hotel with the spate of his bile, whisper in the ear of the severe, kind woman at the shop who had taken him on? He groaned aloud, sat for a long while with head hung, hands hung, metros rocketing past on the peripheries of his sense, factory sirens wailing their requiems for a working day.

Eventually, driven out by the unyielding sombreness of his own self, the random and wandering ghosts of his revitalised past, Mjozi's new and menacing shape, he went down the corridor to Martins' door and it opened to his knock and Martins smiled at him, showing no surprise.

'Can I come in and sit a while?' he asked, sounding, he knew, both desperate and a fool. 'There's ghosts in my room.'

'Well, I have plenty of my own here,' and Martins laughed as though he noted nothing strange. 'But come in, anyway. Make yourself at home,' and he went in, refusing a pouffe, and sat down, cross-legged, on the floor, feeling like a flower child.

Martins padded about the room in slippered feet, silly apron round his hips, busied with a busyness that, to his laggard sense, seemed without sound or form, lulling as a swaying of the wind. A piano's syncopated beat rippled from a small radio beside the immaculately made bed, brimmed insistently against the walls, but Martins did not turn it off, did not even tune it down, did not come to him with intrusive offers of coffee or tea, and, at last, the booze ebbing in his veins and drowsiness insinuating into its place, he roused himself and stood to go.

Martins paused then, asking, smiling, 'Problem solved?' But he shook his head. 'No,' he said, his tongue grown thick, 'but thanks all the same,' and Martins came to him, placing his hand on a shoulder that no longer winced, looking at him with eyes that understood, but toughly so as one who shared a gibbet or a cross. 'Problems are like that,' he said, his voice flatly matter-of-fact. 'Never go away by themselves. Wait for you to kick them up the arse. Sometimes music helps. Sometimes not. Come again. Any time,' and was already again busied with his petty tasks as he glanced around, shutting the door.

After dark, he went for a walk down Main and back, feet splashing through rivers of neon, arms alternating through starbursts of signs, eyes seeking for affirmation in others' eyes that he was seen and, thus, *was*, albeit not known. But the eyes were but glass, unlit from within, sheened and blind as the eyes of predators momentarily snatched by a car's light, or, he thought with a shiver, the lifeless, unintelligent eye of Mjozi that he had begun not to see and that now suddenly was all that he saw. Music – sinuous and persistent as the flesh passing him on either side – passing him by – tentacled out from discos, car radios, strip joints, ghettoblasters in perilous lanes, slid from him then as did the flesh, left him walking with only the pale gauze of his shadow on the paving and tar.

That night, seeking sleep, he knew the torment of laughter in the late streets, drifted between fantasy and fact, sometimes seeing, not seeing, Jason immensely black against the window's subliminal square, turning his head, then, to find Ray's face beside his on the pillow, then seeing only the pillow, sleeping briefly, Mjozi's eye whirling like a soundless yell down through layers of dream to wrench him back into his lonely lying alone. Towards morning, he was again awake, not really expecting yet anxiously waiting for Mjozi's knock on the door, knowing that Mjozi knew that, for the ensuing week, he would be on late afternoon shift and, thus, available for jogging at the usual time. But he and the sorry surround of the room's furnishings surfaced through first greyness into full light and the door stayed mute, and he knew, with a sickening lurch of the stomach and heart, that Mjozi was lost to him and very soon now, perhaps that very day, the axe of the other's tongue would reduce him to ruin. But the day passed with a sameness that was hardly less frightening than the feared reverse and, with less hope than ever then of hearing any knock on his door, he nonetheless each morning again waited for just that, lapsing thereafter into a new day of repetitive and stupid despair.

Then, on the morning of the fifth day, there *was* a knock on the door and he hurried to open it and it was as he had hoped.

'Tell me,' and Mjozi's voice was everyday calm, though the eye that still lived was wrenched by a tearing inside. 'That knife. Did you take it with you *meaning* to kill Sep?'

'No!' and he turned away, disappointed and hurt. 'I *told* you. I took it to cut the telephone cord and *frighten* Sep. Not kill him.'

'You're not telling the truth,' and now Mjozi's voice was heavy and sad. 'If you were going to use Sep to help you open the safe, you would have *had* to kill him, or they would have had you in jail almost as quick as getting you at the gate. And you would have had to kill your mother too – even if she *hadn't* found you at the safe – because you went to her before for money and she said No and would have known that you had come to *take* what she wouldn't give. So you lie.'

'It's still no!' he hissed, whirling round, hysteria perilously close. 'I was going to give the money to Fiona and run. Never see Ray again. Nobody knew of my connection with Fiona except Ray and she would have used the bucks to look after him till he died. For my sake, as I said. For *me.*'

Mjozi nodded then, his eye quieting, though it still did not smile. 'That's more like the man I thought I knew. Let's go.'

And he went, dressing with trembling hands, heart hammering and glad, but anxiety began to seep back in as they ran the usual course but Mjozi did not once speak to him, nor look back when, at a quickening of the pace, he began to lag behind. Almost he slowed to a walk, abandoning the jog, thinking with a resurgence of pride he had not thought would stir again so soon, 'But fuck him! Why must I be treated like a child? It was he who asked me to tell him what I did. I didn't want to, but he kept *on*. It's *he* who should be hanging onto *my* heels, not this way around.' Fortunately, reason returned to him in time to prevent him from, indeed, acting like a child, and, although not able to quite restrain a petulance of the mouth and eyes, it was with a fair measure of composure that he, at last, rejoined Mjozi who was waiting for him on the steps of the hotel.

Mjozi, however, was quick to assess his true mood and, gripping his shoulders with an astonishing openness and suddenness, blurted out, 'No! *No!* It is *I* who should be feeling that way. Not you. I was wrong but my tongue was finding it hard to *say* I was wrong. But now it's saying it. I was wrong and you must not worry. It is as it was before and what you shared with me, I will not share with anybody else. I swear!'

Overcome with gladness and relief, he instinctively drew Mjozi to him and Mjozi, as instinctively, slotted his crotch into his in an embrace that, despite its urgency – indeed savagery – so transcended the parameters of mere gender and lust, that even the ordinarily meddlesome phantom of Jason stayed appeased.

It was doubly disconcerting, therefore, that Mjozi should as suddenly and violently withdraw, whispering, 'Shit!' and he was readying to take offence afresh when Mjozi added, his voice angry and perturbed. 'He's seen us. Seen us do what we just did.'

'Who?'

'That little shit in reception. I saw the curtains move and *know* it's him there because he's been watching us like that for a long time. Do I have to spell it out?' Then: 'Look, don't come and shower with me this time, or he'll make a serial out of the whole thing and get so fired up by what he thinks he's got, that he'll, maybe, forget I told him once that I won't *fuck* him but I'll fuck him *up* if he goes around playing games with my name. Tomorrow we'll start ending up behind the quarters so's we can get to the showers without being seen. Okay?'

It was a measure of his renewed trust that he agreed because, shunned and disparaging logic argued, Mjozi could just as well have made the whole thing up and tomorrow there would be some other excuse to prevent them showering together, Mjozi having grown secretly averse to their being as intimate with one another as they had once been. The next morning, though, they did, indeed, shower together, Mjozi's hands soaping him with a new zest as though – what? – he wanted to show him that no hesitancy over their relationship remained, or – less promisingly – he wanted to expunge from the pale skin his hands so slapped, the last trace of a past that had caused him to agonisedly reconsider their friendship for four days?

The ensuing weeks seemed to rule out the second possibility, if not the first, there being several more sessions with girls to which Mjozi committed himself with an even fuller abandon and acceptance of him as a co-player than before. Then, other than that, there was a *pride* in having him as a friend that had not been quite so apparent in the time preceding the four watershed days – and a subtle but present – and by no means displeasing – *possessiveness* that evidenced itself in such gestures as Mjozi resting an arm on his shoulders for long periods during group conversations in the quarters or elsewhere – and, slowly, he began to convince himself that he had arrived, not in the *eye* of the storm, but in the wider, only dreamt of calm beyond, his heart unburdened by his having shared it with another and the winged creature of a new self risen from his past's grim cocoon.

Once, though, a breath, no more, shook the clear glass and a sediment rose up, fouling the wine, and he was reminded anew of the transience of happiness, the underlying ubiquity of grief. He was in Mjozi's room and they *were*, in fact, drinking wine, and he happened to mention Martins' name and Mjozi passed the usual derogatory remarks about him and he felt impatience stir in him at the almost tired mindlessness of the tirade.

'But why,' he asked, '*exactly* why do you so dislike this guy? *Deep down inside,* why? Telling me it's because he is what he is – is that *really* all there is to it?'

'What else? Look,' and the other leaned forward with a simple earnestness that both chilled and appealed, 'I told you before, and I tell you again now, I *hate* what these guys do to other guys or have other guys do to them. It makes me sick when I think of it and it makes me sick when I have to smile at them in the bar and take their money from their hands when they pay me for the booze.'

'Is that why,' and for a moment he paused, appalled by the audacity of the question that had come to him and that *must* now be asked, 'is that why it took you four days to decide if you still wanted me to be your friend?'

Mjozi stiffened at that, taken by surprise, and his eye, fleeing his, fastened on his hands, and he sat for so long, silent and unmoving, that fear shook the cage of his gut and he thought, 'Christ! I have done it again.' But then Mjozi sighed and, looking up, tiredly said, 'Yes,' and laid his hands, backs down, on the table as though surrendering a shame.

'And how do you feel about me now? Again – deep down – how do you feel about me *now?*' and he gritted his teeth at his sailing so close to the wind, but knowing that this, too, must be asked, be laid to rest. Once and for all.

But he need not have feared. Mjozi's hands stayed open on the table and his eye did not falter as he said, 'I could pretty it up for you, but I won't. Every time I see your bare arse in the showers, I think of what that cunt in the cell did to it and I could kill. But it doesn't make me sick anymore – although at first it did, me remembering what Martins said about you that first night you met him in the bar – but too much had happened between us since then – the girls, the showering together when you never made a wrong move – for me to go on thinking of you as a Martins, or any other of those creeps out there.'

'But why do you want to *kill?* It was *my* arse, not yours. Or is it *in general* that you want to kill? Like God doing his thing?'

'No, it's personal too,' and for the first time Mjozi smiled, but there was a shyness to it and his eye slipped aside. 'I don't know how *you* feel about friends, but, to me, they are *mine*. Private property, you might say. The *whole* of them. Belly, buttocks, balls – you name it. The works. So now, when I see you in the showers, think of that shit doing to you what he did, I could kill because he's been having it off with what's *mine*, even though *I* don't want you that way, don't want to even *think* of you that way. Am I making sense or do I sound like I'm queerer than the queers?'

And he thought, 'No, he's making sense. The way Ray always made sense,' and, aloud, he said, 'No, you're making sense,' and Mjozi let out his breath and poured them more wine and the silence between them was as comfortable as it had once been between him and Ray.

But then: 'What was it like?' Mjozi asked, his voice alien and strained.

'What was what like?'

'Having that guy on you all those years. How did you *feel?*'

Taken aback, unprepared, he floundered around for a way to answer that, knowing that the complex, complete reply would not be understood, would, indeed, only affront and estrange. Perhaps even precipitate a return to the impasse of the four last days.

At last, equivocating, he said, 'I felt like I felt. Like a man being *fucked*. Like *you* would have felt if it had been done to you. What more must I say?'

'Sho. But if it had been me, I would have wanted to kill myself. Did *you* ever want to kill yourself? *Try* to end the thing that way?'

He laughed then, genuinely amused by the other's inexperience and naïvety. 'Wanting to and trying to were two different things, my bra. Hell! I couldn't even *shit* in private, let alone cut my wrists with a blade I didn't have, or hang myself from the cell bars without a dozen do-gooders running to save me for another day of being worse than dead. You never been in jail, James?'

The other shook his head as though confessing to a shameful deed, shook it again as he drained his glass at a single gulp, sat back, saying, 'For fifteen fucking years! Jesus, I can't even *begin* to think what that was like for you. Or, if it comes to that,' and he paused, drawing in a breath, 'what it was like for the guy that *did* it to you. What went on in *him?*' and he stared at him – and yet *not* at him – eyes brilliant with the horror and fascination of one who watches a snake of loathsome beauty coil and uncoil in an Eden of desire he had supposed forever closed.

❋ ❋ ❋

The following weeks passed swiftly as the friendship between him and Mjozi attained a new fullness, then maintained it, and he was happier than he had been in even the peak times of his days with Ray, about whom – as about Jason – he now hardly any longer thought or dreamed. The good-natured banter of the quarters about the friendship did not offend him as once it might have done – imbued him, rather, with a sense of acceptance and pride – and there was such a reaching-out in him towards others that he found himself, at last, asking the reception clerk what was his name, and the latter, taken unawares, blurted out, 'Achmat!' then turned to him the usual thin slouch of his shoulders and scowled as though betrayed.

At work, too, matters went well, his relationship with his employers and co-employees becoming ever more cordial and relaxed and he only once – on night shift – having to fire a shot to ward off would-be robbers, for which he received a small addition to his pay. His past receded from him like the ebbing of a drain and the future came to him over the shining roofs of the town, the thick-as-a-wheat grass of the plains beyond, with a sound as exciting as the rushing of a sea – and, yet, a small cynicism remained as he remembered that twice, in his association with Ray, there had come these summits of arrival – of completion – and then the immediately following descents into disintegration and despair. The first time had been when, in bed together, talking, he had come as close to Ray as he had now to Mjozi, and then, with his next breath, Ray had told him that he had Aids and death was but the snatch of its hand away; and the second time had been at the end when he had fled, exulting, with the cash he had stolen from Sep and the bloodied dummy that was his mother, and the police had been waiting to cast him into the van – as into the fifteen years of death-in-life that the van's small space had so impossibly enclosed. What guarantee, he asked himself, lying awake and defenceless in the chill sanity of the nights, did he have that it was not to be the same now?

As though addressing his dread, a late afternoon knocking on his door brought him to it and it was no shape of terror that stood there, but Sharon Berry from whom he had, of late, become almost wholly estranged.

'Hi!' he said, too jovially and knowing it. 'You looking for me?'

'Who else?' Her tone was sharp – a hint of triumph in it that he found strange – and unease twitched in him like an alerted prey. 'Can I come in?'

'Sure,' he said and swung the door wider and she went in and, unasked, sat down on the bed.

'I have news.'

'Good or bad?' and again he gave the silly two-timing laugh that sounded what it was in even his own ears.

'Depends,' and she looked at him with a severity that stopped his flippancy in his throat. 'Depends on whether you want or don't want what I've got that's yours.'

'You mean –?' and he stared at her still flat belly and she nodded, emotionless save for her thin fingers' ceaseless struggling with themselves.

His breath roared out, cutting off his speech like a strangling hand, and he caught her up and hugged her, but without affection, only a selfish gladness for himself, and she sensed that and did not respond.

'Okay,' she said, flatly, releasing herself, sitting down again. 'So you want it. But, as I told you at the start, it will *cost*. So let's talk about that lovely stuff that makes me a whore and gets you shooting up some poor bastard that's maybe *got* to steal to eat.'

'How much?' he asked and flinched, too late, at the mercenary sound of those two words, body and voice stretched long in their uncertainness as to what she would demand.

'Well,' and she laughed, but bleakly, unamused, 'it would cost you the least if you were to *marry* me, but I can't see you doing that – you and that Mjozi having it off with those black women like you are. Or did you think the whole hotel doesn't know? Not that I had a chance from the beginning, anyway. Even the big emotion that first time around's starting to look like a fake to me from here. So you will have to settle for the sugar daddy deal, which is pay for my room – *plus* what our kid and me must live on – till the six-seven months are over and I can get back to the beat. And if that sounds tough to you, count your beads again because I made a side deal with the Indian that, if I decide to go through with this, I can still have the room for the usual rate but, after that, his commission on my take must go up to forty percent till I have made up what he would be losing by being so soft in the head. Which are his words not mine. And if you are wanting to ask why *I* am being so soft with *you* by not making you pay full board and lodging till I'm back on the beat, it's, straight said, because I only got to look at you to know no ways can you fly that high. But, before you get any ideas about *that*, the *real* thing is not that I'm being soft with *you*, but with *me*, because,' and now the hardness was out of her and there was a shyness to her that rolled back the years, 'it's not only the Indian that's gone soft in the head but me *wanting* now to walk the whole road with this kid, to haul a full belly around like I'm a woman again and not just a sex aid for creeps like you. We got a deal?'

But she had it wrong. His mind was on quite another track, grappling with the 'our' in 'our kid'. There had been a stress on that word – slight but *there* – and he knew *that* was what he must question: not who was being soft with who. 'Who is going to keep the kid? Me or you?'

If she was taken aback by the question, she did not show it, but the hardness was back in her – and a slyness that had not been there before. 'What's that got to do with what I asked? Have we or haven't we got a deal?'

He knew that what *he* had asked had everything to do with the deal, but the ground beneath him was soft with betrayal and – even as he weighed his salary against what he still had in the bank, finding it just – only *just* – enough – he felt himself nod, heard himself say, 'It's a deal,' and she nodded back and said, 'Good – here's my hand on it,' and they shook hands with the courtliness of a vanished time. But then she soured it by adding, as much of sadness as cynicism in her voice, 'Not that that means much these days, but I'm trusting you to be the otherwise freak that does not let us down,' and again there was the small emphasis on the 'us', and again it woke unease, but, this time, he let it pass and she left him and he punched the air with ludicrous fists and surrendered himself to the paroxysm of fulfilment he could no longer hold in. 'A *man!*' he breathed. 'A father. *At last!*'

For days, then, he hugged the greater he to himself, walked in a brilliance of his own making, knew that, when the time for looking back came, these would be the hallowed, the never-to-be-lived-in-again days. 'Ja,' he thought, 'but always only *days*. Then a new shit hitting the fan. Never a settling-down. *Is* this going to be any different from then?' and, each time, he argued to himself that now, surely, it *was* different because being a biological father was not something that could be reversed, or even trimmed down to any other size. But already, without realising it, he was *himself* – *to* his own self – lowering his status, denying the excellence of his virility, by finding it impossible to disclose that he had, as his contemptuous, improbably prudish alter ego phrased it, 'put a common whore up the pole.' Weakly, he protested that he was as base a whore as she and, therefore, not entitled to the prevarication of the self-righteous, but masculine pride, as potent as any lust of the loins, bridled at such unmanliness and it was left to rumour, and the ever garrulous Sharon, to – as a result of his own reticence – spotlight him as a sort of stud-on-the-run.

So formed the first cloud – did the Bible say something about as small as a man's hand? – or had that had to do with quite some other scene? – and he had a feeling of being, indeed, on the run, of a wind blowing to him from some far and barren space, as the news of Sharon's pregnancy spread and the reaction to his involvement in it ranged from hilarity to outright disappointment and dismay. The hilarity came mainly from the hotel's not always so charitable other 'girls' and the disapproval was epitomised by the Indian's scowl in place of the previous cigar, while even the youth, Achmat – who should have been pleased by his involvement with someone other than Mjozi for a change – seemed to regard him with an even bleaker loathing than before. 'Probably thinks I'm a bisexual,' he guessed. 'Having it off with anything with a hole,' and, though not caring, could understand the clearly loverless and frustrated youth's reaction to such a gluttonous hogging of the best of both worlds.

He did, however, intensely care about Mjozi's reaction to the news. Excusing himself from the bar on the pretext of going to the toilet, the latter burst into his room, his face a shambles of horrified dismay.

'Johnny! *What* is this I hear? Is it true?' and he nodded, not bothering to ask what the other was on about, noting, as he had so often before, that Mjozi only used his name in moments of closest intimacy or severest strain.

'How old is it? She going to bring it down?'

'Three months. And, no, I don't want her to bring it down.'

'*You* don't want her to bring it down? Christ! are you crazy? What about your *name?* What – if you let me say so – about *mine?* Quarter's going to think I got a crazy for my bra?'

'Please, Mjozi,' and childhood's whine was, hatefully, back with him. 'Don't *you* start on me. Whatever Berry is, what's in her belly is *mine.* Is all I have got left in the world that *is* mine.'

'You got me, haven't you? I ever let you down? Aren't we like we are under one skin?'

'Sure, but you've also got a wife and kids out there in the sticks. It's not the same as with me.'

'You *marrying* her?' and Mjozi seemed to brace himself for the ultimate shock, his lone eye bright with disbelief and alarm.

'No, but I'll pay for her keep till it's her time and she gives me the kid.'

'Now I *know* you're crazy! And, anyhow, why are you so sure it's *your* kid? These women lie like it's a disease. Go for any sucker they can grab.'

'She doesn't let them have it without the skins and mine broke.'

''Others' can also break.'

'I know, but the timing's right. No, Mjozi, it's mine and I want it and it's hitting me, *hard,* that *you* don't understand. Maybe we're *not* under one skin like you say,' and Mjozi checked at that and, turning, went out, his face stricken as though slapped, and he lay down again on the bed, closing his eyes, but still seeing Mjozi's face on the undersides of the lids. Could he, he agonised, afford to alienate a man whose friendship had become the one sure strut on which he leaned? What guarantee was there that the child would be born *alive?* Sharon was in the shadowland between fertility and barrenness and things could go frighteningly wrong and where would he be then? Should he not get up, *now,* tell her the deal was off, that he had changed his mind? 'And dishonour the contract that you sealed with your own hand? Condemn your seed to death?' queried his human self. 'Fuck that!' scoffed the first gene, shambling from the thickets of his flesh, older than time. 'At the beginning it was only me. At the end it will be only me. What the hell should I care?' And, later, walking to and from the 'Gents', he stopped at Sharon's door, heard her moving around inside, raised his hand to knock, brought it down, and, all that night, the schism raged, the lone cloud spreading like a heaven's pus, the wind blowing bitterly over the wasteland that was his brain.

Next morning, early, Martins came to him, took his hand in both of his, said with an intense solemnness, 'Don't mind what they say. You've planted a life and, no matter where it grows, life is life: the miracle that is not a stone,' and he thought: 'Yet *he* does not plant any life, cannot bear any life other than his own. How does he square that with what he says?' But – because, perhaps, of that very contradiction – that was not so much a contradiction as a simple confession of inadequacy and pain – he found himself, despite himself, quite extraordinarily stirred and better able to withstand the insidious pressure of Mjozi's renewed staying away.

A few days later, paging through the morning paper, the name 'Donovan' flared up at him out of the death notices and he learnt from it that Septimus Donovan, one of the town's oldest residents, had peacefully passed away in his sleep at the Fairview Old Persons' Home. Carefully he put the paper down – as carefully as though it might break – and asked himself how he felt? His first reaction was to cynically mock the 'passed away peacefully in his sleep'. 'How could he have done otherwise?' he sneered. 'He was already up off the earth as a balloon!' But then he thought back more clearly to the last time he had seen Sep, and although he did not find grief, he found shame. 'What did I know about him anyway? What do I know about myself?' and wondered with a kind of pitying voyeurism if Sep had been dreaming of Colin when he died? 'Ghost boy's no ghost anymore,' he thought. 'Dead as him,' and, with that thought, came a wash of, not loneliness, but *aloneness,* the sensation that there was still only he on the dark side of a moon – Fiona, Ray, his mother, Sep – now even Colin – all gone, and only in the belly of a woman he hardly knew, could never love, the as yet unborn, barely aware last of a saga as of a line. Most surely, then, he knew that he would not be knocking on Sharon's door, and Mjozi, as though sensing this, was talking to him again the next day – a little stiffly still, but *talking* – and soon he was even more affectionately possessive of him than before, hoping, perhaps, that this added enthusiasm for their relationship could yet wean him away from the 'whore' and the 'embarrassment' of the child.

Suddenly the sky was again uncluttered, the wind of his prescience stilled, and his world that had seemed to so violently swerve at the near-confrontation with Mjozi, righted itself and came back on course. 'It was only a swerve!' he exulted. 'A little thing. Not a putting of my foot into the shit like it was before. The pattern has changed,' and he was back to walking as tall as when Sharon had first come to him with the news of the child and he was reaching for the seven fat years after the seven lean. 'Why so much of the Bible these days?' he sported with himself. 'Sep still around in you somewheres?' and that which went with him as did his shadow – to which the woman at the shop so readily gave a name but for which *he* had never found a name – not sporting, warned, 'There are *other* patterns. Take care.' But his ears were stone from the audacity of their daring to disbelieve and the namelessness, pityingly relentless, lent him the usual seven days, not years.

So it was, indeed, within a week that, coming from the staff showers back to the hotel, he found the reception youth sitting on a box in a corner of the intervening yard, a cigarette angling from the side of his mouth, a glass of something unpleasantly green chiming its ice in his hand. 'Day off,' he guessed, but did not greet, knowing that there would be no reply, that the other knew that the potency of his hostility lay in silence, not in speech. 'Like a goddam monkey on my back,' he muttered, but flippantly, in no mood to be annoyed. But the youth – perhaps a little drunk, perhaps buoyed by the thought that he was doing what so many before him had with impunity done – snickered as he passed and said something under his breath in a tone that spoke a clear language of its own. Startled by the other's unwonted temerity, but still not quite ready to make an issue of it, he turned round and stood over him, noting with distaste the too heavily greased, stretched-back hair, the sallow, pitted face that seemed to draw, all, to a point like the snout of a fox, and asked, 'You say something?'

'Ja, I asked how's mammy, dad?' and the slack lips, oilily wet from whatever was in the glass, widened into an even more astonishing grin.

Rage seized him then and he gathered up the front of the youth's shirt and jerked him to his feet, the shirt's bold slogan crumpling into his grasp, the ribs of the other's scrawny chest rasping like a washboard across the knuckles of his fist. 'You asked *what?*' he hissed. 'Ask it again, poes. Loud and clear so's I can donner you like I've been wanting to for I dunno how long!'

But the youth, his shirt stained with the green liqueur, the still burning cigarette flopped from his mouth, his feet trampling the remains of the shattered glass, wailed, thinly, frighteningly, as the little more than a child that he still was, and he released him, his fury gone, its place taken by a too late and overwhelming shame.

'All right, forget it,' he muttered, and fumbled in his pocket and took out some loose change and slapped it into the other's hand. 'Here, go buy yourself another drink for the one I broke,' but the youth wailed on, his eyes shut tight, his free hand clutching his groin, and, at last a measure of impatience returning, he pushed the other back onto the box and yelled, 'For Chrissake! *will* you shut up? You a little girl?'

The wailing stopped then, but not the crying, and he asked the top of the huddling head. 'How old are you, anyway?'

'Seventeen, and I'm gonna tell Mr Mohamed what you done to me.'

Alarm stirred in him then, but he brazened it out. 'Tell him all you want and I'll tell him all the bedtime stories I've heard about *you*.' It was a long shot, but it worked, and now the crying, too, stopped and the youth raised his head and looked at him with careful, way-back-Javanese eyes. 'Which reminds me – seeing we're talking like we are – *why* do you always treat me like I'm dog-shit you got on your shoes?' But the other continued to stare at him with won't-tell eyes and he asked again, more sharply, 'Go on. *Tell* me. Why?'

But still there was no answer, only a counter-question as the youth, risen to go, snorting his nose with his hand, turned to him, malevolence fully rekindled in face and stance, and asked, 'Why did you have to come here? Muck up the scene?' and went inside, then, ramming the money he had given him into a pocket of his jeans.

'Not too high and mighty to keep the bucks, though,' he thought. 'Would've thrown them back in my face if I had been him,' and found himself quite exasperatingly troubled by the enigmatic question the other had flung at him – a question that now seemed to be no more than the melodramatic throwaway line of an embittered boy, and then again seemed to be the key to something much more sinister and arcane. Within days, however, the *question* ceased to any longer actively engage him and it was only the sense of implacable *malevolence* engendered by the encounter with Achmat that remained. And that did not go away – and could not be *remedied* – as had been the case with the first clouding-over of a happiness he had hardly believed he could attain. But still he could not see the continuance or intensification of any alternative pattern – did not wish to remember that he had read somewhere that men on mountain-tops were also men who would be coming down. Or *was* he, perhaps, *subliminally* aware – and that with a fullness he could not bring himself to consciously confront – and this was being evidenced by the frenzied-ness with which he reached for and lived out the meagre pittance of grace that the shadow that was not his shadow saw fit to again extend?

Never before had he had so much to do. More and more, as the days slotted into weeks, and the weeks into a month, two months, and Sharon's condition could be more clearly seen, did he find himself swopping his observer status for the considerably more arduous role of co-parent of a budding child. Catering for Sharon's needs as well as for his own was not the organisational pushover it had seemed, particularly since they had agreed that they were both too independent by nature – and he, additionally, too unpredictably employed – for them to fuse themselves into a single ménage – although, in the long term, that would have been by far the cheapest and easiest way. Even so, their lives intertwined to a degree that was alien to them both and there were moments of dire crisis that threatened to tear apart the fragile alliance they had sworn to uphold. He had prepared himself for her to be any of many kinds of women and she turned out to be a composite of several of them: as intensely cynical as she could be naïve, often hugely generous and, as often, cunningly predatory and streetwalker-wise. And – always – and unexpectedly so – a mother to the manner born: fiercely protective and possessive of that which she bore – to the extent, even, of cutting down on her already very moderate tippling and giving up smoking altogether, which did not make her any easier a person to endure. Apart from their usually individual fantasising about the child, the other listening with a faintly hostile reserve, her telling him what to buy or what not to buy and his not listening to her mostly trivial anecdotes of the much overrated 'sisterhood of the streets', there was very little meaningful communication between them, although he did, at one stage, again raise the question of her suggesting that he marry her in order to save himself expense.

'Did you love me enough to go through with it if I had said "Yes"?'

'Don't fancy yourself!' she scoffed. 'The only time I thought I *might* love you was that *first* time when you laid on me and cried. After that, you were just another fee.'

'But *would* you have married me even though you didn't love me and I didn't love you?'

'If you had asked me that question *then*, I would have said "yes" because I was believing then that that would be good for the kid and it being easier for you was just bait on the hook, if you know wharramean. But I have been thinking about it since and I don't anymore believe that it would be good for the kid.'

'Why the change?'

'Because I've been thinking again about what you and that Mjozi have been doing with those women and it's gotten under my skin. I wouldn't like my kid to have a father like that.'

'But,' he protested, 'it's no different to what you have been doing with all those men!'

'It *is* different,' she said. 'I'm doing it for money. Because I *must*. You're doing it for *fun*. That's different. And it's *worse*.'

'But for shit's sake, married or unmarried, sleeping around or staying in my own bed, I *am* the kid's father! Nothing can change *that*.'

'I don't care,' she said. 'It's not the same thing,' and he left it at that, finding no sense in her words, yet half understanding what she meant.

But it was not all altercation. There were many moments of almost tenderness and, most certainly, of understanding, and his chores on behalf of the mysterious visitant of Sharon's belly lent a fullness and significance to his life that he had last – in a hauntingly more tragic and negative way – experienced in tending a dying and unrecognisable Ray Willies, and he was, thus, the fool in motley, dupe with a ring in the nose, who that afternoon entered his room and stopped short, knowing that that which, like the spiders of his youth, had been running in his shadow, had just left there and taken what it had found. Could it be merely the cleaner and his senses were playing him tricks? But no, he decided, it could not be her: she had already been there in the morning and he had brought the room back to the way he wanted it after she had gone.

Carefully he checked the room, his ex-con's eyes – grown aware from watching over his few, cherished possessions in a too small space – instantly uncovering the intruder's spoor: his spare shoes kicked deeper in under the bed by an unaccustomed foot, the book he had been reading and had left, face down, on the bedside stand, still face down but opened now to a different page, the wad of paper that had earlier fallen short of the waste tin, now on another part of the floor, and, most flagrantly of all, the contents of his pack trashed around by an avidly seeking hand. Yet nothing seemed to be missing from it, or from the wardrobe's hangers and drawers, and he sat down on the bed, bewildered and disturbed, hearing a missing something crying that it was gone, knowing that he had *noted* that it was gone but a capricious subconscious was refusing to betray what it was.

Unhappily, he again rose, prowled around the room, stood, heavily, at the window, watching a metro pass, watching the brisk seasonal wind, blowing from off the glittering wastes of the dump, whirl dust clouds, papers, birds, dizzyingly into the air, skitter the papers clogging the fences, infesting the streets, till he felt he was trapped in a holocaust of papers: wrappers, newsprint, blown loose posters, papers, papers, of every shape and size – all defiled and unpre-possessing as industrially contaminated snow. *Papers?* The wind shook the window with an appropriately violent gust, sending even the wad of paper in the room scampering across the floor, and he was back at his pack, frantically emptying it of its contents, scrabbling through the disorder with shaking hands, knowing at last, horror moving in his bowels as the child would soon be moving in Sharon's womb, that it was not there – the envelope that had held the money from Fiona, that cruelly, in a single sentence, laid bare his past, gave even his prison number for the convenience of those who would know more.

Who could have taken it – been so interested in him as to see nothing of value in his room *except* the envelope? Instinctively his thoughts turned to the boy, Achmat, but he was not the only member of the staff who had keys to the rooms, could be bribed to give access to those who – in this place that so reeked of desperation and intrigue – wanted in for reasons they had yet to reveal. Or might never reveal.

Achmat, Martins, Sharon: even the Indian, if it came to that. Achmat hung it all out, but although Martins seemed an honest john, what did he really *know* of him, of the complexities of his sexual life, his vulnerability as a result of them? Sharon bore his child, but what did her heart bear in relation to himself? Did she perhaps seek the hold over him that the envelope would give? And the Indian? He was unhappy about Sharon's pregnancy and might be looking for an excuse to kick him out. Or perhaps, being the petty crook and near-pimp that he undoubtedly was, it was his policy to keep tabs on his long-term tenants in case they got to know too much and had to be 'persuaded' to get back into line. Whatever the case, it was clear that he faced a crisis of such dimensions as to cast doubt on his ability to survive.

Pityingly, gently, the unnamed knowingness that transcended his content and form, whispered, '*Now* do you see how the wind blows, how the pattern flows? It is not too late for you to run. Only you are holding yourself there.' But he was the *child* of content and form, could hear only the wind beyond the walls, could not lift his feet from the treadmill that, relentlessly, bore him on through its gargantuan, repetitive round. He was fully aware, though, that the hell that now had him was no ordinary rack for the wrenching of limbs, but an exquisite anticipation of pain whose ingenuity possessed a bizarre beauty of its own. At every knock on his door, his heart would lurch as he pictured the Indian, who bore the name of his Prophet, standing there, pontificating with an oddly rightful sanctimoniousness that, 'This may not be a five star establishment, Jackson, but there is no place in it for swine like you. So hand in your key at the desk and here's the balance of the accommodation you paid us in advance.' Or would he simply pocket that, knowing he would not dare to demand its return? Similarly, every summons from the office at work, brought him to it with all the hidden hollows of his body drenched with a sweat of dread, and his hands clasped behind his back that their trembling not be seen by the suddenly magisterial presence under the picture of the church. Transfixed, he would stare at her like one arraigned, in his imagination already hearing her pronounce that shocking – if somewhat Biblically theatrical – condemnation of him as being of the accursed of the earth, and sometimes he would so belatedly hear what she was *actually* saying, that she would have to repeat herself, looking at him, then, with uncomfortably questioning eyes.

If only, he thought, he could *share* his terror with some other living soul. But he hesitated to attempt that even in the case of Mjozi because privately confessing to another of a past feloniousness was one thing, but to ask that other to become involved, no matter how peripherally, in the *social stigma* attached to such a felony, was another matter altogether, and, as the days passed into weeks and still there was no move on the part of whoever had taken the envelope, he began to suspect that this tardiness was deliberate, that he was being harassed by one well-versed in the techniques of mental torture, of the debilitating effect of silence when there should have been fury, of an inaction that was the *action* of a stayed hand, of a watcher whose eyes surrounded him from every side and went with him into the most secret places of his flight into sleep. Was Achmat, he began to wonder, capable of such a fiendish finesse? Should his place at the top of the list not be taken up by someone else? Covertly, he studied each one in turn, delicately tried to twitch aside the everyman's mask, but Martins received him with the same bland pleasantness as before, Sharon was wont to snap, 'What's got into you these days?' and the Indian, at the most recent settling of accounts, gave him a curt but quite definite nod. Even Achmat, at whom he took a long second look, showed none of the triumphalism of the child and he thought, 'Christ! could it be someone that's not them at all?' But *who*?

In the end – *if* there was any truth in it that he was mouse to a cat – the game went on for too long and the tempting thought came to him – and was grasped – that there was, indeed, no truth in it and that, during one of his frequent rummagings through his pack, the envelope had, unnoticed by him, spilled out onto the floor and the cleaner had later routinely cleared it away. So – the thought mushrooming in the fertile soil of his need to believe – the structure of his fears slid swiftly down into the flood of his hope and his feet more tenaciously than ever trod the rungs of the great wheel that, like him, sought to rediscover its beginning in its end.

As though confirming that he was once more survivor after having seemed so surely lost, there came the longest interregnum yet in which nothing untoward occurred, and Sharon's pregnancy burgeoned, seamlessly, into its eighth month, she coming to him one morning, breathless at the ever new wonder of the womb. 'It kicked again,' she whispered. 'So *hard* this time!' and he put his hand on her belly to feel, but she pushed it away, saying 'No!' a sharpness to that which unsettled but which he immediately ascribed to the moodiness of a mother-to-be. However, if he had not been so inexperienced, so intent on maintaining the status quo, he would have seen that 'No!' for the aberration that it was because Sharon had, otherwise, become almost bovine in her placidity, sitting for long hours knitting midget garments in neutral colours because she did not know whether they were to be for a boy or a girl. Often, now, he would sit watching her, her strong, almost harsh features mellowed by the busyness of her hands, he a hardly noticed presence on the fringes of her vision and mind, and although there was still no question of love between them, there *was* a new feeling of togetherness, of amiableness, even, that had not been there before and that, he hoped, augured well for the antenatal days, and once, passing her, he was moved to stroke the too-often-dyed, brittle hair and she murmured something sleepy that he could not hear. 'Old whore, old kid, all in one,' he thought, coming the nearest yet to something like affection and staring in awe at the grown vast round of her belly that held the life that was the entire justification for his own life, but still, for all that, seeing her more as the incubator of his seed than a woman and a mother and she, sensing that, turning to him her dead eyes.

A last attempt was made to arouse, to warn him, his subconscious waking him one night, squatting, darkly massive, alongside his bed, but he closed his eyes again, sank back into sleep, its waters washing over him, unlit by any dream.

And, the next morning, the wheel demanded that he tread the faster, scenting the completion of its turn.

***

It was late afternoon, and he just back from morning shift, when Mjozi came, unbidden, into his room, and he knew at once that something had gone terribly wrong.

'What's happened?' he asked, his voice tight with strain.

'Fired,' said Mjozi, trying for bravado, for a grin, but betrayed by the grimace that it became. 'Must be out of here by tomorrow a.m.'

'But what did you *do*?' and he felt himself go into free fall, the bottom dropping out of his world.

'Only what I always do. What all the others always do. Took my cut of the bar to make up for the Moslem's kaffir pay. He *knows* that's what we do but makes like he doesn't see.'

'So why now?'

Mjozi sighed. 'Ja, well, yesterday you-know-who propositioned me again and, when I told him where he got off and he got uppity about you, I smacked him one and this morning the Moslem's in my room and there's two bottles of booze he knows I can't buy with my pay.'

'But didn't you tell him what the kid wanted from you?'

'He could care! He's probably so upset because he's got a yen for the little shit himself. That's one real bad Moslem, if you want to know.'

He stared at Mjozi, his whole self in his eyes, not caring that it showed. 'So what you gonna do now?'

Mjozi shrugged. 'Pack up. Take the notice pay I made him give and go back to the nkosikazi and the kids for a while. Then see where to from there. But before I go, I still have two bottles in the room that the Moslem didn't find and a present I've been keeping for you till you came of age, and tonight I'll be back and give you the present and we'll drink out the two bottles and I'll say "Ciao".'

But the other's speech only aggravated his grief and he burst out, knowing that his were not a man's words but unable to curb his tongue, 'Is that all our friendship means to you: two bottles of booze, a present and "Ciao"?'

And Mjozi, already on his way out, turned back to him, his face savage with anger and pain. 'Of course our friendship means more to me than that. What kind of a shit do you think I am? But what do you want me to do? Break down and cry?' and only the almost-slamming of the door perversely softened the impact of his tone and words.

Alone again, he slumped onto the bed and took his face into his hands. 'Christ!' he mourned. 'Another Ray gone. Another goodbye like it's me that's dying there on the top of the wave. Does *nothing* last? Is *everything* just piss-and-wind?' and he shambled like one drugged to the 'Gents' and showered, and came back and chewed through half of the hamburger he had brought from the takeaway, and locked his door and did not answer when he heard Sharon calling his name.

Then the sun set and he switched on the light and let Mjozi in when he heard the other's still heartbreakingly jaunty tap on the door. 'The last time,' he thought. 'The last time for me and for the door,' but tried, now, not to let the thought show as Mjozi dumped two bottles of top-brand Scotch on the bed and handed him something that had been as untidily and gaudily packaged as by a child. 'Your present,' said Mjozi and grinned a determinedly as-usual-grin, and he unwrapped the parcel, mourning anew at each ineptly tied knot and bow, and laid bare a rather scruffy-looking cardboard box, and opened that and stared a trace bewilderedly at the wire contraption it contained. 'Take it out,' said Mjozi, eager for him to be pleased, and he took it out and saw that it was one of the many township toys whose manufacture had become a cottage industry of its own, but this one not the usual windmill or cyclist, but two figures lying on top of each other, face to face and meaninglessly entwined. Then he found a trigger on the side of the contraption and Mjozi said, 'Press it,' his breath quickening and sly, and he pressed it and found that, as long as he held it down, the figures' hugely exaggerated buttocks revolved and they copulated with an urgency that was as comical as it was lewd. 'To remind you of us and the girls,' said Mjozi, laughing and punching him mightily on the arm. 'You like it?' and he nodded, simulating delight, but secretly he was disturbed because the figures had been so skimpily constructed that they were virtually androgynous and reminded him, not of Mjozi and the girls, but, shockingly and repellently, of Jason sodomising him in the cells, and he put the toy down on the stand beside the bed, vowing to rid himself of it once Mjozi had gone.

'What must I give you to remember *me* by?' he asked, but Mjozi waved that away, saying: 'Just be happy with me this one last time and that will be enough for me to remember you by.'

'No ways can I be *happy*,' he protested, resentment again stirring in him at so unnatural a request. 'I can only get drunk.'

'Well, get drunk then,' said Mjozi and they drank, he avidly, deliberately, seeking release, Mjozi solicitously topping up his glass each time he held it out, lone, attentive eye watching him, the whole of him urging him to loosen up, to laugh, to talk, as they had always done when together. But he only became more silent and morose, and, eventually, more stuporous and hallucinatory, Mjozi's face now frighteningly close to his, then distant from it as the room's far wall, voice now loud, echoing all around him as in a cave, then stilled, only the lips moving like an image on a TV screen with no sound. But Mjozi, too – although drinking far less – was changing into some other self, and – from within the bubble that withheld him from the grown unreal world – he watched as the other's good eye glowed with an unfamiliar light and his hands twitched as they reached, drew back, reached, for what dared not be named – saw also how a small sweat seeped out from the aquifers of Mjozi's flesh, sheening his brow, and heard the latter's words drop, syllable by syllable, through a silence sudden and booming as the hollows of his bones, 'Hey, bra, you a partying man or a corpse? This is no goodbye present you're giving me when you are like this! You want to give me something else?' and he nodded because he thought that was the right thing to do, and Mjozi went over to the door, his every step sharp as a shattering of ice, and turned the key that was still in the lock and came back and stood, swaying, over him, his eye glittering like a burnished glass, spittle wetly in the corners of his mouth, and a voice that he had never heard before, saying, 'Unzip me, bra.' And he looked up and it was no longer one-eyed Mjozi towering over him, but Jason with his bull-neck and hands that could break him like a stick, and he reached up and drew wide the other's fly, feeling the penis rising springily beneath his hand, then turned over and bared his buttocks as one bewitched, and cried out as on his first night in the cells when Mjozi thrust into him and he felt the latter's teeth savaging his neck in an access of unbridled need.

When he came to, his head throbbing and his breath fouled, the light was still on, but the dawn was grey and soft as feathers in the fragment of sky the window held. At first, he could not at all remember what had taken place, was conscious only that this was the hour for getting up to jog. But then the strangeness of the light's burning in the room struck home – and the rawness that was his neck – and the anguished cry of his outraged anus – and his own seed's humiliating fouling of his loins – and he lay quite still, thinking with the cold detachment of one in shock of his long seduction by a man whose name his tongue would never again name. Had it all, from the start, been callously planned, or had it been but the ultimate surfacing of a dark undertow that the other had denied? Or, worse still, had always secretly indulged? Whatever the case, should he not now be rising in anger to confront the jackal that Jason had warned must never be allowed to prowl again, yet had struck in a shape of Jason as, previously, it had slunk in a shape of Ray? But that compounding of the question was more than his mind could face and it knotted like a snail and fled and hid in a far corner of his skull.

And it was then that he became aware of a movement just within the limits of his vision and slowly, carefully, he swung his head and saw that the bedside Bible had been placed on the trigger of the farewell toy and the two figures were copulating as though in tireless simulation of what had earlier taken place on the bed, and – as slowly and carefully as he had swung his head – he at last got up and took the toy and smashed it into a meaningless tangle of wires with the heel of one of his shoes. Clearly, as though the figures had spoken *for* him, he knew now that the other was long gone, had probably left the hotel immediately after he had done with him, and, without warning and against his inclination and will, the boyish prankishness – shameless innocence almost – of the pantomime that had been set for him beside the bed, pierced his heart and he buried his face in his hands and wept – not for any shape of blood and bone, but for the fleshless beauty that had never been.

Eventually, the east urgently brightening, he took his soap and towel and, stumbling over the empty bottles on the floor, bewilderedly tried to unlock the already unlocked door – 'Christ! unlocked all night,' he thought, though he did not really care – and walked with the precise steps of one pacing off a length to the 'Gents' and showered, soaping, washing, anus, buttocks, crotch and thighs as though they would never again be clean, remembering, suddenly, his fingers gummy from his own semen, that no condom had been used. A chill did, then, challenge his numbness and he leaned his head against the cubicle's as chill tiles, thinking, 'Do I now go the same way as Ray?' but it was all still too far away, too not there, and he dried himself and looked into the mirror and his bitten neck was an obscenity that demanded that it be seen. 'Shit! I got to go to work with *this?*' he thought and panic flared in him because the marks, whether from sodomist or whore, were too unmistakeably what they were to be confused with anything other, and although his employers might not immediately fire him, they would soon enough find some other reason to and how would he then support Sharon and the child that was the last proof of the masculinity to which, after the previous night's sodomising, he now but very precariously clung?

Back in his room, he buttoned into his highest-collared shirt and, playing it safe, went to a public rather than the reception phone and dialled the shop and, roughening his voice, told the woman who had taken him on that he had a bad attack of the 'flu and the doctor had advised him to lay off work for a few days. 'Not to worry, Mr Jackson,' she said. 'You rest up. We'll make a plan in the meantime.' Then he remembered that Sharon had called to him the previous afternoon and he had pretended not to hear, and he went to check on her, feeling guilty and exposed in his peculiar choice of a shirt, and she, professional that she was, looked at his neck, his crotch, and opened her mouth to say what she thought, what she *knew*, but then she saw his eyes were no longer those of the man whose child she bore and bit down, hard, on her tongue. Her hostility remained almost tangibly between them, however, and he contrived to see as little as possible of her from then on.

On the morning of the fifth day, he thought the marks had altered sufficiently for him to give an acceptable alternative explanation as to why they were where they were, and toyed, then, with his breakfast before going down to the shop and clocking in. But he was only halfway into his uniform when one of the deliverymen stuck his head round the door of the guards' room and shouted, 'Wanted in the office!' and was gone, and he finished dressing and crossed to the office and immediately saw Fiona's envelope lying on the desk in front of the woman with the no longer motherly eyes.

'Yes, we know,' he heard her say through the thunder of his collapsing world,' and here's your notice pay, plus the pay for the days you have worked this month,' and she indicated the money with her head, making it clear that she did not want to risk him touching her hand. 'Leave your uniform in the guards' room and remove yourself and any of your belongings from the premises without delay.'

He picked up the money, not looking at her, and she said, 'The envelope too. It's yours. Came to us anonymously through the post. You should have been more careful with something as damning as that,' and he picked up Fiona's envelope as well and turned to go, but she went on: 'Murdering your own mother was bad enough – yes –,' as he started, 'I checked on your case with the prison authorities so as not to be unfair – but what angers me most is that you *lied*. Naturally, if you had told the truth, I would not have hired you, but, at least, I would have thought you an honest man and what you told me would not have gone beyond these office walls. But now I know you are a *dishonest* and, therefore, *dangerous* man and I will see to it that you don't find any other work in this town.'

Still he did not look at her, did not answer her, and he was passing through the door when she suddenly asked, '*Why* did you do it?' and he turned round and saw that her eyes were as avid as any gossiping whore's and, with a final flicker of his waning spirit, he snarled, 'What the fuck's it got to do with you?' and watched with a savage satisfaction as her face reddened, fully and bloodily as though he had shot her through one of the two ravening eyes.

In the guards' room, one of the old guards that he knew was being relieved by one he had not seen before and who, he presumed, had already been hired in his place. They had been talking when he came in, but now were silent, hanging their heads as though they shared his guilt. 'Jackson is dead. Long live the next shit in the queue!' he said to himself and snickered, a little crazily, under his breath, drawing from the others a quick, alarmed glance. 'They've been told,' he decided, and hurriedly exchanged his uniform for the T-shirt and jeans in which he had come, then tossed his uniform to the guard he knew, saying, 'Be a pal and hand it in for me. Can't wait now. Got to see my mother before the graves close,' and, again, found satisfaction in the others' horrified disbelief.

But, out in the street, his breath caught in a dry, despairing sob, and there was a whining in his ears like he had a hive for a head, and sometimes his vision blurred and he would screw his eyes shut to clear them, and that and the constant shaking of his head to rid it of the whining, must, he thought, be leading people to believe he was a drunk, a spastic or a loon. But what the fuck difference did it make anymore *what* they believed! Things were different now from when he first hit town. Then, he was afraid to fart in case somebody looked twice and remembered him for what he was, but now he might as well shout it from the rooftops because the holy-mary was already doing that anyway and, soon now, the news that he was Jackson the mother-killer would be running through the streets like it was a plague.

He did not go back to the hotel then or at any other time that day. Instead, at last driven by a prescience that the wheel was nearing the end of its turn, he made another round of all the stations of his past: the flats in Fourth, the cottage where Fiona had lived, the mound under which she now lay – and where he took off his cap and pushed a few flowers into the still there sand-clogged vase and said, in the honest voice of one exploding out of pain, 'Sorry, pal, but it looks like that's as much as I'm ever going to be able to do,' – and he even walked past the home that was no longer his home, and the gilded warren that had been Sep's last home as well as the grave in which he had died before he died. And, all the while, there was the whining in his head, and it beginning to ache from his shaking it, and once he went into a bar and hit back two brandies, neat, but his stomach still held only the picked-at breakfast and the headache settled into a dulled, leaden hindrance behind his eyes.

After sunset, he bought a packet of hot chips and what, in his pre-prison days, was called a 'Russian', but which now was called something else, and he tried to remember what that something else was, but it, together with the other trivial – and sometimes not so trivial – matters, kept slipping in and out of his brain like fish in a too coarsely-meshed seine. He tried to eat all of the food, some instinct basic as an animal's insisting that he should, but he ended up throwing most of it into a trash bin, which wastefulness was not in his nature at all, but he was suddenly too tired to look for a beggar on whom to lavish it and bought a ticket into the sleaziest of the old café biòs in town, partly because it was the nearest to him and partly because it reminded him of Ray and the old Rink. 'Ray and the old Rink,' he repeated. 'Sounds like something from a song,' and laughed softly at his cleverness in seeing that and went on humming it till it wandered away on its own.

He had never before been in the place and soon found that he had outgrown the kung fu and slapstick films that were being shown, and his head kept flopping onto the back of his seat, or sideways onto the shoulder of the youth beside him who, tiring of having to keep pushing him away, eventually got up and moved to another row. In between the bouts of sleep, he nibbled at the stale pastry and colour-of-piss carbonated drink he was compelled to buy in order to validate the establishment's claim to a duality that was more farcical than real.

'I'm not enjoying this,' he complained. 'So why do you go on sitting here? Why don't you go back to the hotel?' 'Because,' he answered, portentously, 'I'm having a holiday and if I go back to the hotel – and me with no job – the shit will hit the fan.' 'And then?' 'I don't know. I don't *want* to know,' and he went *on* sitting there, but, at last, his bladder drove him to the toilet and he came out of it having forgotten to zip up his fly, and the doorkeep raised his brows at that, and he simpered foolishly and closed up again, remembering that Ray had once also caught him that way, but had done more than just raise his brows – had, in fact and for the first time, playfully prodded him in the groin – and he chuckled fondly to himself at the thought and did not at all notice that the doorkeep was signalling 'Crazy!' to his counterpart at the door leading out to the street.

He *did* go to the hotel then, his pace slackening as he approached it, his head swinging a little like an unwilling beast's before a race, but the thought of the foetus that Sharon's belly must still surrender to him, and the anxious dimensions to that thought now that he had been fired, drew him irresistibly on. Reception and foyer were deserted and cavernous, it being midweek and bad for 'trade', but, in one of the rooms above him, a radio was playing and he crossed to the foot of the stairs, his steps walking back to him across the echoing floor, and stood, listening, as a woman's husky voice soared out over a driving beat and loneliness and longing came and crowded round him with agonised eyes.

'I liked that,' he said when the singing stopped and a commercial blabbered in its stead. 'And you?' but the other didn't answer and he began to climb the stairs.

Henry Martins came down them, then, hurrying to somewhere, small feet deft and sure, and stopped and smiled. But he did not smile back, only stared at the other, his mind still listening to the song.

'You all right, Johnny?'

The urgency of the question, rather than what it said, broke through to him and his eyes saw and he grinned, his mouth a little slack, foolishly wide. 'You say something?'

'I asked if you were all right?'

'No, I'm fine. You know me. Never a worry in the world,' and he laughed, a high near-whinny that was both facetious and cruel, and made to move on.

'You sure?'

'Of course I'm sure. Why shouldn't I be?' and his tone was suddenly fretful and his mouth heavy with the crass petulance of a child.

'*Okay*,' said Martins placatingly. 'I just asked,' and went on down and he up, and, when he got to the top, he looked back and Martins was still standing on the bottom step, watching him, his eyes speculative and sad, and he waved, the other already whirling away from him as though on an ebbing tide, and turned and rapped at Sharon's door.

She opened it and at once tried to close it again, but he blocked it with his foot and asked, almost dispassionately, 'What the hell's the matter with you?'

'Go away!' she hissed. 'There's nothing for you here,' and started to spit out the bitter rest her eyes held, but, as on the morning after the rape, something in his face stopped her and he pushed his way in and shut the door and looked at her: the petrification of her hair in its curlers, her face like a Xhosa's under the clay of its cream.

'I've something to tell you,' he said, and came up to her and put his hand on her belly, but she struggled it off and lumbered away and stood, her back to him, in front of the curtained alcove where she had brewed him coffee the first time he had visited her room. 'I have come to tell you,' he repeated, 'that I've been fired and will be quitting here soon as I can.'

'That's fine!' she snapped, not looking round. 'You can fuck off right now, far's I'm concerned.'

'Aren't you forgetting I'm the daddy that's got to pay for us and the kid till it's your time? We got to sit down now and figure out how much I must spare you before I take the rest and make tracks for don't-ask-me-where.'

'I'm not forgetting a damn thing' – and now she faced about, her eyes triumphant and cruel – 'I never spent all you gave me each month. Each month put something away till now I've got enough to get by on my own.' Then: 'Why are you looking at me like that?'

But he did not answer her: answered himself. 'Figures,' he said, his voice conversational and calm. 'Achmat lets her in. That's why she doesn't *ask*, you see – *knows* – why I'm sacked. Now it's nearly her time and she's got enough, so she posts it. Smart!' And then he did speak to her, not angrily, conceding defeat. 'You took it, didn't you?'

'What?'

'The envelope. The envelope in my pack.'

'You on drugs?' but her eyes flickered and he knew. 'All I'm saying is what I said: I've got enough now to not need you, so you can shove your bucks where that Mjozi shoved his cock that last night he was in your room. Or do you think I don't know what those marks on your neck mean? That I didn't guess what was going on in there between you and him?'

'It wasn't the way you think,' he muttered, and shook his head: not in negation but because the whining, that had died down after the napping in the café bio, was back in his head and growing louder all the time. 'It wasn't that way at all.'

'I don't care what way it was. I'm not interested in *anything* you have to say. I just want you to fuck off out of my room – out of my life – *now!*'

'Okay, but remember,' and his voice did not threaten: merely conveyed the final, non-negotiable stand, 'I'll be back. I'll be back for my kid, soon's he's here. We have an agreement and I'll be back from no matter where I am.'

'Cut that out!' she raged. 'Our agreement never meant you could take the kid *away* from me after it was born!'

'It meant that to *me,*' he said, his tone still measured and calm, 'and I've paid my dues and I'll come for what is mine, though I have to come from the other side of hell.'

'You're mad!' she breathed. 'Stark, staring, fucking mad! Do you think I'll ever give my kid to a moffie like you? Why,' and her voice shook with the intensity of her spite, 'I'm still waiting for you to tell me how you got it stiff enough to give me what you did!'

He hit her then, smashing her lips against her teeth, his eyes glacial and void, and she staggered through the curtains of the alcove and came out again, a long saw-toothed carving knife in her hand, but he easily blocked it and bore her to the floor, her belly ballooning under him, his hand wresting the knife away from her and bringing its blade to her throat, and she knew, then, that he was going to do to her what his eyes said, and her face opened out to him in a terminal flowering of terror and she begged, 'Please! Don't hurt me! Please! I didn't mean what I said.' But her face was his mother's, mocking his masculinity, and he kept on pressing down on the blade, the whining in his head now a scream, and she opened her mouth to cry out, but he had already severed her breath and only a harsh, last gargling gushed out, and he did not stop till her legs jerked up into his sides in a manner of death and, flopping back, lay stilled.

Coldly, he looked down at her, seeing only a doll painlessly savaged by a puppy or a child, ludicrous woolly dreadlocks starting from the head, straw-stuffed limbs flung wide, and rose up from it, knife still clutched in the red claw of his hand. But then he saw the belly that had never been any doll's and, remembering, threw himself back on her, shaking her by the shoulders, hearing himself snarling through the clamour in his ears, 'Give me my kid!' but the nearly severed head only lolled, helplessly, round and the dead eyes glared at him with a horror and denial that, too, had never been any doll's.

But then the knife spoke to him in the language of knives and, loathing her and adoring what she would not yield, he did as the knife said and, finally standing up from what was left of her, he found that the tumult in his head had ceased and the treadmill had stopped, and he got off from it and went to collect the rest of what was his from his own room, leaving hers opened and howling of what it held.

✹✹✹

He did not see the boy, Achmat, cowering in the door to the 'Gents', as, laden and bloodied, he strode along the corridor on his way to the stairs, and, more remarkably still, creeping through a hole in the fence beside the tracks and dodging past the shunted trucks, he did not hear the other loose shriek upon shriek as Achmat looked into Sharon Berry's room and brought the hotel running to share what he had seen.

Day after day, he waited, growing gaunt and weak for want of food, sustained only by the water he each night drank from the garden tap of a house several minutes' walk away from where he hid, but, on the morning of the eleventh day, the vigil ended and he came out of the ruins of the old shed to greet Henry Martins who was crossing to him over the shimmering expanses of the dump, a brisk wind swirling the dust around him like a shroud.

'I knew you'd come,' he said, swaying slightly on his feet, tongue thick and slurred, and astonishingly then embraced Martins and, desensitised as he was, did not feel the other recoil from the stench of unwashed flesh that, so unexpectedly and stiflingly, clad him as in a second skin.

'Yes, I remembered what you had told me about the shed and I would have come before, but I could not decide whether this *was* the best thing for me to do. Now, looking at you, I'm sorry I took so long and I want you – please, Johnny – to also see it that way. I promised them that I would bring you to them peacefully and they said, fine, then they wouldn't have to get tough about taking you in. Okay?' and Martins stopped then, glancing about him half-fearfully and conscious that he had been talking too loudly in order to conceal his unease.

'Okay. But why all the fuss? What do you think I've been waiting here for, anyway? And don't talk so loud. *He's* sleeping in there and if we wake him, he won't let me go. Wait here,' and he went back into the ruins, carefully as though there really was somebody else there, and came out again, cradling what looked like a rolled-up blanket in his arms, and held the bundle out to Martins, saying, 'Look, Ray. Our child. At last, our very own child!' and Martins unthinkingly took it into his own arms and shrieked, once, and piercingly as Achmat had, then fell down senseless as the shrivelled, rotting foetus peered out at him from the blanket's folds.

They were upon him then, the uniforms seeming to rise up from the barren flats like a battlefield's phantom dead, and, in the melee that ensued, someone kicked the foetus and it rolled away, minuscule black mouth gaping, bleakly, at the bright sun.

The Quarry

For Gus Ferguson
Solid-gold friend I so little deserve

He's crossing the floor of the Recreation Club's lounge-cum-dance-hall to where the boys and I are practising for the usual Saturday night's gig, and I'm liking the way he moves. Clean-cut but thin, with a thinness that's in the genes, his all-bones should be getting in the way, but he's coming smooth as you please, small arse neat and tight as a fist. And, no, I'm not a gay – just like a flesh – woman's or man's – to have pride, and this guy's sassy as I could wish.

'Buddy da Silva,' he says and gives me his hand, and I think, 'Smart. He knows I'm the ou. But how? Is it because I'm twice his age?' But age does not mean much in this game, and there's no big belly and dark glasses to hang my identity on. 'Clive,' I say, not telling him my other name and wishing his hand had felt less like a meat in mine.

Then he gives the other guys five and says 'Hi' to each one, and some answer and some don't. But he's not fazed.

'Can I try out one of your guitars?' he asks and I open my mouth to say 'No,' bridling, because although we are just a hick band in a mining town on a line going nowhere but here, we have our pride and you don't ask to borrow a man's axe, any more than you do his bike, his sheila or his wife.

'You could be surprised,' he says, quick to see which way the card falls, and smiles, and now it is more than his hand that disappoints because the smile is just a little too boyishly skewed, and the eyes too wise for a skin he's either just shaved or hardly shaves at all.

'Go on, try me,' he keeps on, and at last I say to Ginger, 'Lend him yours,' and Ginger grumbles something under his breath, but plugs in and hands him his axe, and the guy doesn't say 'Thanks,' just takes it and tunes and tunes till it seems he will never stop, and I begin to think 'Loudmouth'. But then suddenly he's done and starts to play, and the guitar sings like a bird in his hands, and Ginger's mouth flaps open somewhere in between envy and love.

'You are good,' I say when he stops, and he says, 'I know,' and I should despise him for that, but don't, and he sits down at the piano – which is a Club fixture that nobody plays, save the town dronkie when he's otherwise too shickered to know his left from his right – and he looks round at us with his hands on the keys and shouts, 'Let's go!'

Now I'm human enough to not like it when someone shoves me aside, but the guys are scrambling in behind the kid, shedding wrong notes like a cat its hairs, and I find myself banging away at the drums, making little runs I never thought I could, and getting more and more excited as a crowd gathers and I begin to figure how much bigger our half of the door would be if this smart-arse could pull them in the way he is doing now.

'I sing too,' he says, after a half hour or so, getting up, his voice flat as one of the piano's battered notes. 'Maybe I'll sing tonight,' and my one hand wants to clout the cocky little shit for thinking he can join us just like that, but the other takes him by the shoulder and I hear myself say, 'Have a beer.'

We go through to the bar and belly up. 'Windhoek or Hansa?' I ask.

'Make that a peppermint,' he says, and I think, 'Ah! just a kid after all!' and shudder a little as he downs the sickening green liqueur at a single gulp.

'Give him another,' I say to Jerry who takes over the tough Saturday afternoon/evening shift from me so's I can be with the band.

'I'll have an aniseed now,' says the kid, and I start to think this is not just a kid, not maybe a gold mine either, but a whacko I might well want to do without, but I give him his aniseed anyway, and this time he toys with it and I sip my ginger ale, and – Ja – I *am* one of those – an ex-alky for whom a dop is sudden death.

'Where you from?' I ask, and he says, 'Sea Point,' but bored as though he wished I hadn't asked, and I think: 'It figures – da Silva – sort of olive, not our kind of hands – plenty of Porties there.' I should know: I come from around there myself. But I check him out anyway – ask him questions about streets, clubs, places to eat. He doesn't miss a step.

'Why you here? It's a long way from over there!'

'Need a change. Heard they pay okay here.'

'Where you at?'

'Nowhere right now. Only got here today. Stuff's still down at the station, but there's still no roof to take it to.'

I think a while, turning the ginger ale round and round, suddenly make up my mind.

'You can kip with me till you got some other place to go. Let's fetch your gear.'

But at the door, I say, 'Wait,' and go back into the bar.

'Pass us the phone, Jerry,' I say, and he writes out an IOU, 'Clive – one call,' and gives me the phone. We're honest johns here. Have to be to hold down the job, old Hawkeyes being what he is.

'That you, Claire?' I ask when she picks up the other end. 'Look, love, I got a guy staying with me right now. From the Cape. I will come to you till he goes. Not the other way round.'

'Oh God,' she says. 'Not you too!' and it's only half a joke, the way things are these days.

'Come *on*,' I say. 'It's only for a few days.'

I could not have been more wrong.

❋ ❋ ❋

He says he only has a back pack, so I take him down to the station on my bike, him on the pillion, thin arms clamping me with a strength I would not have thought they had, breath heavy as a whore's from the aniseed and peppermint liqueurs. It's a bit much, but, at least, he's not got halitosis, which is something I *really* can't take, whether in a woman or a man. Like someone's died inside, but must still make like a zombie so's to scare the shit out of the little kid I still am.

The station's at the end of the main road, and, other side the great buffers that say the line stops here, the thorny scrub goes on forever to places that are only names and where I have never been. Now and again, there are stands of taller trees, sometimes even palms, and some have got San names that sound like poems – and, yes, I do read poems in between the schlock and porn which is about all you get these days. Wouldn't, in fact, be surprised if this kid read poems, he being as good with the axe as he is.

Anyway, we go, easy and slow, the way I like to, down Main, which the Yankee owners of the mine, the Club, and just about the rest of town, have tarred for the benefit of us locals and the odd tourist who needs to have his head examined and can never quite believe it when, just past the station, he's back in stones and sand as never before.

I shout out to him about all the places he's expected to know: the mine offices, the mine shaft, right in the middle of town, humming like a queen bee waiting to be pampered and fed, the bakery where the German baker wanks the dough every morning before light and bakes the best bread south of the Line, the two German hotels where mostly only Germans sit in creeper-covered courtyards guzzling beer, the only non-German shop in town where Van Dijk, the Hollander, and his too young, buxom wife sell tourist-trade trash, the gravelled side streets that branch off from only the one side of Main because, on the other side, a fucking great hill gets in the way, the all-the-same transportable houses, no bigger than crates, to which these streets lead and in which the mineworkers live – and in which my Claire lives with her two sons, her husband having been killed in a rockfall three years back, but she staying on as a typist at the mine – which last, of course, I don't tell this kid that's nuzzling my neck and starting shivers down my spine, even though he's not Claire.

I do also, though, tell him about the churches, wondering even as I speak whether he is interested in any deity other than Da Silva, fullstop. We have them all – Roman Catholic, Anglican, Moravian, Apostolic, Dutch Reformed – but no synagogues, temples or mosques. Ja – no infidels: the Inquisition would have found time sticking to their hands like shit from having buggerall to do. Sometimes I go to the Apostolic Church and sit around, waiting to speak in tongues, but never do, and I also like going there when someone's seen the Light that I also never do, and he or she gets dunked in the built-in baptismal bath behind the pulpit by the weedy little Pastor who is the dabbest hand at tipping them over and back that I have ever seen. But then, of course, one weighs less in water – or so it seems – and I suppose they would just bob up anyway, even if he left them alone. Then, after the once-a-week film at the only cinema, the Catholic Church used to be another favourite of mine – what with the spectaculars and chantings that really got to the showman in me, the nunnery rustling in a corner of the courtyard like a stable for the Brides of Christ, and a backslapping old priest in Biblical gear who distils his own brandy from the nunnery's grapes – but I have stopped going there now, partly because the old guy keeps on so that I must share a brandy with him and I don't want to give him the grip on me of knowing why I can't, and partly because when I look past all the lights, and incense, and other stuff, there's still a wanting in me for something that is not there.

This also I do not say to Da Silva, just point out the churches as we pass, and, when we judder over the spur line near the station that brings in the copper, lead and zinc from the mine, I point out the black ghetto where the whites still don't go of a night – that is, if they go there at all – and from which, after dark, the blacks, save for a privileged few, never come out, bound by habit and blood to their serfdom and this place that is for serfs. 'As though they had never won the Revolution,' I say to Da Silva, not caring what he thinks, inviting him, really, to react so that I know where I am with him when it comes to this one territory where I don't take shit from any man. But he does not respond.

We reach the station and he gets off, begins to walk along the track towards the shed, office, waiting room, water tank – no platform, no signals (what for? there's only one line, coming, going, for one train), nothing else at all save the heat shimmering over the cinders and rails – turns then, says, 'Thanks for the info, Dad. You should have been with Captour,' and laughs, a harsh throttling of the throat, like a cockerel trying for its first crow, and I feel my hands clench on the bike's handlebars.

Quarter hour or so later, he's back, toting the pack, running his hand over the Honda's glistening flanks, saying, 'Kiff bike,' with a note almost of reverence in his voice. I make to kick-start, but then he adds: 'You too old for this bike, Dad. How about you hump the pack and I show you how this bike *should* be rid?'

Now anger's tearing around in my gut like a cat, but I don't let on as I lower my foot back to the ground and say, with a calmness that's so goddam so that he knows I'm really running wild: 'Three things. One – don't ever ask to ride my bike again. Two – don't ever fuck around with my constitutional right to ride my bike any way I fucking well please. And, three – don't ever call me "Dad" again because, one, I am not your dad, two, I am not anybody else's dad, and, three, I am not likely to *be* anybody's dad as far as I know right now. You got that, punk?' (And silently, to myself, I say: 'And I've got you by the balls for now because I have a roof and you don't.')

Sure enough, he does not walk off, buckling on his pack as I have the gall to think I would. Instead, the little sneer that my hand yens to wipe off his chops lasts only until I come to the business of his calling me 'Dad', when, like those flicks where the dying monster turns back into a man, something wilts inside him – something so secret and subtle that I only know it's there – not what it is nor why – and his face sets so's it's almost sad, and he says, 'Sorry,' in a low voice and I know that it's for the 'Dad' thing that he is sorry, not the bike.

Then, not looking at me, he humps the pack and mounts the pillion and his arms go round me in a way that suggests we are as we were. Or is it, maybe, that we are closer than we were?

That, somehow, somewhere, I have touched a nerve?

* * *

I'm all set to be defensive when we get to my flat which fronts on Main and is so close to the location that, some nights, when the wind's right,

I imagine I can hear the blacks moving around: which sound, I must add, does not worry me at all. But the kid looks about him and says, 'Not bad,' his face being not as offhand as his tone, and I begin to wonder what part of Sea Point he's from that he can so easily be impressed by a kip whose name, 'Rosenthal', is fancier than it has any right to be. By white standards, that is, there being only a box-size bedroom with not much more than a bed in it, another room like it that can be whatever I want it to be, a walk-in-sideways kitchen with a sink and a cupboard whose doors hang, and a loo that can just about hold the old-style enamel bath with tap for cold water only and no shower for a quick in-and-a-shout when winter's here. There's also a piece of fenced-in ground, back and front, with a few guava and banana trees which I give a lot of TLC because I like trees the way I like blacks, which means I like them a lot as I must have made plain by now, and the fence is covered with morning-glory which looks pretty good when its time comes. There are no roses though and the outer walls of the joint, as opposed to the thin partitions that are the inner walls, are undressed stone and thick enough to stop an army in its tracks, which probably they once did, this being an old barracks from the days when the Germans were the first to come and tell the Ovambos and Hereros about Jesus and the benefits of being slaughtered in a civilised way.

'We can share the bed,' I say, looking doubtfully at its three-quarter size and again glad that this guy hasn't got bad breath or, by my experience of him on the bike, B.O. But he shakes his head and says, no, he will kip in the other room in his sleeping bag, and says it with such force that although, on the one hand, I am relieved, on the other I am upset and struggle to keep my cool when I point out that the floor in that room is just the bare cement and icy as all fuck in this town's often suddenly cold nights.

But he doesn't want to know. 'No,' he says again. 'I'll be okay there. The bag will keep out the cold.'

'But why?' I ask, now as curious as I am annoyed. 'It's a dead right, no-bugs bed and neither of us is what you could call a heavyweight. And we can sleep head-to-toe, if it comes to that.'

'No,' he repeats, and gives me a wide, blank smile, showing good teeth, which I'm fearing could be a problem for me from now on. 'I want to sleep in there.'

Now I can't take it anymore. 'For Chrissake!' I explode, feeling a fool and all the madder because I feel like that. 'What's the matter with you? You think I stink or something?'

Again he gives me that smile that makes me want to sock him one.

'No,' he says, cool as they come. 'I seen the bath in there.'

'Or,' and I'm dredging this up from some pit in me I don't want to believe is there, 'do you think I'm going to slip you one?'

Again his face sets as with the 'Dad' thing when we were on the bike and he picks up his bag and begins to unpack his stuff in the other room, and I look down at my hands and am shocked to see that they are shaking and ask of myself, 'What *is* it with me? With him? Why does this kid rub me up the wrong way all the time? Have I got me a lemon here or is this just the usual nerves before all the shit I got to take from the drunks and other creeps at the dance tonight?'

Slowly I move my fingers, flexing them as though maybe they have been trapped by the web I'm beginning to fancy is being woven round me by a malevolent something I cannot see, but's real as air. But then the kid makes to pass me on his way to the toilet and he's carrying the stuff he's aiming to lay out there – sort of marking out his territory, like dogs do – mirror, shaving kit, toothbrush, toothpaste, deodorant ('Husky for Men'), soap and sponge, hair oil, comb and brush for the stiff, cuffed-up bristle of his hair which I now see is more auburn than just brown – as also I now see that his face has slacked into the tiredness I, too, feel, and his shoulders are drooping a little, so that I put my hand on one in sudden pity and he stops, tensed, head cocked part-way to me like a bird that's not sure whether to stay or fly.

'Sorry,' I say, feeling eased as after a king-size crap, and though he does not answer, I later hear him hissing softly through his teeth as he runs the bath, and I start to fry us some eggs and rounds of German sausage, and butter a stack of this morning's bake of ditto bread.

He comes in from outside as soon as I call him and we sit down at the table in what is now 'his room', but he only picks at his food, saying that he's too tired from the long train trip to eat, but I have this feeling that will not leave me that there is more to his tiredness than that, but as instinctively also know I must not probe.

I pour me a glass of Coke and pass him the bottle, but he shakes his head. 'Too much gas,' he says. 'Bad for tonight.' Then: 'You don't drink?'

'No. Used to, but not anymore.'

'Why? You born again? Got a ulcer maybe?'

'Neither. Worse. I was an alky five years back. Guess you know what that means.'

'Ja,' he says. 'Tough. Me – I can take it or leave it.'

'I also said that,' I say, but matter-of-factly, not pointing anything at him.

But he reacts nonetheless, though not hitting back, simply saying:

'Ja, but we're not all the same.' Then: 'You mind me taking something here? I'll keep the stuff in my pack, if you want.'

I laugh. 'Christ, no! I'm not that weak. You forget I serve the fucking stuff at the Club. You can put your bottle right here on the table, for all I care. Might be better than flowers, if it comes to that. You drinking all the fancy colours you do.'

He actually smiles then – the first real smile he's given me – and I could cheer, hardly knowing the guy he suddenly is. 'Nice place you got here,' he says, looking round, stroking a wall with his hand. 'How come they don't give you one of those hoks you showed me when we were on the bike? This joint's got class. Looks, too, like it's meant for a married oke. But you're not hitched, far's I can see.'

'Was though,' I say. 'Been twenty years in that bar, off and on, but she left me after only ten. Ran away with a dude from where we both from, but the company let me stay on in the better quarters they give those who don't dirty their hands going down the mine. Special treatment, you might say.'

'No kids?'

'No kids. Just the alky that started getting born the morning after I read the note she left behind. "Dear Clive – blah – blah."'

Just in time, I stop myself from telling him that it was not all her fault, that my sperm was water for all the good it could do, that that is why being called 'Dad' is such a sore point with me – but, fuck it, there's a limit to what a man can tell another and why the hell should I be telling this guy as much as I already have anyway?

It is then the phone rings – Ja, I have a phone – and it is the second guitarist, Stevie, saying he doesn't smaak this new oke and if I take him into the band, he's through with me. I know a crisis when I see one, and this is one helluva one – as much for me personally as for the band. Do I choose Stevie who is no great shakes with the axe, but is a through-and-through good guy and loyal, or this unknown with whom I have just shared something of my past for a reason I cannot understand and who is now lighting a cigarette with hands that I am sure did not tremble so bad earlier on? Now he is looking for somewhere to put his ash, something little-boy-lost about the tilt of his head, and I signal to him to dump it on the floor because I stopped smoking when I stopped the booze, thinking to rid me of two devils at one throw, and he looks up at me as though he knows the line's humming in my ear – as though he knows why – and I cry, silently, 'Stevie! Stevie!' to the listening ear, then hear myself say, 'The choice is yours,' and tear the phone from me as though it was a living thing.

Back at the table, I sit down, looking past him at the wall, trying for calm, but feeling my sadness at breaking with Stevie giving way to as hurting a bitterness against life in general that I should find myself making a decision I am already beginning to regret. At last, though, I look at him, watch him finish screwing his stompie under his heel, and tell him what it is all about, but, except for the single, thinking look he gives me when I say I have chosen him instead of Stevie, he shows no more feeling than a flasher I am telling he's forgotten to zip up his fly.

'Where do I get a guitar?' is all he wants to know.

'There's a spare one that belongs to the Club. Not too good, not too bad. Old Hawkeyes will hire it to us for a small fee.'

'It will have to do. Who we still got?'

I note the proprietorial 'we', but let it pass. 'Ginger on the other guitar, Denny on bass, Larry on vocals and the accordion or concertina if the yokels are in town, and me on you know what.'

'Okay,' he says, and pushes himself up from the table. 'I better get ready now,' and heads for the toilet, but before he closes its door, he turns round and adds: 'Don't worry. It'll be fine. He was the worst of the lot of you, anyway.'

'You bastard,' I think. 'Grabbing me low like that.' But somehow I am not as annoyed as I pretend to be and am even feeling better about Stevie as I clear the table and wash up at the sink, then wait to take my turn in the loo.

But there is no sound from there and, as the minutes drag past and the shadows lengthen, I grow anxious and, against my remaining few better instincts, bend down and look through the keyhole, but can see nothing except his still trousered buttocks, close up to where I am, and back off then and shout, 'Buddy!' which is the first time I have used his so-called Christian name.

'Okay,' he at once shouts back, and a tap opens and closes, and there is a chink of glass against china, and he comes out, fresh as you please and steady as a stone.

I go in then, a niggling at the back of my mind I don't want to listen to now, and my trained bachelor's eye noting, without much surprise, that he has left it to me to scrub out the bath, as he left it to me to wash up his fork and plate.

Quickly I shave, trying not to think of anything else, but not able to resist fingering the bristles of his shaving brush, but they are dry, so it could not have been that that held him for so long silent behind the door.

Again my mind nags me and again I shush it, and we go out and, as I turn round to lock the front door, I see a last ray of the sun is striking a brilliant green fire from a bottle of peppermint liqueur he has left standing in the centre of the table in his room.

'Prettier than a flower,' I say, then remember I said that before.

❈ ❈ ❈

When we reach the Club, we're running late. The paving round the pool's still warm from the day's sun, but the deck chairs and beach umbrellas have been taken in and the pool itself is shimmering under the just-switched-on floodlights like a fancy dress some woman will be putting on again when she's finished with her loving on the grass, and, late or not, I stop a moment, as I always do before a gig, to breathe in some flowers and listen to the bats doing their own click dance round my head. As I said, I do sometimes read poems – don't just handle the hard stuff and knock the shit out of the skins.

Inside, old Hawkeye's Ovambo 'boys' (who says anything's changed?) have regrouped the daytime's lounge tables and chairs round the walls and plonked a burning candle in a bottle on each table in a try for romance, when what you mostly get at these do's is throwing-up and lust on the prowl. The public's been shooed out for the half-hour before we start, which we already should have done, but nobody's hammering at the doors yet and the bar's still roaring like the crushers down at the shaft. 'And don't think they are all coming in here,' I say to the kid. 'Most of them are tanking up for grosser things than our prissy little gig.' But again, as at the start, he's not fazed.

The boys are waiting and they are wild. 'Where the fuck you been?' shouts Ginger, red hair flaring like a devil's as the draught, that sneaks in with us when we open the door, gets among the candles like a fox among the hens.

'And where's Stevie? He's not here either and it's time to go. How we gonna sound with only one guitar?' and now he looks at me beseechingly as a kid at the dad I have never been, and I see the skin is white under the freckles that splatter his face like a disease.

But what I'm thinking of now, and that's worrying me more than what's worrying him, is that Stevie hasn't told him or the others that he's quitting the band. 'Oh Christ!' I think. 'This and Hades too,' and draw a deep breath and jump in at the deep end. 'Stevie's quit the band,' I say, trying to make it sound like the non-event that it is not, and knowing, even as I try, that I am wasting my time.

'Quit the band?' they whisper, all at once, like they got it rehearsed. 'Why?'

'Because he thinks I'm a cunt,' chips in Da Silva with all the goddam indelicacy I am learning to expect.

'No, he didn't say it like that,' I object, but carefully, zigzagging between this attitude and that, like a crazy pilot on a high, so's not to set this guy off on another roll. 'He just said he didn't think he and Buddy here would hit it off, so' – and here I grit my teeth a little at having to pretty up something that's ugly as all shit – 'maybe it's better he quits, so's not to make waves for the band.'

But there's no stopping Da Silva. 'He made you choose,' he says, short and not so sweet, and *he's* heading for an attitude, for sure.

'Okay,' I say, and hear myself getting pissed-off. 'So I had to choose and I, for reasons that I, as your supposed-to-be manager, think are right, chose Buddy, and he will be playing the Club guitar while he's singing and the piano when he's not, and don't tell me' – and I look at Ginger – 'that the piano's not going to give us a big enough sound for these freaks who are too sozzled half the time to know a right note from a wrong.'

'They haven't heard me yet,' again chips in Da Silva, and I get the little show-off loud and clear, but pretend I don't – just stand there, looking at the other three, knowing one wrong word from me now and there will be no dance tonight. Which of them, like Stevie, will quit, and which, like me, seeing the writing on the wall, admitting, even though still only to himself, that this kid's going to be the techno, if not yet the manager, of the band, will stay? Ginger? Big and sloppy, he can still be quick as a trigger when he wants, like now, but mostly he's a comfortable guy who genuinely likes music and he's already shown that he smaaks the way the kid handles the axe. Score one. Denny? He seems a stolid john, as much mouse as Ginger is bear, pale face, under the black mop of his hair, long and sad as a hound's, but, actually, he's a raving gay, eyes teasing open your fly when he thinks you're looking the other way, and I seen him watching the kid's like he's really interested in what's there. Nearly I score two, then I remember he's got boyfriends like a high-class whore's got pearls, and I make that the hook with a dot instead. Larry? Here the problem's got me juggling my balls because Larry's all ash-blond male – even his eyelashes are blond – and he's got a ponytail, and his lips are too cruel to be kissed, yet they beg anything with tits to do just that, and the bimbos love him – and the things he sings in his second-hand voice – love them like they love junk food – like he loves himself – and I think, 'No ways. If ever there was a second Stevie, this is it,' and write him off.

So it's even-stephen and I'm teetering, this way, that, till suddenly I am fucking well fed up to the back teeth and decide, 'Stuff the lot of them. Why should I give myself a hernia like this? I still got my job even if the band drops dead right now' – which is selfish of me, but who isn't at times? – and I stop playing with the gons and say, with a seriousness that gets them listening even if they don't want, 'That's it then. Buddy's my choice for leader of you lot. Finish and klaar. If you accept that, give him your hand. If not, screw off and we'll wrap up the show,' and I grab the tickets and cash box from Denny, sending him back a step and feeling the kid give me that thinking look again, and go and sit at the table beside the door and watch them while they mill around like cattle when a strange bull comes to town.

But not long and they're all shaking hands with Da Silva – ja, even Larry – and I'm not going to say I'm not surprised, because I am – and pleased, even though some of the eyes don't match the hands and the kid nearly wrecks the whole deal by saying with that lopsided smile of his that never softens what he says, 'Well, I hope you guys stay happy with this because I'm gonna make musicians of you, though it kills!'

I could throw up at that, but now's not the time, and I tell Denny to watch the tickets and box while I go fetch the Club guitar to hand to Da Silva, who looks at it as though it is something the cat brought in, but plugs in and tunes it all the same. Now there are some couples at the door and I open up and sell them tickets, and nod to the band to start up to draw the rest in, but they look at the kid who's sitting to one side as though he has no business with the band, and I go over and ask him what the hell he thinks he's trying to do.

I get one of those laid-back smiles and he says, 'Play a few numbers without me at first. Larry can play the accordion and sing like a bird to fill up the sound. Then, when I give the sign, announce me and I will come on.'

I stare at him in disbelief. 'You know,' I say, dropping each word into his lap, 'you are the biggest little shit of a show-off that I have ever seen.'

'Maybe I am,' he says, not slacking the smile. 'But I'm also a showman and you better be too if you ever want to make this more than a hick band.'

He's got me where it hurts, but he's right, and he shows all his teeth as I go back and tell the guys what's the score, and they, too, look at him like he's a bad smell, but, like me, they know he's right, and I give a roll on the drums.

Larry's as terrible as ever, which means I can't decide which I smaak less – the accordion or his voice – but some farmers are in from as far away as the Estosha Pan, and they lap up the crap and do a few trots round the floor, while the locals, who like to think they are a little more with it, stay at the tables, and laugh and light up and bellow at the tribals to bring them more booze. Eventually – and I know it's

coming by the way he hitches up his jeans and settles more solidly on
the flats of his feet – Larry swings into his favourite slow number about
a love that went wrong that makes me want to stopper my ears, but the
teenyboppers scream, 'Larry!' – dragging out the tail of the name till
their lungs give out and making little belly-sounds like he's having it
off with them right there in the lounge.

'Encore! Encore! We love you Larry!' they yell, but now the kid
gives the sign – on cue and cruel as a snake whipping its fangs into a
flesh – Larry's flesh – and my gut heaves, but I get up after another
roll on the drums and shout through the mike, 'And now, ladies and
gents, guys and girls, introducing to you a new member of your
favourite band – Buddy Silver from Cape Town. Give him a big hand!'
Which, except for a few claps from those who heard him earlier on,
they don't and I think, 'Serve you right, you fucking little shit,' and sit
down, sweating like a busker who's had a hard day selling his soul.

But I should have known my boy by now. He doesn't break stride as
he slaps down the accordion, bows as though they have given him a
standing ovation and strikes a first, thunderous chord that makes the
old Club guitar sound as though it belonged to the Rolling Stones.
Heads swing up as though yanked by a single hand, chops still
dripping with beer or fouled by the cafeteria's greasy fries, and the
sudden silence in the lounge is as thunderous as the chord – as he
insists that it be – and I think, with the beginnings of respect and
something of pride, 'Christ! all we need now is the coloured smoke!
Don't fall down now, boy.'

He doesn't. He curveballs them one corny, horny pop song after
the other, not pausing even for the applause, voice doing for him what
he wants, but so easy, so cool, it's like he's swallowed a singing
machine, and he's swinging the axe like he wants to kill with it, and
he's Cliff and Elvis and Jagger, and he's snake from the navel down.
'Jee-suss!' I shout like I at last seen the Light, almost missing a beat,
and he turns his face to me and grins – the second real smile he's
given me today – and then he spoils it hardly two struts later when he
leans to Denny and snarls from the corner of his mouth, 'Hot it up
there, fruit,' and the gibe knifes home because the poor guy's eyes
pop like he's been kicked in the groin, and for a moment I really, truly
feel bad, but I'm so wound up now, and pleased I got it right for the
band, that the kid could do just about anything before I nail him to a
tree. Which doesn't say much for me, I know, but that's the way it is.

Then it's interval and Denny and Ginger go for a quick piss and a
Coke – no hard stuff, though, till after the gig, unless a comp drink
comes in from the crowd, when I let them down that in case the donor

feels he's/she's being snubbed. The kid doesn't go because he can't –
bimbos all around him, touching everything save his balls, buzzing like
blowflies that have found a meat – and I don't go because I want to
assess the crowd – but Larry stays because he's one wild and
not-knowing-what-to-do-about-it man, hands hanging down between
his knees, head bowed and the neck beneath his ponytail so red it's
like someone's tried to cut his throat from the wrong side. Poor guy, I
think, but I daren't speak to him about how he feels because that
would make it worse for both him and the band.

At one stage, the kid tries to break loose to tell me something, but
then Anna van Dijk from the curio shop – sitting alone at her table
because her husband, who's a real nice old guy with his baby-soft white
hair and every-kid's-big-daddy-smile, doesn't dig this kind of scene –
beckons the kid over, the heavy rings on her fingers telling him she's
big bucks, and he goes over to her instead, and one of the bimbos
sitting at the table behind me says, loud and clear, 'Didn't take the old
cow long to get her claws into him, hey?' and another one of them
says, 'Cows don't have claws,' and the first one giggles and says, 'Well,
you know whaddamean.'

'Ja,' I think, 'I know what you mean,' and I watch, and don't like
what I see, as Anna draws up a chair beside her for the kid and pats its
seat like he's a poodle that must jump when she says, and he sits down
and smiles his cutest, crookedest smile, and she leans to him, braided
corn-yellow hair flopping down between her shoulder blades like a
worked-loose second spine, and asks him something, blue Dutch eyes
big and wet and one sack-like tit slopping over onto his hand. Then
she snaps her fingers and an aborigine's there like she's cracked a
whip, and he brings the kid something yellow in a long glass which can
only be an advokaat and is as much tarted-up hard stuff as peppermint
liqueur, and I watch the kid sip it and smile and nod, and hate myself
for not going over to him and smashing the glass out of his hand.
Then she's taken hold of his other hand and is fondling it, stroking
the back and palm, always up to the fingertips, as though she's
lengthening his cock, and the fat mouth's now as moist as the eyes and
I know she's already feeling him in her the way she wants, and will try
to get him to do to her, though he asks a ring from her fingers for
every fuck.

Sickened, I at last look away and see Stevie sitting alone at a table
across from me, but there are three other places with empty bottles
and glasses at the table, so he must be with a party that's gone to the
bar or loo. He doesn't see me because he's watching Anna and the kid
the way a cat watches a bird, and I feel a little shiver worming down my

spine. Then, as though he's sensed that he, too, is being watched, he swings his head round, and I raise my hand and shout 'Hi!' but he looks away again and there is no knowing me in his eyes.

Then the interval is over and I sound the drums to get the crowd back in. Denny and Ginger cross over from the bar and Ginger's okay, but Denny's quiet and shrunk into his skin like a snail into its shell, and when the kid leaves Anna and the bimbos start chanting 'Buddy! Buddy!' Larry at last straightens up and says, 'Cunt-snatcher,' loud enough for me to hear. Perhaps the kid hears it too because the first thing he does is ask Larry if he would like to sing, which is really screwing the knife in the wound, and when Larry shakes his head, the kid says he's feeling a mite beat after all the singing *he's* done, so Larry can play the accordion for a while to please the boere while he takes a break, and then he'll take over on the piano and Larry can take a break. 'Christ!' I think. 'Just how cruel can this guy get?' and watch, almost with respect and with something of a little kid's holding its breath, as Larry, who's always been a bit of a dumb hunk, plays on forever, which means until the teenyboppers begin to shout as much for his head as for the new kid on the block.

Or should I be saying the new big frog in the little pond, because even as the kid finishes his stint on the piano, which is okay enough to get everyone back on the floor – except Stevie who just sits there staring into his glass till he's so big in my mind it's like he's the only one in the lounge – and the bimbos yell again as the kid goes into his orgasm with the axe for the final run of songs, there is suddenly enough of poetry and music in me to know, deep down and cold, that what I am hearing is not art but artifice that, though it deserves all my raves, is still only that – an act that's as gutsy and sassy as they come, and as sad as a desert or a woman whose belly will never swell.

And, ja, I *am* thinking of me and her now, and though I don't know for sure what the kid is thinking about, I do know that this is one unravelling man coming to me through the cunts, fat Anna throwing kisses at his behind, and his hands shaking and his eyes wild. 'Let's go home,' he whispers, and I get him out of there and take him to what he has for the first time called 'home', but I'm feeling two ways about that because a man who's grabbing for what he knows he can never get is like a *drowning* man who takes you with him when he goes.

At the flat, he makes for the toilet and locks the door, and stays there till I have brewed the coffee and rustled up something to eat, but he only drinks the coffee when he comes out without me hearing him pull the chain. Then, coffee down, he suddenly turns to me, whole man again, and whacks me between the shoulders with an awkward hand, and says, 'Thanks for the new name,' and only then do I remember that I called him Buddy *Silver* instead of Da Silva when introducing him to the crowd.

'Like I have created a new man,' I think. 'Like God,' and one of these part's little night winds rattles the door like somebody's trying to get in.

❋ ❋ ❋

The next morning, early, the phone rings. It's Larry. 'I quit,' he says, and puts down the phone.

I'm upset and make coffee, strong, to settle my gut, and when the kid wakes, I tell him, saying things like, 'Well, it was a good try, but – ,' and, 'If only we – ,' and am playing with the idea of being honest (and as nasty as I feel) by saying, 'If only *you* – ,' when he cuts me short.

'Thank Christ,' he says, and I look at him and he goes on: 'We don't need that fucking accordion, man. And as for that creepy little squeezebox – shit! Let's rather lose those hicks out there in the bush than louse up our act with crap like that. Not to speak of that voice' – and he gives his cockerel-trying-to-crow laugh – 'Jesus save me – yes! – that voice!'

'You mean we mustn't sully our art?' I say, piling on the acid, still feeling narked.

'Ja, something like that,' he says, and flaps a hand.

But I'm not happy and worry my way through each day till the next Saturday, expecting, every time the phone rings, that it's Denny also putting in the knife. But he doesn't – probably, I think, because playing in the band gives him a better chance of being picked-up by some drunken hunk in this mostly male, girl-hungry town.

I try not to let him see how relieved I am that he's decided to stay because that will give him a hold over me, and I'm wishing to God that the kid would rein in his anti-gay phobia a bit because surely he must see that, without a bassist, we are going to sound too weird for even this dump where you've got to make do with what you can get, even if it's only a penny whistle or a jew's-harp. I got to admit, though, that the kid's right about Larry et al being more of a hindrance than a help because, without the heehawing of the accordion and concertina and Larry's mostly off-key angst, we at once have that leaner, meaner sound they write about in the reviews, and hardly anybody asks where Larry's at and even the hicks come as before because where the fuck else must they go?

Also, one of the Windhoek papers gets to hear of our 'gallant little band, battling it out in the arsehole of the beyond' (the latter part of the quote being more mine than theirs), and sends a guy all those 300-plus k's to interview the kid who's nice as I have never seen him before, save that he refuses to give the guy any details of his past life, just smiling in a can't-tell kind of a way, which means we get quite a good chunk of print about 'Mystery musician Buddy Silver – blah-blah-blah.' The kid loves that of course (what try-for-Elvis wouldn't?), but it leaves me wondering why he is equally close-mouth with me. Does he think that if he tells me more than that he is from Sea Point, I will blab and spoil some little publicity stunt he's planning to keep going till telling it as it is will be an even better stunt? Or has he got something to hide?

That thought worries me for a while, but then other worries begin to worry me more, like how to get the kid a job because old Hawkeyes calls me in and says that though the dances are bringing in the bucks in the bar as never before and Buddy is the answer to a manager's as well as a maiden's prayer – and here he gives that sometimes smile of his that looks as though it's hurting him inside – the kid can't go on staying with me or anywhere else on mine property unless he's on the company's payroll, and what are my plans about that? 'And don't expect *me* to hire him,' he adds, 'because I only hire barmen and waiters, not, as you might say, show business personnel. That is your business, not mine,' and I know he's right because it's the door that pays us, not the Club.

So I fall about like a fowl whose neck you have just stretched for the pot and it's wrestling itself on the ground like the guy who wrestled the Angel in the Book, and though old Hawkeyes does, after all, put in a good word for us at the mine, the kid does nothing to help himself and seems almost pleased when I come of an evening and say that I have seen this boss or that, but still no dice, and I'm beginning to get narked with his just lying around in the flat or letting his fans buy him drinks or a hamburger at the Club. It's like a skivvy, who's had it tough under some shit of a boss, is now suddenly the boss and is saying, 'Now it's my turn. This is how it was,' and I'm saying this because the few times he does decide to fix us something to eat, he does a job as good as any woman could. By which I don't mean he's a feminine: there's nothing like that about him at all.

At last I get him a job as a storekeep at the mine, but he just grunts when I tell him and hardly speaks to me for the two days before he's supposed to start. 'Like I'm treating him shit instead of doing him a favour,' I think, not trying too hard to remember that I'm doing myself a favour as well, and I decide that if he doesn't take the job, then that's it – he'll have to go and I'll have to crawl to get, at least, Stevie back. Larry I really don't think I can take anymore.

But when I wake, late, on the morning of the day he's due to clock in, me being on late afternoon and evening shift in the bar that week, he's gone, leaving his sleeping bag all over the floor, as is his way, and leaving also a note, saying I must put the flat's key under the mat on the front step so's he can get in when he signs off. So that's that, I think, but it's still not roses all the way because he's moaning all the time that (a) carrying all those heavy cases in the store's going to bugger up his hands, and then how's he going to play the guitar, and (b) the bucks are bad, which they are because the company takes on anybody, whether they are from Zaire, or Angola, or anywhere you want to name, and don't even care if you've got no papers because then they know you are desperate and they can pay you even less than they would a local boy, and the kid has no papers – or so he says – because he was robbed of them on the way up and must write for a copy of his book of life.

Anyway, when he gets his first pay, he buys himself a bed and what goes with it, and though I don't feel too happy about this because it's sort of strengthening his grip on the flat, I let it be, thinking, well, he can always take it with him when he goes someplace else and how can I expect the poor guy to go on sleeping on the floor like he's doing time or is a tramp? Not so easy to take is that he's bringing back stuff from the store – any kind of stuff, whether he can use it or it's junk – and sometimes he brings in eatables that can only have been meant for the Club and hands them to me, and though I suppose I should be chuffed that he's at last wanting to give something towards his keep, again I am not because it's a further strengthening of his hold on the flat and Claire's beginning to ask what the fuck's going on, though she doesn't use language like that, but you know what I mean.

When I tackle him about the stuff from the store, he says not to fret because he's signing for it, but I have my doubts about that, like I'm beginning to have my doubts about a lot of other things, like he's having been robbed of his book of life, because, one morning – he being as sloppy as he is about everything except his music and his looks – he's left his birth certificate and other papers on the table alongside the usual bottle of peppermint liqueur, and I can't help but read the name on it even without picking it up, as I can't help but wonder why it's only the book of life that is gone. Quickly, not feeling good about it but knowing I'm going to do it all the same, I shuffle through the other papers and a photo drops out – a jazzed-up studio shot of the kid when he's a little younger, but still definitely the kid, and his name's written on the back of it in the leaning over backwards scrawl of the note he left me about the key – and now I'm *really* worried because the name on the certificate is not the same as the name on the photo, and neither is the same as the name he's using right now, and I'm thinking, 'Shit! this guy's got names like a cat's got fleas!'

I say nothing though because I have had a hard life that's given me a hard crust with a soft heart somewhere underneath, and I live by the principles of don't poke your nose into other people's affairs when you don't want them to do the same to yours, and don't judge a man (or a woman) until you know all there is to know about them, which you never will, though you and they live to be a hundred years. Which is why I feel bad about having gone through the kid's papers, and why I feel bad about the morning, a few days after that, when he, not meaning to, surprises me into again not being the guy I am trying to be.

That is the morning when I am on day shift – like he permanently is – and I get up before him and go to sit on his bed, where he's still lying staring up at the ceiling, so's I can talk to him about an idea I have for the band, but he jerks his legs back from under the arm I have laid over them and wrestles out of the bed, blanket and all, wrapping himself in it as though I might get to see more than his bare chest or back, and says, 'No, wait, I got to get up now,' and I think, 'Just like the time we had the row about sleeping in one bed.' The pillow shifts then and something drops out from under it and clatters onto the floor, but he doesn't see or hear it because his back's turned to me and he's busy pulling on his shirt, blanket still around his waist, and I'm wondering what he's going to do about the jeans. It's a knife I hear fall – dagger-shaped blade honed till it sings and handle all ivory and mother-of-pearl – and I pick it up and say with a teasing that's sharper than just that and that I cannot help, 'Some knife. This also from the store?' knowing, as he will know I know, that that could never be. Shocked, he swings round, nearly letting the blanket fall, and snatches the knife from me, his face tearing open at the seams with a rage that's more fear than rage. 'That's mine!' he yells.

'I never said it wasn't,' I say, trying for control, and walk off and don't speak to him till the next day.

But the worry about a job for the kid – and then about how he's handling it – though it turns out to be the biggest of my worries because, in the end, it brings me right back to the Windhoek interview and my worrying even then about the kid's past – is not the only monkey on my back – and, ja, 'monkey' *is* the right word here because the worst of the other worries keeps on at me just like any drug.

Its name is 'girls' – 'Buddy Silver's girls' – and, in the long run, it has to do with me and Claire.

At the start, after each of the first few gigs, the kid would leave the cunt that was his for the taking, and come home with me – and, ja, I hear myself also now speaking of the flat as though it's his home too, and still not quite liking what I hear – and go into the toilet and do whatever it is he does to himself there to make himself human again, and perhaps have a sluk of the peppermint liqueur, each time shouting, 'Prettier than a flower', so's it's beginning to get a bit on my nerves. But it couldn't last, and I never thought it would, because he's randy and young, and even I, who am so much older than him that he cannot believe he will ever get to be here, must have the old testes cleaned out more now than then.

So it comes that, on the last Saturday of the month, I don't get back to the flat till first light, old Hawkeyes asking me to stay on after the gig so's to help him check the bar and bottle store stock, the auditors wanting the figures the next day, and I take the key from the cracked-open kitchen window's sill, which is the way we do it when things get as complicated as this and me not at all ready yet for the kid to have his own key, and open the door and go in, and it's quiet, and grey with the dawn, and the kid is making little puffing sounds like he does when he snores. But there's something else – something that's only here when Claire's been here, which she hasn't since the kid's moved in – and the old cock lifts a little as it smells woman-scent and man-scent and knows there's been a lot of fucking done while the cat's away, and when I go into the toilet for a piss, I see there's two condoms in the bowl that he's been too don't-care to even flush, but that's okay by me because now I know that, at least, he's wearing the skins and not rolling the dice with death.

I don't say anything the next morning since it's not my business, and, in a way, it's better so because the kid is hard enough to handle without him being sex-starved as well, and I'm only hoping *he'll* remember it's not my business and keep his sex life to himself so's not to make things more dicey for me than they already are. But I should have known Buddy Silver never does things by halves and, since he thinks my saying nothing means it's okay by me, it's only a matter of time before, straight after every gig, there's a bimbo in the next room for as long as she can stand it, which means not for very long, and I'm going gaga from wanting him to go and do his fucking where I can't hear. I try to solve the problem by once more doing the rounds of the big boys, pleading with them to now give the kid a place of his own, but they say, no, the mine quarters are overcrowded as it is and if I don't want him to stay with me anymore, then he will have to find work someplace else and they'll take on a local boy who doesn't need a roof that's the mine's.

So I'm stuck and must go on listening to what I, at first, don't want to hear, but that, at the end, is sucking me in like a quicksand that wants me to be sand like it's sand and won't let me go till I am. I have my principles, as I said before, and I don't like talking about what I do to my women in bed, any more than I like talking about what other guys do to theirs, but if I don't tell this thing like it is – or how, to me, it is – it's going to sound like it's not for real. The trouble is not *what* the kid does to his bimbos, but *how* he does it, like he *hates* them rather than loves them, biting their necks, lips, breasts, all the while he's ramming his cock into them like he wishes it could nail them to the bed, and then rolling them over, while they fight and moan, lust turning into terror and tears, and giving it to them from the other side, and going on and on without, it seems, ever spitting out what's worrying him, that he hates as much as he's hating them, till at last they break from him like he's a devil and flail off through the dark like crippled birds, and never speak of what happened to them because what were they doing in his sack anyway?

Ja, that's the way it is – that part of it anyway – but there's more, and this part is harder to tell, and I still don't know, concerning it, if what I am feeling is wonder at a beautiful thing in a shape of shit, or a shame that will be scarring me for the rest of my time. All I know is that, because the wall between us is so thin that I can hear every thrust, whisper and last cry, it is becoming more and more as though I am right there with the kid, *am* him, fucking these women till their flesh sucks between my sweat-wet thighs, turning them then over, doing it from that side, and, with each thrust, growing closer to him in another way – a way that has nothing to do with desire or flesh, but is just a sharing, a knowing that, together, we are not alone. And it seems to work both ways, because although he's got no more to say to me than before, he now sometimes comes up for me, like when, maybe, we are in a bar, and someone chaffs me because I'm drinking ginger ale, and he'll say, 'So? It's his gut, isn't it?' and I'll smile inside though I say, 'Cool it. It's okay.'

Anyway, to tell the all of this while I still feel I can, I get so horny from what I'm listening to, that I go to see Claire for the first time since the kid's hit town, and she opens the door, and because we're more careful than this when it's at her place, the boys being too young to accept what is going on and she too bloodyminded to marry me, though I have asked her to often enough, she looks surprised and says 'Hi!' but like she doesn't know if she shouldn't rather close the door. Then she sees from my eyes I must have it, and I see from her eyes that she wants it like that too, it having been quite a while, and she says, low, 'Wait till the boys are in bed,' and I wait till she shuts their door and we go into her room, and she takes off her clothes and I take off mine, and we lie, side-by-side, on the bed and she begins to play with my cock like Anna played with the kid's hand.

But I'm looking at her and seeing what is there to see – a growing grey English girl who came to this country to marry her man, then stayed on after he died because she said she felt sorry for the blacks and wanted to show them that she was not like the other whites who were giving them a bum deal, but can't remember now when last she was in the location or compound – and I touch the English cheeks with their don't-wash-off apple's red, the cropped like a man's anyhow hair, the springy thighs that bounce her round like a hockey mistress at a school for girls, and there's nothing there for me anymore because, although she's no slouch in bed, she only knows the missionary position and I am listening to the wilder couplings of another world.

So the old man doesn't come up under her hand, though she's breathing hard from wanting him to be in her and her cunt's like oil when I start playing around with it like she's playing around with me, but nothing works till I start thinking she's not Claire but one of the bimbos, and the kid and I are doing our tandem act back at the flat, and then I am up and away and she's panting 'Yes! Yes!' and opening up wide, but I'm not me anymore and I'm turning her round so's I can take her from behind, and at first she doesn't know what's going on, then she does, and she's rolling away from me over the bed and screaming, 'You dirty queer! So that's what's going on over there!' and she's out of the room, bare-arsed as she is, and into the toilet and I hear her sobbing behind the door.

The crying gets to me and although I know it's all gone dead for me as it's gone dead for her, I want to tell her I'm sorry and that she's got it all wrong when it comes to me and the kid, and I knock on the door and call her name, but she screams, 'Get out! Get out!' and I cover up quick and do just that because any moment now the kids will come running out of their room and then the shit will *really* hit the fan.

That Saturday, at the gig, I'm still feeling bad and banging the skins as badly as I feel, and the kid's hissing at me like a snake to for Chrissake wake up, and I happen to look out over the floor and there's she sitting, all on her own, the first time I ever seen her at a gig, and her eyes are like stones.

And I look further and there's Stevie and Larry, teamed up again, and their eyes are the same, and though fat Anna's still smiling, I know she's only biding her time as she watches the kid and the latest of the bimbos he's calling 'his girl' and lets sit next to him while he's playing like she's a good luck charm, and I get this feeling, that is more than just a feeling, that it's time for me to be getting out of here while I still can.

But I'm a stubborn ou and the next morning I phone Claire to ask her for her duplicate key to the flat, and she tells me to get stuffed, or words that mean that, so I go down to the locksmiths and have another key made to give to the kid and pretend I don't hear the howling in the hills.

* * *

So I stay put and feel a bit of a cunt for even thinking of pulling the plug, because suddenly we are hitting a good stretch and the wheels are humming and we are on a high. Or perhaps I should change that to 'on a roll' because the kid is not doing what I was scared he would and that I was bracing myself for, which is walk in the shit as well as the shadows of the big ones who die before their time. Instead of stepping up his taking of whatever it is he takes behind the flat's toilet door, he seems more and more to be doing without it, and is even putting on a little weight, which he needed to, although he moans that he is getting fat. What it is he takes, I still don't know and may never know, because except for sharing a dagga-zoll now and again and, when I was younger, trying a little LSD, I am not with it when it comes to the druggie scene and not interested enough to want to know more.

But I *am* interested in why the kid's getting to what, in these parts, is the top – though in the real world it is still pretty much near to the bottom of the pile – does not make him freak out more instead of less. Is it because there is no competition – because he is so far ahead of a lousy field? Or is it because he's seeing things in quite some other way – is seeing himself not so much hanging in there at the top as coming in from the cold, of being *accepted*, of getting right what, in spite of his 'look no hand's, Dad' show-off, he secretly feared he never would?

Something chimes in me, deep down, wanting me to go on, but I'm afraid it's a mirage, that if I get too close, it will be gone and there'll be only me, and then, as I said, we have hit this good stretch and I'm feeling like you do when summer's back when it shouldn't be, and I just want to take off and enjoy it and not play shrink and try and sort out why Buddy Silver's the way he is. Besides, I have now got some *real* managing to do because it's not just here I'm talking about when I talk about a good stretch, but all the even smaller dumps stuck away in the bush, and once even Windhoek itself when old Hawkeyes gives me a whole weekend off to set up a gig and get the band, and some of our fans, down to there with anything that's got wheels. 'Go for it, Clive,' he says. 'Maybe you'll make us a down south Sun City yet,' and he smiles one of those smiles of his that look like he's been grabbed in the gut.

Ja, that Windhoek paper for sure opened the doors for us and I'm feeling two ways at once – worried because I have got so much arranging to do and younger than I have for a long time because I *have* got so much arranging to do – and I'm enjoying *getting* to the gigs as much as the gigs themselves: the kid and I on the Honda and the heavy stuff under a tarp in Ginger's old van. And when I say 'old', I mean *old* – mudguards fluttery as an old man's hands and a jerry of water with the gear for the radiator when it boils.

Sometimes the roads – like to Grootfontein, Otavi, Windhoek, and even to Ondangwa in Ovamboland – are thumbs up, but the branch-offs to places like Abenab and Tsintsabis – both just about making it onto the map – can be the pits and you got to grit your teeth like they're going to fall out and a guy on a pillion gets to hang on like he's humping the guy in the seat. And it's then I think back to when the kid didn't want to sleep in the same bed with me, and yet he's clawing into me now like I'm one of his bimbos after a gig, and how does he square that with whatever funniness is in his blood? Well, you could say he doesn't mind if *he's* doing the clawing, but it mustn't be the other way around, but that doesn't wash because he's liking the bike so much, and I'm feeling so different about him these days, that sometimes (though he never *asks* like on that first day) I give him the seat and let him stand my hair up straight, and then it *is* the other way around.

Weird! – as when we stop beside the road (where else?) for a piss, and Ginger and Denny stop further back and wait, or maybe also piss, and the kid doesn't turn around from his bush till he's zipped or buttoned up his fly, depending on what kind of jeans he's got on at the time, but I turn round still stuffing mine back in and carry on talking like pissing is just the another kind of chore that it is. Or sometimes, mostly when I'm up front, I will stop for no reason other than to sit still for a minute or two and listen to the cicadas screaming like crazy in the sun, or watch the air, that seems old as Whatever's up there, shimmying over the leaves – or maybe it's just the stones or the sand – and that's all there is to see and it goes on so forever that I want to turn round and touch the kid to make sure he's for real, and he will say, 'Scary,' or something else like that that shows he understands and feels the same, though every other time all he thinks about (other than how to wow the crowds) is cunt, junk food and peppermint liqueur.

Or so it seems, and it never seems more so than when we get to wherever we are going and the maestro could be anyone of us: the T-shirt under his arms dark as blood with sweat, his hair gone blond as Larry's from the dust and his face like some tribal who's geared himself for love or war. It's the only times that I hear him ask for beer instead of peppermint liqueur, and the Husky for Men's long gone and he's smelling just like the rest of the animals around, and we've never been more easy with each other like it's that golden time that never is because you know from the start that it's got to end.

Windhoek, of course, is not that kind of scene – little big city, airport, casinos, ice in the drinks, settlers grinning like they don't hate it when there's a black man alongside them at the bar – but I'm not remembering it the way I am those places where you've got to make do with anything that's over your head, and the piano is an animal that died a trillion years ago, and it's just drums, bass, guitars, and the kid belting it out non-stop till he's sounding like he's getting a hernia in his throat, and I'm close to loving him more than I know I should. Sometimes we get twenty couples, sometimes less, and though this time the door's all ours, we still make a loss, unless you count in the drinks – beer, hard stuff, my ginger ale – that, like with the grub, is for free and don't be shy, and that I let the band pig out on like I don't at base, because the night is long and, by dawn, the locals will have their arms around our necks and we'll be swearing blood brotherhood with guys whose names we don't even know. And – ja – though it's not as up and coming at you as at the Club, there's here and there even a bit of cunt – usually in the back of the van – and though, as I said before, I don't like flashing what I do, I also don't want to make like I'm any better than the rest and not confess that I take the latex along and also drop my pants when the chance comes my way. Which it does more often than I expect because booze and me being on the drums makes lust love me like I'm half my age, and though I know this is not me, but the me she left me with when she fucked off with the other guy, I go for it, what with me being now without the easy lay that was Claire.

Back on the home turf, which is usually late on the Saturday, we doss down, quick, and catch all the kip we can before the usual dance at the Club, and it is then that the kid still sometimes gets in behind the toilet door, and I can guess how he feels because I know how I feel, and sometimes I'm wanting to get right in there with him, but, old alky that I am, I'm scared as all shit now of anything that grabs me instead of me grabbing it. I can hear the band sounds a bit rough after we have been out of town, but it's still pretty good and we have a reputation now that goes further than here, and we're learning to lean on that a bit – though not too much – just enough so's we can rest without going off the rails.

Claire's still not on walkabout, telling everybody I'm a queer, or I would have heard it by now, and I try to tell myself that everything's back to normal after the few fuck-ups that seem to have done us more good than harm, but I know I'm lying and that, inside, I am still as jumpy as that night I looked round the lounge and saw them all sitting there, watching me like wolves and wishing I was dead. And I know that's the way I still am because sometimes I'm looking at a shop window, or anything else that catches you like a charm catches a witch, and Claire's face is suddenly there behind my shoulder, staring at me with those eyes like a stone head's, and I don't turn round when it jerks aside because to know it's real, or to know I'm seeing what's not there, is either way as bad as it can come. Or I will again look around the lounge at a gig and see Larry and Stevie are not there, but I know their cars are standing outside, and I get this feeling that they *are* in the lounge, but sitting where I won't expect them to – or they are wearing other faces that they can put on and take off when they want so's they can watch the kid and me from right up close like flies on a wall.

Which last part sounds pretty weird, I know, but that's the way it is when you are old as me and been kicked in the butt so many times, you keep turning round to see who's the next to put in the boot – and what I am *very* sure about is that Anna's breaking cover as I all along knew she would, because, one Saturday afternoon before the gig, the kid and I are sitting in the lounge sharing a paper from down South, and Anna passes and touches my shoulder and says, 'Let me buy you a drink, Clive,' and goes and sits down two tables away.

'Like I'm her rent boy,' I say to the kid, but he doesn't look up, and I say I better go find out what she wants before she makes trouble for me or the band, and don't go away because I'll be back.

'Bring me a gin-and-lime, one cube ice,' she says to the tribal when I sit down, 'and bring him a ginger ale, no ice,' and I tip the hat I don't have on because she knows my habits like she knows her own, and she signs the card for the drinks when they come and looks at me over the rim of her glass and says, 'Skol!'

I raise my glass and mutter something, but don't ask me what, and she lights a cigarette, not offering me the pack because, again, she knows, and I pass her an ashtray when she hunts around.

'Bloody kaffirs,' she says. 'Can't even set a table right. God knows what's going to happen to this country now,' and I seethe but keep my mouth zipped because this is one raw racist looking at me and I don't want to be all shaken up before the gig.

'You were wanting something,' I say, rather than ask, trying to keep the acid out of my voice, and she nods, appreciating my not beating about the bush.

'Yes,' she says, 'I want to do something for the band.'

'Such as?'

'I want to buy Buddy a guitar. A decent, professional's guitar. He's too fine a talent to have to struggle with that horrible thing he's got now.'

'That horrible thing,' I say, deliberately echoing her and not caring anymore how my voice sounds, 'is a perfectly okay guitar that we hire from the Club and that will do until Buddy decides to buy his own guitar, which will maybe be in another month or so,' and I don't turn a hair as I lie like this to her face and swear to myself that, if I must, I will add my all to Buddy's nothing before I let her buy him a guitar.

'Buddy can never afford to buy the quality guitar I have in mind for him and that he deserves,' she says, and leans back and stares at me with the bright, try-again eyes of a bidder at an auction for slaves.

I do try again. 'You said you wanted to do something for the band. Now it seems it's more for Buddy than the band. Tell me' – and I lean forward trying to find her eyes in the smoke she's blowing round her like she's on fire inside – 'is it that you want to buy a guitar for Buddy, or is it that' – and I pause a moment, feeling rage uncoil in me like a snake till its tongue's saying for me what she's not going to believe she hears – 'you want to buy Buddy for what's between your legs?'

Her eyes pop as though I have grabbed her and I think the silence between us will never end and I might as well get up and go. But then she takes a sip of her gin-and-lime and asks, almost sadly, 'Why have you always hated me, Clive?'

'I don't hate you,' I say, thrown now and knowing she knows I lie. 'It's just that I don't think a kid like Buddy should get mixed up with someone so much older than himself,' and despise myself for backing down and sounding like the prissy old cunt that's suddenly taken over my chair.

She laughs, then, not putting on. 'Come now, Clive, that's not you.

Why didn't you say what you wanted to say. That you don't want Buddy
to shack up with an old whore like me? But isn't he already shacking
up with an old whore like you? Or what makes you think you can sleep
with that Claire, and probably other women too, if I know men, but
you are not a whore? But if I sleep with more than one man, I'm a
whore. Or does the fact that one of them is married to me make me
different from you? Woman or man, Clive, you and I are whores,
whichever way we turn. And, anyway, what is it to you if I sleep with
Buddy Silver or I don't? And don't tell me it's because he's a member
of your band. You wouldn't have had the nerve to ask me just now if I
wanted Buddy between my legs if there hadn't been more to it than
that. Is it because he's to you like a son? The son you couldn't give to
the woman you couldn't hold?'

I try to answer her, but my tongue's in a knot and I'm staring at her
like she's a light, and she laughs again and says, 'So! I may be a whore,
Clive, but I'm still a woman, and women know. And I'm sorry for you
that that is what it is,' and she leans over and pats my hand, and I'm so
out of my mind that I don't take it away, 'because I want Buddy Silver
like I haven't wanted a man for quite a time, and though my mirror
tells me straight what no woman wants to know,' and she looks down
at herself like she hates what she sees, than back at me, and for a
moment there's a dead girl somewhere behind her eyes, 'I have what
it takes to buy what I want and – since you asked me – yes, I will buy
Buddy Silver if there is no other way.'

And at last my tongue unties itself and I hear it say, 'And so make
him not only a whore, but a *paid* whore. That is what you want?'

'Why not?' and she mashes her cigarette in the ashtray like it's a
living thing. 'To borrow a phrase from you – I'm interested in what is
between his legs. Nothing else,' and she spreads her hands on the
table to show me her rings, and smiles like we are the best of friends.

I can see now that she wants me to leave, but I can't just let her
have the last word or I'll never get her hand off my balls. But what can
I say? Then it comes to me: a little bullshit, a little the way it is. 'Three
things,' I say, and I'm right back at the station helping the kid fetch
his stuff in the faraway. 'Three things you forgot to think about. One,
you've shown me your hand, but I haven't shown you mine. Two, it's
opening to me that maybe you're right, that maybe I do sort of feel
that Buddy is my son, which means that I'm going to *fight* for him like
he's my son. And three, the way that kind of love is, you're not going
to know which way it jumps if you win.'

But she's not fazed. 'I'll not be going to him,' she smiles. 'He'll be
coming to me. Again – I'm woman – I know. Your fight will be with

him, not me.'

Now I *have* to go and she's had the last word, because what can I do to her if it turns out the way she says? I walk a hundred miles back to where the kid is folding up the paper and she shafts me one last time when she shouts, 'Don't forget the guitar will always be there if you change your mind.'

'What's this about a guitar?' asks the kid, and I think, 'Bitch!' because she's worked it so's *I* have to tell him, not her.

So I tell him and he lays down the paper and smooths it with his palm. 'Save for the udders and the lard, and probably a cunt like a tunnel, it could be not such a bad idea. Maybe I'll think about it sometime.'

'Don't think about it too hard,' I say, and I see my hands beginning to shake like they do when I have had as much as I can take for now, 'or you'll be giving away a fucking sight more than your cock,' and wish, too late, that I had handed it to him straight and said 'selling' and not 'giving away' his cock.

He, too, sees me shake and cackles, knowing by now what that means. 'She's got you worried, hey?' he says, and pushes up from his chair. 'Well, that's what women are for, or where've you been all this time?' and goes into the bar, leaving me hanging and nervy as all hell.

✳ ✳ ✳

A week later and Anna's still with me, running around in my mind like it's a cage, and I'm getting as moody and uncomfortable to live with as the kid, only I feel bad about it, while the kid couldn't give two fucks and even steps up the sulks if he sees he's getting under your skin. The next gig comes around, but Anna, worryingly, is not there – the first time that I can remember that she is not – but Claire is – teamed up now with Larry and Stevie whom she got to know through me before the Fall, and she looks like what she is – a housewife at a Woodstock for punks – and she's laughing too loud and making like she's having a great time, but her eyes are in the back of her head, watching me watching her, and I'm wondering who's looking after the kids.

Then, the Monday after the gig, they send the kid down to Windhoek for some emergency stores and he says he'll be away for a few days, and I'm on afternoon/evening shift, which means that in the mornings I have the flat to myself and either stay there or do the rounds in town. On Tuesday, I stay there and am brewing a late coffee, when there's a knock on the door. It's not Ginger's 'Hey, you there?' ratatat, or Denny's never more, never less than five bangs like it's a secret code only he and I use, but the 'should I, shouldn't I?' tap-tap of someone who hasn't been to the flat before.

I open the door and he's a very small man – all bones, but like that's the way he always is – like a cricket's the way it always is – and I'm thinking he would be just about as quick as that, though he's old. Well, he's older than me, but how much I can't say because though he's wrinkled like a paper you grabbed and threw away, and the natty little moustache is white as a scut against his skin's brown as my shoe, his eyes are bright as buttons and younger than I feel. He's wearing a faded khaki shirt and pants that have been washed till they ache, and the pants are hitched up with braces, which is something I haven't seen since I don't know when, and when he takes off his old-style cloth cap, I see his scalp, shining like he's polished it, is pushing up, high, through the last of his hair.

'Good morning, sir,' he says, turning the cap round in his hands, his voice soft and respectful, but his eyes not shying away, and I say, 'Hi,' liking him like you sometimes can someone you don't even know.

He says he's looking for somebody and gives me the names, and my heart flip-flops like it's a fish he's hooked, and I'm trying not to show my mind's running around, because the names are the names on the kid's birth certificate and I do not know what I must do. Must I tell him he's come to the right door because maybe he's got something to say that the kid must hear, or must I play dumb – which I can because I'm not supposed to know these names – and maybe save the kid from this nice little guy that's no nice little guy at all, but a devil from the past with a tail in his pants long as my arm? I play for time, saying, 'Williams? Vernon Williams?' like I'm thinking out loud, watching the worn-through hands turning the cap, then my mind gets it right and there's no problem because I never saw that certificate and that's how I got to play this thing, but I also got to know more so's there's light in the road and I don't let the kid maybe walk into a bad place and his blood's on my hands.

'No,' I say at last, 'I don't know any guy that's calling himself by those names,' and think that's not a bad try at telling a lie that's not a lie. 'But why did you come to me?'

'Well, you see, sir, it's like this,' and the hands are turning the cap faster now, 'Vernon wrote his ma, saying he's playing in a band up here, though he didn't say where, and so his ma asked me when I'm up here – I'm driver in a transport company, sir – to look around and see if I can find Vernon and tell him his ma got his card and she says to take care.'

'You come all this way from the Cape?' I ask, and could bite my tongue for saying that because why should I think he's from the Cape when I'm not supposed to know where this Vernon is from?

But it doesn't click with him, he probably thinking all whites know everything anyway. 'No, I'm not in the Cape anymore, sir. I'm in Windhoek now. Came here with the independence because, down South, it was trouble all the time and I could see the boss was thinking maybe a younger man would be better for the job. Vernon's ma was born in Windhoek, sir, and it was she that said I should try my luck here, and I must say, praise the Lord, it's worked out just fine and I've never had it so good as now.'

'And Mrs Williams? Is she still down at the Cape?'

'No, sir, she's come back to her home town, although it hasn't helped her the way it's helped me. You see, sir, she's a very strong-minded woman and we belong to the same Church that doesn't care what's the colour of your skin, and she's not afraid to say or do what she believes is right, and a lot of people, here like down South, don't like her for that and walk round her like she's not there. But I can tell you, sir, she's a very fine white lady, she is. Not like so many other white ladies I meet up with, if you don't mind me saying so, sir.'

'I don't mind at all,' I say, 'and I wish you would cut out this "sir" crap. This is a new country, you know.'

He smiles. 'Well, you wouldn't always think that, sir. Most times, here or down South, I still have to remember what I am, or be told what I am in the way it always was.' But there's no bitterness in his voice and it's like he's telling me it's not such a nice day, but that's my white man's God's will and so be it, Amen. 'But I thank you all the same, sir. It's very kind of you to say what you did,' and I know I can forget about him cutting out the 'sir' because this is a born fucked-up last of his kind who would go on kissing my arse even while I'm kicking the shit out of his, which would take a bit of doing, I know, but you get what I mean.

But he's also a sweet old guy that some women would like to cuddle without wanting him up them, and I see the coffee in the mug in my hand is getting cold, and all this while we're standing on the step like I'm just another white racist who's not wanting him further than my door, and I take him by the arm and say to him to step inside and have some coffee and rolls. He holds back, saying it's only another hour before he must be on the road again, but I say, 'Time enough,' and let him sit on the chair in my room because I'm not sure what sort of stuff the kid has left lying around in his.

Then, from the kitchen, where I am making fresh coffee, I suddenly remember something and shout out to him through the 'serving hatch' that is just a chunk left out of the wall, 'Hey! you haven't told me yet why you came to *me* about this Vernon of yours,' and I think, 'Ja, "yours" is right, because no ways yet can I feel that Vernon Williams is the Buddy Silver I know and am hanging onto like in a bad dream.'

'Is true, sir. Must have slipped my mind,' he shouts back. 'You see, sir, I went to the Club first but the old boss there said, no, there's no Vernon Williams playing in their band, and I must try the hotels, or maybe you, sir, because you know all the musicians in these parts. So I go to the hotels, but there's only Germans playing in their bands, and then I came to you, sir, and now I don't know where else to go.'

'But surely,' I say, remembering now also the card, 'the postmark on that card to Mrs Williams could tell you where it's from. *Was* it from here?'

'No, sir, it wasn't from here. It was from Abenab, and I already been there. But nothing, sir. Nothing. So I thought, well, maybe he *posted* it there, but stays someplace else. So now I've been asking at other places as well.'

'Sounds like Mrs Williams's boy is on the run,' I laugh, but not really laughing, if you know what I mean. 'Is he a bit of a wild one, this guy?'

There is such a long silence from my room that I look through the 'hatch' to see if he's still there. And he is, sitting quite still, staring at the wall. At last, carefully, he says, 'Well yes, sir, you might say he's that. To tell you the truth, sir, his ma's gone quite grey because of him and many's the time I'm thinking he's going one way.' He doesn't say what the 'one way' is, and I know I should press him on that – as I should press him more about Mrs Williams – or about himself – but if I'm already getting so close as to make him pause, then I am getting *too* close and soon now he's going to start suspecting that I know more than I am saying and I'll be pointing him back to the flat instead of away.

So I take in the coffee and some rolls and cheese and I see he's hungry though not wanting it to show, and we talk about other things, and, eventually, without me trying for it, he tells me more about himself, though it's only to do with how hard it is to be what he is, but without getting angry about it – without *doing* anything about it – till I'm despising and liking him more and more at the same time. And every now and then, he tilts up his head and his eyes hide as though he's listening to something only he hears, and I know I have seen that way with the head before. Or he passes his hand over his nearly all gone hair, or holds his groin like nervy men do when fear is grabbing them there. But he does not seem to be a nervy man and there's nothing to fear, and I know all this I too have seen, and I get the feeling that if I go on looking at him long enough, I will find some quite other spook growing out of him on my chair. But then he says he must leave, and gets up and offers me his hand, but shyly, like he expects me to slap it down, and puts on his cap and hitches up his braces and, halfway down the street, turns to wave because he senses I am watching him go, and it is only then that it comes to me that I never asked him his name.

Thursday the kid's back and he's tired and cheesed off from the long ride, and I fix him something to eat while he takes a bath, and all the time I'm cracking eggs into the pan and slicing the bread, I'm asking myself, 'Must I tell him? Must I shut my mouth?' Then the food's fixed and he's sitting down to it, and I decide, 'Fuck it, it's his *mother* we're talking about. How can I *not* tell him that his mother reached out her hand?' and I step off into the dark, but casual, like it's nothing to me, and say, 'A guy was here. Tuesday. Asking for you. Didn't give me his names, like he didn't give me yours.'

Sharp as a fox, the kid looks up, 'Then how did you know he was for me?'

'He gave me other names.' I say, looking past him at nothing at all, wanting to keep this calm.

'*Other* names?' the kid repeats, trying for dumb, but it doesn't wash because he doesn't ask, as any other guy would, what the names *were*, and it's like that's a snake he had best leave alone. 'Then, still, how did you know he was for me?'

'He described you like you are,' I lie, holding the certificate to my chest like it's a card and I'm in the game. 'But I said there's no guy by those names living here. And I said that' – and for the first time I look at him, hard, because I can hear from his voice that the shit's going to hit the fan no matter what I do – 'I said that because, you using different names, maybe you don't want to know this guy anymore.'

But the kid's still under control, only pushing the food around in his plate like there's a bug there he's got to find. 'So you don't know what it was he had to tell?'

'I know all right. We had a conversation and he happened to say he's from Windhoek and the guy with the other names, who's a muso, has a mother there, and the mother says she got the card and he must take care.'

'How did he know he must come here?' asked the kid, still pushing the food around and his voice thin as a hair.

'He didn't. The card was stamped in Abenab, but there's no one there, so he reckons this guy with the other names is hiding someplace else,' and I say *"hiding"* like I'm banging on the big skin, 'and he tries old Hawkeyes and old Hawkeyes says to try me because I know all the musos in these woods.'

'Describe him to me,' says the kid and his voice is harsh as two irons rubbing in the wind.

'Short, thin, little white moustache, head going egg, khaki shirt, pants, braces for the pants, praises the Lord like he means what he says.'

So suddenly that I jump though I'm ready for it, the kid slams his fist on the table and eggs and wors splatter over the cloth like a bullet's blown out a brain. 'Stompie!' he snarls. *'That* little hotnot shit? Why doesn't he fucking well leave me alone!' and he lifts up his head like he's listening to something only he can hear, and I see his hand's going for his groin like it's piss or bust, and suddenly Tuesday's back on the chair in my room and I'm thinking, 'Christ! how could I have been so blind!'

'No,' I say, and can't believe that I'm sounding this calm, 'It's not *him* that's the little hotnot shit. How can you talk like that about your own dad?'

At first I think he hasn't heard me because his face doesn't change. Lip peeling from his teeth and head stuck out like it is, he's like some sad, wild thing, back to the wall and listening for if its time has come, and, crazy like I sometimes can be, I'm thinking of my own long gone old ma who always used to say, 'You pull your face like that and the clock strikes twelve, you will never get it back the way it was.' But no clock strikes and, quicker than I can wink, his face suddenly is blank, but blank like it's blind, and he's up, tipping the chair over, hard, and running – ja, *running* – for the door, which is shut, and he rams into it, full-face, like he doesn't even know it's there. 'Christ!' I think and want to look away but can't, and he's round and staring at me, but eyes so squint it's like he isn't, and I want to turn to see who's watching me watching him, but don't because that's crap and I know it, and blood is pouring from his nose where it hit the door, and it's running all over the clean 'Peace' T-shirt he put on after he bathed, and he doesn't lift a hand to it because his mind is back where his body's not and I am never going to be.

'*All right*, then,' says Vernon Williams, and the little hairs in my neck are standing up straight because his voice is far-off and flat like a ghost's, though I never yet seen a ghost, let alone heard one speak. 'So he told you. The little creep told you. So go on, whiteboy. Go tell the world there never was no Buddy Silver. That's what you got to do, isn't it? Got to keep your yours-only john clean. See no little coloured shit like me's pissing on the tiles. It's like my ma always said – and she's a whitey, too, so she ought to know – "Don't do it Vernie. Don't go gate-crashing their party, because they'll get you in the end. The law's changed, but their hearts haven't. Won't, maybe for another hundred years. Maybe never, if I know them." But I didn't listen. Wanted to see what it's like to walk without my head hanging like my cock, do the things I never done before, move in the places where they *say* I can now go in, but where, if I'm not Buddy Silver, I'm still on the outside looking in even when I'm in. So when she follows the creep she let be up her, so's there's now another reject dragging itself around like a dog that's been under the wheels, and she says, "Come with, it's better up there," I say, "No," though my heart wants because I don't know how long she can still hold out, what with her missing her own kind and them walking long ways round her because she's shacked up with this coloured stud that's praising the Lord even when he fucks. But it doesn't work out, so I come up here, straight from down there, so's "daddy" doesn't know where I am and can louse up my act like he's just done, and I got to say,' and he smiles, but like a shark smiles when it smells the meat, 'it was great for so long as I got it right. My head wasn't down there by my balls anymore, and I fucked the tits off your little white whores because it made me feel like I'm wearing their skins, and I knew if they knew it's a black cock they got stuck in them, they'll be spitting on me though I sing like a bird.'

Then he's out of breath, and he smoothes back his hair like he's his dad and it turns red from the blood, and he looks at his hands and sees them for the first time, and his eyes tell he's at last feeling the pain in his face, and not just what's deeper down, and again he smiles, if you can call it that, and pushes away from the door and says, 'Well, I better clean up now and get my things together so's I can go,' and he opens the door, and is passing through it, when he turns around a second time and makes a fuck-you kind of little bow like he's playing his dad for laughs, and says, 'And thank you, Mr Clive, for having me here,' and is gone.

I sit very still, looking down at my hands, hearing a bird making sad sounds in the banana trees, hearing him wash his face, gather up his gear. Then he's coming back for a clean T-shirt, bloodied one rolled into a plastic bag so's he can wash it wherever he's going to now, brown skin from the waist up – now that I *know* – clearly a brown man's, and I think of the card I'm still keeping close to my chest and say, 'Hold it right there,' and he turns and comes to the table and looks down at me, his face like the wall.

'You must do what you feel you got to do,' I say, slowly, thinking ahead of each word, 'but before you get so far, there's no turning back, there's something you need to know, and that is that this guy you so hate, though there's so much of love in *him* that he's hunting like crazy for you all over the goddam map, *never* told me what were your real names. I knew them a long time ago because you left your birth certificate right here on this table, wide-open and stupid, so's I could not help but read it, and I never told anybody about that, so why should I tell them now that you're not white?'

'Because having two names is not the same as being not white, that's why,' he hits back, face still like the wall.

'Okay,' I say, giving in on that because it's a smart point, but still seeing the way forward, another card suddenly in my hand, 'but if I'm such a racist – if I'm seeing you like you're just an animal – or whatever else it is you think I'm seeing – why should I care about you bad-mouthing your dad?' and now he's looking at me as though I am there and I go for the vein. 'Buddy Silver, or Vernon Williams, or whatever the hell else you want to call yourself,' and I am thinking now of the photo, but holding my tongue, because now's not the time to start another devil running around in this room, 'nothing's changed, and nothing's going to change, unless you walk out of that door, when you can go fuck your hand, for all I care.'

Slowly he sits down, holding my eyes, wrestling them, like it's my arm he must make hit the table first, but it's a draw and he leans over and picks up the bottle of peppermint liqueur from where it always stands, and screws off the cap and brings the neck to his mouth and swallows till the liqueur is dribbling all over his chin. Then he re-caps the bottle and carefully puts it down where it belongs, but doesn't say, 'Prettier than a flower,' as he used to do, and I'm wanting to think his eyes are wet with more than just the washing of the blood from his face, or the sting of the liqueur in his throat, but I can't be sure.

Then he gets up and goes as far as the door and stands, back to me, wrestling now with something more than just my eyes, and at last says, 'Thanks,' his voice harsh and sharp as a bark, but I know it's the best he can do and I let out my breath like it's been a long day, though it's still only an hour after noon. It's also only three more hours to my shift, so I lie down on my bed to kip a little before the long haul to midnight, and sometimes later if there's a party going on, and I hear him washing the shirt and putting his gear out again, and, when I wake, it's time and so quiet in the other room that I fall over my feet in my hurry to check, thinking that, after all, he's gone.

But he's still there, lying, fully dressed, on his bed, his face to the wall, and somehow I know he's awake, but wanting to be alone, and I go out and the heat's like a hand round my throat and there's thunder in the air.

***

The way the kid was, lying there on the bed, staring at the wall, quiet as though he's lost a love or a hope, stays with me. I say to myself, 'Not to worry. He'll come right. Just give him time.' But he doesn't, though you wouldn't know it, looking at him just on the outside. At the Club, he still bullshits his fans, putting his arm round the girls, talking to each as though she's the only one for him, cuddling her with a hand that's just missing the tits and she hoping he'll dare. But, somehow, it's more than ever before like pulling the chain and there's water in the bowl, and when he gets back to the flat, he takes it all off like he's taking off his shirt, and he's looking at the wall again without lying down.

It's not so much that he is *moody* – although he is still that too – but more like he is *busy* with something that's got nothing to do with anybody but himself and if you talk to him about it, he'll slap you down. But again, you sense, he won't do that by telling you to go fuck your hand, but just look at you like you're a little kid who's talking shit and please don't worry me now. But it's *me* that's beginning to worry now as the weeks pass, and his head keeps lifting like he's listening for something at the door, and he's more and more like a glass you dropped and you can't stick the pieces together again. 'Something's going to break,' I think. 'Something's *got* to break. It can't go on like this,' and something *does* break, but not as I expected and in the most gross possible way.

We are playing at the Club, the night the shit hits the fan, and the lounge is packed like I haven't seen it for a long time – mostly with hicks from the bush who look like they should be at a Gospel meeting rather than in our sham palace of not so sham sin – and a guy from up near the Pan, who's brought his wife and all six kids, calls me over between numbers and asks if I'll play something slow, so's he and his wife can dance, she getting heavy in the haunch and not so quick on the floor. I say, 'Sure,' though I'm not liking it, because the kid has been listening to the door all day and is strung up as all hell and showing it, and he hates playing stuff like this ou wants and this might just be the one more grab that's too much to stand.

But the hick's a regular, and regulars you got to keep, so I tell the kid and he grinds his teeth like he's a boerboel tasting the flesh – the hick's flesh – and hisses, 'Fuck it! that's all I need!' and drops the guitar and moves to go to the piano, which he must do to give the guy what he wants, and Denny's just then crossing over back to his bass and they slam into each other, groin to groin, and Denny's hand must, somehow or other, have got tangled up in the kid's jewels, because the kid snarls – and the mike right there and live so's the whole lounge can hear – 'Get your hand off my cock, you dirty little fruit!' and lets fly, hitting Denny in the mouth with his fist, splitting his lip. At once, Ginger's there – big, red Ginger, all fired up because, although he doesn't like Denny's lifestyle, they've been playing together for a long time and he understands – and *he* lets fly and smashes the kid across the chops with his big open hand, and the kid crashes over backwards and into my drums, making it sound like I'm giving them a roll.

Now the tribals are here – and old Hawkeyes – and the security guard – but Ginger doesn't hit the kid again, just, worse still, shouts with the mike going on booming like the Last Day, 'Who're you to call him names, you fucking little creep? Since when you better than him? Sticking your cock into every cunt in town?' and I switch off the mike, though it's too late to do any good, and the lounge is so quiet, you'd think there's nobody there, and old Hawkeyes is looking at us, one by one, but hardest at the kid, who's picking himself up, dusting himself off, smoothing back his hair. *'All right,'* says old Hawkeyes, showing his steel. 'This happen again, I'll throw you out of here. Every mother's son. Even you, Clive, though you have been with me such a long time. And as for you,' and now he's looking only at the kid, 'play, boy! Play, sing, dance, make like an ape, do anything you bloody well like, as long as you get the bad taste out of my customers' mouths. Do that or I'll take you outside and donner you up myself, old as I am,' and he turns and walks back to his office, smiling and nodding at everyone he passes as though this happens every night.

And I got to hand it to the kid – he's a real trouper too – doing his best – right till the end – even though half the crowd leaves at interval and doesn't come back, and Ginger's passing Denny his handkerchief to wipe the blood from his mouth, and we're all coming loose at the seams.

And although it doesn't get any worse, it doesn't get any better either when the gig ends and we pack up the gear – the kid going home on his own without even a 'Ciao', although I feel this is not so much because he's still cheesed off, as because he doesn't know what the fuck else to do – and no bimbo hooked into him, as none have been since the skeleton knocked on the flat's door like the traveller in the poem.

I see Ginger and Denny want to talk to me, so I sit down and listen till they've blown off steam and have tied it all up by telling me they want out, Denny looking at me with his hurt, wet eyes and saying, 'I just can't take it anymore, Clive,' but I put my hand over his, though not leaving Ginger out, and say, 'Give it another try, guys. For me. For the band. And don't be as hard on Silver as he is on you, because he has problems that I know about and that make me take as much from him as would you if you knew, only I'm not going to tell.' And I say a lot else over my ginger ale and the drinks I buy for them like any other haggling old fraud, and, in the end, the anger has gone from Ginger's eyes, but although Denny then also says, 'Okay,' I can sense the woman in him is not going to let this thing get away.

Back at the flat, I see the light in the kid's room is still on, but I don't go in to talk crap as I normally would have done, because although I'm not meaning to speak to him about this thing, now or at any other time, I want him to know I feel bad, and when I say 'bad', I mean *bad*. So I lie there and listen to him laying into the peppermint liqueur till he's all green inside – and maybe quiet like those traffic lights that get stuck on the lonely roads I have been on so many times before him – and the bed's springs whine as he flops down on them and begins to snore.

But still I can't sleep, because suddenly I am seeing faces like I am seeing nothing else, faces that the flip side of my mind has all along been wanting me to forget – the faces of Larry, and Stevie, and Anna, and Claire, as they watched the band tearing itself apart, snapping at its own flesh like a wounded beast, and they circling round it, grinning with their teeth, closing in for the kill.

'Goddammit, No!' I shout inside, and though I know that that is a cry from my heart, I also know it is not a cry from any strength.

* * *

At the next dance, a lot of the regulars from the farms are not there, and, the dance after that, it's even worse, and I'm fearing these guys and their women will never be back because they are chained to their Church like they say the Bible was chained to the altar in the days of the priests, and it's for sure that our slugging it out at the mike and, in particular, what Ginger had to say for everyone to hear, is going to make them think that Silver is nothing less than Old Nick himself. So our halfies of the door has never been so low, and that each week's less rands in the hand, and the empty tables grinning at us like goons, are reminding us all the time that we have shat on our own step, and the shit's going to stay even though we clean it up, like the blood on the old dame's hands in the play.

But even without that – even if every last hick came back and said, 'All's forgiven: let's kiss and make up,' and even if there was only standing room in the lounge again – we would go on reminding *ourselves* that things are not the same and maybe will *never* be the same again, because we're wearing each other like we're hair shirts, so very careful, so very polite, like it's between me and the kid even at the flat, and he not caring anymore if we get a note or a beat wrong. Ginger is maybe the nearest to being what what he was, because he's a *big* guy who doesn't bear a grudge for long and – this always surprising me – he *likes* Buddy Silver for something he sees in him, and not just because of the way the kid plays and sings. But that woman in Denny is having a field day because she's sensed the kid's scared of her now – or, rather, not so much scared of *her* as of what he has seen she can *do* to him by just sitting still and letting him bash her around – and it's a sick thing for me to watch this switcharound that's like a cornered beast being dragged down, and there's times when I want to chuck away the sticks and leave them to it while I go and throw up in the loo.

So much I'm hoping that, at least, this is the *bottom* of the pit and we can only start going up again from here on, but, one morning, early, there's again a knock on the door that does not sound like anybody's I know – that *can't* be anybody's I know because this is a Sunday and nobody from my scene goes rousting out a band member after the night before – and I get up and open the door and go out, knowing the kid won't, not even if the flat is falling down, and it's two guys, one black, one white, and while the black could be anything you want because the blacks are still not used to this kind of thing, the white looks, smells, like what he is even though he's not wearing a uniform, but natty blue shorts and bush jacket to match, and even as natty a felt hat with a feather in the band. I look down at his legs and – ja – the fur on them is blond as his hair, his brows, the chunky little moustache, even the lashes round the blank, blue, coming-out-at-me eyes, and his long socks stretch up from the suede shoes to just below his knees, and there's a comb stuck in one of them like it's a brother to the feather in the hat.

'Good morning, sir,' he says, and his voice is soft, though there's no real respect in it, and his eyes are going over me like I'm hiding something I shouldn't have. Then he flaps open his I.D. like he's a crook flashing me a stolen watch and I ask him if he and his shadow would like to come in, which docsn't mean I *want* them to, but I'm trying for cool while my stomach, which smells a bad thing a mile off, is beginning to squeegee so's I can hear it and won't hush. But he shakes his head and, instead, takes what looks like a photo from a folder the black guy is holding and passes it to me, and I see then that it is an identikit, head and shoulders, of a man, and it means nothing to me and my stomach quiets, and I look at the cop, my eyes asking why.

'Name's Val Roman,' he says. 'Last known address, Sea Point, Cape Town. You seen him before?' and my stomach turns right around and tries to run out through my arse, because the names are the names on the back of the photo of the kid I found lying on the table in his room, and I know the skeleton is back at the door and is hammering harder than ever before to be let in. Almost I piss myself trying to clench up, tight, so's my hands won't show the shakes they feel coming on, and I look at the 'kit again, wondering why I was so blind the first time round, because now I'm looking past the too flat nose, the too thick lips, the too cropped hair, the too skewed San kind of eyes, and it's the kid all right, staring up at me like a drowned man from the bottom of a water that won't hold still.

Again, as with the kid's dad, I'm asking myself, 'Do I say yes? Do I say no? Is this an identikit of a missing person or a criminal on the run? Whichever way – and fuck morality – where does my loyalty lie?'

'Never seen him before,' I say, and hand him back the 'kit.

'Or maybe you have seen this,' he says. 'Maybe seen someone flashing it around,' and he shows me a drawing of a dagger-type knife that can only be the one in the kid's gear, and again my gut's going bananas and again I'm shaking my head and saying, 'No.'

But now I'm asking *him*, 'This guy done something wrong?' and he says, 'Not for us to say. It's Cape Town wants to know. Asked us to check if perhaps he's come up to these parts. Perhaps could help them with some information he's got and they don't.'

'But why have you come to me?' and even as I ask that, I'm thinking, 'Christ! this is like a replay of the kid's dad!'

'Well,' he answers, 'it seems he's a musician of some kind. Played and sang in a nightclub down there. So we've just been to your Recreation Club. Asked the manager about him, showed him what we showed you. But he also knows nothing. Only recommended we see you, because you manage his band and travel round a lot. So it's sorry for worrying you, sir, and have a good day,' but there's still no spark in his voice, like he's a tired machine, and he doesn't offer me his hand, though the black man snaps me what's supposed to be a salute, and I jump because it's so sudden it's like a black stone's come alive.

Then they're gone, and I go inside and back to bed, and let myself shake till all the shaking's out and I'm no longer thinking of the kid's peppermint liqueur with a yen that terrifies me more than anything else so far has done. And, after that, soon's I hear the kid's gone out for his Sunday morning swim, I go through his gear, not caring whether I leave a trail or not, till I find the knife and, for safety's sake, wipe it clean, and carry it in a paper to the blind other side of the hill, where I bury it under the stones and the scrub and smooth the place over like it's a grave for a murdered soul.

Back at the flat, I see the kid's still gone, and I wash my hands like there's more on them than soil, and sit down and begin to shake all over again when I think of me standing there on the step and lying to those cops, and all the while the kid's just a pace or two away behind his door, and any time he can open it and walk out and, cops being what they are, they will question him too and he will break, because he's been running and he's scared.

Then I remember the other guy who's got snarled up in this thing, and that's old Hawkeyes who also said, no, he didn't know the face in the 'kit, but he *must* have because he's quick as a fox and when the cops told him, as they told me, that this Val Roman comes from Sea Point, Cape Town, and plays and sings, he would surely have done his sums and looked at the 'kit again and seen what I saw. So why did he cover up and send them to me? Was he doing a Pontius, washing his hands, saying, '*You* do it, not *me*?' or was he being a friend, liking the kid and me more than he ever showed, saying, 'Look, I can't *tell* you I'm covering up, and I can't *warn* you unless I do. So I'm letting *them* be the warning and still giving you a chance in the only way I can. Grab it, guys, or be dead.' And I sit here, just *knowing*, the way one sometimes does without proof, that that's *it*, and I'm loving that hard, sharp old man like I'm not ashamed to say.

One o'clock, the kid's back, bringing burgers from the Club cafeteria, and I brew coffee and we eat. He smells of clean sweat and chlorine from the pool and his hair's still damp and unbrushed, and although his face has grown thinner and his body bonier, and he's again taking his stuff behind the toilet door more often than I like, and there's a fresh bottle of the green piss on the table too many times a month, he's still looking almost like a boy when the light's right, as it is now, and we are easier with each other than for some weeks, though we don't speak much. But then I look at his hands – the fingers long and a little round at the ends like a frog's toes, and the nails cleaned and trimmed as a girl's and yet still very much a man's – and I cannot help but think – and flinch as I think – what those hands might have done with the knife I have buried behind the hill and what he will say when he finds out that it is gone. That he will say a lot, and say it one helluva loud, is for sure, and for a moment I think to tell him right away and get it over with, but I have had about as much as I can take for one day and the kid is humming as he brushes his hair – which is something I haven't heard from him since I don't know when – and I decide, 'Fuck it, let it slide for now,' and lie down to catch up on all the sleep I have lost from the week before's late shifts in the bar.

At first, I think I'm having a bad dream and claw up out of sleep, my ears singing and my lungs yelling for air that isn't there, but then my eyes open and the kid's face is inches from mine, and it's out of shape as a rubber pulled all ways at once, and his eyes are falling out of his skull. I try to struggle up, but he's mounting me like I'm a horse, gripping me, tight, with his thighs, and his hands are round my throat, squeezing it like he wants the last juice from a fruit. 'You bastard!' he's screaming. 'Where's my knife? Give me back my fucking knife!' and he shakes me till my head's flopping round like a doll's.

Now my body's heaving under him, wanting air, wanting the life that is air, and the kid's not the kid anymore, but Old Death's-head himself that's riding me to my grave, and it's getting like it's night and not afternoon, and I'm scared, but quiet-scared because this is *it* and I'm knowing getting scared is no ways the way out, and I clamp his wrists and draw up my legs, then kick them out, straight, and tear and throw him off me like he's a leech, and he falls off the bed and onto the floor and I'm on him, hanging onto the last of a strength I shouldn't have, and he hisses and whips under me like a cat and grabs for my balls, but I know that one and block his hand, then pin both his hands to the floor, and he spits in my face with all of the gob he's got and lies still, staring up at me, hating me with his eyes and the all of him that's hard as an iron under my knees.

'My knife!' he snarls. 'You've taken my knife! Give me back my knife!' and now he sounds only half his age because, under the snarling, there's a pleading like a little kid that's wanting back his toy.

Not slackening my grip, because I'm not knowing which way he's going to jump, I say, counting out my words so that he'll hear them through his rage, 'I have buried it other side the hill in a place you'll never get to know.'

'But why?' he asks, and now the whine is more clearly there. 'What did I do to you that you must take away my knife?'

'It's not what you have done to me,' I say, still speaking slowly, holding him with my eyes. 'It's what you are doing to yourself. Look' – and I relax my hold a little, testing him, but he doesn't grab at what I give – 'the cops were here. Two of them. A white and a black. They showed me a 'kit of a guy they want, and it's a bad 'kit because I can't see it's you till they tell me this guy's name is Val Roman and he comes from Sea Point, Cape Town, and he sang and played in a nightclub down there. But it's only the names Val Roman that made me *sure* it's you they want, because you wrote those names on the back of a photo of you that you left lying alongside your birth certificate on the table in there,' and I nod towards his room, 'and I said then that you were stupid about the birth certificate, and I'm saying now that you were just as stupid about that photo, and I am also saying now that you were *most* stupid when it comes to something else,' and I pause and look at him even harder, and he seems to sense what's coming because his eyes start sliding away, 'and that's that knife of yours that they show me a picture of and that you are keeping right here in your gear, and that someday you will also be leaving alongside your goddam peppermint liqueur, or cleaning your nails with at the Club, or doing any other stupid thing with that only stupid cunts like you *can* do.'

He slumps then, and I get up, quickly, and sit down on the bed, but he goes on lying on the flat of his back on the floor and stares up at me like he hasn't seen me before. 'That's the second time you covered for me,' he says at last, carefully, like he's walking on a strange turf. 'Why?'

'Well, I could say it's because of the band, but that would not be all,' and now it's me that's walking on a strange turf and I'm not knowing how I must go on, and he's quick to see that and says, flat and sharp, the hard look back in his eyes: 'You wanting me up you? You wanting to chain me, like he done? It's that?' and his lip curls.

Rage flares in me like a wind's fanned a coal and I'm thinking I would have hit him had he not been lying down, because, although I am no holier-than-thou and leave each to his own, I expect others to leave me to *my* own and not tag me as something I am not and never have been, and I'm getting a hernia keeping calm as I look down at him, deadpan, and ask, 'Do I look like that's what I want?'

'Nobody looks like what they want,' he shoots back, quick as they come, and I got to think he's got a point, though it's twisted as all hell.

'Okay,' I say, getting tired now and showing it. 'Have it your way. And since your mind's working like it is, perhaps I shouldn't say what I was going to say, which is maybe I keep walking behind you, picking up your shit, because *I'm* stupid enough to be getting too close to you than's good for me.' He chews on that, though making like he hasn't heard, and I creep up on him and suddenly ask, 'And who was it that wanted to chain you like you thought I did, and why?'

Now he's hearing me, loud and clear, and his head rolls to one side and he stares, stubbornly, at the wall. 'Forget it,' he mumbles like someone's slugged him in the jaw. 'It's no big deal anymore.'

'Then why did you say what you did?' I ask, and suddenly the whole buggered-up Sunday's coming at me and I'm roaring so's his head jerks back like I grabbed it by the hair: 'Don't give me that, you little shit! Ever since you been with me, you're bleeding all over my floor and not telling me why. But it's me that's got to swab up the blood, like I got to scoop up the shit. So be a man, instead of a poes, for once in your life and lay out the cards so's I know what's the name of the game!'

He sits up then, hands hanging between his knees, head low – 'Like Larry that last night he played with us,' I think, and there's that bad taste in the mouth that nothing helps, and the silence is a thousand-k's-thread that thins and thins, and that damned bird is making sad sounds in the banana trees again.

'When my old lady came up here,' he says, and his voice is dull and blurred as those old discs they made in a studio for ghosts and that even new needles don't bring back to life anymore, 'and I stayed back there, I tried to find work – a white man's kind of work – but I never made it through high school and, anyway, my papers said I wasn't white and, though they're real nice about it nowadays, that's still the end of the line and fuck you. So I stole a bit, and begged a bit, and sometimes dossed down with the street kids on a doorstep or under a bridge, and sometimes I tried for rent boy and got a run of one-night stands, when the guy would make me bath and give me a good meal with booze, and I would do the job and get my pay and kiss his arse goodbye. And one of them took me to this nightclub before I give it him, and I was a little drunk and asked their crummy band if I could play one of their guitars and sing for the crowd, and they let me, and though it's a long time since I done my stuff at the Church bazaars, they see I'm the voice they been looking for and can handle the strings and, later, even the piano that's been standing there doing nothing for I dunno how long.

'So I become Val Roman and nobody knows I'm not white because there's no papers I have to show, and I'm happy and thinking I got it made. But then, one night, *he* takes me home after the show and he's got it all: Jag, flat in Sea Point, dough that he chucks around like it's the paper in his loo. And, before long, I'm shacked up with him, he being a loner and liking me more than anybody who's given it to him up to then, and me not minding him either, though I'm hating what I have to do to him like he's never going to get his fill. Looking at him from the outside, you'd think he's all he-male, handsome like a woman would want a man to be, lots of muscle that he keeps trim in the gym and uses to put me down with when we play, and not so much older than me like most of the others before him have been. But when he sees I'm getting sick of shafting him like I'm a machine, and want to break with him and enjoy this scene I have always dreamed about with someone that's not thinking of that one thing all the time, things change.

'Then he tells me he's known all along that I'm not white because whites don't have cocks as black as mine, and he trips me up about my name and where I come from, and I try to stick it out because I'm scared of what he says he's gonna do. But even though I stay, that woman in him that you would never know is there, is running scared as me, thinking all the time I'm having it off with one of his friends when her back is turned, and now he's putting me down so that it *hurts,* and he's calling me names every night that hurt me even more, and doing things to me and my manhood that I don't wanna talk about, if you don't mind. So, there comes the time that he stakes me out again so's she can play with me till I howl like her little "tottie boy" that she says I am, and then he takes her into the toilet to pretty her up for sex, lipstick and all, and I take out the dagger we are talking about from the glass cabinet against the wall and wait outside the toilet door, and, when she opens it, I – ,' and for the first time he stops, and his head droops lower and begins to swing, and I finish for him, 'And you slip her the blade,' but saying it casual, like it's an everyday thing, though my nails are slicing into my palms from holding in what I feel.

That steadies him. 'Ja, I do that, and I feel it going in somewhere soft, and she screams and falls down and her arms and legs are banging about like it's an abattoir. But I don't stop to see the end of it, just run, not knowing the knife's still in my hand till I get down to the beach, when I wash it, and in the morning, soon's the banks open, I draw out all the money he's given me and I banked, and buy me a gear and a ticket on the first train out of town.'

He gets up then and begins to walk towards the door, but, before he reaches it, he turns around and says, 'It was a lekker blade. About the only pretty thing I ever had,' and though there's nothing in his voice except the words, I want to go to him, put my hand on his maybe, say any stupid thing that comes into my mind, but I know I must not dare because, right now, he's like one of those old artifacts that look whole when you dig them up, but, when you touch them, they are dust in your palm.

So I stay where I am and try again for sleep, but my neck's hurting me now and I am wondering if this is the way you feel when you try to hang yourself, but they cut you down in time.

❋ ❋ ❋

The signs come quickly then, but I read them the wrong way round because they are the reverse of what I expect. The kid is suddenly much easier with me than for a long time, though a little careful about it, and *that* is a sign that wants me to hear, but I let it pass. In fact, the kid is *generally* easier with everybody he knows – or even doesn't know – and this should be worrying me because, after the cops called, I thought – and was afraid – that he would be needing the biggest crutch in town, but I'm so wanting *not* to be warned, that I bullshit myself that the kid is stronger than I thought and that we have broken through the shit into sweeter days. And even when he is often not at the flat when I come home after late night shift, and, in the morning, he doesn't say where he's been and I don't ask, I don't worry because, ever since he stopped bringing the tail to the flat, we have gone our separate ways and no questions either side. It's only when he sometimes comes in just before dawn and there's hardly time to wash and get to work, that I begin to feel that, maybe, something's not quite right, but then I tell myself it's better this way than that he should be listening to that goddam door and gnawing away at his own bones. Very nearly I wake up, though, when the coming home so late turns out to be those are the nights in the month when a car hoots outside the flat and he drops everything and says, 'See you later,' and is off. And when he starts coming into the bar when I'm on shift, and stays just long enough to stand me a ginger ale while he downs his peppermint liqueur, it gets really hard for me to hang onto that peace of mind that's battling so to get away, because the kid has never before stood me anything, either at gigs or any other time.

But I stick it out and go on living in my never-never land of, deep down, wanting peace at any price and not asking other questions such as why is the kid also snuggling up to Ginger the way he is to me, swopping whoring jokes with him like he's one of the boys, and why, if things are so okay with him again, does he not start bringing the tail back to the flat as before? And so, when I wake up one morning and the kid opens the door, never so late as now, the sun already up somewhere behind the hill and the guinea fowl chinking in the scrub like the glasses in the bar when it's full, it's my own fault that I look at what he's holding in his hand and feel like he's let fly and kicked me in the groin. He grins when he sees me, but he's dog, belly to the ground, wagging its tail, knowing there's hell to pay, and I turn my back on him and say, 'Get that thing out of here,' and my voice is sick and tired as the old man's I suddenly am.

'Come *on,* Clive,' he says, jollying me along like I'm a little kid, even saying: 'Be your age!'

Slowly I turn round, raging now, look at him. His hands are on it like they've never been on any girl – or man – and it's glittering like a hail, and it's lean and mean, and its strings are singing even before he's touching them, and it's the most beautiful guitar I have ever seen. But still I say, meaning it even more, 'And get *yourself* out of here. Go find some other roof for you and your whore's pay.'

'Careful there, Clive,' he warns, and his voice is cruel and it's like he's never come closer to me in all this time. 'Chase me out of here and somebody's gonna say you're like the Sea Point daddy that didn't want anybody else to play with her tottie boy.'

Disbelieving, but knowing, deep in me, that what he's saying, is so, I back off, look at me, rather than at him. What *is* it that is firing me – burning me up each time I look at the guitar? *Is* it only concern for a guy I'm wanting for my son, when all *he* wants is to have my skin? Or is it something else? Something with a bad smell? Like jealousy that she's giving him what I never can? And what do I mean by 'giving him what I never can'? Is it only the guitar? And who's going to do the saying like he said about him and me? Her or him?

He sees I'm standing still, shocked like someone who's walked into a wall. 'Look Clive,' and his voice is so reasonable that I know I should feel like a heel, but don't. 'You don't understand. Can't, because you're not me. It's not you that's feeling the covers coming off him, one by one. First it's Stompie, smousing around with a name I don't want to hear, then the cops, doing like the dogs after the name that's running away. What do you expect? I told you maybe I'll think about it sometime. Now's the time. Anna's my new cover, my new skin, and the bonus is the guitar. You done a lot and I'm saying thanks, but you can't make me feel safe, like I'm someone else, like it is when the ou,' and he fingers his crotch, 'is in her and she a woman with the bread and the clout. So why don't you feel happy for me, like you should if you're my friend?'

'Because I *am* your friend in a way that you don't seem to understand,' I find tongue enough to say. 'I want for you more than you shaking like you got the hots behind a piece of wood with strings,' and I gesture at the guitar with a disgust it's hard for me to feel. 'And I want more for you than a skin you are never going to wear, though you fuck every white cunt in town. Why don't you' – and now I'm

pleading with him and hating to hear myself whine – 'listen to what
your mother said: "Don't gate-crash their parties, Vernie. They'll get
you in the end"?'

'Don't say that name!' he shouts, and I could halve my tongue for
being such a fool. 'My old lady's not *God!* She doesn't know *this* thing!
This thing's different, man. This thing's gonna work. You'll see. And,
besides, why's it you don't mind me gate-crashing the party when it's
your band that's figuring in the con?'

He's got me there and I change tracks, quick, like I'm a fowl you're
chasing for the pot. 'Ja, you give me such a long sob about the psycho
in Sea Point, yet now you go and shack up with a woman that'll hack
off your cock when she hears you're not white, and who wants it so
much, she'll suck you dry as your psycho ever did.'

'Nah!' he laughs, and it is, unbelievably, almost a boyish sound.
'She won't find out what I am. It's all in the dark, man. You forget
she's hitched, and though her guy's old and kaput, he's not gonna
take *everything* she throws. So it's once, maybe twice, a week that she
gets me away in the car and we do it in the bush beside the road. And
as for her being like the psycho – man, you won't believe this, but
she's the worst lay I ever had – only the right side up, if you don't
mind, and – you heard me here – I know – holding out so long, she
doesn't ask for a second time around.'

Strangely, dangerously, that takes something of the sting out of
what I feel, begins to shrink the gap that was widening between him
and me, and I stand here, caught up in the kid's past as much as is he,
wondering if there is a way I can be comfortable with this thing – not
eating shit, yet also not breaking the bond that seems to be tied at only
my end. Then I find the way – the only way – and, as the Books say,
there's a great lamentation in me because, suddenly, in the shifting of
my eye, I am out of the game, on the outside looking in, as lonely as
all hell.

'Okay,' I say, and my voice is so dead that he looks at me, a little
frightened for the first time, knowing something's coming that he's
not going to be able to change. 'You can stay here for so long as you
never bring *her* here, and I will have to go on being your manager, or
old Hawkeyes will turf you out on your ear. But I'm not playing the
drums anymore till that whore's trash is out of your hands. Otto
Schultz – the drummer at the Wilhelmstal – has been wanting to make
a change for a long time. So go see him and he will come for sure.'

'Ja, that's fine,' says the kid – but offhand, as though it's nothing to
him, so why should it be anything to me? – 'Shake on the deal,' and he
puts out his hand, but he's hurt me now so's I cannot take it, and I

leave him looking down at it as though he's wondering what it's done wrong.

Then I speak to Ginger and Denny, giving them a long spiel about it all getting too much for me after the years of long shifts in the bar, and Ginger's feeling bad, but not too much so, because the kid's seen to it that there's another friendship there that's tied only at the one end. But Denny, still bitter and growing more unforgiving with time, wants out, there and then, but when he hears Otto Schultz is going to be the new drummer, he says 'Okay,' as I knew he would because the rumour's going round that he and Otto are lovers, and I think, 'Okay, Silver, so now you have *two* fruits in the band and have a nice day.' I am, in fact, being pretty childish about the whole thing and knowing it, but I don't care, and when Anna – who's not trusting me as far as she can flop a tit and is wondering if I won't spill the beans to her husband, whom I like and who likes me – sends me over a ginger ale with no ice when I'm relaxing in the lounge before my shift, I pour it so's she can see into the nearest tub with a plant, and grin inside like a shark when I see I have hit her where it counts.

As for old Hawkeyes, he doesn't mind Otto Schultz taking over on the drums – reckons it might even be a smart move. 'Could bring in more Germans from the hotels,' he says, and then he looks at me, and past me to the nothing I have said about what is really gone, and adds, 'It's a tough world, Clive,' and knows I know what he means.

The band, though, is not having it tough at all. Silver's steering clear of the two fruits on his flanks that it's now too late for him to do anything about, the new guitar's making like an Angel the Lord's booted out, and Otto Schultz – though I'm human enough to not like admitting this – is playing, at least, as well as – and sometimes even better than – I ever did. Only backstage – at the flat – do the masks come off and the kid and I face each other with naked eyes. Now we do not even cook or eat together anymore, do not speak to each other unless it's do or die, and I know I could get us both back on track again if I would just let go of my tongue, break out of the straitjacket of hurt I clamped around me the day I refused to take the kid's hand – but I'm too stubborn – or is it too vain? – to make the first move, and get even more so – and angrier with *myself* – when the kid ghosts around the flat, not knowing what the hell's the matter with me and too much from another world to understand.

Slowly, things get worse for me, but better for the kid and the band. Worse for me because I am what I am – growing old white boss-man, set in my ways like dough or dung that just splats down and doesn't run into new Clives – and I'm crying all the time inside for life at the flat to be as it always was, while it is me that made it into the little hell that it is now; and crying also for life outside the flat to be as it was, but here it is Anna that is the change and I can do nothing about her, not even if I lop off my balls and become her puppet like the kid.

She's smart, though. Knowing she mustn't start too many tongues yakking in town – knowing, above all, that if she is to prove to the kid that she is a better bargain for him than me, she can't afford to lose him his teenage support – she plays her cards close to the tits at the Club and elsewhere, only heading for the bush with the kid after each gig and saving letting down her hair for the gigs in the other towns, where the usual teenagers are not breathing down her neck all the time. Then the kid rides with her in the Benz, while I bike in alone, and she flashes the kid around like he's one of her rings and nuzzles into his every soft place except the one, till comes the day I can't take it anymore and leave everything to her except for the telephoning and the posters, and, sometimes, a few repairs to the gear.

For the kid – so much younger than me, so often the chameleon that must fit into every new scene or die, so often the bug crushed between the nails that being the bug's become the way it's got to be – it is not the same. Slowly, he gets used to being the leper in the flat, begins to accept this as just another style of life, to suffer it the way he suffers Anna flopping all over him at the out-of-town gigs, or flopping under him for, as he said, 'the worst lay he's ever had'. In the end – and I see it's closing in, but cannot stop it – his coming and going as though the flat has split into two halves like those first jellies in the sea, his carefully not sharing any turf with me at any time, his even whistling and humming a little – not from spite, but simply because he's forgotten I'm around – makes *me* the leper in the flat – makes me want to spend more time anywhere but under my own dak that I was arse enough to let him share.

Evenings are the worst, this being when the dead poet in me comes up for air through all the shit of my life and asks, 'Why did you bury me before my time?' and it is then that even the rough parts of how it used to be with the kid and me seem smoother than a silk, and of the best parts of those days were our sitting together on the bike on our way to the gigs, listening to stones, leaves and silences sing and the kid saying, 'Scary,' or some other simple thing that showed that in him, too, is a could-have-been and a song that's never been sung.

But the kid will not be reaching for that song now – will *never* be reaching for it again, if Anna has her way – and she is making sure that it *will* be her way by pulling out all the stops wherever the band goes – jazzing up its image – and the kid's – high as the skies – as kites of paper in the wind – and not stopping anywhere on the far roads so's the kid can listen to the silences and the leaves.

What old man Van Dijk thinks about all this, I'm never going to learn because he's a real old gent who doesn't talk about his wife to other guys, but probably, like the mantis that eats her own man, she's already got him so deep into her gut that he's past thinking anything at all. Or maybe she's got funds of her own and can do with them what she wants. Who knows?

For sure is it, though, that she's throwing whoever's bread it is around like it *is* bread and there's a famine in the black slums and she's seen the Light in the sky. Whatever, it's new amplifiers, new mikes, sets of differently spangled threads for the guys, and gimmicks and more gimmicks, and hoopla, and a buying a way through to the top in Windhoek and Swakop, and even further away, till Silver's riding one daddy of a wave, and Big Momma's showing her teeth to the press as she watches her little 'tottie', that she still doesn't know is that, signing autographs for little girls for whom the price comes too high.

Which sounds like the man with a grudge that I am, and the weeks pass, and the months, and then it's a year, and still I'm a man with a grudge and learning – like it's a sick joke – like the kid and I have swopped lives – how it feels to be on the outside looking in. And it doesn't help any when the kid's away, making like an Elvis in Windhoek or further down, and I'm sitting, off shift, in the Club's bar, nursing a ginger ale, and Larry comes in and, for the first time since the break, claps me on the shoulder and asks, 'Silver's smell getting you down too, Clive?' and laughs without joy, and I say, 'Fuck off,' but there's no fire in it, and Larry looks at me and knows, and says the ginger ale's on him.

Times like these, I think of those two cops. Are they putting two and two together as they read the papers, making four, or has the case found its grave in the 'dead' files? And Mrs Williams? Does *she* read the papers? If so, surely *she* must have guessed by now that it's her Vernie that's often only her hand's reach away as he does his strut in one of the classy Windhoek joints where she and Stompie never go. Does she then reach out that hand, or does she keep to the rule that you don't shoot down the play-white flying high, but keep away from him or her like you're a disease?

I should feel sorry for her then, but I'm too busy feeling sorry for myself and the ginger ale is flat as my piss on my tongue.

✳ ✳ ✳

But then, so suddenly that now it's there, now it's not, and the kid grown the biggest frog in a little pond I have seen in all my years in these parts, someone puts the pin in the balloon. And who does it? None other than fat Anna herself, though she doesn't know it till it's too late and the balloon's just an old condom in her hand.

I don't know if Anna believes in Anything 'up there' – the funniest people can – but all at once she wants the band to be more than just a joller's band, which is not a bad idea because the jollers, who are usually the brat-pack, are a fickle lot who can turn today's pop star into tomorrow's poes star quicker than the dude can pack his gear. What more solid 'other support' is there, she reckons, than the Churches, particularly when the kid is whipping his pelvis around like he's having it on and there needs to be a watcher with a blind eye tending the flock if there is going to be mutton on the table every day. So she puts it out that the band will be giving 'charity' concerts for any Church that would like to apply and promises that she as 'patron' – Ja, she calls herself that now – will pay a rand from her own pocket into the Church's funds for every rand the band takes at the door. 'Smart,' I think, and hate myself for thinking it. 'She gets the kudos and the band,' which couldn't care less about Churches or charity, as I only too well know, 'gets its pay and, later, even more pay as its support base grows.'

So it is that some Saturdays the band is staging two gigs, one in the afternoon for a Church that needs the bread and just about whips all its followers into the Club, and the usual Saturday night dance when many from the afternoon gig stay on for a double jol. Anna – give her her due – is true to her word and shells out the rand for a rand, and the Churches see they are on to a good thing and begin to hassle each other for the best dates and it's Catholics, and Anglicans, and Moravians, and (a little more fussily) even the DRs, but the Apostolics don't want to know and I got to admit to admiring them for not softfooting round what they believe. There are prayers before and after to make things sound right and the Reverend in charge makes a little speech, thanking and praising the band and saving a special word for its 'Patron,' Mrs van Dijk, 'who is so generously aiding the Church in its work and may the Lord bless her, Amen!' and fat Anna standing there, looking fatter than ever, and *full*, like she's a shark that's just got away with your leg and will find room for the other, give her half a chance.

Then, one day, there is this application from a Church in Windhoek I never heard of before – 'The Church of Christ Aramaic' – or something that sounds like that – and they get their date and, early on the Saturday morning, hit town in a convoy of five taxis and about a dozen private cars, and spend the hours before the gig doing some hot holyhollering in the patch of grass and stubborn scrub that's supposed to be our 'town square'. Then they sit down and eat the packed lunches they brought with them – which doesn't please the two hotels and our only 'restaurant' at all – and, after that, they cram into the Club lounge – and I mean *cram* because a lot of the locals also want in so's they can see these new weirdos who are not shy about showing they've arrived.

Actually, they're nice people, thanking the tribals politely when they bring them their drinks – ja, they don't seem to mind the odd shandy, beer or wine – and taking care not to call them 'John' or 'Boy'; and I particularly like their Reverend: a round, chirpy little Yank with a peeling nose and a straight tongue, whose flab shakes when he laughs, which is nearly all the time. He's no fool, though, because when he first gets to speak to Anna, I sense something moving behind his eyes and know he is seeing more than what she shows.

He it is that opens with a prayer and a 'thank you for coming' speech – short and sweet, but from the heart – and the band is filing in, the kid in the rear, and it is then, as the kid is crossing the lounge, that things begin to happen that I don't understand. The Reverend leans forward and stares at the kid, makes to speak, changes his mind, looks again and very nearly gets up from his chair, then sinks back and goes on staring at the kid as though he's reaching back – back – into what? – into memory? – into time? At first the kid doesn't see the Rev – only does when the Rev moves in his chair – and then – even from where I'm standing in the double doors to the bar – I can see the kid's face drain grey as a dead man's and his hands fist as he forces himself to move on as though there's nothing wrong.

The band starts up, the Rev still watching the kid, still not quite sure, and the kid plays guitar, plays piano, plays guitar, missing notes, fumbling riffs, the other three wondering – as I would've if I hadn't seen the foreplay – if he's drunk or drugged, and even Anna beginning to squeegee around in her chair because – again give her her due – she's not brain dead when it comes to music and the fuck-ups are lasering through her like they are through me. 'Why?' I'm asking myself. 'Why does he not *sing*?' and at last the crowd is shouting out the question for me – baying like they want a blood – and the kid does – but his hands are shaking on the guitar like an old man's and his hips only sway like he's a puppet coming unstuck, a toy winding down, and I'm wincing at the shrillness in his voice – but the Reverend suddenly smiles and nods, uncertainty gone, and leans back and goes on nodding, in time with the tune.

I go back into the bar, then, never having been able to watch a man – or a beast – break down, but when I hear the kid doing his usual last threshing of the strings, I'm out again and he's coming across the floor, guitar in his hand, eyes wide and staring like he's trapped and the jaws are closing in – which they are – Larry's and Stevie's faces, wise and alive as foxes' – even Claire's, pale, coming together like a blade – seeming to stand out from the crowd as though they're the only ones in the lounge – as though they are the only ones that *know*. The kid's eyes meet mine and, for the first time in the more than a year, they are speaking to me, crying, 'Please!' but there is nothing I can do – what am I *supposed* to do, anyway? – as the Reverend jumps up from his chair, shouting, 'Vernie! Vernie Williams, don't you remember me anymore?' and the nice, kind Church people are smiling and dragging the kid back with their nice, kind, blind hands and saying, 'Wait! Wait! Don't go away. Can't you hear the Reverend's calling for you?' and one of them takes him by the arm and leads him to where the Rev is standing, rearing up on his toes, reaching out his hand, running over with the love of the Lord.

Tenderly, he takes the kid back to the mike, wraps his arm around his shoulders, booms, 'Folks, I know we done our preaching this morning, so I don't want to preach again here now, but the Lord has led me back to this young fellow standing here with me and whom I first got to know when he was only this high,' and his hand shows somewhere between his hip and thigh, 'and the Lord is moving me to say a few words about him to you-all before we go home. Now, I *didn't* know him *for sure* when he first came in here this afternoon because he's grown a lot,' and he looks the kid fondly up and down, 'and I see he's got himself a stage name, which I understand, being a bit of a performer myself,' and he laughs and the 'folks' laugh along with him, but the locals don't – just gape, fat Anna's mouth so wide it looks like it's going to stick that way, 'but when he sang, *then* I knew him because he used to sing for our Church when I was still ministering down South in Mitchells Plain where he was born, and I'm praising the Lord that he has grown into such a fine young man, and I'm praising the Lord that, when they transferred me up here to you-all, He led me also back to Vernie's momma and dad who left the Plain before me to come up here and hardly said a word to anyone at the time. Now why did they do that, folks?' and he looks around like there might just be a bright kid in the class that will surprise us all. 'They did that, folks, because, as you know, our Church teaches that the Lord made all men and women from the same mould,' then he pauses and adds, 'well, the ladies perhaps a *little* different from the men,' and winks like he's one of the boys and the 'folks' nearly wet themselves laughing at his little joke and loving him for having the same devil as them between his legs.

But still the locals sit like stones, Anna the biggest stone both ways, only a kind of fright beginning to show in her eyes, and when the folks settle down again, the Reverend goes on, 'Well, as I was saying, the Lord makes us all one shape before He gives us skins of so many different colours it's like Joseph's technicolour dreamcoat,' again a laugh runs through the flock, 'and Vernie's momma, who's the finest little white lady you're ever going to meet, goes the whole way with what the Church says and marries this finest little *brown gentleman* you're ever going to meet, and they don't live happily ever after because that racist tribe of Satan that the sword of the Lord has now laid low, keeps on snapping at their heels like a hound-dog that's got nothing better to do' – 'Shame!' shouts the flock – 'and they sell up the little they got down there in the Plain and come up here to the new Promised Land' – 'Hallelujah!' shouts the flock – 'So, though Sister Williams and her man, not knowing who was here,' and he looks, chuckling, at the kid who's hugging his crotch and watching his feet going nowhere on the floor, 'didn't want to come today' – 'Don't shoot down the play-white flying high?' I ask of myself – 'let's give their son Vernie here a great big hand and may the Grace of God go with you – which will also be my last prayer for today – Amen!'

'Amen!' roars the flock, and they rise to give the kid a standing ovation which is the funniest not-so-funny thing I've ever seen because the locals just go on sitting where they are, not moving even the little finger of a hand, just staring at the kid who's trying to smile through what's left of his face, bowing his head more like it's waiting for the axe than acknowledging the applause, looking like he's wishing the guitar was a cap he can turn round in his hands the way a slave should – the way Stompie *did* – and the whole of him – in a reversal of that day his dad sat on the chair in my room – turning back into that dad – into that 'coloured' man's brat they can now so clearly see he is, that leaves them shocked – and *raging* – that they should not have been able to see it till now.

And none more so than fat Anna who, more so than any of the rest, has had what's swinging between his legs, between her thighs, and is staring at his fly with her face twisted up like it's caught in its zip, and who turns and walks away from him with a spine that says it all when he makes to cross the floor to her and suckle pity from her tits turned hard as iron. Desperately, he looks at the band and Ginger's eyes *are* pitying, but Denny's are speculative and alive, and he faces round again and begins to move across the lounge – searching – searching – like a man in a maze for whom all the familiar turnings have, suddenly, inexplicably, closed. But only the Church people are reaching for his hand, while Larry and Stevie are hugging each other like lovers and whooping out loud, and Claire's thin smile is that of a woman I've never known, and, at last, there's only me, and the kid comes up, close, and whispers, 'Take me home, Clive,' and again, 'For Chrissake, Clive, please take me home!' And my heart cracks so's I hear it when he pleads like that, and I hustle him onto the bike and off-load him at the flat, telling him to lock the door – why, I don't quite know – but not saying more than that because it's a long time since we last *really* spoke to each other and I don't even half know where to begin.

At the Club, old Hawkeyes is waiting for me, looking at me, hard, as he asks, 'And so, what about tonight?' but I'm ready for him there, having thought the problem through on my way back with the bike.

'Not to worry,' I hear myself say, feeling strangely light-headed and in no mood for a nag. 'I'll go down and sober up old Thomas who used to play around with the piano before Silver came. He won't be an answer to a prayer, but he'll be better than anybody else I can think of right now. The main worry will be keeping him off the booze, but I'm hoping that if I pay him something extra out of my own pocket, he'll last the night.'

'Fair enough,' says old Hawkeyes, and he doesn't suggest that I take, at least, Larry back because he knows that I won't, and knows also that Larry's time is past after the kid showed him up for the dud that he is, and I make to go, but he names my name, and I turn back. 'I was born and bred here, Clive,' he says, very quietly, like we're in a church, 'and I know this lot. Before independence, I was the only liberal in these parts and there are times when I think I still am and nothing's changed. They'll forgive *you*, Clive, but not Silver, and I would recommend that he get out of here. *Fast.*'

Suddenly, it all comes together for me and I'm saying to him in the same Sunday tone, 'I know that, sir, and I'll be leaving with him when he goes.'

That catches old Hawkeyes off guard and it's one of the few times in my working with him that he's scratching around for words. 'You mean that?' he asks at last, and when I nod, he adds, 'Then give me your notice now so that I can arrange for you to get your pension and other benefits in full.'

'I'm giving you my notice now, sir,' I say, and he shoves me a form and I sign.

Then he gives me his hand and I take it, and he says, 'If I were younger, I would be doing the same. Now get out of here before I break down and cry – or maybe go out of that door and shoot every single bastard of them that I can find.'

I fix things up with old Thomas, who is not as far gone as I had feared, and who is so chuffed at being asked to play with the band, that I nearly don't offer him the bonus of my own bread, and, when I leave, I hear him already shouting about a clean shirt to the common-law Herero wife that everybody pretends is not there. Then I call the band together in a corner of the lounge, trying to ignore the opposition in the opposite corner who are still whooping it up and shouting out bad-to-worse racist taunts as they soak up the beers, and Denny immediately starts whining about taking Larry and Stevie back and Ginger turns round and, quietly as old Hawkeyes, says, 'Shut up, Denny,' and Denny does – quick – like he's been smashed across the mouth. I explain the setup for the dance, telling them that old Thomas will be coming for a run-through an hour before time, and they better like what I'm saying or they can fucking well all go home, far's I'm concerned, and they can see I mean it – Otto Schultz, in particular, looking very spooked and very girlish in his fancy shirt with the frilled cuffs – and they don't even ask me what's happened to Silver, though that's the one question that must be boiling like worms in their skulls.

But it's all a waste of time. Though not without its excitement if you like that kind of thing. The opposition go on rioting in their corner, refusing to button up, or to fork out for their tickets, till old Hawkeyes gets the waiters and guards to throw them out, and, since the waiters and guards are all black, this doesn't help ethnic tensions any and insults are flying around like feathers when the fox is amongst the fowls. Then the opposition lolls around on the lawns, yowling like cats and spreading hate like it's a disease, and when others start to join them and there's a mob up and running, old Hawkeyes calls in the police and there's another one moer of a snarl-up that's going to hit the headlines for sure. As for Anna, she doesn't come near the band, though I know she's on the premises because, once, she passes me in the cafeteria, wearing shades – at night, if you please! – and looking the other way, and later I see her talking, arms shouting, to a group on the lawns before the police come with the vans. But, inside, the band is playing to an almost empty lounge, the music booming and banging back from the walls, all the Buddy Silver magic gone as the guys just do another job, and only old Thomas at the piano having the night of his life, pounding away at the keys, humming under his breath, scattering wrong notes like a porcupine its quills. For sure, there is a boycott on – the public probably thinking the kid will still try to weasel his way in – but the music is a boycott of its own, and I'm glad when the last of the not more than twenty die-hards leaves well before time and I don't have to go on listening to a once proud band beating itself to death with its own hands.

Biking back to the flat, passing all the places I pointed out to the kid on that first day when I took him down to the station to fetch his gear – the churches, the bakery, the hotels, the shop of the Van Dijks, the little hoks of the houses for men who have come only to grub the guts out of the earth and move on – I suddenly stop halfway and sit there, not knowing why. It is after midnight and quiet, the shaft, the crushers and the flotation plants closed down – as they do each week – for repairs and the observance of a Sabbath that mostly the old, the lonely or the sad observe – and I think of the baker that will soon be up to bake his own sacrament of bread, the little Apostolic dunker of 'born again' souls, the old Catholic priest with his belly still warm from the last cognac before bed, the rustling, tongueless nuns who so unexpectedly can smile when they walk into the blank wall of the infidel that is me – and I realise that this is a place I have learned to *love,* that it is not *only* the place for beerbellies going bananas on a lawn because they want the head of a poor little mulatto who has dared to want to be them. There is no moon but the stars are close and bright, and the bush is a shining all the way northwards to the Kunene or westwards to the desert and the sea, and I think, 'Christ! what am I *doing,* latching – at *my* age! – onto a blowing-with-the-wind kid with too many names that I hardly even know, giving up this safe rut for the wild trails that probably lead nowhere but to hell?' Then I think again of the beerbellies, of fat Anna who's maybe even now fighting off her old guy's fumbling hand – or is it her own hand that's groping in the pouch that's holding less of lust now than hatred and hunger for revenge? – and I think of the kid saying, 'Take me home, Clive. Please take me home,' and kick-start the bike, looking up and in me one last time to Whatever's there, hoping for a Sign, but nothing comes.

At the flat, there's only starlight in the windows, but I'm not worried because of the place being built like a fort, windows high-up and so narrow, you couldn't wriggle through them without making fuss enough to wake the dead, and only the kid and me having the keys. So I stash the bike in the little shed at the back of the flat, go round to the front, unlock the door and walk in. And fall over a body on the floor.

My heart stops so's I think it will never start again and I leap for a switch and flick on the lights. It's the kid, face-down, naked as the day he was born, snoring like a hog, and I look across to the table in his room and see there's an empty bottle standing on it and another that's still half-full. 'Drunk,' I think, but there's no anger in me, no contempt, just a pity that's so big and flooding I can hardly hold it all in, and I roll him over and pick him up and lay him on his back on his bed. Then I stand there, looking down at him, thinking this is the first time I have seen him as he is now – oddly black cock flung, slackly and innocently as a child's, across the olive of the flat belly's skin – and I look closer and pity becomes anger as I see the small scars clotting the lower belly and the insides of the thighs. 'Cigarette burns,' I think. 'Or a playing with a blade,' and know that this is a branding by the Sea Point psycho that the kid never wanted me – nor anybody else – to see and that the darkness mercifully hid from Anna and the lays before her turn. 'But which is worse?' suddenly it comes to me. 'Who must I blame more? The lone psycho in the south, in the dead time, or the wolf pack that is baying for him – here – now?'

As though conscious that the defences are down, that he is exposed to my eyes, the kid threshes round onto his belly and I shake his shoulder, say his name, but he's a meat that does not hear, and I begin to draw the blanket over him when I see something like the tip of a tongue that's just showing between his buttocks, and I spread them and see he has piles, and has them *bad* because – like me when I was younger – he thinks he can just wish them away. Quickly, I get the jar of smelly but sure-fire salve that an old black herbalist gave me in the long ago, and spread the buttocks again and wipe the piles clean with a moist cloth, then gently push them back in and follow them up with my finger coated with the salve, and the kid stirs and moans a little, but whether from awareness of distant pain or a dream, I do not know.

I wake to the crash of splintering wood. Thinking *they* – do I not name them in the hope that namelessness will keep them at bay? – are battering down the door, I scrabble out of bed, but then I hear the racket's in the yard, and I look through my window and it's the kid. Still unsteady from the booze, he's smashing Anna's fancy guitar against a post in the fence, swinging it right back, then letting fly like it's a living flesh he hates, and when there's only a last piece left in his hand, he throws that down and tramples on the glittering ruin till it is returned to where it began, and his face is twisted and strange. But *is* it hate? Or is it pain? Is it not perhaps that he is mourning this slaughter of a beauty his heart and hands loved, but has proved to be as deadly a blade as the knife I buried behind the hill?

Sick at heart, though this is as much a triumph for me as it is a final humiliation for Anna van Dijk, I leave him to it and go into the kitchen and fry enough eggs and wors for two, which is something I haven't done for almost a year and never thought I would be doing again. Then I set it out on the table in his room and begin to eat, and he comes in and reaches for the half-full bottle of peppermint liqueur, and downs a great gulp and shimmys all the way down into his shoes. 'Prettier'n a flower!' he shouts, which is also the first time in a long time, but his eyes are as blind as they are bright, and his hands are shaking, and his bones are trying to push up out of his skin.

'Eat,' I say, as though this was our usual morning scene, and point with my knife at his plate, and he sits down like any obedient child and slices through an egg, and the yoke oozes out of it and he stares at it like it's a pus from a ruptured boil. 'Nah,' he says, and pushes his plate aside. 'Too early for me.'

'Have it your way,' I say, keeping my tone even and going on eating as though I'm enjoying it, and he watching the fork pass to my mouth and back to the plate till I feel like an ape in a cage.

'You fix my arse last night?' he suddenly asks, and I brace myself for the usual row, but his voice is mild, even a little shy. 'Feels good,' he adds, and I pass him the jar of salve which is still on the table and say, 'Here. It's yours.'

He takes it, not saying anything further and not mentioning the scars on his genitals, though he knows I must have seen them and will be human enough to want him to explain. Instead, he says, 'Looks like I'll have to beat it out of here, first train back,' and his tone is flat and offhand, but I can hear the despair behind it and ask, 'Ja, where would you want to go?' He thinks a moment, then shrugs his shoulders, 'Back to old CT, I guess. Where else?'

Now the moment has come – as last night, on the bike, I knew it would – to *finally* decide – tear up the resignation form before old Hawkeyes can get it to HQ, or do the bungy-jump into the beyond? But last night is a thousand nights behind, and now there is nothing for me to decide, and my head is already lifting, and I'm snuffing the wind. 'Ja, where else?' I agree. 'But don't be in such a hurry. Give me a week or so to get my pension and other breads from the Club. Then it's non-stop all the way.'

Now he's very still, like a bird you've flushed, but it's still waiting for your first, next move before it flies. 'You wanting to give me bread?' and he shakes his head. 'No need. I can get me down the line with what I've got and some over till I find a way – *if* I find a way,' and his mouth twists, light years from a smile.

'You're hearing me wrong,' I say, and suddenly I am worrying that he might not *want* me along. 'I'm going with you. I already handed in my time.'

For a moment he looks at me like he hasn't heard, like I'm not there, then he simply says, 'Nice,' and again, 'Nice,' and puts his face in his hands and comes apart like he's an old doll you have chucked against the wall one time too many and the sawdust's running out through the seams. But I make like I'm not hearing anything and go on eating though the food's tasting like the sawdust in the doll, and it's only when he quiets and I think he's got it all out, that I ask, 'You okay now?' and he says, 'Okay, Dad,' and that's one 'Dad' I don't mind him saying because it's not the 'dad' that it was before.

Then I tell him how the dance flopped and how there was a ruction on the lawns the previous night, and don't like and don't dislike either the fear that comes into his eyes because if he's running scared, he'll be taking care and not walk into the beating which my gut warns me is being planned. Later, Denny caps what I've been telling him by phoning to say he and Otto are resigning from the band and it gives me pleasure to say, well, that's too bad but he better tell old Hawkeyes rather than me because I, too, have resigned, and when he wants to know more, it's me that puts the phone down for a change. After that the phone gets the sulks and not even Ginger's knocking on the door, but there's no real peace because all those stomped-on egos and suddenly sanctimonious cunts are crowding round the walls like it's chow time at the zoo and we're the chow.

At the right time, I go to work and nobody's coming at me with knives, though the looks of some of them are sharp as that and most don't look at me at all. In fact, only Ginger and a few my age German guys – who can be as cliquish as most Germans when they are in the mood, but also, again like most Germans, don't mind a bit of black tail from time to time and sometimes even openly have a black mistress on the side – come up to me and talk to me like nothing's going on.

To be fair, one of the unfriendlies also comes up to me – Stevie this time – but he's about as polite as a puff adder when he says, 'Better get that tottie boyfriend out of your flat, Clive, because we're gonna hurt him and there's no guaranteeing that you won't be hurt along with him if you get in the way.'

'You guys forgetting there's a new Government in this country?' I ask, looking at him like he is what he is, thinking, almost tiredly, 'Claire. Playing her ace at last.'

'What Government?' he laughs, and it's an ugly sound. 'Have *you* forgotten this is the bush, pal? Here we make our own laws and one of them is no location shit can come fucking our women like Silver's done.'

'Fine,' I say, 'and here's one of my laws for mouths like yours,' and let fly and slap his face with my open hand so's he falls back against the wall, and he shoots up, swinging his fists, but then sees my eyes and turns round and walks away as I knew he would, and I count 'One'.

But there's no counting 'Two' because they keep away from me after that and I can only watch from a distance as they sit around in the corners, talking in low voices, having their drinks sent in to them if I'm on duty in the bar, and Anna the busiest of the lot, going from group to group, jiggling her tits, flinging back her braid, making like a Latino with her hands. But then, on the second day of the week I want us to wait, they're again close when the phone rings at three in the morning and I pick up and a voice whispers, 'We're coming for you, Silver,' and the line goes dead before I can speak.

After that, the voice – or voices – are whispering in our ears all the time, whether it's in the daytime or the nighttime, whether it's me that's picking up or the kid, and it gets so's the phone's like a ticking bomb and the only thing in the room, and at last I pull the plug on it and they've cut us off from the world.

Well almost, because on the fifth day, and I'm on shift and it's late, the kid plugs in and says, his voice shivery as the chill that's running down my spine, 'They been here. Trying the doors. Moving round.'

'They still there?' I ask, trying to keep my voice calm.

'Nah, I shouted what do they want and they shouted back a lot of shit. Then I heard a car start and now it's quiet.' Then, 'I can't take it anymore, Clive. Can't we go now before I blow my mind?'

'Hang in there,' I urge, hoping he can't hear how I'm blowing mine, boiling up inside with as much of rage as fear. 'Only two more days to go. Just keep the doors locked. Repeat j just keep the doors locked. Only you and I have the keys and they can't break down the doors without waking up the whole town. Not *everybody* here's our enemy, you know. Okay?'

'Okay,' he says, but his voice is tired and lonely as a child's.

Then it's the last shift and old Hawkeyes is giving me my cheque and his hand, and wishing us well and not just making a spiel, and Ginger's standing me a last ginger ale and we're laughing at how funny that for the first time sounds, and he's saying it's a pity we can't get drunk together in memory of the better days, and hugging me and going away with wet eyes. Almost I phone the kid to tell him the moola's in my hands and tomorrow we'll be on the bike going South, but then I remember the phone's unplugged and swab down the counters and stack the glasses in the sink and get down to the flat faster than is my way.

When I try to unlock the door, another key is blocking mine, it, too, inserted *from the outside*. At first I think the kid's been out and back and forgotten to take out the key and lock himself in again, but even the *thought* is too complicated to be true, particularly when the kid is on the run and as careful as he is now. So – and the knowing blinds me like a light and my breath stops dead in my throat – this is a *third* key. But whose? And then it comes to me. Claire's. She never gave me back her key and I never changed the locks and she – and I – in a last unholy union of omission and commission – have thrown the kid to the wolves.

Crazed, I crash open the door and plunge into the dark as into a death, and something hits me in the face, and swings away and hits me again. Frantically I grope for the switch and flick on the lights, and the something is two naked feet, and they're the kid's, and the kid is naked as the feet and hanging by his neck from one of the old beams on the roof. Sobbing, but still holding in as much as I can, I pile a bankie on a chair under the kid and fetch the bread knife and cut him down. He flops onto the floor like a sack, the old, frayed rope knotted so tightly into his neck that I can't get it loose, and his eyes are coming out of his skull like a crab's, and his lips are peeled away from his teeth, the stench of excrement and the salve I gave him tell of him fouling himself as he died. I cradle his face in my hands, but he's not like anybody – or anything – I have ever known, and I pick him up to carry him to his bed and only then notice the gaping red emptiness that is his crotch, and, on the table in his room, neatly piled, the horror of the manhood they lopped from him – *live?*

He crashes out of my hands then – they forgetting they are holding him as I lift them and howl till I am done – then pick him up again and lay him on his bed, gently, as though he would know, and go into the toilet and retch till there is nothing left in my gut and silence seeps back into the flat as into a tomb.

Calm now, emptied with the emptiness that is death's – that is his – I walk over to the table, pick up the bottle of peppermint liqueur, unscrew its cap, hold the bottle up to the light, whisper – to what? – 'Prettier than a flower' – and drink till there's only the neck's chill penis on my tongue.

The Trap

For 'Grysie'
who also slept beside the sea
and loved a bird called 'Fly'

He awoke to a world awash with mist.

'Sea just a "shish" now,' he thought, mist squatting there like some broody hen, feathers fluffing her up to twice her size. For a moment the image of the hen had him back on the farm, he still a boy, sneaking a hand under some fowl, searching for the new-laid eggs, flesh crawling with fright at the thought of what Oubaas would do to him if he found him there, but still, desperately, driving himself on. For him, his mother, father, two girls younger than him, hunger had been more than just a word.

Even then, though not clearly formulating any thought, he had understood – understanding being as much acceptance as anything else – that his father was a good but weak man. Only at the end of every month, small wage in his hand, would he exert his will. Fired not so much by any moral fervour as by a longing to escape the self that everybody told him he was – and that so repetitive a telling had convinced him he, indeed, was – he would pocket the price of a jar of Tassies before handing the balance of the money over to his mother and, sheepishly but tenaciously, stand then his ground as she railed against him in the high, nagging voice that would eventually bring Oumiesies to the back door of the 'big house'. His mother would stop then as though Oumiesies had clapped a hand over her mouth and, unexpectedly – and almost companionably – stay silent for the rest of the weekend, while his father – sometimes with one of the other labourers, but mostly alone – would work his way through the wine into a state of vacuous exaltation that, in the end, left them with only the inanity of his grin.

Sobered up, he would not again drink till the next payday, resisting even the temptations of the grape season when Oubaas would frequently pass around a free 'dop' in the hope that this would spur the pickers on. His father would accept the splash of 'poeswyn' into his mug, but then pass it on to either Kortbooi or Namaqua, his two best friends, and he, being closer to his stolid, uncommunicative father than to the reverse that was his mother, once dared to ask why the for free 'dop' was not drunk while the unaffordable jar was so savagely drained every month end. His father had stood a moment, staring at him with unseeing eyes, turning the question over in his careful though illiterate mind, then said, 'When you want to kill yourself or lie with a woman, you don't just put the point in and take it out again. You put it all in – sommer so – and the job's done.'

The sexual allusion in those words – barely covert as it was – had not escaped him, nor had it confused or even in any way titillated him, because his mother and father, though not amoral or even habitually foul-mouthed, had known but too well that for them to be discreet about the mechanics of sex would have been not only ludicrous but a battle lost before it had begun. The farm animals had provided enough of a pantomime of what sex was all about and, at night, in the tiny, two-roomed mud-brick labourer's cottage with its flat, iron roof, the sound of his parents copulating had been loud enough to trouble his subconscious and bring him, lusting, out of sleep. Inevitably – and instinctively – he had begun to masturbate in step with his father's thrustings and eventually ejaculated his first seed in a bizarre tandem intercourse that had left him sated and – by the nature of his upbringing – wholly without shame. Later, both swimming naked in the vlei at the bottom end of the farm, he had boasted of this ultimate experience to his friend Pietie, Namaqua's youngest son of about his own age, and was deflated when Pietie laughed and said he had already done it 'he didn't know how many times,' and he punched Pietie for laughing and they had fallen to wrestling in the soft mud and Pietie had said, penis erect as his own, 'Hey, you play ma and I'll be pa,' and he had let Pietie roll him over and had been sodomised for the first time. Again, there had been no shame, only an intense pleasure, and when he told Pietie this, Pietie said 'his was better,' but both had, nonetheless, remained curious as to which *was* actually 'better' and, on another outing to the vlei, they had swopped roles and, so, hung, balanced, between two genders until Hettie, Kortbooi's teenage daughter, practically told them she was ready for anything in pants and they for some weeks then made a threesome at the vlei and mated, turn and turn about, with an innocence and abandonment that all too soon ended in sexual rivalry and the severing of a friendship the like of which he was never again to know.

He had never seen his mother drink wine, except for the Nagmaal sip she took at the nearby village's inordinately imposing Church.

'Nobody can shine the brass like Saartjie,' the fatherly, white and quick-off-the-mark Dominee would say, and his mother would glow with a radiance that rolled back the years and spend the Saturday night before the service polishing every metal appurtenance that the Church could subject to her busy Brasso and rag. Come Sundays, she would routinely berate his father for only attending Church for christenings and on the 'higher' Holy Days, and then, humbled by being allowed to stand before God together with Oubaas and Oumiesies and all the other whites from the surrounding farms, would sneak with him and his two sisters into the pew nearest to the door. There she would sit, quietly listening, tall, bony frame fumbled into Oumiesies' cast-off clothes, and, watching her – workworn hands folded in her lap and too heavily powdered cheeks beginning to mottle with an anxious sweat – he would sometimes feel that softness for her that he more often felt for his father and for which he had had no name.

No, he thought – even now warily circling the word – love had rarely dared to show its face in a home that had held twilight even at noon, the largely glassless windows blanked out with tacked-on sacking or board. Ancient whitewash peeling from the walls like a sun-raddled skin, what was left of it soiled with the smoke from the wood-burning stove, the guttering oil lamps that were the only lights from late afternoon till after dawn, the cottage had not been conducive to emotions as alien to it as pity or love, tolerating no more than a hand on the brow, a sharpening of awareness of him, that time when he had nearly died of the 'flu.

The immediate environs had been even more repellent: sentry-box-with-door and a seat over an open pit that served as a latrine and that had stunk with a pungency to turn all but the most seasoned of guts – and that, eventually, had always brought Oumiesies grumblingly out to order that a new pit be dug and the old one filled in. The stench from the appropriately adjacent pigsties, however, had been a problem beyond even Oumiesies' capacity to solve. Or, he had even then wondered – deep down, beyond words – had Oumiesies not *seen* this as a problem, had thought, rather, that the pigs' shit stank less than the shit of his father who had had to tend them and feed them with a profligacy he was never able to extend to his own kind?

Shivering a little as the mist seeped in under the oblong of cardboard on which, wrapped in his two tatty blankets and a 'plastic', he slept, he let his mind dwell on the pigs. Trapped in their pens of sturdy stone, the giant boars had incessantly mounted the keening sows, and there had been an almost primal heaving and threshing in as primal a slush of excrement that deepened into a quagmire of abomination when it rained. But the shrillest cacophony had come from the pens when Oumiesies – needing bacon and kaiings and lard – gave out the order to 'kill', and a boar would be wrestled, shrieking, from a pen and Oubaas would silence it with a neat hammer-blow between the eyes. Then the carcass would be wrapped in sacking and doused with boiling water that Oumiesies dispatched from the kitchen in a seemingly endless processional of pails, and, with bristles and skin softened up enough, he and the other labourers' teenaged boys and girls would be issued with spoons to scrape the bristles from the skin. Sometimes his stomach would lurch at the stench of shit and piss still clinging to the skin and he would quickly go to one side and vomit while the others mockingly howled. Oubaas would always give those who helped some portion of the pig that he did not want and, shortly before his leaving home for good, the younger of his two sisters, Rosie, had reared a tapeworm in her gut from eating meat from a pig that Oubaas should have known had the measles and later died of it because the tapeworm was a rare, not-showing-itself thing and the doctor, just out of college and not caring all that much anyway, had got his diagnosis all wrong.

Again he shivered, but this time from thinking of that leaving home after Rosie died.

It had all been so unexpected, so *at once*, he standing up from stealing an egg from a still warm nest and Oubaas towering over him with the face of God. Stunned with fear, he had not even tried to run – where to, anyway? – and Oubaas had hauled him by the scruff of his neck, the now crushed egg forlornly dripping its yolk from his fist, and flung him, face down, at the feet of his father who was irrigating the wheat. 'Beat him,' Oubaas had said, handing his father his own massive belt. 'Beat him as hard as I want and until I say "Stop". That, or you and your family will not be sleeping on my land tonight.' So his father had beaten him, on back, belly, legs, as he, rolling, tried to escape – beaten him till he fainted and Oubaas still didn't say 'Stop' – and it was his other sister, Naomi, who had been watching, stricken, from a corner of the field, who later told him that his father had then thrown the belt back into Oubaas's face and walked off, uncertainly and blunderingly as one blind.

It was also Naomi who ran to fetch his mother and, together, they had got him home and laid him on his bed. His mother had been gentle with him as she tended him, but her face had given no indication that he was other than a flesh under her hands, and, when his father came in and went to their own bed and, still fully-dressed and muddied from the field, laid down on it and turned his face to the wall, she still had said nothing, only stared down at her usually busy hands as they sat and waited for Oubaas to come and tell them to pack up and go.

But there had been no Oubaas at the door and it was only *he* that then had left. That very night, bundling all he had into a plastic bag, taking the coins from the bottle on the shelf above the stove, finding his mother's eyes, wide-open, watching him, but he not caring anymore, thinking, unjustly, bitterly, 'You used the eggs, did'n you? Never asked me where from. So pay me now for getting me the belt.' And went out then, not even quietly closing the door.

Had he later regretted that? Did he in any way still *care*? Did *they* in any way still care about *him*? Were they, for that matter, still *alive*, still *there*? Hurriedly his mind swerved aside from that, its very swerving betraying that it knew that that way lay pain, that he did, indeed, still care. 'What's the use of it anyway?' he thought, trying to face up to himself. 'There's no going back. Not the way things are now. Not the way *I* am now.'

In the city, he had fared better than most: had taken longer than most to slide from the fringes into the final abyss. The farm school had struggled him into literacy, if not much else, and that, allied with his mother's aggressiveness and his father's physical bulk, had soon gained him the leadership of the various street gangs into which he had drifted with the restlessness – had he but known it – of one seeking – and not finding – that which had been lost. Sniffing petrol or glue, drinking 'meths', had at first been alien to him, but sodomy – as a result of his encounters with Pietie at the vlei – had meant no more to him than his urinating against the nearest wall, and he was soon renting himself out to mainly white paedophiles with a willingness that earned him the final sanctification of always having money to spend. So, many times, he had found himself as in and out of jails as of the street children's 'homes', some of which had abused him and all of which he had, in his turn, abused, the carapace around him having, by then, grown more organic than assumed and he recognising kindness as but another loophole in the armour of a world to which he not only no longer belonged, but both hated and opposed.

But the frail, evanescent bloom of the boy had soon left him – all the more swiftly because of the life he had led – and the paedophiles had, then, too left him, rising from him with the pitilessness of blowflies abandoning all but his bones.

'But not to worry!' he boasted. 'I don't need them no more. Got

other money now. Not as much but I get by. Bush over me's for free.
Sea's for free. Maybe I'll go to the streets just now and get me some
cardboards and papers and stuff. Sell them to 'Scrap'. Or maybe I
won't. Hey, I'm like whitey, man! Do what I want. Just don't have the
suit. Maybe someday I'll have the suit too. And a car. Not just the old
trolley I gotta have for the scrap,' and he snickered with something of
the boy still in him, as also with something very old and very sad.

***

When he again woke, the sun was level with his eyes, shimmering as if
hung from an unsteady hand. And the mist gone – so much so that he
might have thought that he had dreamt, were it not for the wet of its
squatting still drying on the sand. And, in that patina, startlingly, the
fresh tracks of the cat coming to within the reach of his arm.

'Getting tame,' he thought and remembered the night that he had
first seen the cat, it stepping with its careful, ghostly tread down the
narrow track from the fringe of the city above, pausing as it sensed
him in the bush, running then back as though pursued. But he had
seen it – clearly – fur white as the sugar-white of the sand, only the
black markings on it giving it away, one patch, smeared across the
eyes, the nose, lending it a mask of audaciousness that pleased. It had
also been pitifully thin. 'Street cat,' he had told himself and had
begun to put out the odd scrap of food which either it or the rats took,
it never revealing itself to him again.

Now fully awake, he heaved himself about, lay rigid with surprise.
The cat was sitting on that side of him, watching him with its lambent,
malevolent eyes. For a long moment they stared at each other, locked
in a dialogue without words. Then he said, 'Kietsie,' in the high,
wheedling voice of his youth and incrementally advanced his hand.
The cat looked at it as though it held something astonishing and
strange – looked, then, back at him – back at the hand – slowly
lowered its head as though driven by a memory of what once had
been. Confidently, then, he bridged the gap – the precipitous pit that
was mistrust – reached out further, gently fondled, scratched behind
the alien ears, felt a stirring almost of lust – or was *this*, perhaps, love?
– in his loins as the cat's head yielded to his hand, began to nudge,
butt at it with a sensuousness that matched his own. Then it purred – a
grumbling noisiness kick-started out of its long disuse – and flopped
over onto its back that he might scratch its belly – which he did, and it
clawed and bit at his hand till he thought to end the play, fearing a
blood. But the cat suddenly stopped of its own, leaping up, ears laid

back, tail lashing, as it glared up into the leaves of the kaapsebessie bush that was his home.

'Uh-Uh, not "Fly" you don't,', he said and the cat, as though understanding the tone behind the gabble of the words, turned and ambled off with the forward-sloping slouch of its distant lion, and 'Fly', the wagtail he had tamed, came down from its flirting in the leaves and sat on his shoulder, tail swinging, up, down, with the unthinking regularity of a breath.

'Watch it, Fly,' he said, running a finger over the bird's head, it closing its eyes. 'I got me a friend, but you got you a death, you not watch out. So, *watch* out, bird!' and Fly hopped from his shoulder and darted abandonedly about, sometimes leaping into the air and angling a fly from it with a dexterity and accuracy that had earned it its name; and he flung aside his coverings and brewed some 'moerkoffie' in the fire-blackened tin with the wire handle and chewed on a hunk of close-to-mouldering bread. 'Gotta get bread,' he thought, and stripped down to his too large, as terminal underpants and, taking down a plastic bag from the branches of the bush, went down to the sea, Fly not following him because that was beyond the bounds of its secret bird's domain. There, knee-deep, he harvested the mussels for which he had brought the bag, squeegeeing with his feet in the cold sand, enjoying the flailing of his genitals in the too loose scants, feeling as free as the bird.

Back at the bush, he poured sea water from a bottle into the same all-purpose tin, put the water on to boil, added the mussels when it did, left them to cook and gape while he bared his crotch and searched the pubic hairs for nits, muttering as he found one and cracked it between his nails. He did not find any more, but nevertheless, driven still by the nagging of a mother who had convinced herself that only frequent scrubbing with a so barely affordable soap could lessen the shamefulness of their skins, he returned to the sea and, fully dropping now his scants, vigorously rubbed his crotch with handfuls of shale and shells – a fastidiousness, this, which had always set him apart from the rest and earned for him the not entirely mocking soubriquet of 'Duke'.

The two horses had almost passed him before he became aware of the soft plod of their hooves in the sand. Startled, he tried to whip up his scants, but they tangled round his knees and irretrievably tore, revealing, then, more than they concealed, and he looked up to encounter the full scorn of the one rider – a woman – raven-haired, imperious, white as a bone, curling lip lashing out at him with a savagery to match the riding crop that dangled from a languid hand.

Glancing back at him from her own horse's rump, her companion laughed and he tried to see her face, but they were already distant and the sun blinded him and all he had of her was the laugh – nothing of the mockery or spitefulness in it for which he searched, but a genuine and delighted appreciativeness of his plight, and, though he hissed, 'Hoere!' from between his teeth, he did not really include her in the plural as he went back to the bush, holding the remnants of his scants together with one hand.

For a while he sulked, squatting in the mild sun, letting it warm him, comfort his scrubbed groin. Then he thought again of the girl and how she had laughed – 'girl' because he had decided that that was what she was – and quite suddenly himself laughed, primitively as the bare-arse boy wrestling Pietie in the mud rather than the getting-to-be-thirty-something 'Duke', beating a fist softly on the sand. 'Hoer!' he said again, but now it was an endearment rather than an epithet and he lay back and toyed with her till he slept, Fly busily about him, sometimes perching on him, and he loosing a gentle seed, needing a woman again.

Later, a lone autumn cloud moved across the sun and he roused. 'Hey!' he said, reprimanding his penis as though it was an entity of its own, fingering the wetness in his groin, and peered up over the circle of rocks that fronted his bush and concealed the evidence of his sleeping there from passing eyes. The position of the sun showed that it was now nearly noon, and a few mostly whites in hats, sandals and shorts were exercising their dogs on the small spit of rock-littered beach that he had claimed as 'his own' and from which the long, immaculate 'holiday' beaches curved away to the left and right. The rocks, which stepped monolithically into the sea itself, barricaded the pit from both surfers and bathers and it was only the occasional horse-rider, walker with or without a dog, or couple copulating under an overhang in an abandoned unawareness that they were being watched, who sometimes required that he keep his head down for a while.

The authorities undoubtedly knew that he was there, but let him be because he, in an unwritten and unspoken contract with them, kept the spit free of litter – both his and other's – and did not make his presence known as, earlier in the day, he so inadvertently had done. So now he waited till the dog-lovers had gone before he slipped down to the floret of minor rocks just within the high-water mark where the incoming tide would wash away his shit and there defecated, then sank down into a rock 'bath' hard beyond, but carefully, fearing the shell-encrusted sides that could slice into him like knives, and, clinging to the last remnants of his scants, let the cold, bitter water surge over him till, benumbed and unable to endure more, he as carefully edged out again.

Back behind the screen of his own rocks, he laid down and let the sun dry him, noting – though trying not to – the growing scrawniness of his legs and arms, his ribs' emerging skeleton, the beginning-to-round, once flat-as-a-board belly as it rebelled against, not indulgences, but abstinences and, too often, the ultimate abuse of being fed scraps that the dogs or cats had overlooked in the city's numberless rubbish bins. Dried, he crawled in under the bush whose arch of thick, bright-as-a-metal leaves he had buttressed – invisibly from the inside – with a heavy, green-as-the-leaves sheet of plastic he had filched from a factory's loading-yard. There, he neatly folded up his bedding, hauled out a plastic sack from deep inside the bush, took out the last pair of scants he possessed – had saved, actually, for the 'fancy times' – and dressed himself in that, some workman's cast-off dungarees and a pair of sneakers whose replacement was the next and imminent problem to be overcome.

Fly followed him halfway along the path up from the beach, then dropped down again into its own territory as he went on and bought a loaf of bread from the nearest neighbourhood shop, carefully counting out the needed copper coins to the barely restrained irritation of the surly Greek owner's as surly son.

Returning, he remembered that he had forgotten to check on his traps in the bush bordering the beach and turned aside into the dune scrub and backing Port Jackson trees – one of the latter of which he had felled in order to break the stranglehold it had begun to establish over his kaapsebessie bush – and visited his three contraptions of chicken wire, sticks and twine, finding, in the middle one, a guinea fowl. Lured by the handful of crushed mealies he had scattered as a bait, it had blundered into the trap, got its neck stuck in the mesh and – as the tight wrap of the wire round its body revealed – died a particularly violent and agonising death. 'Trap not done *that*, though,' he thought, staring down at the stump of the neck, finding the severed head a metre away, noting the cat spoor all around. '*Tiger* done that,' then repeated, 'Ja, Tiger done that,' savouring the name he had, thus, instinctively decided was the right one for the tom he had that morning noticed was so very truculently – indeed enviably – hung. 'Chewed through the neck and the bird all fussed, then the feathers and the wires stop him so's the big feed's for Duke.' But he was not angered by what the cat had done: began, instead, to find a very real affection for it and, after he had plucked and gutted the bird, he set the entrails aside for it, trying to convince himself that his budding relationship with the cat was not a one-way affair.

The sun was now mellowing into the west and he hurriedly ate the mussels he had earlier cooked and all but forgotten about, stolidly munching, not particularly enjoying, the meagre sea-flesh, he being – despite the more than a decade between – still an upcountry boy whose mouth only urgently salivated when he looked at the cleaned, rough portions of the fowl he had set out for a braai. But food was food and one did not throw away food – not even when it was turning mouldy or beginning to smell – and it was not the sea's fault that it could not yield him the honest, red meat that he so craved. But why then, if the sea could not service one of his most basic needs, did he still want to sleep beside it, be alone with it, instead of huddle with the others for companionship and warmth in bus shelters or doors where the wind and the rain were less of a pestilence than they could all too often be under the bush? He had, in moments before sleep or waking from sleep, asked himself this question, turned it over in his father's slow way, and had more or less decided that it was because there was as much of that silent, walking-alone father in him as his brash, garrulous mother and this what-he-was was *him* and as *fixed* a him as the great rocks of the sea. Sometimes, also, he had found himself telling himself that the sea was 'pretty' or 'nice' and he liked it for *that*, but this was about as far as he could go in that direction, he being wary of replacing the triteness of 'pretty' or 'nice' with a word like 'beauty' which – like 'love' – sat uneasily in the meagre clearing house of his thoughts and words. More positive was the third inkling, namely, that the sea was powerful – the most powerful thing he had ever known – and – unlike the knuckling-down father who had beaten into him a bitterness nothing cured – would protect him against invasion on at least one side of the vulnerable island that was his life.

Mussels eaten, cooking-tin emptied and scrubbed with sand, he took the latter to fetch sweet water from the nearby spring, Fly darting about him all the way, snapping at flies, knowing that soon the sun would be down and it, like some fabled creature a spell had bound, must be done with its foraging and die the small death of its sleep in the kaapsebessie leaves. 'But not me,' he thought. 'Can stay up till I drop if I want,' and wondered, with a rare fancifulness, what it would be like to be a bird, then bent down and looked into the small mirror of the spring water where it briefly pooled before disappearing again under the sand. His father's tight pelt of hair, as tightly-curled mottle of beard, flared nose, generous, soft lips, contrasted strangely with the San angles of his mother's bones, her glittering, restless eyes, and he –

as he usually, childishly, did – grinned a grin that he meant to be macho, but that only betrayed the sad oddity of an old man's teeth in young gums. Then he dunked in the tin, shattering the face, emptying the pool which would only very slowly seep full again, and went back to the bush, whistling through his teeth, and there brewed coffee and, after the sun had set and the last, stray passer-by had vanished with the light, he kindled a fresh, discreet fire and nursed it down to a small round of glowing coals on which he braaied the pieces of the guinea fowl, salting each piece with the grudging hand of the very poor.

Sitting on the rocks, watching the waves caterpillar in under the new moon and the first scatterings of the stars, he slowly, savouringly, ate the guinea fowl, pinching the last vestiges of flesh from the bones, sucking the bones dry, wanting the taste of them never to end, replete with a happiness that was as flawed as it was full because he knew, better than most, that the other – the *certain* – face of repletion was the return of emptiness and pain. Finishing, licking his fingers, he looked up and the cat was watching him from the fringe of the embers' glow, eyes intent but not asking anything of him, and he threw it the entrails he had saved and, after the first, slight flinching, it lowered its head and began to eat with the fastidious intensity of the beggar that is both desperate and proud.

In its turn finished, it squatted, wiped its forepaws over its face and stalked off into the darkness in the direction of the sea, not once looking back, and he thought, 'Just like the rest. Don't care but for his self. Thank you, mister, and fuck you!' and felt an unaccountable and quite ridiculous sadness that no amount of self-berating would allay. But the feeling was premature because, later that night, after he had wrapped himself in his bedding and was about to draw the plastic over his head, he looked around for the last time and the cat was sitting right alongside him, staring at him with its dispassionate eyes. 'Tiger,' he said, softly, a catch in his voice, and put out his hand, and again the cat submitted to it and, this time, came and lay down next to him, roaring with satisfaction, kneading the plastic with its paws.

Later still, the night reaching for the nadir of its dark, he was awakened by the cat's leaping up, and he uncovered his head and the cat was standing as it had that morning stood, ears flat, tail writhing, eyes ablaze, and, when he heard Fly again twitch in the leaves, he said to the cat. 'Hey!' and it glared at him with something of the balefulness meant for the bird, then relaxed and lay down again, but not taking its eyes off the leaves.

✳ ✳ ✳

By the end of the following week, the furthest of the three traps had yielded him a second guinea fowl – this time alive, unscarred by the cat. Blue, bold, oddly Jurassic head tightly caught in the mesh of the trap, it stared up at him with a bird's inscrutable eyes, only the body's spastic twitch pleading its powerlessness, beseeching that it be released. But it was only that body – deceptively plump under the flattering of the speckled feathers – that he saw, and he untangled the bird from the mesh and, pitilessly as any raptor, wrung its neck and bore it, exultantly, back to the bush.

Something like discomfort did, however, stir in him when the day passed and he realised that Fly had not once sat on his shoulder – had, in fact, quite noticeably avoided him – and he wondered if the fowl's death still clung to his hands like a curse. The thought troubled him, stayed with him, despite his little-boy-whistling in the dark, and, the following day, when Fly again sat on his shoulder, he was quite disconcertingly relieved. Which was not yet the end of it because, two weeks later, there was the jackpot of a porcupine in the traps, quills scattered like lances on a loser's field, and when he killed it with a single blow of a heavy wood, Fly seemed quite unperturbed and he knew he was never going to be sure whether he had had to do with a randomness or the surfacing of something beyond his understanding from which he shrank and fled.

His first ever trapping of a porcupine was an event to be celebrated – the thick bacon on the back being a particular prize – and he drank deeply of a small jar of Tassies while preparing it, even teasingly putting out a little of the wine for Tiger who, though ranging by day, never failed to return to the bush at night. The cat was growing sleek, he even buying it the occasional can of cat food which he could ill afford but the giving of which expanded him in spirit as much as it contributed towards the sleeking of the cat. 'You mine, huh?' he said, stroking the cat with the rough possessiveness that he knew it preferred, rolling it over onto its back, yelling as it instantly sank its teeth into his hand, it having lost none of its tigerishness, as it had lost none of its ominous enthusiasm for Fly. 'One bad thing you got there,' he said. 'Fly mine before you. You kill Fly, I kill you,' but his tone was more playful than threatening, and the cat knew that and set to comfortably licking itself while he stared into the embers of the 'braai' and listened to the 'shish' of the sea.

Then the foot slid into the circle of the embers' glow and stopped, close to his side, and he at first did nothing, pretending to be unaware. Then, when he sensed the other's growing perplexity, he seized the foot and yanked at it, and she came down into the soft sand, hissing like a cat, cursing his mother's cunt.

'Why'd you do that?' she yelled, untying her doekie, brushing the sand from the frizzy bush of her hair, tying the doekie back on. 'You forget who I am?' and she glared at him, slit-eyes black as the spaces between stars, but he saw that her lips remained full, trembled on the brink of a smile.

'You lucky I did'n do worse,' he grinned. 'Sneaking up on me like you did.'

'But you knew it was me. Don't tell me you did'n know it was me!'

His eyes ranged over her, familiarly as flies. 'Maybe. Maybe I got eyes in the back of my head. Maybe you got a smell that says it's you. Or,' and again he grinned, 'maybe I just know those shoes. Heels like a hoer's. You on the beat again?'

Again she cursed his mother's womb, but the stock phrase was robotic, toneless: did no damage to his mother's honour – or his. '*So*? If you knew it was me, why'd you do what you did? And me Hendrik's wife! Man-of-God's wife!'

'Feeling good,' he said and indicated the still half-full jar of wine. 'Dê,' and he leaned over and sloshed some of the wine into his own drinking-tin. 'Drink up and forget you're Hendrik's kêt for a change. Had some porcupine but Tiger and me finished it before you come.'

'Tiger?'

'My cat,' he said and looked across the embers to where the cat had sat, but it had vanished, as suddenly and soundlessly as though it had never been – as though, in fact, it had fled from a shape beyond his perception and hers.

'Where? I see no cat. What you want with a cat anyway?'

'You asking means you would'n understand if I told.'

'You think I'm *stupid*?'

'I did'n say that. Hey! look,' and he leaned to her 'you knew what porcupine taste like before you *ate* it? You would know if I just *told*? Come on, drink your wine,' and he held out his hand for the tin. 'You not the only one drinking here,' and she drained the Tassies and gave him back the tin and, after he had again drunk, he poured some more for her and said, 'Tiger's like the Tassies when it's a cold night and you got no fire and the Tassies is lying warm as you want down there in your gut. Only Tiger's not in my gut. It's like it is now. He's out there – somewhere,' and his arm swung, indicating dunes, sea, rocks. 'I dunno *where*, but he's *there*. I just *know* the way you still *don't* know,' and he got up and blew the embers back into a tired flame, then stood looking around as though for the cat and sat down again.

Drinking now more slowly, she considered him, the light of the fire glancing from the beginning-to-surface bones of her face, contrasting shadows emphasising the seams and hollows that scarred her as they did him, that marked them as unwilling kin.

'You're not us, Duke,' she said at last. 'Some of the men got dogs. Look after them like they was their kids. But that's fine by us. Dog *works* for you, *fights* for you, tells you when the cops come. But you got a cat. Now you said something about that, but what *good's* a cat? All we got to do is keep alive. Does the cat help you keep alive? And they say you've got a bird that sits on your shoulder like you're a man who's a witch. And look where you live. Sleep here by the sea all by yourself. Don't want to come and sleep with us up there in town. I also come from the farms. Had to sleep around for a while. Sleep around, like you just now said, like a hoer to keep alive. Like you also done but I don't call *you* a hoer. So now I'm no more Lydia from Vaalbessievlei but the Lydia who's *us*, who's *town*. But you still the farm boy, Duke. Still looking for your farm – here,' and, as his had done, her arm indicated dunes, rocks, sea, and she finished the wine and gave back the tin.

But he did not this time drink, fearing his overpowering by sleep, the neutralising of his tongue and loins. To her, however, he passed another generous, full tin of the wine, urging her to drink, his eyes not leaving the fullness of her flesh under the too tight dress, a surging in his genitals that he did not try to curb. But she put the tin down beside her on the sand and laughed: a shrill, unfunny bark.

'What you laughing at?' he asked, his voice harsh with desire and haste.

'You trying to make me dronk, hey? Want me under that bush!'

'Anywhere you like,' he said, brutally, abandoning pretence. 'It's what you came for, is'n it?'

'I never let you do it with me before. Why now?'

'Woman don't come to a man this late and she not wanting what's between his legs.'

'Well, I'm not wanting nothing from you. Not even this wine,' and she handed him back the full tin and stood up to go.

'But, fokkit, Lydia, *why*? You think I won't come on strong? I been with others. You women talk. All the time. Others not tell you I come on *strong*? Fokkit, woman, I'm in the mood tonight. Look,' and he gapped his fly. 'Let's go!'

The almost boyish note of pleading in his voice stayed her. 'Nay, I don't think nothing like that. I like you, Duke, but I'm not putting Hendrik one side for you. Or *anyone*. I don't get a price on the beat anymore, so I got to have a man like Hendrik to tie me to. He prays nice when there's bad things and the Street *respects* him for that. And respects me too because I'm his woman, only I mustn't sleep around anymore. That way I'm safe. Other way I'm bitch and the dogs after me all the time.'

'But I can look after you too. Better'n Hendrik can. Look – porcupine, wine, zoll if you want. This' – and again he gapped his fly.

'Nay, Duke, You no one-woman-man. With you I'd go one way. Down.'

'But Hendrik is bones. *Bones! Old* bones! And you still *woman*. You letting his thing tickle you till you *die?*'

'Or *he* dies,' she corrected, sombrely, not meeting his eyes. 'He's thirty years older'n me.'

'Hah!' he taunted. 'He could live to be a *hunnerd* yet! I gotta wait that long?' but she did not answer him and a small silence settled between them, resonating like a bell.

Then he was pleading again. 'Hey! If we do it now and you don't stay, he won't know. Come *on!* What's wrong with having fun? Yirrah! You act like I'm giving you the blade!'

But she shook her head. 'Nay. He will know. He will *smell*. He's old and the old know and they smell. Nay, I must go now. I already stayed too long,' and she turned. But he was on her, like the cat yearned to be on Fly, tripping her onto her back in the sand, gripping her between his knees. Frantically, she struggled to be free, uttering no sound, but he wrestled her, getting a hand up her skirt, finding only nakedness underneath, slipping the hand then between her thighs, finding her flooding and ripe, stretching then down over her, hissing, surprised: 'You *want* it! Like *I* want it!' and, for a moment, a hunger equalling his did, indeed, stare up at him from the wide, acquiescing eyes, and she stilled, seeming to melt inwards as he bared them both and sank down for the irreversible thrust.

But then the voices of late strollers suddenly came to them from other side his shield of rocks and she whispered with a deadly and implacable calm, all lust gone, 'Loose me or I scream,' and he rolled away from her and lay, face down, his head on his arms, his erection unabatingly pinned between his belly and the sand. Dully, he heard her get up, rearrange her dress, the rustle of the cloth impossibly loud – heard her hunt for a shoe that had fallen off, put it on – heard her come across to him, felt her touch his shoulder as though she would – what? – apologise? – finally curse his mother's cunt? 'Fok off!' he snarled and did not raise his head as she crunched away over the sand, rolled the stones on the path up from the beach to the streets that were home.

Her steps stilled, the voices of the strollers drawing away again, he rose, joylessly masturbated, knowing he would otherwise not sleep, and washed his penis and hand in the sea. Then he rolled himself in his bedding under the bush, heard Fly rouse, again sleep, tried to sleep himself, instinctively stretching out his hand to stroke the cat. But it still had not returned from some near or far place of the night, and this, being no longer the way of it, troubled him and he lay, for long and dismally alone, torn between fear that something had happened to it and the chill remembrance that his mother had once said that cats fled those who walked with the Devil in their hearts. Had the Devil that night been in Lydia's heart or his? Or in both?

He woke to a presence at his side, senses flailing in the still undiminished cocoon of the dark, and it was the cat – tensed, uncertain, watching him with eyes that seemed huge and lit as a lion's. But it came to his hand when he called to it, though uneasily so, and he fondled it, watching a star plummet into the sea, hearing the previously tranquil waves splash in a midnight surge, feeling sea, sky, earth, the thunder of the dark, crush him as he a nit between his nails.

And when he again slept, last haul to dawn, he dreamt of the farm, of home, each image bright and stilled as an arrested slide.

✳ ✳ ✳

For the five years since she had first arrived in the city, he had 'coveted' Lydia, he still thinking in the Biblical terms drummed into him by the Church. Why, he was not quite sure. She had been pretty and – though a softness was settling in her now as in him – a softness of rottenness in a too-ripe fruit – she was still not to be compared with the rest of them with their pendulous dugs and mottled skins, the splaying feet and spindly shins that struggled them so painfully over the least unevenness of paving or tar. She still had her teeth, could still recognisably smile – not gape in a final disintegration of the face – and her breasts, he thought – pert still and round – were so clearly shaped for a holding in a man's hand. But was that all? Or was it also that the hardness of her – the imperious nose, almost savage lips, the tongue that could be as quick and as stinging as a lash – reminded him of the knife he so cherished, had so long scrimped and saved to buy from the shop that would not relinquish it to him till he had counted out the last small cent of its price? Or, most slyly of all, was it the sallowness of her as compared with his own swarthiness that attracted him as rattex a rat, that bade him possess it in a sad coupling with a whiteness – however illusionary – that he vocally reviled but – in his deepest self –

revered?

Whatever the case, he now desired her more desperately than before, lying awake nights, savouring again the near-intolerable pleasure of her nakedness's momentary yielding to his, his straddling her, poised for the locking into her that would shudder them into a coitus beyond recall. But she would not be visiting him again for a long time – maybe never – she being now as scared as she was hard – and, so, driven and against the grain of common sense, he went in search of her, found her in the only place where she would be: beside Hendrik in a little lean-to at the end of an industrial lane. It was a grey drizzle-day, autumn teetering into the big chill, and he lifted up the plastic flap of the lean-to's otherwise doorless opening without announcing he was there, eager to get in out of the rain, and she raised herself, startled, eyes betraying her alarm, then her anger as she lay down again and turned her face to the wall.

But Hendrik was not fazed. 'Hey, Duke!' he roared, sitting up and back against the factory wall, reaching him a giant hand. 'First time you been here! You got troubles, boy?'

'Nay,' he said, lie ready on his tongue. 'Just come to see your new kip.'

'Ja, the Lord has been good to me, boy. You still under the bush?'

'Where else?'

'Plenty places else. Look at me. Praise the Lord and He says to the boere, "Hey! that Hendrik's a good man. You better look after him for Me!" So they give me this kip and all I got to do is keep an eye open when they gone.'

'You *heard* God tell them that? How do you know it's not just the boere who give you the kip because they want your eye?' and added, not meaning to, but it slipping out, 'For free!'

Hendrik looked at him, shaking his head. 'You don't believe in the Lord, do you, Duke?'

'Done nothing for me.'

'You *asked* Him? Nay, Duke, you don't get nothing, you don't ask. Now I ask – all the time – and I got the Power and the Street come to me because they *know* I got the Power – not just to see how's it with the new kip,' and the towering, still powerful bulk seemed to draw itself up even higher and, though the voice was gentle, the eyes were brilliant and fierce.

Unwillingly, he felt awe wake in him, shrank before the other's face as before a steep of rock as elemental as fire or air. 'But he's *old*,' he thought, reasoning with himself. 'Must be going for that seventy years the Bible says,' and he searched the knobbly hands, their veins surfacing under the thinning skin, exposing themselves to a nick of blade or nail, but the awe remained and he glanced away at Lydia's still turned back, suddenly, agonisingly, possessed by an image of Hendrik coupling with her, penis – mammoth, no doubt, as the rest of him – replenishing her from the inexhaustible reservoirs of his lust.

And, as though intercepting a signal from him as subtle as a pheromone, Hendrik reached out a hand to Lydia and, grasping a buttock, massaging it with a harsh possessiveness, smiled at him with a lazy slyness and said, 'So now you've seen how good the Lord's been to me, giving me this fine kip. But that's nothing, Duke. The Lord opens His hands *wide* when He's got to do with them that praise His Name. He's not just counting out a few cents for the cardboards like the boer at Scrap. He's giving me also my woman, Duke – this Lydia I got here now under my hand. And the Lord has been good to her too because could be she'd picked a young bull like you and missed out on what a *real* man is giving her now. What do you say, girl?' and his grip on the buttock tightened till she whimpered and tried to push his hand aside, still not turning round. 'What's wrong with you, woman? Why you not greeting our Duke that's come to visit us all the way through the rain? You two had a fight the Lord's not telling me about? Hey, Duke?' and the great head swung back to him, the eyes unsettlingly not questioning, reminding him that she had said that he could *smell* what was hidden before it was told.

Desperately he strove to stay calm. 'Nothing *my* side,' he said, sensing, too late, that the indifference he feigned was *too* wholly achieved, too devoid of a natural inquisitiveness and surprise.

Hendrik grinned. 'Well, that's fine then, Duke. Thought a minute there you'd been trying it on with my girl and she saying, "Nay," because she's loving what I'm giving her and the Lord's showing her the Way. Not that I'd be blaming you, Duke. I been young myself once – *am* still young, boy, when it comes to what counts – and, if I was you, I would also be looking at my Lydia like I shouldn't and be thinking those things that are an abomination to the Lord. So, *if* the Satan been at you, boy, speak up – any time – and old Hendrik will get right down on his knees and have that Satan out of you quick as a flea. Understand?'

'Ja, I understand, but,' at last back on track, the scattering of him again reined in, 'why you keeping *on* like this? I *said* there's nothing like what you thought.'

'Ja, I heard you and I'm thanking the Lord that there's still a young bull on the Street that's not all the time lusting after what the Lord forbids. I'm proud of you, boy, and I'm trusting you so much, I'm letting you do something no man done before. Look,' and the hand went out again and, this time, lightly, sensually, stroked the buttock within its reach, 'as I said, you seen now my kip and you sat in it and it's nice and warm in here and you not caring about the rain. So you seen *and* felt it, but you only *seen* my woman, Duke, so I'm saying to you now, put out your hand like it's my hand and *feel* my woman, Duke. Feel how soft and nice and warm as the kip, is my woman, boy.'

Shock and fear lanced through him as though the hand on the buttock had shot out and crushed his genitals, but, somehow, spurred by desperation, he managed to clutch about him the tatters of his calm, heard himself as from a far distance say, 'Don't want to do that. That don't sound like a Lord's thing.'

'Who are you to say what is a Lord's thing, boy? The Lord given *you* this kip, this woman I'm asking you to put your hand on as a friend? Come on! What's wrong? I'm trusting your hand. Or is your hand saying your tongue lied?'

Hesitantly, driven by the very gentleness of the other's insistence, he stretched out his hand, laid it, inertly, on the buttock's as rigidly unmoving curve.

'*That's* not feeling her, boy!' Now the coaxing voice was commanding, cruel, and the other's entire presence seemed to be arrowing in on him with the ominousness of a countdown nearing its end. '*Feel* her, Duke! Let that hand you say's not wanting her, *feel* what a fine woman I got from my Lord. Feel her or your hand will be telling me it touched her before, that you are a fornicating satan-seed I must throw out of here in the Name of the Lord!'

Convulsively, almost of its own volition, his hand obeyed, gripping, kneading the buttock with no trace of tenderness, his desire for her doused as though it had never been, and she, at last also driven beyond recall, whipped around and cursed his mother's cunt with the intensity of the deranged, then buried her face in her hands and wailed.

Hendrik laughed then – abrupt, strange bark that said nothing at all – stared at him with challenging eyes, but he rose to the challenge, her reaction sobering, shaming him, driving him to his feet, hands balled, fear drained from him like a poisonous blood. 'Dog!' he breathed. 'Fokken shit from a pig!' and the grin slicked from Hendrik's mouth like a wiped-off grease and they looked at one another for a long moment of hatred as passionate as love, then he turned and slammed out of the lean-to, letting the wet plastic door-covering whip back and scatter its wetness like a spewing of spittle into Hendrik's face.

Outside, the rain was tailing off, a wan sun struggling to break through the clouds, and he took the stolen supermarket trolley from where he had left it alongside the factory wall and went on his round of central city dumping sites for papers, cardboard and, very occasionally, even the odd metal part from a reconditioned machine or car. Soon the trolley was piled to wobble-height with what he had found and the whole perilously held in place with wire or string, and he trundled the trolley with an unusually suicidal defiance of the traffic through the streets to Scrap, his spirit still outraged by what had taken place in the lean-to and his mind grappling with the puzzle of why Lydia had reacted as she had done.

Had she come to hate him to the extent that she could no longer tolerate even the touch of his hand, or had she *acted* that way in order to convince Hendrik that nothing untoward had occurred between him and her? And, if so, had she meant to protect *him* as well as herself, or only herself? – in which latter case, he inwardly snarled, 'she might as well fok off for good,' for all he cared. Or was it that he *would* still care and that that was why her wailing in his ears would not go away? And then there was also the question of *had* she actually convinced Hendrik that it was all in his mind, or had her reaction – excessive as it had been – convinced him the other way around and even now he was donnering the shit out of her with those great hands? And would he care if *that* was the case, and, if so, what was he doing here, now, instead of helping her back in the lane? – and he hurried the trolley faster and faster along the streets until he was almost running with it – running as his mind was running from a complexity of speculation and emotion he was wholly unfitted to resolve.

Scrap sold, he pushed the empty trolley back to the beach, pausing to ferret in the trash tins strapped to the lampposts, irritably littering the pavement with what he did not want, eventually striking it lucky when he found a packet with a handful of crisps still in it which he at once wolfed, and, later, an almost whole meat pie of which he saved a small portion for the cat. At the last cafe before the descent to the beach, he bought a loaf of bread and the 'tailpiece' of a polony at a reduced price and then rattled the trolley down the path to the bush, whistling for the bird, but not expecting the cat which would be doing its own scrounging in its own incommunicable and solitary ways.

But Fly did not come to him, nor could he see it foraging about the bush which seemed to huddle in a silence unnatural to it, that even the ceaseless whisper of the sea could not breach, and anxiety surfaced in him as he was reminded – as so often before – of the essential fragility of a small bird like Fly – the uncertain refuge of its low-level flights, the breakable as china slivers of its bones. 'Like a woman,' he thought. 'Klap her and she breaks,' but that spawned the hardly less unsettling thought of Lydia being beaten up by Hendrik and he summarily thrust that image from him, only to find his mind blundering into the hideous conjecture that maybe the cat had at last caught up with Fly, and he pushed the trolley deep into the Port Jackson scrub in which he always hid it and hastened to the kip, hopefully again whistling up the bird.

And stopped short.

Tracks – smaller, narrower, than those of his own broad, sneaker-shod feet – roamed – inquisitively, disturbingly – through his kip, indented deeply as someone crouched to inspect his fireplace, indented again as the same someone squatted to peer under the bush, stretched out, then, to inspect his meagre possessions – to disarrange them – not spectacularly, but clearly enough under the censure of his accustomed eye. 'Yirrah!' he thought, 'the cops!' and traced the spoor back to a massive concrete block, an iron pipe inexplicably jutting up from it, that had been left behind by some aborted breakwater scheme of long before his time. There the tracks both started and *ended* – why *that?* – coming, going, along the side of the block – but it could have been that they started as they ended *other side* the block, only the incoming tide had already surged in up to there and smoothed out the sand, and he had to jump back as it again surged to within inches of where he had stood. The firmer sand in the region of the block did, however, show the tracks up more clearly and he could now see that they were those of a *booted* foot and, because he had always associated boots with officialdom, he was further – and depressingly – convinced that someone from 'the Law' had been prowling his kip. 'But you *know* I'm here, boer,' he said, addressing the unknown, trying to shake off the long shadow of the day. 'So why you fokking me around now?' and although Fly, clearly frightened off by the alien intrusion, returned before nightfall, and the cat came to eat the scrap of pie and a piece of the polony that anxiety had robbed of its taste, he was only partly comforted and lay a long while, listening to a gull sleeplessly patrolling the sea, before he himself knew sleep.

The next day, coming back at the same time, he found fresh tracks overlaying the old, but not, this time, rambling around – going now straight to the bush, then returning to the concrete block where the tide had again wiped them out, leaving the puzzle still maddeningly unsolved. Fly – no longer so fearful of the mysterious intruder? – was still there, answered to his call, but his own previous unease lurched, sickeningly, into terror and his hand reached for his crotch as though to restrain the flooding urine of his fear. '*Fok you!*' he cried, as though the harshness of the words, the loudness of his voice, could armour him, flush out into the open that which no longer seemed gone, that lurked, rather, in the dune scrub, the contours of the sand, anywhere that was tantalisingly just beyond the parameters of his sight. Startled, it was he that Fly then fled, though not going too far, cowering in the leaves of the bush towards which he now edged, watchfully, ears alert as his eyes, spine aware as one who slunk amongst foes in a darkened place.

At the entrance to the bush, he stopped as he had stopped the day before, rigid with shock. But now it was shock of another kind – the shock of delight of the child upon whom an improbable beneficence had been bestowed – and he sank to his knees before the groceries that had been neatly stacked alongside his bedding-roll – sugar, salt, "moerkoffie", samp, condensed milk, meat cubes, soup powder, rusks – and a packet of boiled sweets which he immediately and plunderingly breached, eager for the sweetness that his palate so craved. 'Yirrah!' he said, and again: 'Yirrah!' and screwed up his face, tight, and sucked at the sweet, hard, because there was a something in him like a weeping, but it was all too long ago and he did not quite know anymore how to let it all out.

That night, he diluted some of the condensed milk with water from the spring and set it out for the cat in a king-sized polish tin's lid that he had thought to use as a plate, and the cat sniffed at it with a fittingly tigerish mistrust, then dredged up a memory from way back and, hunching over the lid, began to lap up the milk with noisy slappings of the tongue. It finished and settled at his side, he then again – as on the previous night – struggled to fall asleep, his mind still bemused by the gift of food and his curiosity as to the identity of the donor grown to fever pitch. '*Must* show a face now, hey?' he told himself, excitement rowelling him, but a week passed in which nothing further happened and it was as though a cloud had passed overhead, loosed the small cargo of its grace and, emptied, dissolved itself beyond recall.

❋ ❋ ❋

Sun barely up, he kindled a fire and hunkered over it, racked by an occasional bout of coughing from the first of his usual winter colds. 'Gotta get me a mix,' he muttered, but knew he would probably, coffee brewed, roll himself back into his bedding and sleep on till the importunities of bladder or bowel drove him out and up the path towards the clinic and a belated round of the bins.

He was also moody from not having smoked a zoll for several days as a result of the pain in his chest, and, when mucus flooded his nose, he irritably blocked each nostril in turn with his thumb and snorted onto the sand. 'Fok it!' he growled and rose to fetch fresh water from the spring, then whirled at a sudden heavy threshing from the direction of the sea.

She was tying the reins of the restive horse to the pipe in the concrete block, patting the proud arch of the beast's neck with a gentling hand, speaking to it in as gentle a tone, and it quietened and stood, nuzzling her hand. 'Hey!' he breathed, meaning the horse, not her: *knowing* the horse with a farm boy's knowingness, but not knowing *her* because he had not seen her face that day.

Then she was coming towards him, twin saddlebags sagging from an arm, her smile a little hesitant, but warm.

'Remember me?' she asked, the playfulness in her voice as slightly flawed, her eyes ruefully admitting that that was so.

Warily, avoiding her eyes, he studied her: the thin blouse that revealed her feminineness, the jodhpurs that distorted it, the fine leather riding boots that had left their telltale impressions in the sand.

'Nay,' he said, his voice curt and unmannerly to even his own ears, but he not meaning it that way, the impact of her intense otherness – blue and blonde of eyes and hair, pallor of the skin under its bluff of her tan, a lankness, a flowing, where he knotted and coiled – addling his tongue. But she could not know that and he, sensing the ebbing in her as from a wound, said again, 'Nay,' but now less harshly, and added, 'Only the horse. I know only the horse.'

'But I was *on* the horse!' she laughed, the ebbing stayed. 'How is it you remember the horse, but not me?'

'Did'n see you. Saw only the other one. She with the little whip.'

'Oh, mommy?' and again she laughed, but now a little more measuredly – as though she shared a secret with herself. 'Yes. People always remember *her*. She sees to that.'

'You bring me the food, miss?'

She looked at him uncertainly, the suddenness and directness of the question taking her by surprise. 'Did you mind?' she asked, sidestepping a flat 'Yes'.

The evasion confused him and he looked away, shaking his head, his tongue unable to rise to the challenge of adding anything of its own.

'Good,' she said and put the saddlebags on the sand and took from them a fresh supply of coffee, sugar, milk, smiling up at him with a genuineness that both warmed and nonplussed. 'If I had had to take this all back, it would have spoilt my ride. Not that I would not have understood, though. *She* would have thought nothing – if she ever *did* anything like this – of dumping stuff on you and expecting you to kiss her feet. I know I had no right to scout around under your bush when you were not there – same thing as breaking into somebody else's house – but I wanted to find out what I could bring you, what you needed most. And even *that* was wrong because how did I know that you *wanted* anybody to bring you anything? Like you give somebody something without them asking you to, and they take it because they really *do* need it, but at the same time they are ashamed that their need showed itself the way it did. You understand?'

But he did not answer that, instead asked, eyes careful and speculative as Tiger's that first time, 'But *why* you bringing me all this stuff, miss? You only seen me that once, there by the sea.'

'Maybe it's *because* I saw you there in the sea,' she said, and laughed, and he thought the laugh had a good feel, like a sudden sun touching him on the cold days, and he grinned with such a sun's suddenness, the grin both impish and shrewd and his eyes alerted and male.

'You like what I showed?' he asked, and his arousal reached to her though he did not move.

But she did not respond: bridged any awkwardness with a stride as easy as her smile. 'That? No, that was nothing new. I'm at UCT. Hope to be a doctor next year. So I can't think of anything, male or female, that I haven't already seen. Or had under my hands. No, I wanted to make up for *her* looking at you the way she did. Like you were something that smelled.' She paused. 'And, yes, because of your face. Like a little boy that had been caught with his pants down. In more ways than one.' Again she laughed. 'So forget what showed and that I saw. It's no big deal. Just what you've got to have, is yours. Like a leg or an arm.'

'More powerful than *them*,' he countered. 'More powerful than *anything*,' and his voice was sullen as the little boy's she had seen him to be and she reached out a hand and quickly touched his shoulder, then sat down on the sand and hugged her knees.

'I didn't mean it that way,' she said, but didn't explain in what way it *was* meant, sensing the chasm between them that could not be wished – or argued – away, and he was seized with a paroxysm of coughing that left him breathless and squatting, head hanging low.

'That's a very bad cough,' she said, her voice more than cursorily concerned. 'You had it for long?' He shook his head, wiping his nose with the back of his hand, scrubbing the hand on the sand. 'No matter. It could get to be something worse. You taking anything for it?'

Again he shook his head, not looking up, liking her sympathy, with unconscious cunning conning her for more. 'Nay. Must go to the clinic today. Get me a mix.'

'You do that. Or I'll have to be back. Playing doctor this time.'

He considered that, uncertain whether he also liked – or resisted – the not entirely playful bossiness of her tone – deciding that he liked it less than the sympathy and he – wholly sexist male – must watch it or this woman would be telling him what to do, and that – the example of his mother and father under the thumb of the as white Oumiesies vividly before him – must never be allowed. So he merely grunted – noncommittally – more than a little irritably – and again she heard and was warned, and he looked up, his mind – never concentrated for long on any one thing – veering off to quite another concern. 'That other one. The one you call your "ma". She really your ma? She don't look like no old woman. More like you.'

For a long moment she looked at him and he waited – patient with the patience born of having nothing better to do. Then she said, almost inaudibly above the rustle of the sea, 'Well, what am I waiting for? I came around, messing in *your* life without even asking and you are *asking* – so – no, she's not my real "ma". She's my father's second wife. He likes them young. Young as me. Or younger if he can. Young as the one who *was* my ma and who he put out with the cat – though only the cat was let back in – when she was all burnt-out from doing the circus tricks he calls "sex" and "playing it cool", and he going on for fifty-four. Real stud is my dad. Won't catch *him* looking like a little boy with his pants dropped, down there in the sea.'

He nodded. 'Ja, I know somebody like him. Praising the Lord all day. Your pa praise the Lord?'

'Christ, no! The last time he was in church was when he got hitched. This second time around, that is. The first time, the court was good enough, but stepma's a Catholic who's no Virgin Mary, believe you me, but she goes by the rules when it comes to the big stakes like birth, marriage, death. Give her credit for that. And you? Do you praise the Lord all day?'

'Was raised that way. But now – I dunno. Got too much else on my mind these last I dunno how many years. Us bergies live hard, miss' – angrily, too late, he tried to curb his kind's habitual whine – 'and the Lord – *if* there is a Lord – most times seems to have too much on *His* mind to worry about me.'

Impetuously, she reached across, held his hands, loosed them again as he sat down flat, at a loss how to respond. 'Cut out the "miss",' she urged, her eyes intent and without guile. 'Call me by my name. "Shirley". There! I have given you my name. Will you give me yours?' He told her his name and again she briefly took his hands. 'So who knows, Duke – and I *don't* know – me not knowing any more than you *what* to believe – but still *believing* in some kind of a way – maybe – at the end when it really counts – whatever is the Lord *will* find the time to think of you and you will be the one that's laughing while I cry.'

'Would'n want that, miss,' he said, buttocks squirming embarrassedly deeper into the sand. 'Feels to me like you crying too much right now. Your pa treat you bad?'

She stared at him, a little scared. 'What made you say that?'

He shrugged. 'You got crying eyes. Like all bergie people got. Even when they skel.'

'I have?' and she laughed, but uncertainly, her hands reaching for each other as though in need. 'Well, the answer to what you asked me is, "No". My father is very *good* to me, Duke. Gives me all I want. Or *don't* want. My private wheels, a horse with a pedigree longer than my own, a flat to myself in a house big enough for *ten* kids instead of the only one that's me, and anything else I can think of and all for free. Even she's not what you could call cruel. Just having to go around with her so much so's she can feel young as me – and so *look* young as me – and maybe, then, daddy won't be getting tired of her as quickly as he did of my mom – *that* gets me down. Gets me down the way everything else under that roof gets me down. And why? Because I hate both him and her for what happened to my mom, but I have grown hard enough – *hating*-hard enough – to know I must stick it out till I have my degree and don't need them or anybody else anymore. But that's not for crying over, Duke. Bergies can cry, but little rich girls like me don't have to cry. So what's all this about me having crying eyes?'

Challenged to prove his point, he forgot his shyness – and her whiteness – and, leaning swiftly to her – she starting back, but not too much – he seized her hands and turned them, palms up, and indicated the thin lines of stitched skin across the wrists, then rubbed the circlet of similarly paler skin around the finger where a ring had once been and said, something of the heartlessness of the triumphant child in his voice, 'Look!'

Quickly, she took back her hands, her eyes stricken and trapped. Then, as quickly, she laid her head on her knees and only the shaking of her shoulders showed that she wept. Stolidly he watched her, not trying to comfort her by either word or touch, as inured to the suffering of others as he was to the endemic misery of his own life. Only the noiselessness of her weeping – as opposed to the extravagant lamentations of a bergie woman – seemed to him remarkable and he waited with a vague sense of discomfort, scrabbling with his toes in the sand, wishing she would have done. Which, quite suddenly, was so, she raising her head from her knees but still not looking at him as she fidgeted in the pocket of her blouse for a tissue and blew her nose into it with a small, desolate snort.

Confronted, then, with the ridiculous impasse of what to do with the tissue, she glanced around with something of the desperation of a smoker seeking an ashtray in a non-smoker's house, then, with an equal ridiculousness, shuffled it out of sight under the sand. The irony and banality of the dilemma seemed to steady her and she at last again looked at him, eyes determinedly expressionless save for the brilliance of the just shed tears.

'You are very clever,' she said, her voice flatly matter-of-fact as one busied with the next sentence of a conversation in which there had been no break, 'and if I ever thought otherwise, I'm begging your pardon for looking down on you the way *she* would have done. Of course, you were right. We fell in love in our second year at UCT and he bought me a ring which I always wore when alone or with him. Even now I wear it when alone, though I don't when I'm out *riding* alone because I might meet other riders who know me and the ring and will go and tell *them* and I just can't face up to any more of what happened back then. You see, he was an Indian and, the way things still haven't changed for you since Mandela got to be the man, so things haven't changed for my father either and I knew he would rather see me married to a dwarf with two heads than anyone not white, so I laid low, but then one day I forgot to take off the ring when I got home and my father saw it and the sky fell in. I have always been scared of my father – you see him and you'll know what I mean – and he got Ali's name out of me and went straight to the campus and confronted Ali as only my father knows how. Ali's parents could have sued my father for what he said but they, being Moslems, were as against Ali going out with me as my father, so they did nothing and Ali went into a tailspin I couldn't talk him out of, and, next thing I heard, he'd hung himself, even though he had told me that, in his religion, anybody who did that, or shot himself, or whatever, would have to go *on* doing that for all of his time in Hell. Well, I didn't have any sick ideas like that, so I did this,' and she held out her wrists, 'the thought of stringing myself up with a sheet the way Ali did, being more than I could take. But they got to me too soon and – hey! – look! – I'm still here. But only *just*.'

'You want coffee?' he asked.

'No,' she said, and stared down at her boots, trying to hide the hurt she felt at his not having anything other than that to say.

'Ja. Got no cups anyway.'

'I didn't mean it like that,' she protested, a sharpness to her tone now that warned of a stretching too far. 'I don't worry about the fancy stuff anymore. That's for *her*. If I wanted your coffee, I would drink it out of anything you've got. No matter *what*.'

'Uh-huh. What about all that fancy stuff you been telling me about? That you still got. You don't worry about *that* anymore?'

'You don't understand,' she muttered and wished, too late, that she had held her tongue.

'Ja. I don't understand. It's like your new ma says. I'm stupid. That's all. Just plain *stupid*. I can understand you feeling bad about what your boy done. But to go cutting yourself the way *you* done? That I *don't* understand. You still a fine body of a girl, miss. Like that horse over there. Go ask *him*. *He* don't cut himself when a merrie dies. He knows there's lots more for him to put it in. Like there's lots more boys for you, miss. You just got to say, "come *on*". And then there's all this fine living your pa's giving you for free and you say you don't want to have it because of what happened between him and your ma. Now I can see that that *was* a bad thing that happened back there – or maybe it wasn't because it was your ma-and-pa's thing and *you* don't know it all – but – good or bad – you hating your pa's not gonna bring your mama back, so why not relax and *enjoy* what *I'm* never gonna have though I live to be a hunnerd years. *That* I understand, but not this other story you been telling me here.'

'Fine living doesn't always bring happiness,' she retorted and hated herself for the preachiness that was not her at all.

'Try me,' he said, and grinned, widely and wickedly, but she sighed, conceding defeat, and lowered her head back onto her knees.

'I shouldn't have told you all I did. But I came here feeling sorry for myself and looking for a shoulder to be sorry *on*, and I was hoping yours – you having had it the hardest of any – would be the one. But it isn't and I'll try not to cry on it again.'

She waited, then, for him to say something in return, but all she heard was a busyness of hands, and, at last, curiosity overcoming her, she again raised her head and saw that he was fashioning himself a dagga-zoll, was licking it into a shape that would stay. Again he grinned as he saw her watching him, and, finished, stuck the zoll between his lips and lit it, and, its tip glowing steadily, drew the sickly-acrid smoke deep down into his lungs as in a sacrament, and the lungs, inflamed and mucus-clogged, exploded in revolt, and he hacked and wept and, wrenching the zoll from his lips, glared at it with a blending of desire and despair.

'Got to get me a mix,' he mourned and, with an almost old-world ceremoniousness, passed the zoll to her.

At last she understood. 'You lit it for me, didn't you? You knew you couldn't smoke it,' but the returning grin, now mischievously won't-tell, was his only response and she took the zoll into her mouth, slipping the spittle-slicked end between her lips with an unwitting sensuality that transformed a simple act of smoking into the ultimate intimacy of fellatio, and his grin froze into a humourless grimace and his penis kicked into an erection so powerful that he had to cover it by wedging his hands between his thighs. 'Smoke! Smoke!' he soundlessly insisted, his hands hungering to claw down the last barrier of the blouse, seize the unspoilt, pampered breasts, a far corner of his mind wondering if she was still a virgin, but finding no compunction – heightened desire, rather – at the thought of that, remembering then the Hettie that he and Pietie had bloodied in the long ago, who had howled that it hurt, then wanted more of the same than either of them was ever able to give.

'Got me a Hettie!' he illogically convinced himself, sides of his wedged hands slyly inciting the erection to an even crueller pitch. 'Go *on!* Smoke! Let the ganja tell you Ali's back. Only now his name is "Duke"!' and he giggled inwardly with a mindlessness that had no face.

But then the horse whinnied, tugged at the reins around the pipe, and she rose, hastily, glancing at her watch. 'Hey! I must go, or she'll come looking for me. Thinking I've been raped! Or robbed! That's all whites like her – *and* him – think about these days. But I'll be back. Soon as I can. That is, if you don't mind. *Do* you mind, Duke?'

'Nay, I don't mind,' he said, but his tone was sullen and estranged. 'Bye, miss.'

'Call me Shirley,' she urged. 'Come on. It's not so hard.'

'Shirley,' he said, but the sullenness stayed and she, misinterpreting it, leant down and gently touched his cheek, then gathered up the saddlebags and, mounting, galloped off, hair bright and streaming on the wind.

'Shirley,' he said again to himself, fingering his cheek, but the name still sounded alien on his tongue and her touch was fading from his skin as quickly as a spoor in tidal sand. But the cleft between her breasts as she leant to him, the breasts' laundered swell, the gold flash of the watch as she checked the time, these stayed with him – the breasts more lastingly, more vividly, than the watch because, for a bergie, gold was a flying-too-high and what would he do with it anyway? How explain it away? No, he thought, lifting washing from a yard where there were no dogs and the walls were low, was about as far as he could go. And the breasts? 'Those white-as-Oumiesies tits?' How far could he go with *them*? 'Yirrah, Oumiesies – if *she* wants – *fokken* far!' and when he came back from the clinic with the 'mix' and found Fly was again around after steering clear of the girl and her strange beast, he said, 'I got me a Hettie, Fly,' and that night, still determinedly creating his world-according-to-Duke, he told Tiger the same thing, and both Tiger and Fly stared at him with their bright, interested eyes that were just eyes.

And the next morning, when he woke, there was a rushing about him as though the sea had suddenly advanced to the fringes of his kip. But it was only the first of the true winter rains and he knew that the 'heavy time' was again upon him and would have him by the throat for sometimes as long as half a year.

For ten days, save for brief intermissions of hardly troublesome drizzle, the rain pinned him down, demanding of him his utmost commitment as he battled to keep dry his bedding, provisions and meagre extra clothes. Fatalistically as any seasonal animal, he submitted to the pitiless necessity to survive, banishing from him all fanciful lusting after a Shirley as Shirley or she in the even more unattainable persona of the Hettie of his youth. Predictably, there were no visits from her during that time because who, he reasoned, would be so 'toe' as to come down to a sodden, weed-strewn beach, whether on horseback, threading through the thunderous surf, or even via the fancy 'wheels' he had not as yet been privileged to see? His never *quite* chastened libido did, however, occasionally again stir when he glimpsed Lydia in one of the soup queues for refugees and street people and instinctively sensed – though neither admitted to knowledge of the other's presence – that she was as acutely – and carnally – aware of him as he was of her. Why, he wondered, did he still feel like that about Lydia when she was nothing but a 'spook' compared to the 'white poesie' who brought him food and touched his cheek as though he, too, was white? Confusedly, he strove to define – hold to – whatever raw and elemental strand of – what? – sharedness? – sameness? – it was that still linked him to one so sadly shorn of all the mystical connotations of her name. But then the sand would be churning about him again under a fresh assault from the skies and he would be back to sexlessly, mindlessly, wrestling the beast that was the rain.

On the morning of the eleventh day, the clouds took flight even as he watched, jostling each other as though in intelligent terror of some shape only they could see, and the waves, surfacing from a last recalcitrance of mist, rolled in from forever under a sun brilliant as summer reborn, and yet a tissue-thin chill still to it that prickled the skin. Fly was instantly about, foraging, chirping his thin, sweet note, and Tiger, released from his cowering under the bush, streaked out and away over the dunes, not so much in search of food – he having had his fair share of what there was – but because he was a cat and a tom who loved the feel of being free.

Inevitably, his bedding was damp, though not soaked, and he hurriedly draped it over the bushes in the dunes where it could not be seen and so raise the ire of any passing beach patrol. Then he built a careful fire from the still dry wood that he had hoarded – more jealously than gold – under plastics in the lush heart of the bush, and lingered, blissfully, over the first decent brew of moerkoffie he had had in ten days. Then he made a frantic round of the trash sites, knowing the weather would not hold, and sold what he could find to Scrap and, so, replenished the meagre cash reserves that the rain had compelled him to all but spend.

Coming back, a loaf of bread in each hand, he paused at the head of the path leading down to the kip, knowing without being told that the shiny red sports coupé, parked alongside the oleander stand, was hers. Then he went on down and she was waiting for him, an anxious smile on her face, and, at her feet, a sack of provisions and two woollen blankets which he caught up and held to him as he would a woman, grinning with delight, and she was discerning enough not to still offer him her hand because he had already taken it in a very special way. She also had the sense not to stay too long because he was heavy-eyed from the long, sleepless nights of battling the rain, and, as soon as she had left, he brought in his bedding from the dunes and blanked out till, towards evening, he again awoke to find that the mist was creeping back in over the sea.

For the rest of that winter, she almost always came to visit him in the breaks between the rain, the car bringing her rather than the slower horse because, as she explained, the rain could so suddenly return and the beach was increasingly becoming strewn with the wrack from the deep-sea storms. As on the occasion after the first storm, she never stayed long because she realised that he had to take every opportunity to 'trade the trash' and, with an even rarer wisdom, sensed that he must never be made to feel – or be allowed to *accept* – that he was a 'kept man'. But the visits were frequent and long enough for her to be told the inevitably edited and dramatised version of his life and to discover the strange, almost magical relationship between him and the cat and bird. From his side, he increasingly came to accept that he had to do with an entity that would never be a Hettie, that was as guileless as the cat or bird, and desire gave way to respect, to the affection that he harboured for Tiger and Fly, and the otherwise ever predatory penis remained quiescent in the small, miraculous sheath of its restraint.

But the visits were also frequent and long enough – and the sight of the car at the oleander stand memorable enough – to alert other eyes and ears, and there were times when it was not the wind that stirred the oleander leaves, but that which caused the cat to crouch and still in a clear indication that he had, after all, become too indolent to perceive and understand.

※ ※ ※

It was in the first week of a still uncertain spring, flowers beginning to bud in the dune scrub, that he realised that some of the tracks milling about his bush were not hers. Erratically skewed to one side, they were clearly distinguishable from the usual neat prints, and that they were also not random was evidenced when they eventually veered off to under the bush itself and a packet of moerkoffie and a packet of sugar were found to be missing when he checked. 'Fokkit!' he cursed, his tone as edgy as it was angry when he recalled that Fly, who had grown used to Shirley, had increasingly not been about when he returned from town. He did not tell her, though – much as he wanted to share his uneasiness with someone else – because he was afraid that she would take fright and he would not see her again. 'Shit thought!' accused his innermost self, but his cynicism was still not quite gone.

The immediate problem, of course, was what to do with the remainder of his supplies. He could not possibly carry them about with him wherever he went and to hide them under some other bush that the Street knew was not his, was to strip him of his claim to them and abandon them to every hungry predator in town. So he had no option but to leave them where they were – only pushing them so deeply into the heart of the bush that he was forced to crawl on his belly, head butting the twigs aside, in order to get them out again. 'Fokkit!' he would again hiss – and some days yell – as he each time wrestled his way through, and, often – desperate to catch the unknown and so resolve the problem once and for all – he would hide out in the dunes and watch the bush from there, pretending he was in town. But the trap remained unsprung and it was, he thought, as though the intruder watched him as he watched the bush, and, once, his eyes strayed to the oleander stand and, a connection sparking, he rushed up the path to the street. But there was nothing there – only the wind stirring in the long, indolent leaves.

So, a month passed in which the alien eyes bored into his spine and there was a soft giggling at his side that did not leave him even though there was no further filching of his supplies. At variance with his mood – as though mocking it – the sun strengthened and the flowers – flooding now the dunes – tinged the salt breeze off the sea with their own subliminal yet pervasive fragrance of honey and spice. To his left, the far mountain and its flanking hills rose up as though surfacing from the sea, but to his front and half-right, the waves rambled without hindrance, pellucid and placid, yet cautioning that theirs was a power restrained. And it was from such an ambience that she again came to him, but this time on horseback, the sea, in the gentler season, taking back from the beaches the long winter's ruin.

He was still in his bedding, half-asleep, the sun but a hand's-span up, and he was not aware of her coming till her shape, trim in the usual jodhpurs and blouse, blocked the entry to the bush. Thinking it was the intruder that had got it wrong for once, he sat up, reaching for his knife, but she laughed and gently pushed him back down and, for the first time ever, startlingly lay down beside him on the blankets and stared up at the sun-dappled canopy of the leaves.

Bewildered and ill at ease, he glanced at her, waiting for her to speak, to explain, but her profile was suddenly as remote from him as it was near, and the minutes passed and she made no move, spoke no word, was as one wrestling with herself, and he saw, then, that her face was drawn, that there were lines of tiredness about her mouth and eyes. 'Did'n sleep,' he guessed. 'What's fussing her? What's she *want*?' and, inevitably, the thought came to him that maybe, at last, she wanted *him*, the one thing he could give her that she didn't have, and his eyes moved to her breasts, the soft trap of the groin, and although there was the beginning of an excitement in him, there was also an odd, confounding chagrin that the dream of an otherness should so easily dissolve itself into the mundane.

'No,' she said, as though answering him, not turning her head. 'I have come to say goodbye.'

The waves stilled – then rolled again – and a gull yelled, swooping low, wings soundless as the air. 'Your pa know you coming here?' he asked, and wondered at the alienness of his own tongue.

She shook her head. 'No, I am going overseas. For a year. I have been given the chance of a lifetime to complete my hospital training in the UK and I'll never forgive myself if I don't go.' Now she looked at him, but he turned his head aside and she said, placatingly, 'It's only for a year.'

'Man can die in a year,' he muttered, his voice both genuinely bitter and petulantly that of a child.

She laughed and almost the laugh rang true. 'You won't be that man, Duke. I am the one with a skull for a head. Not you.' But he did not answer, did not look back at her, and at last she seized his hand and rose, urging him up, her voice peremptory, almost harsh, as she said, 'Come on. Let's not draw this thing out and make it worse than it has any right to be. I want to remember you as you were. Not the way you are now,' and he got up then and they stood together at the entrance to the bush, looking out to sea, and Fly passed in his foraging and studied them, head to one side, eye black and glistening and devoid of all humanness as an oil.

'Fly,' she said, her voice soft and fond, but the bird, unusually, took wing, and she looked around and asked, 'Tiger not here?'

'Nay. Went out first thing. Won't be back till night now.'

'Then you must say goodbye to him for me,' and suddenly she was facing him, her eyes bright with the tears that she would be shedding anywhere but there, her face taut and pale under the still uncertain spring tan. 'Ciao,' she said, in a low, firm voice, and, rising up on her toes, she as firmly, sensibly, and for the first time, kissed him fully on the lips and was gone, heading for the horse that she had tethered to the usual makeshift hitching-post of the iron pipe on the surf's fringe. Bleakly, fingering his lips, he watched her place a foot in a stirrup, bow her head preparatory to vaulting up onto the horse's back, and the youthfulness and vulnerability of the back of her neck was bared to him as never before, and his breath caught and there was the softness to him that he had felt when Fly had first sat on his shoulder and Tiger had submitted to his hand, and, almost not of his will and with a selflessness strange as speech to a stone, he heard himself shout, 'You find yourself another Ali over there, you hear?'

Smiling again, she turned and shouted back, 'And you see you're still here when I get back! Okay?' and he nodded and she mounted and galloped off, not once waving or looking round.

Alone, he kicked at the sand, booted a rusted tin into the dunes, sat down in a full return of his sullenness on the nearest of the rocks. 'Fokkit!' he snarled and glowered up at the clear sky as though expecting That in which he disbelieved to descend from it and give Its accounting of why he should again have been so summarily deprived. But it was only the oleander stand at the top of the path to the beach that suddenly threshed where there was no wind and, as once before, he was up and running, his disconsolateness momentarily forgotten, his feet scrabbling in the loose shale. And again as before, there was nothing: only a faint sourness of squatting flesh, the sharper tang of excrement and cats' pee, and he went back down the path and Fly came and rode on his shoulder all the way to the bush, and he reached up a finger and stroked it, whispering, 'Only you and Tiger now, Fly,' and, that night, he drew Tiger into an even closer intimacy beside him, conscious as never before of his own littleness and aloneness between the city and the sea.

In the morning, he garnered and sold his trash with a challenging irritability that left him isolated and deprived of the violent catharsis that he sought, and, eventually, he bought a bottle of Tassies and took it to a bench in the municipal gardens where the remote, imperturbable trees only intensified the targetlessness and unreasonableness of his rage. Wine downed, he smashed the bottle, uncaringly, on the paved path and then, as brutally, sprawled the full stretch of the bench, seeking sleep – but the wound he could not reach constantly nagged him back into wakefulness and at last, weaving a little, he got up and made his way back to his kip.

She was waiting for him there, sitting on a rock, drumming her rickety shoes against its sides, finally come down from her covert in the oleander stand.

'What you doing here?' he growled, his moroseness sharpening into anticipation of a letting of its bile. 'There's nothing for you here.'

'There's you,' she said, her heels quickening their drumming against the rock, her eyes blackly watchful as through the slits of a mask.

'You forget that night?' he asked, coming up close, bringing her to her feet, her legs braced, her body poised between response or flight. 'What you said? How you treated me like shit? Or has Hendrik gone and got himself another poes? Or,' and he very slightly paused, 'he's dead?'

'Nay, he's alive and we're the same and I forget nothing of that time.'

'Then, like I said, there's nothing for you here. Or,' and his lips drew back into a grin that, bleakly, showed only his teeth, 'you come to steal more of what's mine?'

'Ja, I took what I took,' she said, her eyes, defiant and unashamed, holding his. 'You eating yourself full like a pig and it getting to look like a store here under your bush and you not thinking anymore about the Street. I took what I did so's you'd know the Street knows what you're doing and the Street don't like it the way it is now.'

'So why you sitting here waiting for me? Why did'n you just take what you want like before?'

'I did'n say *that's* what I'm wanting *now*.'

'So *what* is it you want?' but she only stared at him, her eyes inscrutable yet, somehow, persuading him to what the tongue would not disclose, and suddenly, the wine lifting a little from his brain, he remembered and let out a breath longer than his lungs. 'You been watching me from there?' and he pointed at the oleander stand. Still she did not answer him, did not turn her stare aside, but there was an almost imperceptible shifting of it that told him he was right. 'You hoer,' he said, his voice low and flat – and all the more menacing for being that. 'You *fokken* hoer,' and made to leave.

'Ja!' she yelled, stopping him, her eyes, her entire self, startlingly again animated as at the flip of a switch. 'I seen her bringing you all she did! Feeding you like you was her pet dog! Paying you for fokking her there under that bush!'

'You lie!' he raged back. 'Never was nothing like that. White women don't sleep with bergies like me. You been smoking the pipe?'

'*You* lying, Duke! I seen her *kissing* you right where we standing now. And she just come with you out of the bush!'

'That don't mean I been fokking her!'

'Huh? You got to *lay down* under that bush, Duke. You know that. So you and she just laying there talking and you not on top of her, quick as a snake? You wanting me to believe *that*? *You* forgetting what you nearly done to me that other time and me another man's wife?'

'As though you wasn't ready for it!' he mocked, and laughed, harshly, humourlessly, as the hawking up of a phlegm. 'Seems to me you jealous of this other one! Want it now like you wanted it then, only you was too scared of that old fake you call your man to let me through. Well, I don't knock twice on the same door. So you fok off out of here and go give what you got to any that's wanting it because I'm not needing you anymore.'

She came at him then, spitting, clawing for his face. 'Your ma se poes!' she howled. 'What makes you think I can't fok as good as that white hoer?'

Instantly he slapped her, arm swinging the hand round in a wide, violent sweep that knocked her sideways into a tangle of limbs on the sand. For a long moment she lay motionless, clearly winded and dazed, ragged print dress rucked up to over the wearing-through knees, the cocky doekie slipped down over her eyes, the shrewish fury of her features smoothed into vulnerable repose. He tried to tell himself that he had not meant to hit her so hard, but he knew that

that was not true, that, in his anger at her calling Shirley a whore, he had, indeed, meant to hurt her, could for that single, explosive second have killed her for all that he cared. But where was that anger now? Why did he now look down at her with something of the penitence and guilt of one who had been betrayed into a battering of his own kind? Why – more bewilderingly still – did he for a transient – yet *existent* – instant feel resentment towards she who – however unwittingly – had brought him into confrontation with that which was *his* – in bone and blood, circumstance and shared degradation was his – no matter how often it might be evaded or denied?

Then she stirred, sat up, touched her cheek which was already beginning to swell, and wailed, eyes screwed shut, tears like water on her face. The keening – its agelessness, its harking back to a root from which they both had sprung – harassed him afresh with a sense of having turned against his own kin – his own and inescapable *self* – and he stared down at her, confounded as much by the thought that it was *his* hand that had wrought this thing as by the intensity – or affectation? – of her grief. He was no stranger to physical violence – had on numberless occasions been involved in the fumbling scuffles or outright exchanges of a community that was as quarrelsome as it could be clannish and solicitous of its own – but always it had been *men* that he had struck as he had now struck her and he shrank – as from the pandemonium at his feet – from the remembrance of his father's quiet yet implacable condemnation of such an act. Also, watching her face's almost perceptible slewing to one side, he began to wonder what explanation she would be forced to give a man whose self-proclaimed prescience he outwardly mocked, but in which, secretly, he more than a little believed. Worse still, *would* she have to be forced to give an explanation – whether lying or true – or would she *willingly, vengefully,* point the finger at him, desiring for him the full retribution of her possessor's wrath? The thought chilled him and his mind, scuttling for his knife, resolved that that must go with him from now on.

And still she wailed as one whom violence still engaged, and still he vacillated, hesitant to speak or touch in case that goaded her into a fresh paroxysm of distress, and it was only when he heard voices rounding the bend into the left-hand long beach, that he desperately toed her till she opened her eyes and he – feigning a resurging rage – swung back his arm as though to strike her again. Instantly the keening stopped and, her eyes distending in terror, she scrambled to her feet and fled, hobbling as though tethered in her awkward shoes.

***

It was only some days later, his eyes instinctively alerted by a stirring of the oleander leaves, that it dawned on him that he had not told her that Shirley had gone 'overseas', would not be back for a year. Querying this in his own mind, he tried to shrug it off as being 'no business of hers anyway', but he knew – his tongue's protestations of innocence notwithstanding – that it was really because the macho male in him secretly *wanted* her to believe that he had slept with Shirley – would, in fact, still *be* sleeping with her – so why pluck the sting from the essential elements of jealousy – not to speak of vitiating his new desirability as the 'ou' who was sleeping with a 'boer' girl – by telling her – or anybody else, for that matter – that Shirley was actually now in a place so distant from him that she might as well be on the other side of the moon? Worse still, she might think that Shirley had broken off with him – had had her fill of him – and he was lying about her going away so as to cover up his shame at being dismissed as more moffie than man!

The possibility of her no longer being interested in him – his hitting her having brought the matter to an end as well as to a head – never occurred to him, partly because, again, the macho man refused to entertain such a thought, and partly because – on the occasions when their paths still crossed, each going about their peripheral business of the Street – he was sardonically aware that their eyes' never meeting was less a shunning on her part than a carefully timed turning aside of a covert stare. His own sly glances showed that her face was back to normal and still no change in Hendrik's habitual shark-grin and facile calling down upon him the blessings of the Lord, but he still continued to keep his knife within reach of his hand because Hendrik was notorious for pouncing upon an opponent under cover of even a prayer or protestation of undying love.

The pretence that Shirley was still there and sexually on tap, was not only a childish and, ultimately, unsustainable conceit, but one that kept her at the forefront of his thoughts and, by so doing, perpetuated his sense of loss. All in all, he found himself slipping ever deeper into an isolation and loneliness that, actually, had begun long before the advent of Shirley in his life. Of the few who were reasonably literate, he often read bits and pieces of the newspapers he found stuffed into trash tins or fleeing the south-easterly gales, and, from these, he had become more aware than most of his community that death – twinned though it was with the supreme delight of sex – lurked between the legs of a woman like Lydia who, before her shacking up with Hendrik, had been a whore. Which, he knew, was an unfair distinction because most of the women on the Street were little different, drifting from one relationship to another in search of security and material betterment rather than at the prompting of such exotica as lust or love.

Condoms and their use were not alien to him and he had on occasion bought them when the choice between sex and food was not as critical as usually was the case and he had been sufficiently primed with weed or wine to not care that he was a bergie and as out of place in a pharmacy or clinic as a dog turd on a public bench. Even then, he was usually too embarrassed to use them, fearing – almost as starkly as he feared his death – the banter of a people for whom Aids was only a word and the sight of one of their kind grappling a condom onto his cock enough to spark a hilarity that was as uninhibited as it was hell. So, gradually, almost unconsciously, haunted by the horror of pictures he had seen of the otherwise faceless beast, he began to practise a measure of restraint that was as unnatural to him as it would have been to his seemingly phlegmatic father who, without ever knowing it, had initiated him into the rhythms of an act that had then yielded only pleasure – the unalloyed, unplunderble pleasure that had been his as it had been everyman's – not the now desperate spasms over which loomed a shadow as long as the God's.

God? Did he – as he so often before had asked himself – believe or disbelieve? He did not know: knew only that restraint was not abstinence, that each time his loins with a terminal implacability summoned him, he would not resist them, would savour the sweetness of his seed being drawn from him as though it was for the first time. Or was it that that sweetness was now even sweeter as a result of his restraint, of the element of forbiddenness, of guilt, that the act now embraced? The answer to that did not require any formulation because it was embedded in the deed itself, in the intensity of his reaction to it, and – from the strengthening vigour of his early morning tumescences, his mind's conjuring shapes of beauty from even the most slovenly and unlovely of flesh – he knew that soon now he would again be abandoning all restraint, would be rolling a dice with the beast, playing puppet to the spring as much as did any Tiger or Fly. Oddly, though, he never completed the equation of his heritage, acknowledging that he possessed his father's sensuality, but denying his mother's puritanism and genuine fervour for That which was beyond the flesh, and which, in him, surfaced in the guise of his dread of the beast and only submitted – as had his mother – to the authority of the patriarchal loins. Since there was no acknowledgement, there was no questioning, but the mystery remained: heavy with its undertones of loneliness, of longing to be back, to again be whole, yet flinching from that as from an artefact that threatened pain.

Nowhere was his loneliness so evident as in his relationship with Tiger and Fly. With such a seeming fullness did they respond to him that he recast them in his own image, imbued them with an intelligence, an awareness, that was the clone of his own. Most ominously of all, he ascribed to them an accountability for their actions that was based on a wholly human concept of right and wrong and, by so doing, set in motion a mechanism of consequence beyond his capacity to perceive or control. The more traditional dog, with its attributes of predictability and dependency, would not have provoked quite so rabid an anthropomorphism, but a bird that foraged for itself, took off in winged flight when it so wished – and a cat that was now close as the beat of his heart and, in a breath, aloof as its still untamed kin – these were something else again: secretive and fickle in – ironically – so very human a mould, forever beguilingly demanding that they be pursued.

Fly was still a loner, despite its being spring, but Tiger, fired by the same tumescence as was troubling him, was spending whole nights away from the kip, returning only at odd times during the day to eat the scraps he had set out under the bush before leaving for his rounds of the bins. On the ever fewer occasions that they still met, Tiger was the same affectionate, inclining-towards-brutal friend, coiling round, rubbing against his shins, drawing blood with claw or fang if he wrestled him with his hand. Increasingly, though, he bore the marks of amorous battle – a gouged nose, a ripped ear, a general turbulence of embattled fur – and, about him, sensed rather than smelt, a pungency of wantonness and pee. And once, doing the round of his traps, he found Tiger copulating, black-as-a-blot female under him snarling yet supine, and he called Tiger by his name, but the cat stared at him with eyes that held neither pleasure nor recognition and he left it to its odd, expressionless thrusting with a feeling of rejection and hurt that he had last experienced when his father had beaten him with Oubaas's belt on the farm.

He was to see the black cat several times after that, sometimes with Tiger, sometimes not, and always in the distance as though it sensed that they were competitors and it would not be tolerated on his home-turf, and he would confirm that by shaking his fist at it and it would turn and flee as though it understood what was meant. Unashamedly childishly, he resented Tiger's absence from his side in the still chilly nights, and found it increasingly difficult to fall asleep as he pictured Tiger with the black cat and, as a result, was himself aroused. Sometimes he tried to remember Shirley but her image had dimmed into the strangeness of an ambience beyond his ability to conceive, and he would call out into the darkness of the leaves above his head, 'You there, Fly? Only you now, bird!' and wait for a reply that he did not really think would come, then lie on, hoping each rustle of the sand was Tiger's treading softly, coming home.

But on that last night, he again calling, softly, into the leaves, Fly did suddenly cheep – a single bright note of ineffable sweetness that stopped his breath – and he laughed, delightedly – laughed as he had not for a long time – and slept and rose in the morning, strangely comforted, and gathered and sold his trash and came back to the kip, whistling for the bird to alight on his shoulder, flutter its wings against his cheek. But no bird came to him: only a silence that seized his tongue, bidding that he, too, be still, and, crouching to crawl in under the bush, he saw why and his world shattered, its pieces chiming about him in the clear day. Falteringly, as one drugged, he picked up what was left of Fly, sat down, staring at the tiny mess of feathers and bone, his eyes harsh and burning with a grief too desolate for tears. 'Tiger,' he thought, his mind picking over the word as though it named something alien and without form. 'He done it. He killed my bird.'

Then he scooped a hole in the sand where his head lay in the nights and buried what was no longer Fly, and, with the same deliberate and exact movements, cut a piece from the polony he had just bought and went and sat outside in the sun, the meat in his hand. Patiently, outwardly emotionless, he waited, and, the sun slipped an hour lower down, the cat came and stood a distance from him, snuffing the wind. 'Tiger,' he called, his voice low and gentle, his hand holding out the meat, as gently jiggling it, angling for the cat's eye. And Tiger, hearing, seeing, came up close, trustingly and unafraid, and reached out to take the meat and, swiftly, seamlessly, he closed his hands around the cat's neck and rose, the cat exploding into frenzied struggle, contracting, lengthening, whipping round to claw the blood from his hands. But he felt nothing, saw nothing, hatred brilliant as a nova in his brain, coursing like a purging fire through his veins, and he was aware that he was shouting something unintelligible and ape as he whirled the cat around, striving to snap its neck and, at the last, himself whirling about with it at arm's length, brightness of sea and sand blurring into a circlet as imprisoning as flame.

Something gave then and he stopped, staggering from the whirling round, and saw that the cat was quite dead, the neck stretched to an impossible length, only the skin still anchoring the head to the whole. Vision and sense returning, he looked down at the head that glared back at him from his hands, both head and hands glistening and slippery with the blood that the cat had drawn from him in a last hideous sacrament of love annulled, and he dropped what was no longer Tiger as Fly was no longer Fly onto the sand, but still the eyes glared up at him and the fangs snarled in a rictus of hatred that matched his own. Shuddering, hatred overtaken by the horror of what he had done, he turned his face to the pitilessly impervious sky, and the gulls, foraging in the incoming tide, thundered, screaming, up, panicked by his own primal howl of deprivation and despair.

'You killed the wrong one,' she said, and he spun round to find her standing a long stride from his back. 'It weren't him that killed the bird.'

His mouth worked, but his tongue, huge and leaden behind his teeth, emitted no sound.

'No, it weren't him,' she repeated, thinking he hadn't heard. 'The black one killed the bird.'

But still he only stared at her, mind too bemused, too drained, to want to grapple with what she had said.

'You listening?' she asked, her voice sharpening. 'I said the *black* one killed the bird. You killed the wrong cat.'

Now, at last, the repetitiveness won through to him, filtered then flooded like a water winning through a stone, and his eyes distended, started, as though her words had settled behind them in a mounting tide of cranial blood, and she took a step backwards, suddenly afraid. But his voice, though hoarse, was low, almost calm, as he asked, 'How do you know?'

'I *saw* it kill the bird. Me sitting there on the rocks like I was the rocks, wondering why I'm not seeing the mêrrem visiting you anymore. It waited till the bird went in under your bush, then it jumped it coming out, and the bird fussed and fussed, but the cat had it *so*,' and she pressed a thumb into a palm.

'You did'n try to stop the cat?'

She shook her head, watching the bloodied hands clench, hearing the low voice sink lower still into a growl.

'Why? You knew Fly was like my friend.'

'You hit me, did'n you?' she snapped, the long-harboured grudge betraying her into incaution, her eyes lighting with a malice they could no longer conceal.

'Bitch!' he screamed and was upon her, tripping her as he had once before, hurling her to the sand, straddling her, reaching for her throat with both savaged hands, but her left arm blocked them and her right hand, striving to seize his genitals, succeeded in wrenching down the zip of his jeans before he stopped it, and the jeans flared wide, revealing that he wore nothing underneath, and she renewed her groping for the almost-innocence of his most vulnerable self. But he fought her off, abandoning his attempt to bare her throat when he found that he needed both hands to wrestle back her frenziedly flailing arm, and, at last, exhausted, she slumped, closed her eyes, opened her mouth to shriek, but her lungs were drained of breath and no sound came.

It was then, as suddenly as had been the initial assault, that there was a shift, a moment when he knew that he would not murder her and she knew that she would not die. From towering over her, contorted and possessed, his face dropped close, his mouth meshing into hers, and her hips were lifting to help him in, slick as a silk and deep, and his lungs were gusting in great gasps of pleasure as mindless and purely carnal as his flesh, and, towards the end, he heard – and she heard – her cry out, 'Wait! Wait for me, Duke!' and he did, idling till they locked into long spasms of ebbing lust and breath.

Voided as she, he lay on her for long moments, listening to a skirl of voices passing other side the screen of rocks, then, only the lisp of the sea still sounding, he rolled from her, stood up, handling his genitals back into his jeans, zipping up the fly, and went down to the tidal pools to wash the blood from his hands. Coming back, he saw that she, too, had risen, was struggling her doekie back into place, but still he did not engage her with eye or tongue, and, taking up one of his wire-handled tins, went to fetch fresh water from the spring. On his return, he found that she had kindled the fire, and he brewed coffee and they sat sipping it, looking different ways, apart yet not isolated, bound by the very silence that they shared. Then he cast the grounds from his tin, unashamedly farted and went and lay down under the bush, hands behind his head, eyes closed, and, after a while, she, too, came in and lay down beside him and, within moments, slept as did he. Waking first, a fresh erection straining at his jeans, he slid a hand up her skirt, waking but not affronting her, and toyed with her till she was moist, then rolled over onto her and achieved a second coitus that was hardly less fulfilling than the first. Again slack, he turned his back to her and shaped a zoll, lit and smoked his half of it, handed her the rest, and she smoked, staring up past the fringes of the plastic 'ceiling' into the leaves.

'Could be I'm sorry now about the bird,' she said, her voice toneless and detached, barely bridging the long silence between, but he did not react, his eyes again closed. Then: 'Where's the white one that was here?'

'Gone,' he said, his voice as emotionless as hers.

'She'll be back?'

'She'll be back.'

'She do it better'n me?'

'I *told* you,' he grunted, mellowed enough to resist the temptation to be cruel. 'There's nothing like that.'

'You lie,' she said, but not bitterly so, content now as he. Then, musingly! 'I think I'm better'n her.'

'*All right!* Have it your way. But don't say I did'n tell you, hey? And anyway,' and now he looked at her, a beginning of teasing in his eyes. 'What about how's it for *you*? Who's better: Hendrik or me?'

She studied him, her face stern. 'You done a bad thing with me today.'

'Hey? You did'n *like* it?'

'Did'n say that. Said you done a bad thing that's a bad thing *because* I liked it. Now I'm remembering what it was like before I tied me to an old man.'

'Well, *untie* you. Tell him to fok off. Plenty of room for you here.'

'And when the white one comes?'

'Fokkit, there you go again. Like all the other women. Gwarra-gwarra-gwarra! Always the same old kak! Like a brak with a bone. Only you's tying you to Hendrik. Only you's gonna get you loose.'

'You know that's not true. You know he'll kill me before he'll let me go, and if I run, he'll kill me where I am.'

'Hey! Come on woman! You talking wild now. Old men don't do things like that. Old men of *God* don't do things like that.'

'Hê? You sleeping with Hendrik or me? We all get a devil in us sometimes. You just got to find out when. No, Duke, someone else will have to loose me from Hendrik. Someone with something like this,' and his eyes widened with shock as she reached out and touched his knife where it hung by a thong from a branch above their heads. Instantly, the silence that had been between them was back, but now there was a different quality to it – a mumbling secretiveness of the sea talking to itself – and he turned his back on her in dismissal as much as disbelief.

'Crazy!' he muttered, but more to himself than to her. 'Plain fokken *mal!*'

Quickly she rose, curt movements showing that she was upset, 'All right. So I'm mal and so I'm going now. Back to my old man. So you just lie there, Duke, and think about him and me doing what you and me done here today. Maybe then – if you any kind of a man – you won't be resting so easy anymore. Be thinking maybe of that blade you got hanging over there – it wanting a blood the way you was wanting me,' and her head brushed against the overhead plastic and the entry to the bush darkened and lightened, and he lay listening to her shoes crunch over the sand, clatter over the stones of the path leading up from the beach to the city beyond.

Disturbed, no longer wanting sleep, he, too, rose, went down to the sea, gapped his fly and washed his genitals, flinching at the salt-sharp lash of the spring tide. Only then, drawing back the foreskin of his penis to wash – as his mother had always put it – 'the head of the snake', did it come to him that, in the fury of the day's events, he had not once thought of using two of the condoms he still had, and a chill far sharper than the lash of the water struck him as he considered not only the possibility of Aids, but the far more immediate possibility of his having impregnated Lydia and, by so doing, saddled her with a final, inescapable evidence of her guilt.

Would she declare the child to be Hendrik's or his? Unbidden, coldly, the blade glinted in his brain – for whom? – but he thrust it from him and came back and stood over the now stiffening corpse of Tiger, reluctant to touch it again, but knowing he could not leave it lying there. Gently he toed it over onto its back and saw that the wind had glazed the glare of the eyes with sand, and sand clogged the snarling mouth as though it had eaten of the earth in its frenzied refusal to be torn away from its own so small a portion of sense and sun. Choosing a spot next to his bush, he scooped a hold in the sand as deep as the stretch of his arm, then – steeling himself against the bobbing of the head on the elongated neck – took up the cat as though it was a human shape and laid it in the hole, and filled the hole in again and marked the grave with a seemingly random pattern of stones and shells.

Then he sat down next to it and, at last, silently, bitterly, wept – wretched with a loss that was not of the flesh – touched by the long shadow of the lonely nights to come.

✴ ✴ ✴

Never before had his sexual desperations been so conveniently and readily appeased. At least once a week she would slip away from Hendrik on some pretext or other and visit him at the tail end of the day. These visits rarely lasted longer than an hour, partly because her fear of Hendrik bestrode her throughout, and partly because – the brief intimacy of their coitus past – they almost always lapsed into petty bickering which soured both and led to her flouncing off with vague threats of estrangement that she as well as he knew would never be kept. 'Why don't you get you a kip in the Street?' she would grouse. 'Then I would'n have to come all the way to this fokken bush,' and he would reply that Fly and Tiger were buried there and there were his traps that caught him meat, and she would taunt, 'Fokken little meat you get from *them* and the worms already eaten up your cat and bird!' but he would not be swayed because he knew that these were not his real reasons at all – that the real reason – which he dared not divulge – was that he had promised Shirley that he would still be there when she returned.

Once, however, she came startlingly close to baring the truth when – he again refusing to leave the beach – she suddenly asked, 'Hey! that white woman of yours *really* gone? You not lying to me and that's why you don't come up to the Street?' and he felt that he hesitated for tellingly too long before he mumbled something about why should he lie when there was nothing to lie about and when was she going to start trusting him for a change, and she shot back, 'Me trust a *man*? I must be mal!' and he did not listen to the rest of what she said, thinking of Shirley, missing her in the exalted and painful way in which he still missed Tiger and Fly, comparing her to the carping of his own kind even as he turned to that for a fresh assuaging of the no less rude imperative of his groin.

Over nothing did she grow so vociferous as over the question of his using condoms: he insisting on this at their very first assignation after the day on which Tiger and Fly had died. 'Do you think I'm still a hoer?' She had demanded, her eyes more than ordinarily slitted and aroused, and, when she saw he was adamant, added, 'And what's the good of it anyway? You already spit in me twice!' but she knew that that was no argument and, as relentlessly driven by desire as he, restricted herself thereafter to the occasional expletive or a silence as he prepared himself that was as eloquent as any sneer.

Ironically, it was her earlier experience as a whore – an experience that had taught her the erotic techniques of such countries as India and Taiwan – that made her the consummate practitioner that she was, that shocked him into frenzies of response that fulfilled her as they fulfilled him and fused them into a single unit of satiety that was as mindlessly beyond flesh as it was all of flesh. For days after she left him, it would seem to him that the very pores of his skin exuded a musk that was the amalgam of her carnality and his – their heat and sweat, the ancient mustard and ammonia of sperm and womb – and he would bring his hands to his face and she would be in them as though she had never gone. And yet – dimly but obtrusively – he sensed that something was wrong – that he was drifting towards where he should rather not be – and, at such times, Tiger and Fly would again be searingly uppermost in his mind – as searingly no longer at his side – and pale, sad Shirley – sad with a sadness that, deep down, he knew he shared – would seem to be watching him from the shadows between the dunes. And sometimes, in the evenings, he would walk along the beach and see a sea-bamboo, fronds splayed, lying on the fringe of the surf and, with something of an odd child's fantasising, say to himself, 'Hey! that's Shirley lying over there. Gone and drowned herself, she so sad. Waiting now for me to come and say, "Hey! wake up, Shirley. No good drowning yourself for that boy. He's dead, girl. Dead as old Tiger and Fly. So get up, Shirley. The sea's no place to be",' and he would come up to the bamboo and kick at it, laughing at himself with something of a child's wildness and all of the heartache of an inarticulate man.

Then it was that sometimes a more honest if not necessarily wiser self would exclaim, 'But that's *it. That's* what is wrong. Which do you want, Duke? Fairy-tale-girl no ou has touched or one-time dockside hoer who knows all the tricks and is giving it to you like you never had it before? You can't have it both ways, boy!' and then she would be back, bewitching him with an eroticism that drove all else from his mind.

But for her there was no such dalliance with shades, pandering to doubt. No matter how ferocious her grappling with his need, she never once lost sight of the goal towards which she strove, would, at every opportunity, needle him, recounting with seeming relish how Hendrik had vented himself in her on such and such a night, would be doing it again when she got back from him, and, all the while, gauging his reactions with the fine antennae of her instincts rather than with any scrutiny of the traitorous eye. Experienced enough to guess that she was goading him, that she was probably lying more often than she was not, he tried to attain – and to maintain – the indifference which common sense said he must, but her constant nagging wore him down, built up in him not only resentment, but that darker other for which she aimed.

'What is it with you?' he at last burst out. 'For what I gotta keep on hearing about your old bag of bones?'

'Huh? You did'n say that to *him*, that one time you was there. You getting jealous, Duke?'

'Jealous? Of *him*? What you doing here every time if I gotta be jealous of him?'

For a long moment she said nothing, then she reached up, touched the knife dangling from the branch, watched it swing on its thong. 'Then you *better* be getting jealous, Duke, or else' – and she looked at him, her eyes triumphant and cruel – 'I *won't* be coming here anymore. I'm not your hoer, Duke, for you to be playing with like I'm back on the docks. I'm not asking you nothing and you not paying me nothing for the good times I been giving you. It's like it's your wife that's coming to you and a wife don't like it when the man don't care like you don't care about Hendrik putting his in me.'

'What you trying to say?'

'I'm not *trying* to say anything. I already *said* it. Straight. Right there at the start. And you understand me now like you understood me then. So don't lie there playing games.' Then she again touched the knife and it swung – and now he, too, watched it – watched it as though it had a life of its own.

'No,' he whispered. '*No!* Do *that* and there's not even a *fight* between him and me?'

'You hit *me* quick enough, did'n you, that time? Was *I* fighting you then?'

'Was different, that,' he muttered and she sneered: 'Ja, *would* be, would'n it?' Then, more placatingly: 'Anyway, you come *fighting* Hendrik and he'll whap you like you was a fly. No, look' – and she lay closer to him, her breath urgently on his cheek, her voice lowered as though she feared the leaves would tell – 'my way's the only way. I thought it all out after that first time. Soon now's the big days. Oujaar, Nuwejaar. Oujaar, Hendrik will already be dronk as the dead man he's gotta be and no trouble at all to you and me. So, Oujaar night you bring him' – and she flicked the knife for the third time – 'all nice and cleaned like you never touched him before, which is just in case – just *in case*, you hear? – he drops somewhere outta your hand and you gotta let him lie. Then you hang around till you see I put out the light in the kip, which means Hendrik doesn't know what's his name anymore, and you and I can sukkel him out to the end of the lane where he won't mess up the kip, and you can say, "Okay, Hendrik, you not Hendrik now – you just a bok back there on the farm," and then you cut him – so –,' and she drew her finger across her throat, 'and you get back to your kip and I get back to mine, making like I'm asleep, and when they find Hendrik, I come out screaming, "they killed my Hendrik! What am I gonna do now?"'

He stared at her and his lips moved, but his tongue found no words. 'You like it?' she asked and, incredibly, smiled, her eyes bright and mischievous as any girl's. Then words did come to him: 'There's a devil in you, woman,' he said, his voice thick as with a lust, his side shrinking from hers as from a disease.

Instantly she was enraged. 'Your ma se poes!' she spat out. 'Don't you go calling me names! What about the moffie devil in you that lets you hit a woman like she's a man, then says, "Eina!" when it's got to cut the one that's taking its woman away? And the cat? Ja, what about the cat? Devil's not too fiemies to pull its neck just because it ate a stupid fokken bird that was *meant* for it to eat anyways!' He reached for her then, overtaken by a cauterising rage, but she had been expecting that and was up and out of the bush with a fluid swiftness he could not match, pausing only to say, 'Oujaar, or you can find you another devil to play with your piepie for all I care!'

He tried to brazen it out, to convince himself that now she had gone too far, that he could never entertain the scenario she had sketched, that the relationship between them was at an end. But, from the start, the odds were stacked against him in the shape of three factors of overwhelming subtlety and strength. Firstly, there was no longer a Tiger, a Fly or a Shirley to allay the loneliness and isolation that stalked him during the long nights; secondly, *she* intensified the already barely endurable into the intolerable by cutting off her visits to him and, by so doing, giving him a foretaste of the sexual frustration that would be his if he did not toe the line; and, thirdly, the scenario was still only a scenario, was not fraught with the terrifying *actuality* of something that had already taken place – or was *about* to take place – Oujaar being still a full month away.

So it was that there was time enough – as there was *excuse* enough – to slowly modify his stance, to ever less vividly recall the almost sexless amorality with which she had presented her plan, to increasingly revive his hunger for the wantonness and abandon of her earlier sexual greed. Outwardly, he continued to pretend that there was no change, that there was absolutely no prospect of his participating in her horrendous plan, and there was still an echo of this mantra sounding in him when Oujaar dawned and his hands, as though obeying some higher edict they alone heard, carefully polished and cleaned the knife, hung it by its thong around his neck, stuffed an old sock into his pocket with which to glove himself when the knife must again be held.

During the day there was much proffering – and accepting – of Tassies, and even the 'fancier' stuff for which money had somehow been found, and he rolled and shared several dagga-zolls and, once, drew hungrily on a 'pipe' that was doing the rounds. Throughout, the dichotomy of intent within him persisted: the gullible, accessible self assuring him that he was merely celebrating Oujaar, the darker, fugitive being that refused to lock eyes with him, demanding the anaesthesia of booze and drugs that alone would enable it to bridge the abyss between purpose and deed, that eventually found it turning into the late-night factory lane, the light from the lean-to dimly flickering at its further end.

Walking by numbers as one programmed, he settled down into the pitch-dark behind a row of rubbish bins halfway along the lane, his breath beginning to sharpen and his heart to sound as the realisation that he was, after all, at the appointed place at the appointed time, filtered down to him through the thinning carapace of dagga and wine. A clock proclaimed the hour, but he was still too befuddled to count the strokes, and a security guard suddenly stood at the entrance to the lane, blackly silhouetted against the city's glow, menacing as an avenger in a child's comic-book-tale, and his heart began to pound with a thunder that he thought must surely be heard, but, as unexpectedly as it had appeared, the poised, perceptive figure vanished and only the receding footsteps evidenced that it had ever been. Then a cat leapt onto the bin behind which he crouched, stalling his heart, staring at him with lambent, horrified eyes, leaping away again, and he resettled himself behind the bin, his hands shaking, sweat trickling down his spine as much from shock as from the windless, midsummer air. 'Fokkit!' whined the gullible self, still not quite subdued. 'Why you sitting here? You not going to do this thing, anyway. You *know* that, Duke. So get up. Go home,' and he did get up, listening to the continuing, distant revelry, almost resurfacing into the world of normality and triviality to which, rightfully, he belonged.

And, as at a signal, the light blinked out and the darkness, rushing in to reclaim its space, swept him with it and her arms were taking him into the lean-to, to her breast, and she was whispering with a genuine joyousness, a generous warmth, 'I *knew* you'd come, and – listen – he's like I said he would be,' and he became aware of Hendrik's stertorous breathing: its unsettling closeness to where they lay. And became aware also that her breath was sour-sweet as his own, and she was more than a little drunk, and her breasts and genitals were bared, and she was zipping open his jeans and sleeking his penis into an astonished erection with impatient hands. 'Not *now!*' he whispered, frantically trying to disengage, torn between desire and fear as Hendrik suddenly threshed round, ramming a knee into his side, but she hissed, 'He won't wake now,' and drew him into her and it was as it had been that very first time when, fuelled by blood and violence, his lust had flared into an intensity he had not thought to again attain. Oblivious now of the snoring hulk whose knee jiggled in time with his every thrust – seemed to strive for inclusion in a coitus of which it had unjustly been deprived – he abandoned all restraint, driving her back against the abutting factory-wall, feeling the buttons of his shirt work loose, the knife about his neck flop out between her breasts and ride there like a second Duke – the Duke that was not sheathed as the knife was sheathed, but no longer cared – and lay, then, spent as she was spent – desiring, now, nothing more than to lay his head where the knife lay and flee in sleep the shape of terror that the night still held – and demanded that he still face.

But for her there was no such flagging of energy and intent and, within moments, she was pushing him from her, covering up her nakedness, surging to her feet, saying, 'Come,' her voice brisk and businesslike as though she was summoning him to the most mundane of everyday routines. Obediently, he then, too, rose, zipping shut his fly, caught up still in the slipstream of events, their surreal immediacy that gave him no pause in which to think, to resist – and yet, deep down, something which, for once, she had not foreseen: a faint flickering of post-coital irritation that he could not be left in peace.

But then they had hoisted Hendrik to his feet, his head lolling as from a broken neck – 'Tiger's,' he, sickened, thought – and were struggling him down to the lean-to's exit from the lane, one arm about his shoulders, the other about hers, his toes skittering on the tar. And they were lowering him, face up, into a streak of white streetlight, insanely solicitous that he should not bump his head, and she was pulling at the head so as to lengthen the neck, bare it to the sacrament of the knife, and he heard her whisper, 'Quick! Do it now before the guard comes!' and he was taking the sock from his pocket and fumbling his knife-hand into it – fumbling excessively so that it would seem that it was the fumbling that was shaking his hand and not his fear – but, when he looked up, her eyes stared mockingly into his and he knew that she was not fooled. Goaded by that, he jerked the knife from its sheath, gripping its haft with the covered hand, and brought the blade to Hendrik's throat, clearing a way for it through the skimpy beard, and he heard her draw in her breath, anticipating the final bearing-down, the yielding of skin, flesh, veins, the gusting out of the last of life, the imagined became the irredeemably real.

But still he did not move, his being splayed against the wall of what he was, had ever been, faces, voices, a cat's mewing, the sweetly liquid cheeping of a bird, staying his hands, and again she whispered, 'Come on!' the whisper frantic now, sibilant as a scream, and, reflexively, he gathered himself: suddenly, desolately, wanting to have done and be freed. And Hendrik – revived perhaps by the fresher air of the lane? – the feel of the chill steel against his throat? – opened his eyes and said, 'Duke!' then crowed, 'Happy! Happy!' and hooked an arm about his neck, almost causing the blade to slice into his skin, and brought his face close and kissed him, slobberingly, on the lips and fell straight back into the black hole of his 'Oujaar'.

Slowly, he got up, wiped his lips, stared at the knife in his hand as though wondering what it was doing there, then sheathed it and a sob shuddered through him as though something alien and malignant within him had threshed and died. But then she was coming at him, raging, her nails clawing for his eyes, her face stripped bare as her skull. 'You poes!' she hissed. 'Give me that knife! If you're too pap to cut him, *I* will!' but he struck her hands aside and she stood, panting, a pace off, her face contorted, her doekie truculently skewed. And then he did again unsheath the knife, levelling the blade at her, coming close, and she backed away, the beginning of fear in her eyes, but he followed her, placed the tip of the blade under her chin, delicately stopping short of any letting of her blood. 'Witch,' he said, his tone almost conversational, the word no more than a meaningless sound. 'I'm seeing you now. You come lolling by me again and you'll be getting what I'm not giving him. Ja, I'm seeing you, and I'm seeing me, and I'm seeing him what's down there on the ground. He done nothing to me that I must cut him! No! He's kissing me here for the Oujaar and me fokking around with his woman and she fokking around with my balls. Well, it's finished now. Finished and klaar. So don't cry for me, baby, 'cause you not my baby no more,' and he rammed the knife into the sheath and set off down the lane.

For a moment she was speechless, stunned, then she cried out, 'Wait, Duke! Wait!' and there was real pain and pleading in her voice, but he did not turn around and – a more habitual anger reclaiming her – she yelled, '*All right*! Fok off then! Go back to that white bitch what's waiting for you. You think I don't know you been lying to me all along? But it don't end here, Duke! *It don't end here!*'

But still he paid no heed and it was only when he was rounding the corner into the main road, that he at last did glance back and saw that the security guard, alerted by her screaming, was helping her get Hendrik back into the lean-to, and the guard was laughing and saying, 'Best you get you a new man now, Lydia!' and the words and the laughter were booming with an almost spectral hollowness down the narrow conduit of the lane.

✳ ✳ ✳

On reaching his kip, his first action was to wrench off the sock that still, senselessly and forgotten, gloved his hand. Then he unslung the knife from his neck, took it from its sheath and – deliberately, angrily – fingered its blade and haft, forcing it to a witnessing of the innocence of his hands, stripping it of the anonymity, the tracklessness, that had marked it as an instrument of infamy and shame. Then he hung it within the usual easy snatch of his hand and – rolling himself into the blankets Shirley had given him – shuddered with the shock of what he had so nearly done.

By morning – having eventually blacked-out into a soddenly unrefreshing sleep – he had steadied sufficiently to reclaim the outward shape of that which bore his name. But, inwardly, it was as though a small but vital spring had snapped – had left a yawing, a slack, he was too wearied – was, indeed, *unwilling* – to even *reach for*, let alone mend. So he lay for a long while staring blankly at the mesmerising repetitiveness of the waves, listening to their hushed, hollow roar, underlying sibilance, that so dismissively overrode all alien sound: roistering of the last of the revellers from the night before, a helicopter's ratcheting overhead, a beach buggy's bucketing over the dunes. And even when his eyes did veer from the compelling turbulence that yet lulled as did a chiming or a chant, and rested on a yellow-headed youth, bathing briefs below his knees and buttocks slowly and contentedly undulant under the overhand of a dune, the voyeur in him did not stir: watched the gradual build-up into brutal orgasm with the detachment of one for whom an artefact, primed and set upon its course, performed its passionless routine.

Later, he brewed coffee – black and charged as the darkness that lay just beyond the fringe of his conscious mind – drank it sugarless because he had spent all his money on dagga and wine – chewed, uninterestedly, on a chunk of bread – thought, without meaning to, of Tiger and Fly, his eyes straying to where Fly lay buried under his head, then further on to the pattern of stones that penned down Tiger's bones. Immediately his torpor was pierced by a pain as sharp as on the day that they had died, and he held his face in his hands and cringed into the blackness of their making until the pain went away and he could do the round of his traps which, all their cunning outstripped, yielded not so much as a feather or a fur. Then he hung his knife about his neck, concealing it under his shirt, and took a long walk along the left-hand beach – the first of many such that he was to make before the end – and listened, all the way, to the sea saying, 'Shish – shish – I am mussels and fish – mama that washes you clean – woman when all women are Tiger and Fly – when I spit Shirley out like the

sea-bamboo and there's only a you and a me.' And he said, 'Shish –
shish,' and she echoed that, then added, 'But remember, boy, I am
older than old. You are not me and I am not you. I was at the
beginning and I will be at the end, and only I will be knowing then
that once upon a time there was this man called Duke who's walking
alongside me now, trying to tell me things I already heard before he
was born.'

And he should have come to his senses, then, snapped out of the
fanciful mood born of the previous night's strain, because the sea did
not speak of its *power*, of the board that warned against it near his kip,
of the current that – silent and unperceived as a drowned man's hand
– plucked the new drowned that would not be warned all the way
across to the right-hand beach's far end and splayed them out like
angled fish on the horrified sand. It was not that he did not *know* of
the sea's power, was not subconsciously *aware* that the sea, by not
speaking of that power, was speaking with a fudging tongue, was
betraying that it was a perilous love to be walking beside, to be spoken
to – and to be given words with which to reply – as though it was a
human love and not a mindless phenomenon subject to the whims of
winds and moons. But the sea had not spoken of she who had brought
him to the brink of murder and the death of himself, and he thought
that that was kind of the sea – and understanding – because the very
thought of her, a single sounding of her name was enough to set the
night's horrid sequence in motion again – and, apart from that and
most importantly of all, he wanted to be *comforted,* and the sea, as so
many times before, comforted him and, on his return to his kip, he
took off his shirt and, sprawled on the flat of his back in the warm sun,
hovered halfway between sleep and a companionable consciousness
that the sea was *there.*

Sadly, he could not see that the intensification of his relationship
with the sea was more illusory than real – was, indeed, but a reaction
against the *animate* that had caused him pain – a reaction, moreover,
that had been developing over as long a period of time as from the
day when his father had beaten him with Oubaas's belt on the farm
and that had, then, come to a head with the bizarrely inverted Biblical
kiss of the night before. Illusory also – and transient – was the small
peace he experienced after his communing with the sea because the
skewing of him, though subtle, was also radical and profound and to
think that he could wish away all thought of her who, principally, had
engineered that skewing, was tantamount to thinking that he could
debar the sea's susurrus from its invasion of his ears and mind, and,
indeed, it was not long before his awareness of Lydia – of the entire

grisly scenario in the lane – had revived in a measure that was close to obsession, and he began to see her in still distant shapes that, on his unwilling coming closer, proved to bear no resemblance to her at all, and, in the nights, he would increasingly wake from a recurring dream in which he finally pressed down on the blade at Hendrik's throat, only to find that it was *his* throat that yielded to it and gave vent to a scream as thick and turgid as a bubbling of his blood. Or – more terrifyingly still – he would wake for no reason that he knew, but immediately be convinced that, as his eyes opened, a shape of black and watchful menace had just vanished from the opening to the bush and was waiting beyond its frame for him to sleep again, and he would seize his knife from the branch overhead and, still half-swathed in bedding, stumble out to find not even a track on the wind-slicked stretch of the sand. Then, lying down again, dead bird under his head, dead cat to his side, only the sea alive and crawling under the ultimate silence of the sky, he would curse himself for a fool, but, nonetheless, be unable to close his eyes for fear of summoning back the spectral figure he had just proved beyond doubt was no more than a figment of his mind, and sometimes, in these lonely nights of facing up to his own face, he would hear again the last words he was ever to hear from her, 'It don't end here, Duke! *It don't end here!*' and coil foetally tighter as they echoed and re-echoed in the hollows of his brain as they had echoed and boomed in the narrows of the lane.

As summer weakened into autumn and autumn cut its first teeth of the winter-to-be, it became increasingly clear that Lydia, wielding her not inconsiderable authority as Hendrik's wife, was turning the Street against him. He had always been a little aloof, but the aloofness – being not contemptuousness – had won him respect rather than dislike, and it had been accepted that he was something of a loner who wanted to live his life – odd though it might be – in accordance with his own rules. Now, however, there was a looking up at him from under brows, a shrinking from him that was sometimes blatant, sometimes merely sensed, and the occasional snide remark that it was intended he should hear, but that culminated in no more than a bland, inquiring stare should he turn his head that way.

It was from these remarks that he gathered that Lydia – for who else was there to blame? – was spreading tales calculated to brand him, not as the loner he was already known to be, but as a 'doekoem' or wizard after the manner of the local 'Malays'. So a whispering arose – spread like a disease from cupped ear to cupped ear – that birds sat on his shoulder when he called to them, that he spoke to them and they spoke to him in a language only they could understand, that he strangled cats with his bare hands for strange doings under the moon and slept on the beach under a bush, not because he wanted to be alone, but because he fornicated with she-devils whose loins would burn the hide off any other man who dared to try such a thing.

In consequence of this, he began to drink more, eat less, to wander ever more aimlessly about the dunes, along the beach, the loner's habit of occasionally talking to himself now becoming a distressingly something other that prompted the further whisper that he was possessed, that the she-devils were now speaking for him with his tongue. He tried to convince himself that all these stories, and the Street's voracious acceptance of them, meant nothing to him, that he had never depended on the Street for company and, so, did not have to crawl on his belly for it now, but time proved that voluntary isolation was not the same as that which was imposed, and he grew thin and hollow-eyed and even his once impetuous libido sickened and waned, contenting itself in the end with the odd, joyless emission in sleep that he then, with some irritability, even tried to curb instead of satisfiedly abandoning himself to it as he once would have done.

Occasionally, his and Lydia's paths would cross at the trash sites and, although she never looked directly at him, he would persuade himself that, somehow, she was assessing his condition and would put on his most braggart face to deny her the frisson that she sought; but then, one day, Hendrik accompanied Lydia and came across to him and, with the odd blend of unctuousness and arrogance of the self-appointed Godsman, said: 'Hey! Duke, what's happening to you, boy? Best come to me, Brother, and let us pray because I see there's a Satan in you and the Holy Spirit in me's wanting to take it by the tail,' and he, upset at being so exposed, quite forgot that Hendrik had kissed him for the Oujaar and, with a flash of his old self, snarled, 'Go take your own fokken tail!' and fled, his trolley still only half-filled.

He had been sorely tempted to leave then, to find himself a kip in some far other corner of the city where he was not known, but the graves held him – and the sea – and she who had asked him to stay till she returned. So, he was still there when, on a bright but icy day in full winter, the woman descended the path to the beach, treading carefully, almost fearfully, clearly on it for the first time. Down at last, she came to where he was sitting on a rock, thick-ankled legs driving deep tracks into the sand, matronly hips and full, free breasts liquidly moving as water in a skin. Stopping a pace from him, she coughed, nervously, and he looked at her body and decided that she was actually quite young – maybe even a little younger than himself – and that her hands, brown with the brownness of birth rather than from the sun, were those of a woman who raised children, scrubbed floors, did her washing without the aid of a washing machine. Then he looked higher – up over the shabby, too thin coat, her quiet trembling from the cold – to the face with its pug nose, too heavily rouged, full lips, strangely eloquent eyes, and – marking her as of his own class – the modest doekie that confined her unstraightened hair.

'You Duke?' she asked, her voice a little breathless, her hands clutching a too large, too shiny handbag as though a parting warning still sounded in her ears.

He nodded. 'How's it you know my name?'

'A woman up there told me,' she said, sitting down on a facing rock, drawing the coat closer round her with one hand, the other still holding onto the bag. 'I been all over, asking, but nobody could tell me what I want to know. Then I asked this woman sleeping in a door up there and she showed me the path down to here and said, "That's Duke over there. Go ask him. He talks with devils and birds and maybe they told him what you want to know." You talk with devils and birds?' she asked, eyes widely more curious than afraid.

He laughed: a curt, dismissive fart of the lungs. 'Nay. It's only them like her that talks with the devils, not me. But what's it you want to know?'

'I'm looking for a man who left where he was born when he was still a boy and I was still a girl and who must be here because he did'n have the money to go further'n here.'

'But who was he? What was his name?' and she gave him the names that nobody had called him by for fifteen years and he quickly turned his head aside that she not see how deeply the names hit into the place where once his heart had been. Then he turned back to her, his face blank as the sand: 'So what's it you want with this ou?'

But she did not answer that straightaway. 'But do you *know* him?' she asked, leaning forward, the bag almost slipping from her grasp.

'Ja, I know him, but he's not here now. Gone away over the sea. Won't be back till it's spring.'

'Gone over the sea?' she echoed and there was a crying in her voice as of the child that had not thought to cry again. 'What's he doing over there?'

'Got him a woman – a white woman that's crazy for him. She gives him grand clothes, a car like you never seen. Now they riding around over there other side the sea.'

'A *white* woman!' she exclaimed, her voice hushed with awe. 'You playing with me?'

''Strue,' he said and grotesquely puffed with pride at the

impression he had made, the hurt inflicted on him by the Street during the past months momentarily salved. 'So, now, what was it you was wanting with this grand gent that's riding around where he can't hear you though you yell fit to bust your sides?'

For a moment she said nothing, her face withdrawn and sad. Then she asked, 'You seeing him again when he's back?'

At first, the braggart in him, whose true other face was the twin of hers, wanted to say something like, 'Ja, of course. I'm like a brother to him. With him all the time when he's home,' but, looking at her, he was suddenly as sick of the game as he was sick of the sad clown of a self that had been leading him by the nose, and he did no more than grunt and nod and she reached out and touched his sleeve and said, 'Please then, Mr Duke, will you tell him his sister was here to let him know that his pa's just died and his ma's now very old and wanting him and will he please come home?' Then she asked, 'Are you listening, Mr Duke?' and he looked up from where he had been furiously tracing patterns in the sand with his toes and his face, which he had again not wanted her to see, was back to being blank as the sand as he said, 'Ja, I heard you and I'll tell him what I heard,' and she rose, saying, 'Thank you and God bless you,' and, after rummaging in her bag, handed him a photo, adding, 'Here's a photo of his ma with a number on the back that he can phone when he's coming home,' and he took the photo and her hand and she turned to go, but he said, 'Wait,' and she turned back again and he asked, 'How did he die – your pa?'

Clearly distressed by the question, she looked past him and out over the sea. 'He, my brother and the Oubaas of the farm where we still stay had a trouble and my brother ran away. Pa also ran away, but only inside his head. He got sick in his head. Stood out in the fields all day with his spade, but not working and talking to hisself like there was two of him. Oubaas let him stay on because he also felt bad about the trouble and ma worked in the Big House, but pa never came right and now' – and she paused and looked at him, her eyes bright with grief and something like resentment that she should be telling him such a very private thing – 'he's just gone and hanged himself up with his own belt.'

Then she turned and said, 'Bye,' with her back to him, and he said, 'Bye,' and nearly added, 'Naomi,' under his breath, but then decided against it because, even now, knowing who she was, he still felt that he had never before seen her, that she was nothing but a random stranger who, somehow, had gate-crashed his own sorry celebration of a life. But then, as in a frightening postscript, she paused halfway up the path from the beach, and looked at him for a long moment and called, 'Mr Duke, you know there's something about you ... We never met before?' and, for the blink of an eye, he stalled, then he called back, his voice measured and dull, 'Nay, we never met before,' and she went on and the oleander leaves swayed as her hip brushed them on the last heave up to the street beyond.

Only then did he look at the photo that she had given him, and the gaunt, ruined face, eyes almost simian under the beetling brow, mouth propped by too large false teeth that he could not remember her having had when he was still a boy, was also one that he had never before seen, for which he felt no affinity at all, but he nonetheless, moved by an impulse he denied even as he gave in to it, searched for and found his only small stub of pencil and, under the telephone number on the photo's reverse side, painfully scrawled, 'Sorry I got to be such a bum,' and signed himself, 'Duke,' so that Naomi would know that he had lied. Then he added it to his scant treasure of trivia in the usual supermarket bag and, that night, went on thinking about it, wondering – the nothingness of the dark getting to him – if perhaps he *should* go home and, if so, when? 'Well, I gotta wait for Shirley, haven't I?' he reasoned with himself, but that reasoning only went *that* far and his instinct told him that he would *not* be going home, that he did not fit anymore, would only be a pig-shit in a nice people's lovingly cleaned sty.

Then he thought of his father, lying there on the double bed, his face turned to the wall – thought of his lonely talking to himself, his last desolate reaching for the death about his waist, the earlier pacing of him with a masturbating hand – and, emotion relentlessly engulfing him, he whispered, 'I forgive you, Pa,' and began to cry: the thin, high snivelling of a broken man or an abandoned child.

* * *

And, quite suddenly, the flowers were back on the dunes and the ghost of Tiger was rolling in them and snuffing the air, and the red car was parked alongside the oleander stand and she was coming down the path to the beach, her hair a brightness all about her and her feet in their sensible sandals confidently threading through the stones. Squatting beside a just-lit fire, nursing it into a further flame, he only saw her when she was halfway down and sprang to his feet, his breath fluttering in his throat like a bird that had blundered into where it should not be, and she waved and he barely managed not to run as he went to meet her, his face alive as it had not been since the deaths of Tiger and Fly.

'Hi!' she said, laughing, and kissed him, lightly, on the cheek, not – as he had half expected, had hoped – on the lips, and he was prepared to be disappointed by that, but then she hooked an arm through his and walked with him to the fire which had slumped into a swirl of smoke, and he awkwardly disengaged himself and knelt down to puff it back into life.

'You want to go inside?' he asked, meaning under the bush, looking up at her from the fire, trying to identify something he sensed in her that had not been there before.

'Oh no!' she exclaimed, and that was it, he thought: a certain skittishness, a striving for a girlishness that had outlived its term. 'It's far too lovely a day to be anywhere but in the sun!' which, indeed, it was and he grudgingly conceded her that, but then, looking at the car, at her, brilliant and groomed as the car, both compelling as signs pointing the way to the drabness and inappositeness of his kip, he felt his flesh crawl with unease as so often in the past the oleander leaves had crawled with watcher or wind.

'Anything wrong?' she asked, his distraction communicating itself to her, but he laughed and said, 'Nay,' striving to make himself heard through the booming of the voice in the lane, and she looked around and said, 'Something's missing,' and then, 'Yes! The bird! The bird is not here. What was its name?'

'Fly,' he said, surprise bordering on reproach stirring in him that she should have forgotten so vital a name, but she was not aware of that, went on: 'And the cat. There was a cat you always had to warn away from wanting to eat the bird,' and she laughed in fond remembrance of that, horrifyingly not knowing that the cat's by now picked-clean bones lay within the stretch of her arm.

'Tiger,' he said, his voice now clearly vexed and his eyes avoiding hers. 'Both gone. Long time now.'

'Gone? You mean something happened to them?'

'I dunno,' he hedged, suddenly and brutally realising that he could never tell her the truth. 'One morning, the bird don't come. Another morning, the cat don't come. They was wild things, them. Even though Fly sat on my shoulder and Tiger ate from my hand, they was wild things. Maybe they dead, maybe they someplace else. I dunno.'

'Shame,' she said and her voice was as warmly comforting as he had remembered it and he felt good again. 'It must have been very lonely for you here after that.'

'Ja, but I was always thinking of someone over there, other side the sea,' and he grinned with an audaciousness just short of a come-on, and she again laughed and sat down, tucking her long, tweed skirt under her and checking that her jersey – red as the car's red – was buttoned up to her throat, there being still an edge to the air. 'It's *all right!*' he thought. 'She's just the way she always was. It's me that's changed. Not her,' and he stoked the fire with fresh twigs and asked, 'You want I make us some coffee now?'

'No, please!' and she held up her hand, the gesture a trace histrionic, her eyes uncomfortably pleading that he understand. 'I can't stay long. There's still so much to do.'

'You just come?'

'No, I've already been here a week or so, but, as I said, there's so much to *do*. Even now, I shouldn't really *be* here, but I just had to find out if you were still around. To be honest, I more than a little believed that you would be gone.'

'I *said* I would stay, did'n I?' and now, for once, she listened to his tone as well as to his words and her eyes widened with genuine bewilderment and dismay.

'No, Duke, no! I did not mean it *that* way! I know you said you would wait for me here, but I did not mean that you must make me a *promise* that you must *keep*! We all have our different lives to live and life sometimes takes us anywhere it wants.'

'Don't take me nowhere *I* want!' he suddenly, shockingly, howled, and she shrank from the nakedness of his anger and despair, not understanding the why of either of these, knowing only that, somehow, she had blundered into a minefield of another's being through which not even the credentials of her own slashed wrists qualified her to pass. Covertly she studied him as he sat, now silent, hanging his head, and lambasted herself for not previously noticing how emaciated he was, how the first malignant signs of malnutrition and alcohol abuse were beginning to mottle his skin. 'Duke,' she said, but he did not lift his head, and the silence continued to swell between them like an inflatable beast, and the sea lisped, 'shish – shish,' fanning out over the sand, speaking in tongues like a holy fool, and she said again, 'Duke!' louder now, and he did then lift his head, but only a little, fixing his stare on a point to the left of her and on a level with her chin.

'Duke,' she said, stretching out her arms, baring her wrists with their pale bangles of scars. 'Remember these? Surely they give me the right to ask you what is wrong, why you are looking and acting the way you are now? Or is it I that am doing something wrong?' but he gave no sign that he heard her, even saw the scars, and she took back her arms and hugged herself with them and said, a hint of impatience in her voice for the first time, 'Well, as I told you, I have got a lot to do still because I am leaving for London again as soon as my bookings come through – for good this time – to finish my studies there and to get married there, because, you see,' and her voice grew arch as though she was cajoling a child, 'I did what you told me to do: I got me another Ali, even though he's white, and daddy's pleased for a change and has given me his blessing and a pat on the behind. So you, too, be happy for me, Duke, and, because you are my friend, I'll tell you something that even daddy doesn't know' – and she laid her hand almost reverentially on the belly the jersey hid – 'there's another me in there now – three months old!' and she laughed her girlish laugh that was no longer a girl's. 'And now I *must* go,' and she stood up, smoothing down her skirt, coming round to him, kissing him on the ear. 'Goodbye, friend, and – though I am not a one to preach – go slow on whatever it is that's tearing you up the way it is and thank you for the good advice that's made me into a woman instead of that stupid girl that came bleeding all over you last year!'

For a long moment she paused beside him, expecting some response, but he did not turn his head, shift his glance, in any way relax the rigidity that had seized him like a stroke, and she made a small sound of either impatience or disquiet and began to move away across the sand, then stopped, came back, fumbled in a pocket of her skirt, said, her voice featureless as from a widening of water between, 'I brought you this,' and dropped a large slab of chocolate into his lap. Now, at last, he stirred, took up the chocolate as it slid from the too short, cheap packet that had enwrapped its lower half – a packet he at once recognised as being from the supermarket immediately across the street from where she had parked the car – and hurled it at her back as she hastened to be finally gone. It struck her between the shoulders and she whirled, her frown inquiring and alarmed, and he said, his voice quiet, almost conversational, terrifyingly at variance with what she had feared, 'Pick it up, Shirley,' and that, too, was terrifying because he had used her name for the first time – used it despite her not, as always, insisting that he should – and, thus, was now tearing her from an eminence which an earlier Shirley would never have claimed. Compelled, sickeningly aware that she had been summoned to an accounting where she still did not know what it was that she owed, she leant down, picked up the slab and he let rage and hurt have its way with him and snarled, 'Now feed it to that hoer-kind you got you by that ou over there!' and she was girl again, staring at him in horror and disbelief, clutching the chocolate to her as though it was the child he had cursed, running, sobbing, then, over the sand to the path.

Instantly as the devils they said he housed, his rage fled him and pity and remorse cried out to her, 'Wait!' but she was already dead to him, scrambling up the path, hair wild as a lamentation at a grave, and he knew that, as he had strangled Tiger, so had he just strangled something born of himself which he had once felt for his father, but had never again felt until now, and he turned, blindly, to the sea and began to walk along beside it, only dimly aware that the more vociferous of the Street, attracted by the glittering opulence of the car and cruelly indifferent to her distress, were pressing round her, sucking the dry dugs of her compassion till they bled.

* * *

The sun climbed from early morning to late morning, and still he walked till the groomed beaches gave way to the trackless wild and he crawled like a beetle up a high dune's side and sat on its uneasy summit and stared out over the sea. There was a hint of mist like a breath on glass on the sky's far rim and the waves came smoking in in long languorous swells, but the sea was not speaking to him, withheld as all else, and he came down again from the dune and set out on the long return, a brisk wind nudging the small of his back, urging him on as though he was an emptied package or the last of winter's leaves.

Robotically his feet thrust into the fringe of the surf, the wet sand starting up between his toes, and it became noon and hot and he tugged off his shirt and knotted it around his neck and at once sensed that there was something about him that was wrong, that was not *there*. He tried to think what it was, watching his lengthening shadow as noon passed, but could not and, slowly, annoyance that he could not rooted itself in him, and grew, and proliferated, rupturing the grey, almost soporific monochrome of misery that was his mind. What *was* it that was not there? 'Watch *me*, watch *me*,' whispered his shadow, and again he watched it – the swinging of the arms, the pistoning of the legs, the thrusting, forward, back, of the head, the swaying in the wind of the shirt about his neck – and, all at once, he *knew* what it was that was not there and urgency and panic erupted in him like an incontinence of the bowels and he began to run, the sand dragging back at his heels, gulls rising before him in spiralling clouds, his shadow yelling, 'Go! Go!' as though it possessed a sentience of its own.

Inevitably – and ever more frequently – his body rebelled, forcing him to a standstill, hands on knees, head down, breath roaring from his mouth and nose. Sweat sheened him like an oil, a second skin, his blood thundered in his ears, blocking out even the ceaseless insistence of the sea, and the dog-walking strollers, the occasional early spring bathers, stared after him, then turned to see what was pursuing him, he being so clearly a hunted and haunted man.

But, at last, he was rounding the bend into his own small spit of beach, was staggering up the slope to his bush, falling to his knees to peer in under it, covering, then, his face with his hands, rocking back and forth as though he had run, full tilt, into a wall – for it was as he had feared: the knife that the distress of the encounter with Shirley had caused him to forget, that he had left hanging from its branch in the bush, was gone, and tracks that were not a man's showed, clearly and insolently, in the sand.

Then, too intense to be sustained, the shock passed and he lowered his hands from his face and his mind cleared: focused with the cold intensity of one driven too far, no longer wholly sane. It was, of course, she who had taken it: so very carefully – with a covered hand – as she had insisted that he do before the murderous tryst in the lane. That way, his prints would be preserved on it as she slit the sleeping Hendrik's throat, then took it to the police, saying she had surprised him in the act and he had dropped it as he fled. That way she would be rid of Hendrik and – aroused into a fresh fury by the sight of Shirley's so clearly parked car – or perhaps even by the sight of Shirley herself – would carry out her threat to him that their parting in the lane 'was not the end'. Yes, it was certainly she. Should he confront her? With what? He had no proof that the tracks were hers and, even if he had, where was the proof that it was *she* who had taken the knife? How little, indeed, was it that he could *afford* to do when he had as much to hide from Hendrik as she and the Street had been poisoned against him by her slandering tongue.

When would they come for him? Suddenly as a footpad from behind, the question was upon him and, involuntarily, his eyes scuttled about and up to the head of the path, half expecting to find a police van already driving in. But then he reasoned, no, although the knife was an unpredictably perilous thing to hold onto, she would not use it *now*, would probably – if she used the sense he knew she had – do it that night, but, even then, only in the small hours before dawn when an assassin was most likely to brave the grown-slack vigilance of the factory's security guard.

And what could *he* do? Frantically, panic again befuddling his brain, he considered that. Flee? Where to? How far? He had no money, the Street swarmed with those who had branded him as no longer of them, who would betray him for the least pittance of a reward. No, the net had been flung about him with a perfect cast: not a mesh of it too large, not a strand of it with a knot that would yield. Hugging himself, he rocked on his knees, thrusting forward, back, as his head had done, coming along the beach – as the quarry in his traps had done before he granted them the final grace of a strangulated neck or a crushed-flat skull. 'But I'm not a porcupine or a guinea fowl,' he suddenly, furiously, rebelled. 'Yirrah! What can I *do*? Am I not, then, still a man?' And rage rose up in him, irrational and blind as a goaded beast's, and bellowed at a sky that would not heed.

But the sea heard and, for the first time that day, it spoke, summoning him to it, licking his feet with little tongues of lascivious surf, and he listened to it, staring out over it with mad, exalted eyes, and came back, charged with a chill purposefulness that matched the sea's own immutable surge. 'Get me a Tassies now,' he murmured, as though it had been just another day, and took the last of his cash and bought a bottle at the nearest store, then sat drinking it, quietly and reflectively, until dusk and the first star, when he rose, resolve still iron in him, and drained the bottle and flung it as far as he could out into the dunes.

And Naomi was coming down the path again, but slim and fleet of foot as she had been when she had run to tell his mother that his father had beaten him with Oubaas's belt, and Fly was settling down in the kaapsebessie bush, fluting a single, unsettlingly sweet note, and Tiger was rising up out of the sand, shaking it from his fur, readying himself for the rigours of the night ahead, and, when he went down to the sea, Shirley was lying there in the surf, face up, beautiful and quiet and pure as he had created her and she had never been.

Then he waded out into the sea, further and further, the wine singing in his veins, and the current snatched his feet from under him and swept him out to the far beach where, at peace and beyond reach, he would be his own proof – and only at the end, going down for the last time, fear and cold overriding the wine, did she, too, come full circle as he cried out loud for the familial wild warmth of her loins.